DRAKONIA  BOOK ONE

CHRONICLES OF THE

DRAKYN WAR

DAP DAHLSTROM

Gardland Books

Dedicated to my dad, the original transmogrifer.

This is a work of fiction. Any similarity to actual persons or events is purely coincidental. All of the characters and events portrayed in this novel are either products of the author's imagination or are used fictitiously.

Published by Gardland Books

Printed in USA

Book design, cover design and map by Dap Dahlstrom

Library of Congress Control Number: 2022920534

ISBN: 979-8-9872044-0-5 (Ebook)

ISBN: 979-8-9872044-1-2 (Paperback)

First Edition

Apakoh Ice Shelf

Temple of the
Ice Queen

Inkuiuk
Tundra

Yaglin Kareth

NORTHERN
CONTINENT

KARSIK RANGE

The Thousand Isles

Kjarik Point

Malgrin's Isle

The Lonely Isle

EASTERSEA

Gozlin

Kren

Kara

Gorin

Suz

Bay
Isle

Two Moon
Bay

Keln

Palace of the
Drakyn Queens

Bay Towne

KRAIDA

Cara
Bay

Flying River

HARTBONE RANGE

Forest

Tia Cara

Valley of the Legong

Dmisi

DRAKONIA

Dageki Lands

Forest

Volcano Lands

(CHARTED LANDS)

Krasa Ktel

Cygnan
Lake

RUNNING RIVER

WESTERSEA

Great
Waste

Escarpment

River Cyn

The
Maze

DRAKYN'S TEETH RANGE

Ancient
Keeps

Mistra

Kjndry

Cyn

Lygr City

Southern
Isles

CHAPTER ONE

Last Meal on the River, Plus One

Blood oozed from the sky. Kodo watched, mesmerized, as it fell softly to sprinkle the firs below with a sparse crimson rain. Though he would never admit it, the challenge hadn't gone his way. Everything hurt. His wings were shredded, and ragged wounds marred his once-perfect skin. Blood and bile congregated in his throat and spewed a lovely pink mist when he coughed. One lung had collapsed, and the other was inclined to follow. Every breath was torture, every wingbeat more unbearable than the last.

He had to find a place to rest soon. It wouldn't do to appear at the palace in his current state. Then he saw the cabin; its warm flag of chimney smoke waving him in. With relief, he wheeled and dropped maladroitly from the sky, only to discover that he stood before a skragling house.

"Just perfect," he groused. He had to hope this wasn't the home of a warrior like the one he'd just escaped.

With the last of his strength, he transmogered, assuming the visage of his enemy, the lucky skragling bastart who'd ruined his day. He tried to laugh at the irony of this, but the effort skewered his chest with an explosion of agony. He made it to the door before collapsing, his energy spent, only to lapse into dreams of swirling magenta skies and clouds weeping the last of his blood into the thirsty ground.

In the loft bedroom of her Zaladz River cabin, a clammy chill permeated every surface, courtesy of the wily fog that had crept in overnight. Though her frayed trousers were clean, it felt to Wren like she was slipping her leg into a freshly gutted carp.

"Gardamn, it's shaping up to be a fruckin' miserable day."

Her curses resounded eerily in the empty room. Today, she had to decide. She'd finally admitted to herself that the battle was about to overrun her, and it was time. Tomorrow. Tomorrow she would leave.

Outside, she hoisted the carrier to her shoulders and trudged down through the leafless alders along the path that ran beside the silent porker sty and chickers' coop. She hurried past the dock to which the water-logged rowboat still clung. There at the river's edge she dipped her buckets to collect water for the day's washing and cooking.

As she did every morning, she stood there for a moment to catch her breath and look back up the hill to the familiar shape of the cabin. Its warm trickle of chimney smoke flirted with the chill morning fog; its face of wood and stone only slightly more organized than the surrounding terrain that had birthed it. Was this her reason for staying; her protection against the coming war? She realized that the cabin anchored her there, forbidding her to leave with its stone-cold heart, but offered only a liar's promise of safety.

As she stared, she recognized that the cabin's face was contorted in a way that at first, she couldn't define. Then she saw it. A form lay on her doorstep. Was it a fallen tree branch, a hungry barr, or something far worse?

Wren considered running away, maybe finding others like her downriver. Safety. Warm fires and welcoming arms.

But no, this was her home, as cold and uncaring as it was. She lay the buckets down haphazardly, spilling water on her feet. Picking up a crusty, worm-embossed stick, she marched up the hill with purpose, hurrying to make it to the top before this unaccustomed bravery could desert her.

When she reached the cabin door, she found neither a tree branch nor a hungry barr. Before her lay a soldier in a once-resplendent crimson and gold uniform, now torn and stained with blood. The medals, ribbons and gold-fringed epaulettes told her he was a colonel or maybe even a general. The man was lithe yet muscled, with olive skin and ink-black hair, except for an odd streak of gold that appeared to be his natural, untransmogered shade. His face was handsome, but severe, with a prominent nose and arching ebony brows.

One leg had collapsed beneath him at an unusual angle, and Wren recalled a bow-shot stag that had fallen limb over limb down the hill. She'd had to use her knife to end its pain. The soldier appeared near death, yet had the strength to look up to her, pleading for help.

Blood trickled from his lips as he spoke. "Take it away. It burns!"

"Take what away?"

His chest wheezed like a leaking bellows as he reached for her. She jumped back when he thrust trembling claws toward her face, then exhaled loudly when she saw that they were only his hands, charred and twisted by burns.

She considered leaving him there, to bleed out like fallen prey, but how could she let another human die on her doorstep in the cold? When she tried to lift him by the shoulders, she almost changed her mind. He felt heavier than ten men! Had she listened more closely to her mama and her confusing talk about "mass" and "nothing being lost in the change," she would have known what she faced, but she hadn't listened. She didn't know enough to be as afraid as she should have been.

With great effort, Wren managed to drag him into the cabin and up to the fireplace. She made him as comfortable as she could. It was a warm place to die, at least.

Even before her mama and granpapa had passed, Wren had thought about death more often than was probably healthy for a young girl. She remembered watching a chicker run around the farmyard without its head. When she tried to ask her papa a question, he motioned with his blood-stained axe at the flopping hen and said, "They die, we live, girl."

She understood that. The real question she wanted to ask ran deeper. Where did life end, and death begin? If the chicker could run around dead, was she running around dead right now?

She sat by the fire for a while in silence, except for the popping of embers and the distant cry of a vixen calling to her mate. The soldier's breathing grew shallow, and soon she could barely detect the rise and fall of his chest. She cleaned up the blood on her arms and clothing as best she could and went about her day, expecting to have another body to bury in the morning.

To her surprise, at dawn the next day, the soldier was sitting up, poking aimlessly at the residue of the fire with a stick. For a long moment, she stood at the base of the stairs, unable to make sense of his recovery. She approached him cautiously, unsure whether she should stay or run.

She leaned down to observe him more closely. "You seem to have healed, but...overnight?"

With a nonchalant glance at his stained and disheveled uniform, he waved a manicured hand dismissively. "Oh, most of this blood isn't mine. I just needed a good night's rest away from the challenges."

He spoke with a slight accent, but Wren couldn't place it. His voice was silky and rich, almost mesmerizing with its tone of casual intimacy.

She glanced at his body, where tears in his clothing revealed smooth, touchable skin and an athletic physique. Embarrassed to be caught observing him so closely, she turned away and busied herself adding logs to the fire.

She heated an iron skillet on the fire and made him a simple breakfast of fried goldenbell shrooms, taters, wild scallions and herbs, all crisped to perfection in the last of the turken fat. The aroma filled the small cabin with homely comfort.

His chair at the rickety wood table creaked and groaned, threatening to splinter under his imposing form.

Through a mouthful, he said, "This is wonderful. I can't even taste the blood in it!"

She glanced up at him, confused. "Wh–What?" she stammered. "There's no blood in this recipe–if that's what you expected."

"Oh no, you have no idea how tired I am of it. It seems as if there's blood in every recipe at the palace: blood soup, blood pudding, seared raw fletmeat with blood drippings, blood and beets–"

The look of horror on her face stopped him.

"Ha, ha, just my lame idea of a joke, girl," he explained in a stilted tone.

She wondered about his odd sense of humor and bizarre choice of words but said nothing until she took his empty plate away. "You must be feeling better; at least you have a healthy appetite," she said.

"It was delicious! And you made some of this by hand? Maybe that's why it tastes so good." His gaze fell to her calloused fingers, and reflexively, she jerked them behind her back. Berating herself for her tell-tale reaction, she casually let them fall to her sides.

Not knowing what else to say, she pulled upon the lies her mama had taught her. "Oh, well," she stammered. "It's a...It's a bit of a hobby, you see, plus, you know, herbs and spices taste so much better if they're allowed to mature naturally. I create the mix myself, by hand..." she trailed off.

He laughed. "Well, one of my hobbies is eating, and your fare is delicious, no matter how you transmoger–er, concoct it. Have you thought about becoming a professional cook? I think you'd make a great one."

"Oh no, I couldn't cook for more than a couple people, I'm sure. And now I only cook for one," she added quietly. She immediately regretted admitting that she was alone.

"Don't worry; I knew you were the only one here. It must be quite lonely and difficult." He paused, looking around at the meager furnishings of the cabin, as if considering something.

"I'd like to make you an offer; come back to the palace with me. You'll love it there. Plenty of your kind to keep you company, and you'll have the queen's gardens to grow your herbs and spices, plus a real kitchen to work your magic."

Stepping away from him abruptly, she knocked over a chair and the strident noise woke her fear at last. She squeaked, "What do you mean, 'm–my kind?'"

His expression darkened. "Oh, oh, it seems the flet is out of the hat! It's just a short way, but I'll need a more useful form. Or maybe I'll just be myself. I'm told I'm quite handsome." With that humble admission, he grew in stature. His features warped as he struggled to become something else, but it didn't seem to be working. His skin split, and an oozing greenish hide broke through. He screamed in pain and fell back, grabbing at the pustulous mess, as if to force it back into shape. Yellow eyes in a writhing, bloated face glared at her as if to say it was all her fault.

"What have you done to me, little git?" The angry words were distorted by his swollen lips. He reached out a pus-draped hand and slapped her with so much force that her head bounced off the rock fireplace. Her eyes closed, and she floated to the floor like an autumn leaf.

She woke to a terrible headache, recalling the dream she'd had of a soldier who contorted as she watched, taking on a grotesque shape. When her eyes finally opened, she found that she hadn't been dreaming at all. Before her was a creature more nightmare than reality. Almost touching the ceiling of her small cabin, its oversized reptilian head sported double rows of needle-sharp predator's teeth and bulging eyes that, disturbingly, tracked separately from one another. Blood-red cartilage appendages ringed its head like proud flags fluttering in the breeze, though there was none. The appendages never stopped moving, even when the creature did. A streak of gold on one side of its head continued into the waving cartilage, and she wondered if every drakyn had this mark, for she knew what this thing was now. Though she'd never seen one in the flesh, her mother had shown her illustrations of drakyn in their firstform.

The body was almost comical; a bloated gray-green bulk that, she would later learn, provided the mass for the infinite forms into which these creatures could transmoger. Its chubby front limbs were tiny in comparison to the body. In contrast, the back legs were massive and delineated by muscle, as if straining to leap from the ground with every step.

Worst of all was how the thing smelled. The putrid stench brought back a vivid memory. One night she'd returned late from shrooming to find her papa sitting on the floor in front of the fireplace, staring into the flames intently, as if they were imparting some great wisdom to him. She noticed the almost empty bottle in his gnarled hand, the tater mash she knew he'd been saving to celebrate the unlikely return of her brother and sister from the war. Despite the fire, he was wasting the last of their precious fuel in the blazing lantern. Her sister Justine had been the only one who could transmoger it, and she was long gone, surely never to return, just like her brother, Seth.

When she'd bent to turn down the flame, her father had grabbed her wrist, and panic filled her. She saw the unfocused look in his blood-shot eyes and knew he was far past doing more than deluging her with fantastic tales and embryonic plans that were destined never to be born.

"Papa, it's hurting. Let me go!" Surprisingly, he obeyed her with a grunt. She rubbed her arm and rose quickly to sort and clean the shrooms. She'd laid them out on the table to dry for tomorrow's breakfast before he spoke again.

"Wren, me darling, you be next, me little gem, just you wait and see. I best impart me pearls of knowledge on yur purdy little head about these gard-awful fruckers afore ya go."

"I weren't always just a worthless fisher with not a crocket to me name, ya know. I fought, oh yeah, I fought in that first war in the North..."

This was the first she'd ever heard of him being gifted in transmo-grifee. As long as she could remember, he'd been talentless, like her; fishing, planting taters, hunting, and even carving the rough wood furniture of the cabin–*all by hand*. Her disbelief must have shown because he said, "Sure, don't be believing me if ya want, but it's all as true as me own ugly dying's nigh. They's gonna act all sweet, right afore they take yur fruckin' head off!" Spittle flew from his cracked lips as he spoke, and a vein pulsed at his temple. "They's yur worse nightmare, little bird. Never, ever trust 'em! They's gonna look purdy one minute, then stench of carrion sat too long in the sun the next! They's gonna tell ya trues that ain't and give ya hope, but there ain't no way but death with dem gardamn mama-frucking, blood-sucking drakyn bastarts!"

His speech degraded into mumbles, truncated by the occasional shout of "gardamn bastarts!" until he crawled off to sleep and left her in peace.

Now his words came back to her in a rush, and with them the knowledge that she knew so little about the drakyn.

The creature noticed that she was awake and bent its head down to hers with a quizzical tilt.

"Sorry about that." The thing spoke with a sibilant rasp, but perfect diction, as the words whistled through its double rows of teeth. "Must be the after-effects of the battle challenge. It was a messy one. I didn't mean to take it out on you, little one. Is your head bleeding?" The monster reached its tiny arms toward her with an eager gleam in its yellow eyes.

She screamed.

"Ouch! No more of that. It hurts my excellent hearing! Hee, hee."

Was that a giggle?

He flared the alarming blood-red appendages, and they rustled like a new dress.

"I mean you no harm. Well, at least no more harm than you can handle. Ha, that was just a joke. I'm very careful with my toys, generally. Now, choose a few things to bring with you. Nothing too heavy, mind. I'm still not completely healed, I think."

Wren sat unmoving on the floor, trying to grasp the reality she faced. Her eyes darted to the door, but the creature followed her gaze and blocked the way so quickly that Wren could hardly track its movements.

"Don't even consider it, little bird. That's what your name means, *n'est pas?*"

She rose and frantically scoured the room for an answer to her predicament. The three little primers, of course, had to go with her. They were the most important things she owned—the only things, really. Then, through her fear and confusion, an idea occurred to her. She picked up the primers and her notebook and stuffed them into the oiled canvas pack she used for hunting and shrooming. Pulling it onto her shoulders, she motioned toward the loft.

"My Congregation Day dress, I can't leave without that."

In truth, she had few clothes other than the britches and threadbare men's shirt she wore, and certainly not any special dress for Congregation Day, but this horrible creature couldn't know that. "It's upstairs in the loft."

"All right, but hurry. We don't have the whole day to dally."

When several minutes had passed, the drakyn snarled and rushed out of the cabin. As Kodo forced his way through a door that was now too small for him, pieces of the shredded casing flew in all directions like ill-formed arrows. At the back of the cabin, he caught Wren just as she reached the ground, having forced her way through a tiny window and down a rope made of sheets and miscellaneous fabric, all tied in a line.

"Resourceful little git, aren't you?" Kodo said.

Wren couldn't answer because he'd knocked her down and pushed her face into the dirt.

As Kodo continued to hold his struggling prize fast to the ground with one clawed rear leg, he preened his crimson cartilage with his nimble front limbs, preparing for one more addition to his almost perfect physique. With great concentration–for some reason, he still felt oddly queasy and hot during the change–he formed the massive wings he would need to carry her weight along with his own. His mind did the calculations and designed the artfully shaped wings automatically. He drew the required mass from his core, and his chubby body grew suddenly lean.

A drakyn began to learn transmogrifee before he could walk. It was innate for his people, though some were born talentless. They were just as often eaten by their parents as allowed to live. In truth, it was probably an act of mercy; for how long could a drakyn survive without transmogrifee?

Kodo thought himself exceptionally gifted, even for his kind. He could draw everything he needed from the tiniest, most basic elements in the air and matter around him. He had no need for the bags of minerals and pigments that the less talented utilized for their creations. In all modesty, he believed he was the next step in the evolution of drakynkind.

His wings popped out with a resounding *thwap* and glistened in the morning light. Each feather sported a sparkling crystal at its tip and was haloed by a misty glow. He was quite enamored with his wings. He'd gotten the idea from a skragling primer about diaphanous creatures they called "angels," which may or may not have existed in their otherworld. The only thing that irritated him was the gardamn streak of gold. Couldn't it just end at his ears? But no, it had to extend even into his beauteous wing!

Transferring the skragling to his front limbs, he ran clumsily across the clearing, gathering speed as he went. Rear claws dug into the earth and clumps of dirt flew. His massive hind legs propelled him at ever-increasing speed until his new wings could carry him and his prize aloft. As he flew, he congratulated himself on his find. A good cook was worth his or her weight in gold–or taters, anyway. Skragling cuisine was one of his many interests, as was just about everything skragling. He knew that some of the more bellicose courtiers gossiped about him behind his back, calling him names like "humanophile" and "critter lover," but he ignored them.

This one was perfect. With her silver hair and delicate features, she was a crystal doll. With little or no talent, she was no threat to him or his schemes. She was a gifted cook–to replace the one lost to accidentally excessive blooding–and had an ethereal, transparent grace about her. Fragile in appearance, but with hints of unbreakable glass within, she might survive the palace longer than most.

CHAPTER TWO

Cooking is in My Blood

How they could call this ugly stone edifice a palace, Wren didn't know. The whole place stank of gard-knew-what, and dank breezes blew through the ill-fitted stones. With all their transmogering ability, you'd think the drakyn could do a better job of imitating human construction methods. Maybe they were incapable of imagining the details, working from illustrations in the primers they collected like dragon's gold. In many ways the structure was a dish with too many cooks; one section resembled an ancient human emperor's pagoda, other sections looked more like a primitive fur-trapper's cabin. Always in flux, its passageways could lead an unsuspecting wanderer into a dead end they could never escape.

The kitchen was the only comfortable room in the entire place, but the master cook managed to ruin even that with her constant criticism and unmitigated bad humor. Teeka found fault with every dish Wren prepared. It probably hadn't helped that Kodo had dumped her unceremoniously in Teeka's care with the statement that Wren was "the best skragling cook he'd ever found." Teeka wouldn't win any popularity contests, even when she didn't feel threatened, but she'd made it clear early on that Wren was unwanted and unneeded in her kitchen *and* in her life.

The other kitchen workers generally gave the head cook a wide berth and got along passably with her, but Wren hadn't gotten off to a good start with the woman. She couldn't control herself around the pompous old fool, especially when she spouted her supposed knowledge of every cuisine and dish known to man or drakyn. Moreover, Teeka was still adapting after recently receiving what Kodo jokingly called a "battlefield promotion." The old head cook had succumbed to some illness and died unexpectedly.

Unlike the stereotypically stout chef, Teeka was thin as a reed, tall, and deceptively strong. She could pull the heavy ceramic dishes that held two roasted turkers from the stone oven with ease, her frizzy mop of white hair escaping her headband to shroud her eyes. She was notoriously prone to fits of temper and didn't hesitate to give her kitchen helpers a good wallop if she thought they needed it. Most often, she just threatened them with a one-way trip to one of the drakyn-run farms, but Wren didn't think that sounded so bad. Having grown up on a farm, she thought she would prefer mucking out stalls to being yelled at all day.

She'd only seen Kodo a few times since she'd arrived, and then only for a few minutes when she brought his food. Occasionally, he summoned her to the cavernous dusty room the drakyn called a library, to answer some question he had from his readings in the primers. Wren was amazed at the number of primers that the drakyn had been able to accumulate. How many primer-keepers had been killed to amass this library? Kodo appeared to be interested in human history, literature, and art, while most of the other drakyn wanted to learn about petty things that drove Wren to distraction, like party invitations and dance steps, how to tie a tie, or how to giggle. The drakyn had even adopted English as their preferred language, though human laughter appeared to be a challenge of the highest order for them. She was terrified at the grotesque sound they made when they practiced, the rustling cackle echoing through the cold stone halls.

Usually, Kodo sported the same human form that she'd first seen him wear, but she would have known him no matter what form he took, as the gold stripe was always present, and he was the only one of his kind that she'd seen with such an aberration. He hadn't hit her again or even said a rough word to her. If Wren hadn't known better, she would almost have thought that he was ashamed of how he'd acted toward her at the cabin. She didn't think the drakyn could feel regret, or compassion, but she knew she had much to learn about these creatures. Kodo was often in the company of the queen, whom she feared and loathed. Jelebron was the biggest, most foul-smelling drakyn she'd so far encountered.

Teeka was trying to teach Wren some of the recipes that the drakyn preferred, but she was having trouble even reading Teeka's scrawled script on the stained and tattered recipe cards. Searching for the recipe for swamp stew, she pulled out one of the most worn cards. She read the ingredients and instructions with growing horror.

It read:
TEEKA'S OFFAL RAW BLOOD SOUP

INGREDIENTS:
1/2 cup fermented adder's venom (can be substituted with fermented herdbeast birth water if available)
3 teaspoons eel sauce (or to taste)
3 litres fresh blood

2 cups finely chopped offal: swine snout, tongue, and small intestine

1 cup worm-riddled tree nuts, crushed

1 teaspoon each chopped lintweed and corniadder

3 sliced swamp carrots

A few leaves baby sty lettuce

1 small bunch rotted cress, mashed

2 tablespoons freshly ground meallybug flour

Pinch of dried windspice

1 cup live mugworm larvae

INSTRUCTIONS:

Mix the eel sauce and adder's venom into the fresh blood (taste frequently to avoid over-seasoning). Set aside.

Chop the swine snout and offal and add to a pot of water. Sprinkle in the crushed nuts, vegetables, and herbs. Cook the offal mixture until opaque and tender. Mix the raw blood and the offal. Stir in meallybug flour until slightly thickened. Let the soup cool until the blood begins to set. Serve topped with live mugworm larvae and enjoy!

She put the recipe card back gingerly and wiped her hands on her apron, as if the action could erase the memory of what it contained from her mind.

Fortunately for Wren, she hadn't been asked to prepare dishes that called for animal blood, and Kodo never requested them. It was Teeka's specialty anyway, so Wren left her to it. Though she knew that some human families made blood sausage, hers had not, and the thought of eating raw blood was off-putting to say the least. She abhorred the metallic smell and couldn't even bring herself to taste the many drakyn dishes that required it.

Fresh blood arrived at regular intervals from the farms, and Wren wondered how they could kill enough animals to provide blood so often. It had to be unsustainable. When she learned the truth, she would look back on her gross ignorance and remind herself never to underestimate the depth of cruelty her drakyn captors were capable of.

For the most part, the other humans at the palace were like her: low talent, or none at all. Most couldn't even light the fire or enhance a sauce using their talent. Plus, when you didn't exactly know what you were doing, transmogering could take a huge toll on your body and mind. In most cases, it wasn't worth it to use a skill that might result in nothing but a headache and a cake that tasted like fish.

One day, when Teeka was in an especially foul mood, Wren destroyed a dish by adding too much salt. The drakyn were especially sensitive to the mineral that humans valued so highly and wanted very little of it in their meals. When Teeka caught her disposing of the dish, she became livid, ranting at her for several minutes.

"So, thees ees zee best cook in zee whole wide world, eh? You are, in fact worthless, n'est pas?" said Teeka. "Eef you could transmoger worth a gardamn, you'd know how easy to remove zee salt. But no, you can't even do sometheeng as basic as that. What good are you?"

Wren had had enough.

"I seem to recall that you did exactly the same thing last week," said Wren indignantly, "and when you tried to fix it, you turned it into a giant brick of mud! You're not such a great cook yourself, are you?"

Teeka said nothing, which was an especially bad sign, while her face turned a ripe tomato red. With blinding speed, she slapped Wren hard across the face with so much force that she was thrown across the room.

The next day, when Wren brought Kodo his meal, he saw the bruise on her face. He dragged her behind him and stormed into the kitchen, towering over Teeka, who cringed as her workers cowered under *her* wrath.

"If my little beauty shows up again with any hurt, be it a sliver, or even dark circles under her eyes, you, *you* Teeka, will pay a heavy price." Leaning close, he breathed malice into her face. "Is that clear?"

"T'was but an accident, m'lord. I promise to keep closer watch on 'er from now on. Eet won't 'appen again, I assure you," she apologized in an overtly obsequious manner. Wren had never heard Teeka sound so contrite, but there was something greasy about it. Why couldn't Kodo see that she would take it out on her workers as soon as he left the room? She wondered how much the drakyn really understood about human psychology.

Wren was amazed that Kodo had become so protective of her. Why was it alright that he had hit her, but no one else was allowed to? Whatever the reason, she was grateful for a reprieve from Teeka's wrath, though she assumed it would be short-lived.

When Kodo left, and Teeka said nothing to her, Wren breathed a sigh of relief. After a time, when Teeka still hadn't retaliated against her, Wren began to think she might be safe, not fully comprehending the depths of Teeka's spiteful nature.

Wren was busy adding the seasoning to Kodo's favorite turken soup, when her attention was drawn away by an altercation in the door to the washroom. Teeka was bent over a scrawny teenage boy with a curly mop of orange hair and more freckles than should be possible on a human face. He sat in a pool of spilled tater peelings, his long-fingered hands held above his head to fend off at least some of the blows that Teeka landed on him.

"You useless, ugly little cretin! Imbecile! *Putain de merde!*" Wren heard this last phrase quite often and wasn't sure what it meant. She had thought it meant "put it in the oven," but that obviously didn't work in this situation. She winced every time another blow landed on the hapless little kitchen grunt. He looked too fragile to withstand the abuse much longer without a broken bone, or worse. Against her better judgment, Wren stepped between them.

"Hey, I think he gets it," said Wren, raising her own arms in defense.

"Get out of zee way! You're as worthless as he be!" Teeka snarled.

"What did he do?"

"What did he do? What did he do? What didn't he do, the worthless nincompoop? Zee oven isn't stoked, zee vegetables–not chopped! Zee dishes–not washed!"

"He's just a boy! I'm sure he's moving as fast as he can."

"Well, that's zee problem, *n'est pas*? 'Cause I told eem to slow down."

"Why would you do that, then be angry with him for doing what you asked?"

Teeka motioned as if she would tear out her hair. "'I told zee little git to slow down 'cause ee's always in a hurry, but no, not in a good way! So clumsy! Breaking things and causing problems I don't 'ave time for. Ee's a menace! I'm thinking now ee's not cut out for this kind of work, and keetchen grunt ees pretty much thee end of the line een theese hell hole."

"No, please don't send me to the farms," begged the boy, his voice breaking. "Nobody comes back from there." He almost whispered these last words.

"Let me work with him," suggested Wren, not knowing what possessed her to step in for him when she barely had time for her own chores.

"Well, isn't that sweet of you," sneered Teeka. "Zen you'll be 'appy to do hees work, as well as your own 'till I can decide what to do with eem."

When Teeka stomped away from them, mumbling, Wren helped the boy to his feet and introduced herself.

"Poppet's my name," he replied.

"That's unusual."

"My mama number two called it a term of...dearment, I think," he murmured. "My third papa said it was 'cause I was always poppin' up where I didn't belong."

Wren couldn't help but laugh. "You're just at that stage where everything is more difficult than it needs to be," she said.

"Well, if that's the case, then I've been in this stage since I was born," grumbled Poppet, brushing at his dirty clothes to no visible effect.

Wren sighed, looking back at her pot that appeared ready to boil over. She was already putting in twelve to sixteen-hour days in the kitchen. She didn't know how she would manage more.

Poppet saw her expression and said, "Don't worry. The old hag will forget all about it next time Mala frucks something up."

"I'm not so sure. She really has it in for me," mused Wren.

Poppet gave her a curious, thoughtful look, an aspect that appeared overly adult on his young features. "I think they like you, or at least you really interest them. They're always lookin' after you when you walk down the hall. And the one who wears the handsome human warrior, he practically drools over you."

"I don't want their attention; it's deadly," she whispered. "And you're more observant than is probably healthy."

She helped him gather the tater skins and went back to her duties, wondering all the while what the drakyn could possibly find interesting about her, a passable cook with no talent, no future, and no hope of anything better happening for her any time soon.

Later that week, Wren was pulling a heavy pan from the stone oven by herself when her hands started to tremble, and she realized too late that she was about to drop the whole thing on the floor. Mala appeared at her side with oven mitts and helped her lift it to the counter.

"Thanks, little one. You saved my bacon. Except this is turken," she added.

Mala giggled. "It's nothing, Wren. I like helping you." She ran stubby fingers through her sleek mane of black hair and her ebony skin glistened in the kitchen heat.

Wren had taken to Mala and the younger kitchen help. Some of the older cooks were not much more than zombies, going about their work in taciturn silence. Or maybe the drudgery had just baked the life out of them. She enjoyed being around Mala. Despite her small stature and rounded figure, she appeared to swim through life, always in fluid, graceful motion. Her cheerful laugh brought joy to the drudgery of the kitchen. She was always upbeat and calm, no matter what drama swirled around her. Her curiosity was prodigious. She wanted to know about everyone's past, where and how they had lived before the palace, and made an effort to learn new words and new ideas. She had a special gift for living every minute fully.

Unknown to Wren, Teeka had seen the exchange between her and Mala. Later, she sent Wren to the garden to gather herbs, and she went willingly. At least the garden, though enclosed by stone walls, gave her a breath of fresh air and a chance to imagine she was back at her cabin, tending her own herbs and plants.

When she was finally released from her long shift, exhausted and dirty, she caught sight of a lump in the shadows of the hall. Curious, she moved closer, until the lump turned into a small figure, slumped against the stones.

"Oh no!" She knelt, almost afraid of what she would find. When Mala let out a moan and rolled over, she almost cried in relief. Then white-hot anger hit her.

"Who did this?" she asked, knowing the answer. Mala mumbled something, and Wren's anger temporarily succumbed to concern. She felt for broken bones but found none.

"Can you walk?"

Nodding, Mala stumbled to her feet. Wren helped her down the hall to the now empty common area and had her sit beside the waning fire. She stoked the flames with a few new sticks, then hurried off to get a bowl of water and a rag. In the deserted kitchen, she added some crushed leaves of cardamom and ground willow bark to the bowl to help the swelling and pain. When she returned, she cleaned up Mala's visible scrapes and bruises, not knowing what other damage might lie unseen.

"It's just some bruises I think," explained the girl. "It's nothing for you to worry about. It's not your job to watch over me. Besides, I probably deserved it. I did drop that pot and—"

"There's no excuse for it, Mala! This should never have happened. It's my fault you were beaten." She told Mala about the ultimatum that Kodo had laid down to Teeka, that she not be harmed.

"She figured if she couldn't hurt me, she would hurt my friends. Teeka has gone too far this time. Something has to be done about her."

"But what?" asked Mala. "She's in charge. She rules us all. What can you do?"

"I don't know yet, but I'll think of something. When I was little, my mama read this to me from one of the primers: 'Never give up, for that is just the place and time that the tide will turn.' We can trust the primers; they came with us from the gardlands, you know. They teach us that every one of us has worth, a great talent, in fact. That's why we're here."

"What do you mean? What's a primer? What's a gardland?"

Wren was thoughtful for a bit, then asked, "Would you like to hear a story?"

Mala's eyes brightened, and she appeared to forget her hurts.

"I can't believe your mama and papa never told you this tale," Wren began. "We all learnt it as babes. My granpapa told me the story, as he learnt it from his elders, and so on and so on, back into time. It's also in the primers, of course, but you would need a teacher to show you how to make sense of the words. I'd be glad to teach you someday. My mama and her papa were primer-keepers. That's why we have the primers, of course. Back in time, everyone could read, but now there're only a few who can still decipher them. Now sit close, and I'll start the tale."

Mala scooted closer to the fire and put her arms around her knees.

"Our people came from the gardlands, a place so far away that it's beyond magining. It was a land filled with laws and rules, bee counters, lawtellers, technologers, and regulators."

"Bee counters," Mala exclaimed. "Who would want to count bees?"

"Well, they did. I guess they counted everything, controlled everyone. Your life was laid out for you even before your birthing; how tall you'd be, the color of your hair, where and how you'd live, even whom you'd join with when you came of age. Now be quiet, so I can tell the rest of the tale."

Mala exhaled loudly and propped her chin on her chubby fingers, leaning in intently to hear more.

Wren continued, "Magination was considered a crime in the gardlands. When someone started to show signs of creativity or be skilled in making things that were not completely utilitarian—"

When Mala gave her a blank look, she explained, "Utilitarian means having a purpose but no joy."

Mala nodded knowingly.

"These people were branded as artistas and thrown into great stone barns called prisons. But over time, more and more of us were born, until the prisons overflowed. That's when one of the technologists got the brilliant idea to send us to this place through the cubes, to live out our lives in exile on Drakonia, never able to return to the gardlands. Here's the part where my granpapa said we had the last laugh on the gardlanders. Though surviving here was hard, especially in the beginning, before the seeds and animals they sent with us multiplied, our people were free to live as we chose, go anywhere on Drakonia we wished, create new lives for ourselves. Then we started to learn to transmoger too. In the gardlands, transmogrifee wasn't even possible."

"No!" breathed Mala.

"Oh yes," said Wren. "In the gardlands, magination lead you nowhere. If you wanted to transmoger something, you had to do it from scratch with your bare hands!"

Mala exclaimed, "I can't believe people could live like that! I know I don't have much talent myself, but we all depend on the creations of the talented to survive! I'd almost feel sorry for these gardlanders, if they weren't so cruel. Are the people still being sent here through the cubes then?"

"No. We think that no one has come through the cubes for generations."

"So maybe they learned their lesson and left the artistas alone."

"I suppose that's possible, but my granpapa had another idea. He believed that when all the creative thinkers were purged from their society, the culture grew so stagnant that eventually, their civilization failed. He said that the gardlanders stopped sending artistas through because there are no more gardlanders left to send them."

Mala nodded and stared into the fire in silence for a long moment.

"But what of the drakyn?" she whispered. "If life is so much better for us here, why are we at war? Why do we serve these beasts?"

With a heavy sigh, Wren said, "My granpapa told me that at first, we lived in peace, at least here in the south. When the drakyn began moving down this way, encroaching on our lands, that's when war came." A moment of silence ticked by before Wren spoke again. "Now it's time for bed, Mala. Kitchen work starts at dawn."

With a mumbled, "Oh, I can't wait," Mala rose stiffly. Then abruptly bent down to give Wren a peck on the cheek before limping down the hall toward her sleeping mat.

A little embarrassed by Mala's unexpected show of affection, Wren touched her cheek gently, thinking of her mother, the last person who'd ever kissed her so tenderly. She stared into the fire, grasping at the tatters of memories too few and faded to offer much comfort, until she caught herself nodding off. Silently, she rose and crept to her own bed.

In a corner of the room, a translucent figure disengaged itself from the gloom and took solid form, watching Wren's departure with a thoughtful expression on its practically human face.

CHAPTER THREE

The Reluctant Emperor

K odo paused at the door to his mother's reception chamber, wondering again if he should have worn the crimson robes or the gold. His mother's whims and moods were legendary in the palace. Her vision was still acute, her judgment of the smallest details always critical. He smoothed the waving cartilage at his ears and opened the door with a heavy sigh. Approaching the rough stone chair his mother called a throne, he bowed deeply. Before he could rise, the queen spoke.

"I like the blue; it highlights your eyes." She twisted in her chair, an expression of pain on her broad reptilian face. "Kodo, you are the only one I can trust to tell me the truth. You come here in your firstform, as is correct. Unadorned but for a simple cloak of the most intense and lovely cerulean blue. A color of truth. The others, I can't tell if they're coming or going, honest or deceitful. And the ridiculous dances..."

As if she really wanted the truth, he thought, but said, "Forgive me, your highness, was there a reason you called me here today?" Sometimes Jelebron needed a little nudging to get her back on subject.

"Yes, Kodo. I was getting to that!" she hissed, annoyed. "Because I have no female heirs, you will be emperor, first son, after I'm gone."

Kodo spluttered, "B–But don't they have kings in skragling culture, Your Highness?"

"I think we will make an exception. If I am not mistaken, skragling kings ruled over their queens, which is of course impossible. We must be aware of the proprieties. You could be called a steward if you would prefer."

"No, Your Highness, the title is fine. I'm just concerned that—"

"Good. It's settled then."

He tried not to show it, but Kodo's mind was in turmoil. Did his gracious mother not realize that making him "emperor," or "king" or whatever she wanted to call it, was tantamount to declaring his death sentence? She might as well give him the epithet of "Kodo the Quickly Assassinated." No female drakyn would accept him as their leader. It just wasn't done. There had been no significant male leaders in the history of the drakyn. Drakonia was a matriarchy. As much as his people could change their individual shapes, they were incapable of societal change. With the best teachers and studying everything he could about history and culture, still he'd failed to foresee this moment. Why hadn't he prepared better? He could have pushed one of the capable female warriors forward, downplayed his own achievements more. Failed more.

How had he missed the signs? Jelebron was past her prime; that was obvious. No new eggs or liveborn in decades. Was she really near death?

"Mother, you have ages to live yet. Why speak of passing now? You still look so young."

"Young? Don't bother with your false flattery. I get enough from the others to drown an eel! It's time to face it; I look as old as the stones of this palace, and I haven't weathered half as well. My end approaches."

"I'm so sorry," lied Kodo.

"There's still time to prepare for your rule."

"Can't I talk you out of this, dear Mother?" he wheedled. "There are so many female warriors far more deserving than I am."

"Don't feign humility, my dear, it doesn't become you. You're the perfect choice. The most intelligent male. The best warrior, the most handsome."

So, my fate is sealed, he thought, finally giving up his attempts to change her mind. He knew how intractable she could be.

"But what of Semli?" he asked, almost to himself. Semli had always thought himself the most talented, the most deserving of accolades. How would he react to this?

But Jelebron misunderstood his question, stirring uncomfortably in her chair. "Of course, after I'm gone, the decision will be yours. If you think he needs to be eliminated..." Her eyes clouded with memories. "When I saw what I had birthed–I'm still amazed that you saved him."

Kodo coughed nervously. "As I am too at times, Your Highness."

She snorted, and her massive cartilaginous ears rippled in the morning light that streamed down on them through the high window.

"Well," she said with finality, "he will be your subject. You can decide what to do with the little fool. But be careful. I fear that his talent for betrayal is as great as his desire for power. He could poison the court against you or cause you distress in some small and petty way."

Semli does nothing that is small. Petty maybe.

"I'll deal with it, Mother," said Kodo quietly.

The queen pulled her considerable bulk up to a more erect position, and inwardly, Kobo cringed. *What now?*

"There's one more thing. You've been keeping that new little skragling to yourself, first son. It's time for a coming-out party. Is that what they call it? Bring her to the grand ball tomorrow evening."

"Which skragling, Your Highness? There are so many."

"You know perfectly well which one, impertinent son." Jelebron's voice had turned to steel. "That pretty silver-haired thing that makes my head buzz."

"But there isn't enough time for Bellon to fashion her an appropriate gown. You know the rules. We can't use our talents to help them."

"Then you'd better get her on it at once. You are excused." Jelebron twisted her massive bulk to face away from him, and he knew that the audience was over.

On his way out, he found his brother, Semli, at the door.

"Mood?" asked the other drakyn, brightly adorned in the human form he had chosen today.

"The usual," replied Kodo.

"In other words, surly, intentionally obtuse and full of gas."

Kodo laughed. "That's our mother."

As Semli walked past him, Kodo couldn't help but marvel at the extent his brother would go to mirror skragling culture. Today he wore an incredibly handsome human form, with dark almond eyes and a muscular frame, which Kodo assumed he needed to bear the weight of his elaborate battle gear. It was complete with chain mail, massive iron pauldrons, and a wide belt that gleamed in all its intricate golden splendor. A crimson cape and ornate samurai sword completed the look. Kodo had to admit that it was impressive. Whether it would have any effect on their mother's mood, he couldn't say. Poor Semli. Always the second son; always the unwanted one. Always trying to please, but never allowed to be anything but a loathsome sycophant in his mother's eyes.

Passing by Semli, Kodo wandered aimlessly down the hall. His mind was far from the gelid stone that surrounded him, but his thoughts ran just as cold. He'd gladly have Semli take his place as emperor. Unlike his brother, he had no desire for rule, no longing to be fawned over by sniveling courtiers and adored by the unwashed masses. He had doubts about where his people were headed. More and more he was beginning to wonder if their treatment of the skraglings was beneficial to either race. Was he growing a conscience? Unlikely. Probably just indigestion from that ghastly blood stew he'd been forced to eat at last night's royal dinner. But the life he had led so far did not make him proud, and the life his mother had planned for him promised to be just as ignominious. As he walked, four words kept playing themselves over and over in his mind.

You don't want this.

CHAPTER FOUR

Multiple Dance Partners

Wren fidgeted on the raised platform while the dressmaker fussed and mumbled. Bellon stuck her with a pin for the third or fourth time and Wren could take it no more.

"Ouch! Bellon! Are you creating a dress or a human pincushion?"

The older woman's hands shook as she replied. "Sorry girl, I'm in a bit of a rush. The bastart wants you ready for their ridiculous grand ball tonight, and I just don't know if we can get it done in time. So, hold still."

"OK, OK," said Wren, wriggling. "What the fruck is a grand ball, anyway?"

"Please don't swear!"

"Sorry," she mumbled.

Bellon continued, "There ain't that much grand about it in my humble opinion, but it's one of the things they love to copy from skragling culture. I mean, human culture," corrected the small woman quickly. The woman paused in mid-poke as if realizing that she had been drifting into the drakyn way of thinking. She shuddered. "Anyway, they just love the old dances and music. They're not that good at it, but never tell them so. It's all kind of stilted, but they try. If you can dance or play a tune, they'll love you. Probably to death."

"What does that mean?" rasped Wren. "And no, I can't dance. Mama taught me a few steps, but I never had the chance to go to a real dance, and I'm sure I don't want to attend this one."

"Well, you don't got no choice now, girl. Do what they ask. You don't wanna see 'em angry. You got me?"

"I guess," Wren admitted reluctantly, then asked, "Bellon, has anyone ever escaped this place?"

"Shhh!" hissed Bellon, pulling Wren down close to her. "There ain't no way outa this gardamn hell hole, hear me? It's flat all around. If they find you gone, they can see you running for miles. An' they can fly! Get me? Ain't no way outa this gardamn hell hole," she repeated. "That's why they pick us what got little transmogering talent. There's no way out. Sooner you face that, the sooner you'll..."

"I'll what?"

Bellon appeared to sag in on herself. Already not much more than an empty sack, her body deflated even more. "I don't know. Accept yur fate, I 'spose. Now hold still!"

Wren didn't want to just "accept her fate," but she was no fool. Without talent, she didn't have much of a chance. Her brother and sister had taught her some hard truths when she was still a child. They knew she would never have the talent they possessed, so they tried to teach her how to use the skills and wits she did have. She fought her brother hand-to-hand until she was exhausted. Then he sat on her until she admitted that she'd lost and quizzed her on what she would do next. Her sister raced her across the fields, letting Wren get ahead and think she could win, then passing her by as if she weren't even moving. She thought they were so cruel. They made her feel weak and stupid, but later she understood. If she had any chance of survival, being untalented in a talented world, then she'd better get used to losing and find other ways to survive. She had to use her wits, her determination. It had worked out so far, but now she wondered how long she could go on hiding her truly impressive lack of transmogering skill.

As the two women huddled together, a great shadow darkened the curtain to the dressing room, painting her silver gown in shades of gray. Then the shadow deflated and was replaced with the shape of a man. Kodo stepped into the small room.

"Is it done?" he demanded imperiously.

Bellon bowed low and almost didn't make it back up again, until Wren gave her a hand.

"Almost, m'lord," Bellon wheezed. "If you could just give us a couple more minutes—"

"We're out of time, dressmaker. Let me see what you've got so far."

"Er..."

"Stand up straight, girl!" he commanded.

Wren stood up straight as instructed, to realize that the gown was obviously only half-finished.

"It's lovely," he crooned. "It brings out the silver in your hair and your enchanting gray eyes."

But his eyes weren't focused on her face at all.

Wren realized that only a diaphanous film of fabric covered her upper torso, and she blanched, crossing her arms in front of her chest defensively.

"I am not wearing this as it is!"

"Oh yes, you are!" he countered stubbornly. "It's perfect. The others will be so jealous. I have found the most pulchritudinous skragling flower on all of Drakonia, and you are my discovery."

*Pulchritudinous? Where did he learn a word like that? It
sounds more like something I'd spit up than say out loud.*

Wren fumed, tempted to try to gouge his eyes out, then remembered her brother instructing her on how to deal with the
talented. "Their egos are their weakness. Pretend to give them
what they want. Make your ideas become theirs, and they'll think
they've won, while you get what *you* want." He'd looked at her
in pity, and Wren realized sadly that she'd probably outlived her
extraordinarily talented brother.

Wren affected her most charming smile.

"Of course, Your Highness, but your supremely talented
seamstress has an idea to make the gown even more glorious. Silver
ribbons, running from here to here."

When Bellon stood looking at her stupidly, Wren surrepti-
tiously gave her a kick in the shin.

"Ouch–Oh yes," stammered Bellon. Groping in her basket of
notions, she pulled out a length of all-too-slender silver ribbon.
With more pins and inadvertent pricks, she managed to attach the
ribbon at strategic points along the length of the bodice.

"Hmm. I don't know," mused the drakyn, his hand to his chin.

"One thing I've learned from your wisdom, master," began
Wren obsequiously, "is that a thing not entirely revealed is so much
more tantalizing than showing everything at once. The others will
be amazed at your ingenuity and prodigious sense of style."

Kodo gave her a questioning look as if perhaps he could see
through her attempts to manipulate him, but then he smiled and said,
"Oh, I see! That is lovely! And so 'tantalizing,' as you put it. Bellon,
finish this up at once. We need to get the rest of her ready for the ball
tonight. It's going to be epic and legendary! My rescuing this jewel of

skragling womanhood from rural poverty and the dangers of war will be the talk of the palace!"

Wren frowned, then nodded tentatively, not sure if she'd just won a victory or surrendered her last vestige of dignity.

The alleged ballroom was a great, drafty cathedral of tumbling stone and precarious arches so tall they were lost in the overhead gloom. The high beams were studded with thousands of glittering black gems, some of which appeared to move awkwardly to the rhythm of the instruments that played.

Two ragged bands battled for ascendancy, playing at once but most assuredly not as one. Each contained a rabble of haggard human players. Their instruments, some of skragling and others of drakyn construction, were of intricate design, with inlaid oystum shell, sparkling chrystala, and lapis lazuli in the frets. The head of one five-string took the shape of a curving drakyn's head, an elegant mahogany visage more graceful in form than any living drakyn she'd ever seen, but perhaps this was how they imagined themselves. Nearest to her played a human band consisting of fiddle, skelighorn, twistflute, and five-string. They were playing a ballad she thought she knew, but it was so out of tune and time that it presented only a grotesque mockery of real music.

The multitude of black gems overhead shifted as if in discomfort at their stations, and a ragged group of drakyn and human dancers stood about, not seeming to know what to do next.

Wren looked about as Kodo led her in, feeling tiny and insignificant beside the flamboyant skragling form he'd taken. She wasn't sure what era, or eras, of human culture he was attempting to emulate, but he'd adopted from them the most extravagant and supercilious affectations he could find. A gigantic peacock feather flopped from his massive hat over one eye. His uniform of blue and gold sparkled with war medals and ribbons. Long bone buttons adorned the front, and she wondered what poor animal had volunteered them. Around his neck, he flaunted a ridiculous sparkling pink boa so long that its end trailed far behind him, an absurd gilded snake's head bouncing along the floor as he walked. To her horror the snake's head hissed ever time it hit the floor. His supple leather boots extended to his upper thighs and sighed with every step he took. The whole costume rippled with his every muscled movement, glimmering and sparkling as he walked. He looked so perfectly ludicrous, yet somehow perfectly suited to this macabre scene of brazenly costumed players set in a musty, dank cathedral of gloom and dissonance.

It's like an opera of the bizarre.

He gazed down at her with a frown, as if the general discomfort of the scene was all her doing. She shrugged, resisting the urge to adjust the all-too-revealing metallic straps on her gown.

Kodo led her over to Jelebron, who stood next to a handsome human prince, or so he appeared.

"Let me formally introduce you to Her Highness, Queen Jelebron. Highest born of all drakyn on this world, and your Grand Leader. You will bow."

Wren did as she was told, trying not to gag from the smell. The queen of the drakyn gave her only a passing glance, but Wren could see a calculating light in her ancient eyes.

"And this is my brother, Semli, second prince of the realm."

Semli studied her intently, and Wren felt as if her clothing was even thinner than it truly was. She knew she was blushing and forced herself to ignore his look and return one as penetrating as his. He let out a snort as if amused by her comeuppance. The arrogance came off him in waves. He was as vain as Kodo, maybe more. Yet there was something else there. Perhaps an intelligence or understanding of her kind that Kodo didn't possess. Semli "did" human better than any of the drakyn she'd so far met. He wasn't overdressed, but he had the details spot on. His uniform was like one her brother had worn when he first joined the resistance: gray doublet, scarlet cloak, and sword belt of simple leather. He wore no hat, and his blond hair was cut short in the rough soldier's way. He smelled like a hayloft, of equines and leather and hard work outside. Wren couldn't think of a better way for a man to smell. Then she reminded herself that this wasn't a man at all, but an abomination of the sort that killed her kind for sport. Confused, she felt drawn to him, despite despising him for what he was. Kodo must have sensed what was going on between them because he pulled her away abruptly and asked, "Can you dance?"

"Well, yes, but not to this!" The words were out before she could stop them. "I mean, when does the ball begin?"

Kodo looked annoyed. "It has begun, foolish skragling. Be aware that you are in the presence of the Royal Orchestra and the best dancers in all of Drakonia!"

Wren realized her mistake. She resisted the urge to snigger and said, "Well, it's off to an excellent start, m'lord." After a pause, she couldn't help but add, "I don't know much about royal ball protocol, but something seems off to me."

He glanced at her coldly, and she swallowed hard. Was she already making him angry? She didn't understand the first thing about relating to these creatures. The smart thing would be to shut up right now.

She hesitated. She just couldn't stop herself. Music had been an integral part of her life before she could speak.

"It's just that—"

"What?" he demanded impatiently.

"My granpapa was a fiddler and five-string player his whole life. He taught me this song that your musicians are playing—or trying to play."

"What's wrong with it?"

"Well, it's out of tune, and the rhythm is off." Seeing his expression, she added, "But other than that, it's perfect. Anyway, with what he taught me, I think I could get your players to sound even more exquisite, if you would allow me."

Kodo relented. "Certainly, my sweet. Please show us how it's done."

Not sure if he meant it sincerely or facetiously, but seeing a twinkle in his eye, she hesitantly approached the first band. A tired-looking gray-haired man handed her his five-string before she could even ask. As he did so, he whispered to her, "It doesn't matter what you play or how out of tune it is; they won't know the difference."

"Yes, but *I* will!" she retorted. With a frown, she took the instrument from him and began to tune it. It was of better quality than she'd expected, and she thought it would hold a tune well. The notes it produced were rich and bright. As she began to strum it, she noticed that the delicate ear cartilage of the drakyn who had retained their firstform started to tremble in synchrony with the instrument. When she had it in tune, she turned to the other musicians. "It's

Euroscale, not Asias. I think that will be easiest for tuning and it fits the song." In a daze, the other musicians nodded and began the process of tuning their instruments to match hers. She had the odd impression that they'd never tuned their instruments together, never bothered to actually *play* together.

"OK," she said, encouraged by this small victory. "Now, let's follow a basic beat. My granpapa called this walls-time. I hope that makes sense. It's also called three in four time." She tapped her toe on the floor and began to play a simple tune. Soon the other musicians joined in, even improvising on her simple melody. The grim dance hall was soon filled with a delicate, fledgling music, perhaps the first it had ever known. She noticed a smile or two on the grim faces of the musicians. Then she began to sing in a hesitant but rich alto voice.

"Down in the valley, valley so low,
Hang your head over, hear the wind blow
Hear the wind blow, love, hear the wind blow
Hang your head over, hear the wind blow
Roses love sunshine, violets love dew
Angels in gardland know I love you
Know I love you, love, know I love you
Angels in gardland know I love you
If you don't love me, love whom you please
Throw your arms round me, give my heart ease
Give my heart ease, love, give my heart ease
Throw your arms round me, give my heart ease
Build me a castle, forty hands high
So I can see her as she rides by
As she rides by, love, as she rides by

So I can see her as she rides by
Down in the valley, valley so low
Hang your head over, hear the wind blow
Hear the wind blow, love, hear the wind blow
Hang your head over, hear the wind blow."

A great sigh came up from the drakyn listeners, and Wren was surprised to hear such a sound from them. *Was that their version of applause?*

When both groups of musicians were playing in sync, Kodo motioned to her, and she returned the five-string to its now eager owner, who, like the other musicians, appeared to welcome the chance to play actual music for a change.

Kodo said, "Well, you seem to have improved our orchestra immeasurably! What else can you do?" He looked at her with those eager eyes, the way he'd looked at her back at the cabin when he'd seen her head bleeding. He saw the fear on her face and took a step back.

"I don't mean to frighten you," he said carefully.

"You don't frighten me!" she replied in defiance, then was not sure if she meant it.

"You're very strong for your size, you know. I mean, for a skragling, and you are quite willful. I find it intriguing."

"No, I'm nothing like that," she said, not wanting him to think her capable of anything, especially escape.

"OK, let's agree that you are at least exceptional, shall we?" He looked at her quizzically, but she couldn't read his expression. Kodo and his kind were so hard to follow sometimes. The more they tried to act human, the more alien they appeared.

"Shall we dance?" he asked.

"Well, I've seen it done," she said, and then felt foolish. In her nervousness, she giggled, and that encouraged him. He took her hand and led her out onto the stone surface that passed for a dance floor, where other couples were attempting to move to the music with varying levels of success. She took his hand and didn't know what should follow. Then she remembered the simple steps her mama had taught her.

She said, "Left foot forward, step over to the right foot. Step back with your right and move to your left. Make a square." She didn't realize that she was saying the words aloud until she saw that Kodo was saying them with her. "I think I'm getting it. How fun. You're a genius, little bird!" Then he stumbled.

"Now, just relax and move with the music," she soothed.

As they danced, the other dancers fell in beside them and duplicated their movements until the whole room vibrated with the rhythm she'd created. The dark gems in the rafters separated and formed a black cloud, pulsating with the music and the figures beneath them. Soon the cloud settled close, joining them in the dance. Now she could see individual shapes; small flying lizards with elongated, delicate necks and heads as fine and pointed as sea equines. Glossy black scales covered their bodies and glittered as they moved. Long, translucent tails and gossamer wings gave them the look of tiny ebony angels.

Watching them move, she was entranced. "What are they?"

"Oh, it's just the flets, you know. Not much meat on them, but not half bad with the right sauce."

"What? You eat them?"

"Well, only when we can catch them. Bloody fast little biters."

"I've heard of them but never seen one."

"Well, you'll rarely see just one. In the wild, huge flocks gather in caves. They invaded the palace; I suppose thinking it was a cave. They shite everywhere. Just a nuisance, really."

"But they're so beautiful!" she whispered.

Looking up as if he were seeing them for the first time, he said, "Yes, they are, aren't they?"

"Look how they move with the music," she exclaimed, mesmerized by their synchronized air dance. "How can they do that, move as one, yet with such individual grace?"

He was watching her closely. She noticed that he'd grown smaller, closer to her own size, and his uniform was less ornate now, more like an ordinary soldier, an ordinary man. The disquieting boa was gone.

"Show me more of this dance," he demanded softly. Without questioning, she increased the speed and variety of their movements, a bit awkwardly at first, but as they moved, they found a kind of balance between them, one reacting to the other, then even intuiting what the other would do next. Soon, the flets were moving with only the two of them. Gathering over their heads, the flets dipping when the couple dipped, swirling as they swirled. When Wren laughed, they emitted a sparkling chorus of echoing laughter. They imitated her speech and even the rustle of her gown with amazing accuracy. Before she knew it, the other dancers had left the floor and her and Kodo danced alone, the center of attention. Wren heard a spattering of applause and the eerie sighing sound that she assumed indicated drakyn approval.

The dark hall was filled with light and warmth and movement and music, and for just a second, Wren was happy. She hiccupped, and the flets hiccupped with her. Disrupted by the sound, she realized where she was and what she was doing, and the spell was broken. She felt her brittle, fleeting joy break as if it had hit the floor with a crash. She stumbled, suddenly unsure of her steps. What was she doing here? Kodo braced her arm and frowned at her in concern.

"Are you all right?"

She blinked and the smile froze on her face, slowly melting into despair. In that moment, she knew she had no choice but to escape this place before it devoured her, as it had consumed so many before her: the ones who had just given up, the missing, the victims of accidents and gard-knew what happened to the ones sent to the farms. But perhaps the worst loss of all would be her will, her humanity. She would not die here, in thrall to these bizarre creatures and their sick games.

Pulling herself up, she said with as much cheer as she could muster, "I am ever so well, m'lord, but it's getting late, and I still have work to do in the kitchen. May I be excused?" Kodo, perhaps as surprised by what had happened between then as Wren was, just mumbled, "Yes dear, run along. I'll see you tomorrow."

Wren, determined that he would *not* see her tomorrow, or any day thereafter, hurried out of the great hall. As she walked, she tried to force her nascent escape plan into solid form, but her thoughts kept drawing her back to the fleeting joy she had felt and the graceful, ethereal dance of the flets.

CHAPTER FIVE

Darkness of the Heart

Wren was lost. These cold, dank tunnels lead nowhere, or so she assumed, because she'd been everywhere and nowhere all evening, searching for the rumored secret exit that obviously didn't exist.

She'd considered the enclosed garden. There were apple, cherry, and drakynfruit trees. Maybe she could climb one of them, then jump from a limb to the stone wall. But none of the limbs were close enough. She assumed that others had attempted to escape this way, so the trees had been trimmed. It had all been tried before. Her plans were half-baked, she had to admit. But there had to be a way out, and she would find it! She leaned against the wall and let out a heavy sigh of defeat. Who was she kidding? She had as much chance of escape as a clawcrab being thrown screaming into a boiling pot of water.

Then she stilled. She'd heard a sound where there shouldn't be any. A scraping, scritching noise that abraded her eardrums. It was coming from the tunnel behind her. She quickly dimmed her lantern. Willing her body into the very stone, she became as still as possible and stopped breathing. A form passed her by, but she sensed that it wasn't moving as a normal creature moved. Most organisms had an internal balance, with two or four, six or eight limbs. Even if they had three or five, there was symmetry and balance to the body. Not so for this pathetic creature, with its haphazard grouping of limbs and organs. She'd never seen or felt anything like this poor laboring thing before her. She gasped as it wheezed and dragged itself past her. She shrank back even farther into the darkness, but it had heard her.

Semli caught sight of the skragling in his peripheral vision as he passed. He would have traveled by it unawares, had he not smelled the pity emanating from its skin. Of course, it was tiny, fragile, and talentless, no threat to him, but it had *seen him* in his firstform. That was not allowed, so it would have to die. Then he realized what it was, and he pulled up just before delivering a death blow. There might be more entertainment here.

"Kodo's pet!" he croaked, doing the best to make skragling words with his deformed vocal cords. "Aren't you a lovely, delicate little thing! Perfect little digits and perfect, lovely knees and elbows. So pretty. My, my. And he values this possession, doesn't he, my dear brother. My dear, dear one."

Wren stood as still as she could, realizing intuitively the mortal danger she was in at that moment. Unable to speak, she felt the hate and grief emanating from this creature like a blast furnace of despair. His malice toward her was palpable, undeniable. She didn't at first recognize him from the evening of the ball. This was something else entirely.

"You know, I owe all this to dear Kodo, don't you?" His limbs stuttered in a painful parody of an actor sweeping his arms in a dramatic arch. "I should not have lived, you know. Brother dear saved me from being eaten at birth by my own mother." He sniggered at the look of horror on her face.

"Oh yes, that's how it's done. If that's how a mother treats her child in drakyn society, how do you think Kodo will treat you when he gets bored? You're just an amusing toy to him, a piece of shiny flotsam to be discarded when he tires of admiring your lovely form. I've seen him do it before." A thought occurred to him. "But I would like to use you just a little, too."

She could tell that something was happening to the creature, but she didn't understand it. Semli cried out in pain; then, as if breaking through some unseen barrier, he extended his limbs, struggling with great effort until there were only four of them. A cloying scent filled the air. Colors coalesced from sparkling and asymmetrical to smooth and complimentary. A shape became itself.

"That was harder than it should've been," he remarked, wiping sweat from his brow. "Must be the moons. They're in alignment right now. Damn hot in here, too, but no matter."

Semli had changed back into the handsome human she'd first met at the ball. He stood tall and straight, and his tanned skin was smooth as silk, tempting her to touch it. Even his scent drew her in, despite her fear. Wren was lost. She'd known at the dance that he wasn't human, of course, but had she known that this grotesquerie lay beneath the surface, she would never have had the courage to even speak to him. The horrid creature had transformed in seconds into this fully formed, handsome, likable young soldier, the one she'd wanted to get to know. Truly, Semli had a great talent at transmogrifee and understood humans better than any of the others.

Too bad it's wasted on a monster!

Semli drew close to her, pushing his muscled torso against her, and Wren groaned involuntarily. He laughed. "You are a spicy little thing, aren't you? Kodo chose well. I bet your blood tastes like dark honey."

"My blood?"

"What do you think we keep you for, silly little bird? Your sparkling wit? Your talent? Your skill in battle? Well, obviously, you have none of those attributes, do you?" He pushed her roughly against the stone and lifted her skirt. As he entered her, he grabbed her wrist and brought it to his lips. Wren felt both exquisite pain and an obscene pleasure pulse through her. Dizzy with a need she didn't know she had, she moaned and was lost to her own weakness. She felt herself slide between shapes in a nauseating parade of lovers and battles and feasts. Tastes and smells and the touch of hot skin burned in her like a bellows-blown fire. She felt something she'd never felt before: power. It lasted forever or ended as suddenly as it started, she wasn't sure which, but when it was gone, she felt bereft and even smaller than before.

When he left her, she lay sobbing, crumpled against the stones. She sat in the dark for a long time, hoping that the pain would end soon, but knowing she wouldn't be so lucky. She wasn't even sure exactly what had happened to her. There was a sticky wetness at her numb wrist, and she realized that it was bleeding. She felt drained, but even in her misery, she realized that she'd felt something else. Lust, yes. Pain, yes. Humiliation, yes, but something more. For a second, she'd shared Semli's power to transmoger, and her mind was spinning in a whirlwind of possibilities she'd never dreamed might exist. Her head buzzed with quiet fire, as if a power deep within her struggled to climb up from the darkness of her heart. Was it her potential, or had she just been sharing Semli's abilities?

Potential. What was potential but a hollow promise, an empty womb, an open sore that hopes to heal, one day? Her mother had said that Wren had great potential. Look where it had gotten her. To this.

Wren sighed and stood on shaking legs. Self-pity was worth even less than potential, she chided herself. Despite her exhaustion and fear, despite her confusion, Wren felt instinctively that she'd learned something about herself this night that could change the course of her life, if it turned out that she survived another day. She had potential still. She just didn't know for what yet.

She limped back to her kitchen chambers with great but undefinable thoughts forming in her beleaguered mind and an even stronger will to survive raising its feeble head in her soul. She'd been the victim of one who had no identity of his own, who cringed away from who and what he really was. Maybe she'd been doing the same thing her whole life. Did she share this disability with the crippled drakyn? She couldn't live in shame and anger anymore for the loss of a talent she would never possess. She would embrace being talentless and live every day to the utmost of her ability, using the meager skills she'd been granted at birth. She would escape the frucking hell-hole these moron lizards called a palace or die trying.

CHAPTER SIX

Into the Deep and Over the Edge

When she brought him his meal, Kodo sensed something different about Wren. He'd smelled that she hadn't been a virgin when he found her. It happened as a natural course of life. A young farmhand on loan, or the brother, or even the father. It happened. But it shouldn't have happened here, on his watch. When he found out who had done it...but that didn't matter now. Now, he needed to help her if he could. She wouldn't look directly at him, or at anyone. He feared that her fire had been extinguished, or at least greatly diminished. It was his fault. He should never have hit her. He didn't know what had overcome him in that moment. Not being able to transmoger, even for a second, was his worst fear. He had reacted out of panic, and he regretted it now. It was still difficult to transmoger if she was too close to him. Was that his own fear, or was there something about her that caused this buzzing heat in his head and the tightness in his chest? She was a mystery, a puzzle that he desperately wanted to solve. Now he didn't know what to do to make her feel better, if even he could.

So distracted was he by his thoughts and concern for her that he didn't notice when she left the room.

In the garden, Wren found a fragile looking branch that might hold her weight and began to climb. A voice rang out behind her, and she almost fell.

"Not that way."

"Wh–What?" Wren jerked back in alarm, then realized it was only Mala. She saw the dejected look on Mala's face.

"What is it? What's wrong, Mala? You look like your best friend just died."

Hearing this, Mala looked like she might cry. "It's Poppet, he's missing. Teeka won't tell me where he's gone, but I think I know."

"The farms?"

Mala just studied the ground. Wren was wracked by guilt. If only she hadn't shown an interest in the boy.

"I need to go home," Mala blurted.

"Home? Where's that?"

Instead of answering Mala just pointed off to the west.

"What's that way?" asked Wren.

Mala's face brightened just a little. "The sea. I think I lived near it."

"You think? Don't you remember?"

Mala just looked confused. "Yes, I mean, it's all a little blurry, like another life."

"Well, you were probably very young when you were brought here."

"Yes, maybe that's it. I don't know. I only know that it's trying to pull me back. It tugs at me, and I must go. With Poppet gone, there's not much reason to stay any longer, and you seem determined to escape yourself, though your ideas seem a bit...What's the term for 'not thought through?'" She studied the tender branch, way too far from the wall to reach by even a prodigious jumper, like a grella. Wren didn't have a chance.

"OK, maybe my ideas are a bit half-baked, but I'm getting desperate. I have to get away from here too."

"Half-baked, that's the phrase I was trying to think of!"

Wren frowned. "Well, do you have a better idea?"

Mala glanced at Wren critically, as if assessing her inner strength. She said, "I think I know a way, but it won't be easy, not for you anyway."

"What do you mean?"

"Can you swim?"

"Sure," Wren replied, "I lived on a river, and we swam every summer. When I was nine, Mama joked that I was more fish than girl."

"Well, the way we're going, you'll need to be." Mala observed her, uncertainty written on her earnest features.

Wren said, "Look, I'm determined to get out of here. If you know a way, I'm all in. I would rather die trying than spend another minute as a slave to these monsters."

"All right," soothed Mala. "We'll meet tonight after dinner in the common area. Bring some food if you can steal it without being caught, but not too much. The way we're going will require we travel light. Wrap up your notebook and primers so they're watertight."

"OK," agreed Wren, not entirely sure what the girl might have in mind, but determined to make it work, one way or another.

At the common area that evening, Wren arrived with the canvas pack that carried her precious notebook and primers, wrapped in oil paper for travel, as well as a couple pieces of stale cheese and a few wrinkled apples that she'd been able to slip out of the kitchen without anyone noticing. She waited nervously for Mala, wondering if she'd changed her mind or lost her courage.

When Mala finally arrived, Wren heaved a huge sigh of relief as the girl wordlessly motioned for her to follow. At first, the route took them into the tunnels that Wren had already explored, and she was about to mention this to Mala, when the girl pulled up abruptly. In the gloom, Wren could see that Mala had brought an emerock lantern and lit it now by pouring lime green phosphorescent dust into a jar of water. It sizzled and foamed, and as it settled, the rock walls around them grew brighter with an eerie jade glow. Mala raised a hand and stood still as if listening for something. In the lantern light, her impish features glowed in shades of celadon.

Finally, she said, "It's this way, unless it's been transmogered. That's unlikely down here. Who would bother?" Mala hurried down an offshoot of the main tunnel that, as they walked, gradually began to smell more and more rank. A cloying dampness accompanied the smell, and Wren wrinkled her nose.

"Ugh! This smells worse than the drakyn, and that's saying a lot. Are you sure this is the way?"

"I think so," said Mala, "In fact, the worse it smells the closer we'll be."

Thinking that Mala had lost her mind, Wren followed tentatively, soon lagging far behind. The feint light of the lantern bobbed in the distance and Wren stumbled in the dark, not sure if she should go forward, or run back to her warm, itchy straw bed instead.

She heard Mala cry out ahead of her. "Hurry up! It's here."

Wren stumbled forward as fast as she dared until she stood beside Mala in the empty tunnel.

"What?" she exclaimed. "This is a dead end. I've already been down this way. It's hopeless!" Wren wanted to stamp her foot in frustration, but when she looked down, the most nauseating smell crept up to meet her nose. Below their feet, a rusted metal grate covered a dark smelly hole. Below that, a dimpled mass of sewage crept by at a turtlet's pace.

"Down there," said Mala unnecessarily.

"You've got to be kidding! I said I could swim–in *water*, not struggle through shite up to our ears!"

"It's the only way, Wren. You said you wanted out and this is our best option. The smell will improve as we go, trust me. Soon it will be more water than shite as it merges with the underground river. That's where the current is coming from. All the sewer lines must join this main line."

"But how do you know it will take us in the right direction?"

"Because water flows downhill, and I've seen the lay of the land from above. Teeka assigned me to clean the upper chambers, as a punishment. I could see from a window that it's slightly downhill all the way to the sea from here."

"And how do we know the tunnel isn't blocked with another grate at the end?"

"We don't," admitted Mala. "But I'm willing to try if you are. What do we have to lose? Besides, I have this." With pride, Mala pulled a small metal tool from her bag that looked like it wouldn't open a box of sweets much less a huge rust-encrusted grate.

Wren didn't see that they had a choice. She was committed to this crazy plan. Before she could come up with more objections, Mala said, "OK, give me a hand," as she strained to lift the heavy grating. After extensive grunting and swearing, they'd moved the grate just enough to allow the two of them to slip through.

"I'm going to regret this, I know it," said Wren through gritted teeth as she lowered herself tentatively into the fetid opening.

"Just hurry. I don't want to end up too far behind you. I'm the better swimmer, so I'll try to help you if you get into trouble."

Before Wren could be hurt that Mala just assumed she was the better swimmer, Mala pushed her fingers away from their steel grip on the edge and Wren fell. She had no time to think about anything else before she was plunged into sewage hell.

The toxic gases threatened to suffocate her before she could drown. The caustic fumes burned her throat and eyes, until she was swimming blind, in sheer pain and misery. All she could do was splash feebly in the slow current and hope that she was going in the right direction. Occasionally, she could feel Mala tugging at her to keep her moving. Wren had to admit that Mala was made of sterner stuff than she was. She was truly at home in anything liquid, even this horrible sludge.

Wren had given up all hope that they would survive, when she felt a wisp of fresher air caress her forehead and it felt like their pace was picking up. The revitalized current pushed them gradually ever downward and outward until the tunnel widened and the water ran cleaner. Wren was exhausted, gasping for air and didn't think she could go any further. She thought about dying like this, alone in a sewer, her flesh eaten away by putrid slime. The water pulled her below the surface, but even as she went under, she felt gentle hands pushing her upward. In her delirium, Wren thought it was her mama, pulling her from the bath.

"You look like a little prune!" she heard the warm voice of her mama exclaim. "Get out of there before you turn in to a mergirl, or maybe a marm. Then you can swim with the fishes all day and live on herrins and kelp salad!"

"Yuck," said Wren, laughing. She let the gentle hands lift her out of the now lukewarm water. The bath made her sleepy and she fell into dreams on a soft, fuzzy towel.

When she woke, the towel had turned into an itchy bed of moss and her mama was gone, long dead, of course.

Mala sat beside her on a narrow shelf that provided barely enough room for the two of them. Frantically, Wren searched for her pack and found to her relief that it had stayed on her back through the swim. To her dismay they were still in the tunnel, but she could see Mala and wondered why for a second, remembering that they'd left the lantern behind. Then a hopeful thought occurred to her dulled brain, and she sat up.

"Yes," said Mala, reading her expression. "I think we're near the exit and light is reaching us from the outside, but you were exhausted, and couldn't go any farther without rest."

"How long was I asleep?" asked Wren.

"Not long. A couple of hours. It must be almost daylight outside."

"I hope so," grunted Wren. "Either that or we're approaching the fires of hell."

"There is no such place, silly," chided Mala. "There is only solid ground and sea and sky and where we are now. I never understood why people need to create other worlds, when this one is perfect."

"You're an odd girl, Mala, but so much of what you say makes sense. I think I agree with you."

After they nibbled on the cheese and apples she'd brought, she told Mala she felt strong enough to swim again and they slipped into the water. It had grown cooler as they floated downward and now the chill bit at Wren with muscle-cramping shock. She struggled until Mala's strong hands grabbed her and pulled her along. Wren was amazed at the strength and endurance in this slight girl; the cold didn't seem to bother her at all. Encouraged by Mala, Wren relaxed and soon was able to swim on her own again.

As they swam, the waterway widened and, almost imperceptibly, the light grew brighter. Wren was beginning to hope it would be smooth sailing all the way to the ocean, when the current picked up, rushing them along at an ever-faster pace. As they were carried along, she felt the walls closing in around them. Fearing what might lie ahead, Wren began to struggle against the current, trying to slow her pace, but it was beyond her power, as the water became a raging monster, with a strength far beyond that of two slight humans. She gave up the fight and just clung to Mala, who appeared to have her own innate buoyancy in the water.

Sudden light burst upon them, and she saw blue sky ahead. Then the water disappeared beneath them. They perched together for a moment, hanging weightless in the suddenly bright morning light, while aerated water frothed and hissed all around them. Then they fell. The foam engulfed them, pulling them down, growing thicker and darker as they descended. The fall went on and on, until they were hit hard by the watery beast that had reached up to grab them. She lost consciousness in the maw of some darkly salted water dream. It grabbed her breath away and pulled her deeper, perhaps to sleep forever in the depths of a sailor's worst nightmare.

Coughing and sputtering, spitting up briny water, she finally came to her senses, realizing that Mala had saved them once again. They lay together on a narrow spit of rough sand and gravel, while a great waterfall raged above them. Mala had even managed to retrieve her pack and it lay at her side, wet and bedraggled, but whole. When she could breathe normally again, Wren raised herself on shaking limbs to gaze up at the monstrosity that had just spit them out.

"We survived that?" she gasped. "What is it? I've never heard of a waterfall that spills directly into the ocean like that."

"I think humans call it a tidefall. They're very rare," said Mala loudly, to be heard over the roar of the falls. "I don't think I want to try that again. Ever."

"Me neither! Thanks for saving me–again. You are an amazing swimmer, and much stronger than you look."

"You did well, too. Don't sell yourself short. I'm sure you could've made it on your own."

"I'm not so sure about that," replied Wren, "but I'm so glad to be back on solid ground."

Mala gave her an unreadable look but said nothing.

Once they'd rested a few more minutes, they rose and made their way along the narrow shore, away from the noise and power of the falls. As they walked, Mala was quiet, gazing out to sea. Wren wondered what she was thinking.

"Do you think we can find your family?" Wren asked, not being able to take the silence any longer. "There must be a village along here somewhere. My papa said he grew up in one of the seashore villages around here. We should look for an inlet or cove. Boats require a safe harbor."

Mala just continued to march ahead, often glancing out to sea. The shore gradually became rocky, until they were struggling over boulders and through tide pools filled with glistening seastars, brightly colored urchins and tiny darting minnows so bright they could have been gilded in gold.

Wren pulled up and watched Mala, who had stopped and was staring up at a rough natural stairway in the rock. Here they might be able to climb up to the grassy headland.

"What is it? Do you recognize this place?"

Mala said nothing but jerked her head around when they both heard a barking call in the distance. It pulled both their gazes out to sea, where a dozen or more shiny black heads bobbed in the waves. Then they saw even more of the sleek figures dancing in the crashing surf, between the rocks and over them, their movements as smooth and powerful as the ocean itself.

A worried, confused look shadowed Mala's features.

She spoke her first words in a while. "We'd better get up the stairs. Now."

The urgency in her voice seemed unwarranted to Wren. The marm pod was harmless, she knew, but she offered no objection as Mala lead them up the rough stairway. Wren struggled up to climb the rocks that could only optimistically be called stairs. She was running out of energy and her tongue was glued to the roof of her mouth from her thirst. Thinking of that only reminded her that, ironically, despite their waterlogged journey, they would need to find a new source of fresh water soon. Though they'd drunk their fill from a stream they found near the tidefall, that had been hours ago. She didn't even want to think about how they would find food.

At the top, they both collapsed in the swaying grass, to lie there panting. After a while Wren sat up and spoke. "After we find your family, I think I'll head inland. Maybe back to my cabin, if it's still there. I probably won't be able to stay long; it's the first place Kodo would look for me, if he decides I'm worth chasing down, of course. Then, I want to look for these farms the drakyn run, or at least find someone who knows where they are. I mean to rescue poor Poppet if I can–if I have the strength. After all, it's my fault he was sent there."

After a while, she thought Mala was sleeping, when her voice filtered up through the dancing grass.

"It's not on you, Wren. Not everything is your fault, you know. Besides, there could be many of these farms, and you don't even know where *one* of them is."

"Well, it sounds impossible when you put it that way, but at least I can try. We never thought we'd escape the palace, yet, thanks to you, here we are."

"Yes, here we are."

Mala's voice sounded so sad that it startled Wren.

"What is it, girl? You've been so quiet since we came out of the tunnel. Are you hurt? Or are you worried we won't find your family?"

"No, I'm fine. It's just that..." she trailed off.

"You can talk to me, Mala. Something is going on with you and I want to help."

"You can't help me. No one can," said Mala, dejectedly.

"Why is that?"

"Because I've finally remembered where my family is."

Wren couldn't imagine how this could be a problem. Were her family members criminals? Were they dead? Was Mala unwanted? Had they thrown her out?

Sudden anger on Mala's behalf made Wren's cheeks burn.

Wren said fiercely, "It doesn't matter. Whatever it is, I'll help you. I don't care what your family says. You're the most amazing girl in the world and I won't countenance anyone saying otherwise!"

"That's just it," muttered Mala, "I'm not."

Though Wren pushed her for an answer, Mala would say no more, and they lapsed into an uncomfortable silence.

Wren was determined to help Mala, but she didn't yet realize how impossible that would prove.

CHAPTER SEVEN

A Dageki and a Gentleman

G rakt was an extremely intelligent and accomplished dageki. He thought himself handsome as well. Dageki were sightlier when compared to the other races. Humans for instance; snoutless little stick-things with thin, scaleless hides and tufts of grass-like foliage sprouting from their heads and groins. He studied the swirling colors in his own glossy hexagonal body plates. Where the sun caught them, their dancing colors held a depth and quality of hue that was pure pleasure to the eyes.

I must be getting delirious with the heat, he thought. With a spluttering sigh, he stuffed the crystal diplomacy primer into his pack with the others and settled his squat torso farther into the shade of the rock outcrop. He pulled his segmented tail beneath him with great care. Though it was a short tail, compared to some truly ancient ones, Grakt was justifiably proud of its length. At home, he spent hours each day polishing the plates and rubbing oil into the tip to keep the tissues viable. It was a tedious task, but necessary if he wished to retain his social position. He'd heard stories of courtiers who had lost major segments of their tails in ceremonial rituals or accidents and had been forced to spend years as virtual outcasts, waiting in disgrace for the regeneration of their tails, in hopes of regaining even a modicum of their former status.

The thought made him shiver, despite the heat. It gave him little comfort when his research told him that the loss of the tail was a genetic predisposition for the dageki, a throwback to a time when the dageki had been primitive scurrying creatures of the desert floor. The cast-off tail could mean escape from a pursuing predator. Better to leave your tail in the mouth of an attacker than your throat!

Grakt had trouble believing this explanation, however. He couldn't accept that the proud dageki race had ever scurried across the desert floor. And what predator would have attacked so formidable and resourceful a creature as a full-grown dageki? The only exceptions were the exceedingly rare grellas. The big cats had been a threat to the young for generations. The sonic deterrent developed by Mageki Kyni Gouzuni had put a stop to their vicious attacks. But now there were the unexplainable disappearances in the outlying areas, and Mageki Kyni Gouzuni herself might be missing.

These thoughts brought back to him the urgency, and perhaps the futility, of his own mission. His patron, the sovereign, had little prepared him for the shocking truths he would encounter. Dmisi, the capital city, was more isolated from the provinces than anyone had thought. How would Sovereign TyKoro take the news he carried, that the provinces had not overestimated their losses to garner royal attention and increase their hazardous outpost stipends? If anything, they'd underestimated the number of dageki who were missing. If these losses continued at their present rate, the whole race might eventually be decimated. How long, he thought, before the royal city itself was under siege? These worries had pushed him farther and farther from the center of dageki lands, past the sleeping bulk of the volcanic Hartbone range, and into the great wastes. How could he return to TyKoro with only vague rumors and fantastical tales of dageki who had wandered from their homes as if in a trance, never to be seen again? And how could he tell her that the same fate had befallen Mageki Kyni Gouzuni herself, the living treasure of dageki scientific achievement?

So, he'd followed the rumors into the desert, where the ephemeral trail had turned to dust and left him literally sitting on his tail, contemplating failure.

Failure. Not a dageki word at all, but a human word, borrowed from the first trade encounters with that obstinate and uncultured race. Grakt had been given the uncomfortable position of interpreter, as his skill with languages was renowned, if not also viewed with suspicion, at the university. In any event, he could never have refused his sovereign's request to serve the crown. He'd soon regretted learning human languages. When he tried to speak to them in their own tongue, he found them exceedingly dull and slowwitted. They could not grasp even the rudiments of proper social encounters, making worthwhile trade with these primitive people all but impossible. The humans had soon given up and sailed away to the north in their floating houses, claiming that the dageki had nothing worth trading for anyway. No one had been sad to see them go. They'd failed to grasp even the necessity of a farewell ceremony.

Now Grakt wondered at the tales he'd heard from the locals. Along the seacoast where his journey had first taken him, whole towns were missing, dinners rotting on the tables, fish decomposing in the nets, as if the entire population had suddenly thrown themselves into the sea and drowned.

He'd found a survivor in one of these towns, but this dageki male appeared unstable, and Grakt had no way to ascertain the truth of his account. The man's short name was Kelz Si Tageki Goz Um, meaning Kelz, male Dageki, Last Grain of Sand. No wonder he was insane.

With such an ignoble Kye stick reading at his birth, life must have been unbearable, knowing all his life that he could never achieve a social level above Garaci, never be eligible for anything other than the lowest and most demeaning of jobs, and never be allowed to fertilize the eggs of a female.

It took a while to get anything out of Kelz, and then Grakt found what he said difficult to believe. Kelz told him that a floating house had arrived at the shore one evening in the fog, blowing an eerie, screeching horn that all harkened to. Soon the residents of the town were at the water's edge, standing as if in a state of sleep-walking. The floating house lowered a ladder, and the townspeople climbed up and were devoured by it, never to return.

"And this horn did not affect you?" Grakt asked.

"No. I don't know why, but it's funny, isn't it," he sniveled. "The whole world is going to heaven, and I'll be the only one left behind, just like my kye stick reading says." Then the poor wretch began to sob loudly. Grakt didn't think the other citizens had been heading to heaven, which he didn't believe existed. He could think of nothing comforting to say to Kelz, so he left him there, huddled miserably against the chill of the night, ruminating on his own misfortunes. Grakt had continued his journey with a growing sense of dread.

He headed inland, hoping that dageki were disappearing only by sea, but the attrition was even greater in the inland communities. Farm after farm he found deserted, with half-harvested crops and animals bleating for food in their pens, or decomposing in the dirt, long past the need for nourishment. Then had followed the lonely and perilous days it had taken to reach the desert.

Far from his city and home, deep in the less charted lands, he came upon the research facility where Mageki Kyni Gouzuni had been working, and his greatest fears were realized. The station was totally devoid of life, except for a couple of hungry equines, who whinnied loudly from their corral at his approach. He couldn't figure out why the equines were here. Perhaps Mageki Kyni Gouzuni had kept them for research purposes. He saw no wagon that they could tow. He probably would have turned back for Dmisi if not for them. After searching the building twice, he remembered the hungry animals and went out to set them loose to fend for themselves, but first, he went to the barn to pull a bale of drygrass for them from the loft. As he opened the gate for them, he tossed it in a line that he hoped would lead them into the fields and to a better life. As he threw the grass, his eye caught sight of a rough trail leading past the corral. It pointed southwest, toward the empty wastes. From the signs that the wind hadn't erased, he judged it to be a wagon, with a couple equines at harness. Some marks resembled the odd tracks that human feet left. It was the best clue he'd found, and he owed it to Sovereign TyKoro to at least investigate.

So he'd thought, two days ago. Now he was running out of food and water, and he hadn't been able to oil his tail in days. He was feeling decidedly unpatriotic. Had he really been chosen for this mission because of his superior abilities, or was he just a disposable member of the lower court? It was true that Sovereign TyKoro had always expressed affection for him, but how far did that feeling extend? After all, he was just another male offspring who could never attain the social standing of a female. Perhaps she knew more about the disappearances than she'd told him, for fear he might refuse to go if he'd known the dangers and hardships he might face.

Getting paranoid now, too, he thought.

Whatever the politics behind it, he was here now, and he would just have to make the best of it. In two days of steady march, he had yet to catch sight of his prey. They could travel faster with the wagon than he could on foot. Riding one of the equines would have been out of the question. No self-respecting dageki would do something so undignified, and besides, very few equines were large or stout enough to carry the bulk of an adult dageki for any distance.

He hadn't considered what he might do when he did catch up to the wagon, but that wasn't his present worry. The trail was becoming more and more difficult to follow. A dust storm had moved through here at some time after the passage of the wagon, and he wasn't even sure he was still on the right track. In fact, he was now completely lost.

Rather than ruminate on his present predicament, Grakt settled back against the rock and let his mind drift into daydreams. He'd walked straight through the night, and he was physically and emotionally exhausted. He filled his mind with the healing thoughts of his childhood. He heard the splash of water, smelled its mineral musk, and felt the cool wash of it across his plates. He was back at the community pool, swimming with his friends. His dream led him into sleep, unaware that he'd passed the camped wagon during the night and was now ahead of it.

Nor was he aware when Dolman the slaver caught sight of him from his perch atop the wagon as it made its dusty way through the desert.

CHAPTER EIGHT

Homecoming, with Fish

"You've got to leave here," Mala groaned. "There's nothing more you can do. Look, Wren, I really appreciate everything you've done for me, but I just don't fit in your world. I'm sorry."

"I'm not leaving until we find your family," said Wren, linking her arms across her chest.

"We have found them. Now go." With that, Mala turned to the rough stairway to the beach and started down.

Wren began to follow, when Mala turned back on her abruptly. "Don't follow me! You don't want to see this, trust me."

"I can't leave you like this! I need to know you'll be OK."

"I will be, but the transition for me is not like when the drakyn do it. Not as smooth. It hurts. A lot. I don't want you to see it, so you'd better just go."

Wren slowed her descent when Mala started to stumble, almost falling down the last few steps. In a blur of untraceable movement, her body twisted and writhed. Limbs groped at empty space and her whole body spasmed in pain as the girl disappeared into a new form, a sleek, black body emerging from the internal melee. A long hollow scream echoed across the beach. The body that fell, hitting the rocks below was not Mala. In her place, a young marm squirmed and struggled to get to the water.

Aghast, Wren clung to the rocks and stared in horror as her friend was subsumed by a creature of the sea. Finally, the struggling marm reached the water and plunged into the surf, not looking back, not giving Wren any indication that Mala was still part of it. The fantastically reborn creature swam quickly from the shore and was lost in the waves for a second, before it rose to the surface in the center of the marm pod. It danced joyfully among similar creatures, except that some were larger, and some smaller. When noses had touched and marine squeals of joy filled the air, the marm pod started out toward open sea. Wren realized that she was seeing Mala's family at last.

Tears streamed down Wren's face as she collapsed on the steps, feeling more alone than she'd ever felt. Memories assailed her of her friend, and things started to fall into place. Little things like Mala's love of smoked herrins, her healing ability and her great strength and skill in the water.

She should have seen it sooner, she now realized. Wren just hadn't known that an animal could transmoger itself into a human. She'd never heard of it being possible. Was Mala unique in her abilities? What great talent and intelligence the creature–no, Mala–must have!

But she was gone now. Poppet was gone. Her whole family was, she assumed, long dead and gone. Could she go on alone? For a bit, she forgot her resolve not to feel sorry for herself and succumbed to creeping fatigue and depression. Doubt and inadequacy crippled her. Miserable and hopeless, she stumbled back up the steps and collapsed in the grass, exhausted and unwilling to leave the seashore. That would mean she would never see Mala again. Finally, thirst and hunger drove her to stand on shaking legs and take the first step in her lonely journey into the unknown.

CHAPTER NINE

My Kingdom for a Contail

W ren found water; a small stream that ran downhill, she assumed, to the Zaladz river. She scavenged food along the way.
She ate crawdaddy's raw from the creek, and grossberries from the
bushes, nibbling on wild lettuce to fill her up when nothing else was
available, but she still felt hunger gnawing at her stomach painfully.
She found a stand of dark firs and under their deep shadow on the
north side of the hill, next to a fallen log, she found a true treasure:
two dozen or more goldenbell shrooms in their prime. She took care to
trim them at the base with the gutting knife from her pack. She knew
that more shrooms would burst forth next season, unless she pulled
them up by the roots, as some shroom hunters did. Even though she
doubted that she would ever come this way again, it was just the way
she and her family had lived. To give back to the land, and any that
may follow. Because if you didn't, someday, there might be no more
goldenbells for anyone. She felt this was important, even though she
didn't really understand why, when there were endless forests and even
more goldenbells.

She came down from the trees and carried on, a little lighter for the
weight she now carried, these wonderful gems of the forest floor that
gave life. She was encouraged to travel on. She'd devised a way to carry
water, by removing her notebook from the oilskin paper and folding it

carefully, she was able to create a crude sack that would carry enough water for a day or two, if she were careful with it and took care not to spill it as she walked.

She remembered her granpapa telling her that if she were lost, to follow a creek down to the river, because the river would always lead her home. Following this wisdom, she started down along the creek, but it wasn't easy. The alders, wild rose, elderberry and chokeberry, not to mention the omnipresent salal and prickly grape, had had the same idea. They crowded along the creek like a herd of children being offered candy. As the brush grew thicker and taller, forming an almost impenetrable hedge, the water level rose until she was sloshing through a mixture of mud and tall grasses that rose to her knees. Obstinately she pushed on, until the brush got so thick that she could go no farther. In panic, she realized that she'd lost her pack somewhere along the way, without even knowing that it had been lifted from her back. In haste, she tried to backtrack the way she'd come, but the pack was nowhere to be found.

The pack contained not only the precious primers and her notebook, but two stones that could mean her survival in the woods. Almost in tears, she leaned against the stump of a vine-choked tree and tried to control the panic rising in her like a deadly gorge. She knew she had to control her fear. Though she was an accomplished hunter and gatherer, she was ashamed to tell anyone that her greatest fear was being lost in the woods. It wasn't a rational fear; she'd always carried enough supplies to spend the night if she had to, and anyway, she was very careful not to wander too far from the areas she knew. When she dared to venture out even a little farther, she always looked back to imprint landmarks on her mind, so that when she returned, she could follow them in reverse.

She hated the fear, forcing herself to go beyond her limits time after time, until she was as good at her woodcraft as her brother and sister, even surpassing them at times. But the fear would not leave her, and a few times she'd panicked, running, stumbling blindly, and breathing hard, until reason had taken hold and she was able to find her way by the position of the sun, or if it was rainy or cloudy as it often was, find a hill or tree to climb and make her way from the landmarks she could make out in the distance. Fog was the worse. In the woods, fog filled her with unreasonable terror.

Looking back the way she'd come, she admonished herself to stop and think. Her gaze traveled around her, up and down. There was her pack, lodged high in the brush. How did it get up there? In vast relief she retrieved it and, admitting defeat, struggled back out of the morass the way she'd come. Maybe following the creek to the river was a good idea in other places, but not in this terrain. In this battle, the brush and marsh had won. She continued on, hoping that it wouldn't rain on top of everything else, glancing up often at the menacing dark clouds.

Let's just hope for better weather.

As if on cue, the rain began to fall.

Wren trudged through the downpour until her skin was soaked and her hands grew stiff with the cold. At least she'd left the lowlands and wasn't knee-deep in water anymore. Tall firs and pines filled the forest and provided some protection from the weather.

After a time, she knew she could go no further and found a spot under the canopy of an ancient fir tree where the branches gave some cover. It was something her granpapa had taught her, as well as how to make a fire in damp weather. The truth was that she'd never been very good at it, though. When their granpapa had tested their skills, her brother and sister had their fires healthy and crackling in fifteen minutes, while she was still trying to light a tiny mound of pine needles and moss an hour later.

"You've just got to be more patient, is all," her granpapa had explained.

"Patient?" she fumed. "Any more patience and we'll all be dead before I get this fruckin' thing lit!"

Her granpapa had just given her "the look," the one that said she would have to grow up eventually.

Well, that time had come. If she couldn't start a fire now, she would most likely die of the cold. She rifled through her pack, praying to the gardlanders that she'd put her firestarting stones back in her pack after her last shrooming trip. Finally, with a sigh of relief, she found them at the bottom.

Willing herself to be patient, as granpapa had counseled, was more difficult than she imagined, with her hands shaking and her fingers numb. She'd gathered what she needed, a pile of progressively larger fuel, starting with the pine needles and moss, followed by tiny sticks, then larger sticks, then fallen limbs. She tried to find the driest wood, but there wasn't much of that available on a day like this one. She didn't have a hatchet to trim the larger branches to fit the fire, but she didn't really care if it was pretty, only if it was hot.

She built the needles and tiny sticks into a cone with space inside, remembering that fire needed air. She began striking the emerock against the sparking stone. Little fireflies of spark reached out to the pile of needles, but nothing happened. Perhaps it steamed a little. Then the pile collapsed.

"Fruck!"

With a deep breath she forced herself to be patient and try again. This time she got a little smoke, but that melted away, consumed by the cold, damp air. On the third try, the smoke came up thicker and whiter, and eventually, a tiny flame erupted.

She wanted to cry or scream or shout to the heavens of gardland, but she was too cold and tired. Plus, she knew she had to baby this tiny flame if she wanted it to grow into the crackling, toasty, life-saving fire she dreamed it could be.

Little things matter, she thought out of nowhere.

"Now I'm really losing it," she said out loud. To her surprise her words were answered by the distant, barking cry of a male fox. She laughed, as the flames grew and feeling returned to her fingers.

"It's just you and me against the world, little fox."

She searched through her pack for the last of the goldenbell shrooms and devoured them quickly, realizing that it wouldn't be enough. She would need food soon. She didn't have the materials to make a snare for a contail, and her bow was back at the cabin she'd so unceremoniously been taken from by Kodo. She had no idea what direction it might lie. She was far beyond the forest she knew by heart and had no idea where to head next. East was what her and Mala had decided, since that was the direction the poor slaves were taken when they were sent to the farms.

When the rain stopped, the fog moved in. Wren, not knowing what else to do, slept. When she awoke, dawn was just starting to make the air glow, but the fog hadn't left her. She gathered more wood for the fire, trying not to lose sight of her tree in the still, milky air.

She tried to call up what she knew about fog. Usually, it lifted when the sun began to warm the soil, but there was another kind, the kind that came up from the coast and clung to the ground like a blanket for days on end, the kind she didn't want this to be.

She spent another uneasy night of sleep on the ground by the fire. She was having to go farther and farther to find wood, and she'd started to carry her pack with her when scrounging, just in case she couldn't find her way back. Though she was warm, lack of food was now the beast trying to kill her.

Soon she would have to decide if she was going to try to find a way out of the fog, or just lie down here and die. The latter was beginning to sound more and more appealing as hunger and exhaustion took over. Some rescuer of Poppet she'd turned out to be; she couldn't even rescue herself. That night she lay down, wondering if the darkness behind her eyes would become permanent come morning.

To her surprise, she did wake up alive the next morning, and she thought the day was brighter. Maybe the fog would dissipate today and she could continue on her journey, but she was so weak from lack of food she didn't know how far she would get.

She stood at the edge of the overhanging branches and stared out into the fog. As if by magic, a small cross-shaped form started to appear. It advanced slowly out of the fog like an apparition. The hair stood up on her neck. Whatever it was, it was being very cautious. Finally, a shape appeared with four legs and a sharp-nosed head. At last she realized that it was a fox, and it held something in its mouth.

She stood perfectly still so as not to frighten it. Then she saw the limp shape with floppy ears held lightly in its mouth.

A fox! And he's caught a contail!

She wondered if she could frighten him and make him drop his prize, but that proved unnecessary.

The fox approached her, closer than she'd ever seen a fox in the wild. She saw how beautiful and perfect he was for hunting and surviving out here, his slight, fast body with large ears and keen eyes. He wore a thick orange coat above with white running from his jowls to his belly, all balanced by a rich brush of a tail. His yellow eyes with slit black pupils like a cat observed her intently, as if to divine her intentions.

"Don't worry, little brother," she said softly, "I won't hurt you. That's your meal, not mine, and it would be wrong of me to try to steal it from you. Though if you were thinking of sharing..."

To her immense surprise, the fox gently dropped the contail at her feet. He glanced up at her for a moment, and she felt the spark of his thoughts appraising her. She remembered now her granpapa telling her that some of the more intelligent animal species were able to increase their natural gifts using an instinctual form of transmogrifee. Indeed, she'd seen that Mala had been able to do just that. She had to believe that this was the case with the fox, otherwise it was some kind of magic. She didn't believe in magic, but that everything would have an explanation, if we just looked long and hard enough to find it.

As the fox turned away to leave, she called after it. "Thank you, my furry friend. Someday, perhaps I'll be able to repay you for this."

She only wondered what had prompted him to save her. She realized she might never know, and told herself not to look a gift equine, or fox in this case, in the mouth.

She hurried to gut and skin the contail and put it on the fire to roast. She soon had warm food in her stomach and a brighter outlook on the day.

She'd been right, and the fog was finally lifting. Now she could see the sun trying to burn its way through the haze and she had a direction.

With the rest of the contail meat secured in her pack, she started out through the forest heading east.

Wren walked and walked and walked, all the while thinking that she could have planned better. An emerock lantern, a first aid pack, more food and a waterskin would have been useful now. But how could they have brought all these lifesaving things along when they would most probably have been lost in the wild ride to the tidefall? She'd been lucky to hold on to her small pack. And how could she have known that her friend Mala would be lost along the way? Another victim of Wren's extremely poor luck. Or was it luck? Was she just a poor judge of character? Did she just make bad decisions? Could she have seen what Mala had intended all along? Yes, if she were a sharper thinker, if she could have interpreted the signs along the way, but she hadn't. She hadn't seen any of it, lost in her own self-pity.

She stumbled on a rock and almost fell, realizing that the terrain had begun to change as her mind was elsewhere. Ahead of her was a land where trees and brush were growing smaller and sparser. Where were all the people? Surely, she should have come across a town by now, unaware that she'd managed to avoid two main human settlements, Bay Towne to the north and Tia Cara to the south.

There wasn't any farmland here. Wasn't that what she was looking for, to find Poppet? A farm run by drakyn? What could they grow in this dry land? What animals could graze on the tufts of sharp yellow grasses that were surely almost devoid of nutrition? She considered going another direction when something attracted her eye in the distance. A thin line of dust, a black speck at its head, like a snake's head bouncing along. She hurried her pace to cut off what she reasoned must be a wagon. She could transect its path if she hurried. Then she pulled up abruptly. How could she know if these were not drakyn or some other danger? But would drakyn need a wagon? Not likely. She wished she'd paid more attention to her papa's tales of the other races on Drakonia. She felt her water pouch, realizing it was nearly empty and made the rash decision to seek out these people. At least she hoped they were people, and not something infinitely worse.

She jogged forward to intercept the path of the wagon that she could now see was much like the ones that had visited their farm, infested by dirty peddlers, greasy hawkers and occasionally, a few honest traders. Her papa had soon sent the former on their way, unless of course they carried something truly worth trading for, like whiskey. She ran until she thought she couldn't go another step. The thirst in her throat made her choke. Whoever drove the wagon must have seen her because the trajectory of the equine-drawn wagon changed, angling directly toward her. She stopped and bent over, leaning on her knees and breathing hard. She struggled to get enough air into her desperate lungs.

When the wagon pulled up beside her, she saw its riders consisted of a stout man who held the reins and a slight boy who sat beside him, squirming in obvious excitement to see another human out here. The man, dark-featured and unshaven, pulled hard on the brake, and without a word reached behind him into the wagon. He pulled out a weapon that Wren recognized from ones the soldiers had carried. They'd called it an arbalest, a cruel weapon that could fire an arrow with great speed and, depending of course on the skill of the bearer, great accuracy. He pointed it at Wren and she cringed away, realizing with dread that if he really meant to kill her, she could never run fast or far enough to escape its deadly barb.

"What are you?" the man demanded in a gruff voice.

"What am I?" Her voice quivered in fear.

"There are many who are not what they appear. Prove that you are firstform human and not one of those disgusting drakyn, or I swear I'll take you down right here."

"But how do I do that?" she yelped. "I assure you that I'm human!"

"Then what are you doing here? A mere slip of a girl wandering in the drylands alone. It's most unlikely."

The boy tugged at the man's arm and said, "Papa! No! She's human, I can feel it!"

The man's shoulders relaxed the slightest bit, but his aim did not falter.

"How come you're here?" demanded the man.

"Well," she began slowly, "I escaped from the palace of the drakyn queen with my friend Mala and—"

The man's hand tightened on the grip. "That's not possible. No one escapes the drakyn."

"It wasn't easy, I assure you. We almost died several times."

"And where is this friend of yours? Mala, you called her?"

Wren was silent for a second, feeling lost and missing Mala deeply.

The boy spoke again, "Please, Papa! She looks hungry and thirsty too. Can't we help her? She's no threat. I'm sure of it."

With a great sigh, the man lowered the arbalest and returned it to its place behind him. Reluctantly, he said, "All right, but know that I'll be watching you. We need a rest anyway. Bryn, check on the equines. Make sure they have food and water and then water our cargo, too. Then bring some food for us and that flask of wine for me. We'll take a break right here, I guess."

When Bryn had finished his chores, he brought forward the victuals along with a worn straw mat that he placed on the dirt. They all sat down and began to eat and drink. The stale, lukewarm water tasted delicious. After a sip, she left the bitter red wine to the man. He introduced himself as Dolman and his son as Bryn. He explained that they were traders with a home base north of the leijong territories, but Wren had no idea where that was or what a leijong might be. As they ate, she heard a low groaning sound, and the covered rear of the wagon quivered and rocked.

Wren asked as casually as she could, "So, what is it you take for trade?"

The man was hesitant to answer, and Wren added hurriedly. "It's no business of mine of course..."

Dolman observed her closely, then took another swig from the wine flask. "It's no secret what we do. It's just our cargo this time–it's a bit controversial, you see."

"Controversial? Why?"

"Some of these animal-lover types, they say the gilamons are actually more intelligent than they appear, which is ridiculous, in my opinion."

Wren wondered wryly if the price he could get for them hadn't influenced his evaluation of their intelligence.

"Can I see them?" she asked timidly.

"Oh, I don't think you want to do that. Their spit is mildly poisonous, not fatal, of course, but you don't want to get it in your eyes. You need to be a professional to deal with these critters."

"OK. I guess I was just curious," replied Wren.

The boy Bryn looked at her and rolled his eyes, but the look was gone before Dolman could notice it. Dolman issued more instructions for the boy, and they were soon back on the trail. Wren sat in the center of the bench and was at least grateful not to be walking, as her feet were sore and blistered. The boy Bryn sat on her left. Between them, she felt confined, even trapped. She took a deep breath and forced herself to relax. When she breathed in, a choking smell assailed her nostrils, which had been preceded by an odd, hooting noise. The smell was so strong that, for a moment, she had to hold her breath.

Dolman laughed. "Yeah, they don't smell so bad of themselves, 'till they pass gas, then all bets're off!"

Bryn giggled, and Wren again wondered about their unusual cargo. Did they really need to be transported in cages? She was determined to learn more about these odd creatures that humans called gilamons.

CHAPTER TEN

A Picnic for Five

The family of four picnicked on the cliffs whenever they could, especially if it was sunny. They returned to this wildflower-graced patch of grasses and heather far above the raging surf. They spread their rough wool blanket and, with care, set out the treasures they'd brought; fresh-baked wheat bread and honey, grossberries picked along the way, and dried herrins, the tastiest treat of all. They sat cross-legged on the blanket and laughed and teased the young ones and joked some more, until the sun dived low on the breakers and rocks far below. The ocean foamed and spit while the sleek dark marms played in the saltwater, unaware of the humans watching them from above, all save one marm, who watched and listened. In this one seagoing mammal, curiosity was born, and this small fact would influence everything that came after.

It began with a tiny, lovely kaleidoscope of brittle colors that sparkled and danced in her vision, eventually fading into mere blindness. But when that passed, it transmogered into a terrible pain. Not even realizing it, she was hitting her head on the rocks, just because it hurt less than this unbelievable pain. Then nausea hit her, and she remembered little until later, when the pain transmogered again, this time into a giddy euphoria. Happy to be alive, she thought. No, not that. Happy that the pain was less. Torture? She thought she was prepared for it after this, but who really knew how much pain a marm could handle? Perhaps only the torturer knew for sure.

Then the change began, and Mala felt the real pain. Her flippers elongated, stretching and splitting into five spindly appendages that moved against each other. Her neck broke and lengthened. Her head jerked upright on a now vertical body. She grew long ebony hair and a button nose. The pain was at last more than she could manage, and she gratefully lost consciousness, lying unmoving on the shore.

She slept for a long time. When she awoke, she saw gravel before her eyes. She was on land. Above her was a rough natural stairway leading up the cliff face. She could climb with these new human limbs, if she chose. She stood up shakily and felt the land sickness hit her. When she was done vomiting herrins, she pulled herself upright again, determined to finish this adventure, wherever it might lead. She had to rest often, as she was still learning how to walk as a skragling and control her shaking legs.

At the top, she collapsed, exhausted. Later she wandered until she found the spot where the grass was flattened from the blanket the family had placed there. She looked around at the low heather and grasses that appeared to go on forever. Then she saw a tiny edifice in the distance, that was in fact a tall stone structure. For a long time, all she did was gaze at the distant creation made of rock and wondered, *who made this*? Is this where her happy family lived? She was wrong, of course. No human family would be content to abide in that inhospitable, drakyn-made monstrosity. Only pain came from that place, but Mala would learn this hard truth later.

CHAPTER ELEVEN

Out of the Sea and into the Frying Pan

It had, for the most part, been miserable being human. No swimming, no sunning on the rocks. No friends, well, except for Wren and Poppet. Now those human friends haunted her, even as the sea called to her. They swam with her in her thoughts, making her clumsy in the water, when she should be free like the others in the pod, cavorting in the waves and diving in the kelp fields. Those humans were her friends now, and she couldn't seem to forget, couldn't shake the feel of flat land beneath her. She missed the joys and frustrations of language, of critical thinking, of dreams, the flavor of anything other than herrins. Like pudding. She especially liked pudding. How could she live without that, or without complicated thoughts, without Wren and her ridiculous ideas, or Poppet and his clumsiness, despite his spot-on insight into everyone except himself? She couldn't. Maybe it was the mistake of her life, perhaps only second to leaving the marm colony in the first place, but she couldn't go back to being just a marm. She was Mala now.

For the hundredth time that day, Mala pulled herself from the waves onto a warm flat rock that she particularly preferred. The warm sun felt good. The chilly seawater felt good. The slick silver herrins tasted good. But something was missing. She'd been born a marm—she realized that now—a seagoing creature that would repeat these actions for the rest of its life. There might be some mating in there, too, at which thought her heart rate jumped up a couple beats. But that was all. She was more than that now. Her experiences in human form had changed her, forming in her a desire to be more than just a consumer of herrins. She thought about poor Wren and the unlikely quest she was now condemned to attempt without Mala's help. And Poppet was probably, at this moment, tripping on a rock for a fall that would require her medical attention or was facing some worse fate at the hands of the drakyn "farmers."

With a heavy sigh, Mala slipped again from the rock, but this time she swam not for the feeding grounds, but in a beeline toward the ragged shore. As she swam, she tried to prepare herself for the pain of the change.

CHAPTER TWELVE

The Formalities Will End, Eventually

Mala had followed Wren's tracks as best she could. It was an obvious trail, and Wren wasn't trying to mask her sign. She saw the camp where the girl had spent several nights and later found her tracks leading in and out of the marshland. Mala figured she could gain some time not having to follow Wren all the way in and out. But now she was worried. The land had grown more and more arid. Eventually, the trail disappeared completely, consumed by another track with many hooves and perfectly shaped marks in a line that she reasoned could belong to the wheels of a wagon. The trail disappeared into the distance and Mala wasn't sure she could catch up with whatever it was that preceded her. She did have one advantage: she could go all night and day if necessary to catch them, and her quarry appeared to be taking frequent breaks. She looked up from the tracks and straightened her back, mentally preparing herself for the ordeal that lay ahead.

Wren listened to the snores emanating from the canvas tent where Dolman and Bryn slept. She'd declined their offer to fit her into the worn tent with them. If the smell of the gilamons was bad, Dolman could have competed with them after a campfire dinner of beans, spiced with bits of some anonymous meat and taters tossed into the coals to bake. She thought it was one of the best meals she'd ever eaten, though her opinion might have been influenced by the fact that, except for the contail, she couldn't remember when she'd last had a cooked meal. The rich food put her out for several hours and she slept soundly, wrapped in a blanket on the straw mat. She'd pulled the cover over her head to hold in the warmth as the heat of the day escaped them, both the land and her shivering body. Now she wondered what had woken her. She held perfectly still for a moment, listening with her whole being. Then she heard it again. What was that? A whimper? Was someone crying?

She tried to ignore it and go back to sleep, but the sound continued. She couldn't take it any longer and pulled herself up quietly, creeping to the back of the wagon. Carefully, she pulled aside the canvas to reveal a massive, locked metal cage that filled most of the space. Dark shapes huddled in sudden silence and Wren remembered what Dolman had said about them being venomous spitters.

"Hey, there," she whispered in the calming voice she used on the porkers when they were restless. "I mean you no harm. I hope you're not hurt. I wish I could help you. I know you don't understand, but I can tell when something is hurting. If my friend Mala were here–she's a good healer–she might be able to help you."

There was a slight movement from the cage, but no further sounds.

The snoring from the tent stopped abruptly and Wren stood perfectly still. After a few seconds, the snoring started up again. Wren let out a heavy breath. "OK, I've got to go. If there is any way I can help you, I will." Wren turned away, letting the flap fall back into place. As

she turned to leave, she heard a sound that could have been, "Wait."
She pulled back the flap again, then dropped it in shock as a huge face
met hers.

"So sorry," groaned the voice, "I had no intention of frightening
you. Everything I am saying is so wrong. It is so wrong."

Wren found the accent unfamiliar. The words were delivered in
a hesitant and stilted way, but there was no doubt that it was human
speech.

"Is there a human in there?" she asked in surprise. "Come forward
so I can see you."

"No, no, it is only me. I would not speak to you like this, but I am
desperate, and you smell unusually non-threatening, for a human."
Wren stared, becoming aware that the words were coming from the
hulking form before her, its dark hide oddly shimmering in the gloom
of the cage. She couldn't discern its exact shape in the dark but felt the
massive bulk of the creature before her.

"Why is it wrong for you to speak to me?" she whispered back. "I
thought that gilamons were incapable of speech."

"That statement is wrong on both of its premises. Not only do I
speak twenty-seven languages and dialects, but we are not gilamons."
He spit the word. "We are the dageki, the master race of this world! But
we need water and food, the rudiments of hygiene, and Hika Si Mageki
Ri Henza Kelz needs medical attention that I cannot provide. What
kind of monsters are you to treat us in this way?" The voice paused.
Was that a sob? It resumed, "But it is improper for me to speak without
introduction. I fear that the heat has made me ill as well."

She forced herself closer to the cage and up to the face of the
dageki who had spoken. In the light, she could just make out yellow
eyes watching her; the head tipped like a bird to follow her every

movement. Like the others, it sat very still, but its small front limbs quivered slightly.

"I am a specialist in languages at Kgiara University. I have learned multiple languages and dialects, including this crude speech that I was forced to learn so that I could communicate with your race. I now realize that I was chosen, even then, not for my ability, but for my social flexibility." He said the word 'flexibility' as if it were the worst possible trait one could possess.

Another dageki sitting at his feet yammered at him in some high-pitched, nasal tongue, pawing at him with its short front limbs in what appeared to be a gesture of reproach. He said something roughly to the sitter, then turned back to Wren.

"Giaranu Wiyhe Si Mageki Ky Sizi informs me that I am required to make at least the minimal introduction if I am to speak with you. However, I have found that your kind lack the patience for such niceties, and conditions are obviously not ideal. I doubt that you would spare the time."

"How long do these introductions take?" she asked, bemused.

"No more than three days. I could use the controversial abbreviated form—perhaps two days and a half."

"Couldn't you just tell me your name?" Wren laughed despite her frustration. "I don't think we have two days and a half."

Silence.

"I'll start for you," prompted Wren. "It's really quite easy. It's nice to meet you. My name is Wren Weatherspring. My family and friends call me Wren. Please call me Wren. How's that?"

A spluttering in the dark. Was that a dageki sigh? Wren wondered what was going on in its mind. So much of a language is culture, social organization, even the dictates of physical structure, all areas where human and dageki obviously differed markedly.

"It is really quite easy," he mimicked. "My name is Grakt Si Tageki Ki Jorfa Kera Ri Jorfa. It means Grakt, Proud Male, Dust to Silent Universe to Dust. My family and friends call me Grakt Si Tageki Ki Jorfa Kera Ri Jorfa. Please call me Grakt Si Tageki Ki Jorfa—"

"Excuse me," Wren interrupted. "I don't think you quite get the idea. It saves time, you see. Couldn't I just call you Grakt? It really has a nice sound to it," she lied.

Silence again. A long silence. Wren shifted her weight impatiently. She was beginning to think she'd pushed him too far.

At last, he said slowly, "Please call me Grakt."

Wren let out a breath she hadn't realized she'd been holding. Perhaps there was hope for communication after all, though it would probably never be easy. She imagined that the slavers had found it all too convenient that the dageki refused to talk. It provided a wonderful excuse for enslavement if the creatures appeared to be nothing more than dumb animals. Few humans would ever take the time to learn their complex social system, and without the required introductions, no dageki would think it proper to say hello, much less learn an alien language! They were so proud. She wondered how many survived captivity.

"I'll answer your questions if I can," said Wren. "I'll bring you more food and water. As for the medical care–I don't know. I'm afraid that I'm little more than a guest of your captors myself. But I promise you that I won't leave this wagon until I've made at least an attempt to set you free. No creature deserves to be treated like this! I'll do what I can."

Wren turned away to get their water and food without further words, her thoughts in turmoil. Behind her, she again heard the other dageki whining at Grakt in their unintelligible, nasal language, but Grakt made only a brief response. Were they berating him for speaking to her without a proper introduction? How could they be so obstinate when their very lives were at risk?

Wren spent another day and night with Bryn and his father, trying to draw out more information on the creatures they carried. Whether they were called gilamons or dageki, it didn't really matter to her. All she understood was that they didn't deserve the treatment they were suffering at the hands of these traders. No matter what she said, Dolman wouldn't listen. She could understand why he didn't believe her. When she led him back to the cage to talk to the dageki, the creatures were sullen and silent. Even Grakt was quiet, and Dolman had good reason not to believe her. He carried a great treasure in that filthy cage. Convincing him to give it up would not be easy.

"I have my son to consider," he said. "We can't live like this forever. With what we've saved and what we get from these animals, we could buy a farm, give up the constant travelling. I intend to make a better life for him."

"I understand that, really I do," she said. "But what's that life worth if it's attained through the suffering of others?" She glanced at the boy who pretended not to be listening, though she knew he registered every word.

That night she and Bryn were gathering wood for the fire, and without a word, the boy slipped a key into her hand. She looked at him in surprise, but he only smiled at her in a knowing way. Later, when she sank into her bed, she felt a lump and discovered a bag, that when opened, revealed a waterskin and a few pieces of stale bread inside. It wasn't much, but she almost cried when she saw it.

When the snoring symphony, boy and man, was in full swing, she left her bed. She wrapped herself in the blanket and took her pack, into which she had stuffed the bag with the food and water.

At the back of the wagon, she drew aside the canvas and struggled to find the keyhole in the dark. When she finally got the key in the lock, it wouldn't move and she panicked, thinking that Bryn had deceived her, or maybe accidentally given her the wrong key. Finally, she realized that the key was upside down. When she turned it over, it slipped in easily and opened the cage door with a satisfying *snick*. The door creaked loudly as it opened and Wren was sure the sound would wake Dolman.

She waited, motionless in the dark, for the inevitable. She could hear the chorus of Dolman and his son snoring. From the cage, Wren heard nothing.

Finally, she called out softly, "Grakt, are you there?"

Again, nothing.

She whispered, "You're free, you're all free. Come with me, quickly." She heard muffled conversation in their strange language. After a pause, a tiny voice answered.

"I am unable to comply."

"Is that you, Grakt? What? Are you crazy? Let's go before Dolman wakes up."

"I apologize. They refuse to go. They say that because I have broken every law of dageki social order, I will be—what is the human word?–ostracized. I will be banned from the Royal Court. They do not understand that I am the diplomat."

"You mean, *a* diplomat," she corrected automatically.

"No, you don't understand. Diplomacy is not a dageki concept, but one we adopted from humans. We have never had a reason to use it before–before me. I am the first, the only diplomat in the history of our kind."

In exasperation, Wren whispered loudly, "Wow, I'm really honored, but do you think we could just get the fruck out of here?"

Grakt half-stumbled, and was partially pushed, out of the wagon. She was amazed at how large he was when he finally stood beside her in the gloom, though she didn't think the dageki were a threat. If anything, they were too passive for their own good. She motioned for him to follow, and she started off into the dark. After a few steps, she realized that he wasn't beside her.

"My pack, the primers. I cannot leave without them," he croaked in a tortured whisper.

She looked back for him in frustration, then saw him rummaging in the front part of the wagon. Dolman must be the heaviest sleeper on the planet! Finally, Grakt let out a grunt and pulled something from the wagon. A large, bulky pack was in his small front limbs. He stumbled toward her, and they started to run.

Finally, Dolman was behind them, shouting. Wren remembered the crossbow he carried in the front of the wagon with sudden horror. Would he waste his arrows trying to hit them in the dark? Hopefully not.

What she didn't realize was that Bryn had hidden the arrows and would pay for it mightily the next day.

Before they made it to the trading post, Bryn and his father would only lose one more of the critters, and Dolman eventually forgave the boy. He mostly forgot about their unfortunate kindness to another human being, though he vowed to be more careful about what innocent-looking strangers they took in next time. The loss of another of the dageki would weigh on his mind only in terms of the lost gravures in his purse. The animal's body plates alone were worth a fortune, and Dolman didn't lose a minute's sleep over the fact that he'd caused the docile creature's death or how they had treated the remaining dageki along the way.

CHAPTER THIRTEEN

Reunited

Mala had reached a crossroads. The problem was that the trail had suddenly split into two and she had to decide which one to follow. Dawn created high contrast, elongated shadows across the land, showing her the story of what had occurred, written in the dust and dirt. She loved this new skill of tracking that she was learning. With the right imagination and logic, she could create a moving picture in her mind of what had happened and when. But here only dust swirled in her vision. This story was shrouded in uncertainty. These tracks gave her only a play without a plot, and characters who didn't know their lines. Beside the wheel tracks were flattened patches in the dirt, as she'd seen before. Where beds had been made? Did this mean that the group had spent the night here? Probably, but the rest of the scene made no sense, just a jumble of tracks, some that looked human and one large bipedal track that she'd never seen before. Beside it was a print that looked like Wren's light step, widely spaced and more pressure toward the front, as if she'd been running, perhaps away from some threat, but then there was no way for her to be sure. Should she follow the larger track or these two?

In the end, she let instinct choose for her and followed the smaller track, the one without the wheels. She later marveled that these two tracks had diverged in the desert, and her choice had made all the difference to her destiny.

Wren and Grakt trudged through the drylands, totally lost, but only wanting to get as far from the wagon as possible. Suddenly, Grakt pulled up and lifted his head, sniffing the air.

"What is it?" asked Wren, fear lodged in her throat.

"I am not entirely sure," said Grakt. "It is like nothing I have ever smelled before. It is almost..." He trailed off.

Wren looked around them apprehensively. Then she could see what Grakt had been able to smell long before it became visible–a tiny, dark shape on the horizon that approached them steadily.

"What should we do?" she asked. "Is it Dolman?"

"No, I am sure it is not the slaver. Whatever this creature is, it is oddly out of its element, as if it carries an essence of the sea within it. I know how strange that sounds."

Wren's look of confusion gradually transmogrified into one of hope.

"Could it be?" she whispered, then cried out with sudden joy. Wren ran forward to meet the approaching figure, who fell into her arms in exhaustion.

"Mala! I don't understand. How are you here? I thought—"

When Mala answered with a parched cough, Wren motioned to Grakt who approached cautiously, handing her the water skin. Mala gulped the water greedily and, in a few minutes, her color improved, and she was able to stand on shaky legs.

"I guess this body wasn't made for the drylands," she quipped, then her eyes went wide, as if she'd just now noticed the monstrous being that accompanied Wren.

"What is *that*?" she asked, staring at Grakt in horror.

Grakt said, in his perfect but halting diction, "I would request to be allowed to inquire as to your genetrics and consequent morphology. Forgive me for being so forward, since we have not been properly introduced. It is a pleasure to meet you. I am Grakt Si–"

"I think we can skip that, Grakt," said Wren, interrupting him impatiently.

"Humans. So rash, so rash," he mumbled.

Wren said, "Mala, this is Grakt, a dageki. He has been a great help to me. In fact, I doubt that I could have survived out here without him. I think Grakt sensed more about you, even before meeting you, than I figured out in all the time we worked together. I get the feeling that his sense of smell is far superior to ours. The first thing he said was that you carried the scent of the sea within you."

"That's very insightful," mused Mala.

"Grakt is of a species similar to the drakyn, but so different! If I'm not mistaken, they don't even eat meat, subsisting mainly on vegetables, grains, and fish."

Grakt nodded his massive head.

"And so nonviolent, they won't even defend themselves when attacked or forced into slavery."

Mala sighed. "I take it they found a champion in one lost, and might I add, equally defenseless, human cook?"

Wren had to admit to herself that Mala might have a point. She quickly changed the subject. Turning to Grakt, she said, "Mala is my friend. She has great transmogrifee talent. In fact, I think the first time she did it, the process was completely involuntary. Am I correct?" She turned to Mala inquisitively.

"That's right," said Mala. "But I have a lot to learn yet. I can't control when it will happen, and it's too painful to do it more often."

Wren asked her, "Why did you change your mind? I thought you'd decided to stay with the marm pod, I mean, your family."

"Oh, Wren, I just couldn't leave you to look for Poppet alone!" Then she added in a sardonic tone, "It seems that, like you, I can't resist the urge to champion the most hopeless of causes."

Grakt gurgled and Wren was surprised that these creatures might have a sense of humor, but why not? Grakt had already proven his intelligence and ingenuity.

As if to prove her point, Grakt said, "I apologize profusely for interrupting this poignant reunion, but we are running low on water and all of us need rest. There may be a source of potable water, a spring a short way north of us, and it offers some shade. I suggest that we head there with all the alacrity that your friend can manage."

Mala asked, "How do you know it's there? Have you traveled this way before?"

"No," replied Grakt. "The hydrolysate and various flora have penetrated my olfactory range."

When the two women stared at him blankly, he explained, "I can smell it."

CHAPTER FOURTEEN

A Book is Only as Opaque as its Reader

As the trio made their way east, where Grakt claimed they would find water and more arable land, Wren got to know the dageki a little better. Though he could be long-winded, both conversationally and intestinally, she came to believe that his claims of being a member of a developed civilization might actually be true. He carried with him many useful items that made life on the trail more bearable, as well as a knowledge of native foods and how to cook them on a campfire. He also possessed several unusual crystal cubes that he spent much time over after dinner every evening. When Wren asked him about them, he called them primers, and she was confused.

"Primers? But primers are books of teaching." She explained that the only books allowed in the gardlands were instructional tomes. No speculative fiction or opinion was countenanced. Works of fantasy or humor could garner the worst possible punishment; immediate and permanent exile to a world so harsh and unforgiving that the new residents had named it Drakonia. The newcomers found a primitive land of unpredictable storms and erupting volcanoes, endless tracts of desert, miles of raging, unnavigable rivers, six-hundred-foot tides and an ocean filled with sea monsters. Not to mention the hundreds of land species that would swallow you before pausing to find out how you tasted.

"Those things you carry don't look like primers," she said uncertainly. "Are you sure that's the correct translation?"

"I think so," said Grakt, suddenly tentative. "Is not a primer a receptacle for the teachings passed down from one generation to another?"

"Yes, that's right, but you need to be able to read them."

He looked at her curiously, handing her the translucent cube he was holding. "This is one of my favorites: Architectural Trends in the Age of Krave Kia Si Tageki Tyco Racentix: A Personal Journey Through Transcendent Life Spaces by Melit Si Mageki Ron Kio Scentorz."

She accepted the disk and turned it over in her hands. It appeared to be constructed of many layers of crystal, but the interior looked scratched, etched or cracked throughout. She tried to open it, but it was a solid piece of stone. There were no pages, no words, no letters.

Grakt said, "Well, I suppose you are unable to read our language, but it is quite logical. I could teach you. With your innate intelligence, I am sure you would learn quickly."

Now Wren was even more confused. "What language? Where are the pages? Where are the words?"

"They're all here. Let us begin with something easy. Just look at the illustration on page four hundred and sixty-six."

"I'm sorry, Grakt, I can't see any pages. I don't know what you're talking about. This must be one of those concepts that doesn't translate between our cultures. This isn't a book, as we know them. It's like nothing I've ever seen."

Grakt took back his cube, turning it over in his nimble hands as he appeared to consider the problem.

"Hmmm," he mumbled. "Perhaps our dilemma is not so much a matter of translation, but of physiology. I think that is the human term for biological functions and capabilities, correct?"

"Yes, that's the word, but—"

Grakt interrupted her and Wren marveled at how quickly he was learning human impatience along with other facets of their culture.

"Yes, I see," he said. "I mean, I see, and you do not. I believe that human eyes lack the ability to focus that we possess. You cannot see page four hundred and sixty-six because you cannot differentiate it from the other pages. For instance, page four hundred and sixty-seven."

"You mean that all the pages are assembled on top of each other?"

"Yes."

"So, you can focus on just one thin page out of..."

"Nine hundred and thirty-seven, in the case of this particular volume," he said.

"They must be so thin!"

"Yes, very. It takes time and great craftsmanship to assemble just one volume. They are my prized possessions, of course."

"I can see that." After thinking for a moment, she asked, "Hey, Grakt, you don't have in these volumes one that contains maps, do you? I would like to see anything that shows the locations of drakyn settlements, the farms they run, specifically."

Grakt said immediately, "Of course I have maps. I could not have made it this far into the wilderness without them, and the compasser." Then he hesitated. "But we generally avoid the drakyn. Evil creatures. Very violent and unpredictable." As he spoke, he scratched under his massive chin with one tiny hand, and Wren had to keep herself from laughing at the simple gesture. He really was the most adorable two-thousand-pound intellectual lizard that she'd ever met. Well, the only one to be exact.

As he looked at her, Wren was sure she saw satisfaction in his beady yellow eyes. "Yes, I believe the maps are contained in the much-lauded Gormz Si Tageki Raz Kendir Saraz Hefner's Travelogue of Least Recommended Travel Destinations for Sensible Dageki, Volume Four."

Mala snorted but stayed quiet after a silencing look from Wren.

Wren asked, "And you think it has the locations of the drakyn farms?"

"Yes, though this volume is a bit outdated. I could not afford volume five on a teacher's stipend. I am sorry." After a few moments in thought, he continued, "It will be dangerous, Wren. Are you sure you want to attempt this?"

He set the book down and linked his arms across his chest.

"Grakt, this is the first time we've had any real hope of finding Poppet, and who knows how many other human workers that have been enslaved. You don't have to come with us. I appreciate everything you've done so far. Your pots alone!" She mused. "I would give my best hen just to be allowed to cook with them one more time. They really are phenomenal."

"Well," explained Grakt, humbly, "they're made of a revolutionary new metal. It disperses heat and—" He paused suddenly, perhaps realizing that he'd been sidetracked from their initial conversation.

"I will not desert you," he said quietly, then continued in a stronger voice. "You and Mala have become important to me in a very short length of time. I will not leave you to rescue your friend alone or face the drakyn without my aid." He bent his head as if to bow to her, and Wren was deeply touched by his sincerity.

"Us too, well me, anyway." She glanced at Mala who nodded. "Both of us have come to appreciate your beneficent presence as well." Was she starting to sound like a dageki herself? Maybe that was the soul of this new diplomacy they now practiced, for the two cultures to not only embrace each other, but change places, becoming the other, if only for a moment.

Always practical, Mala inquired, "Which way and how far to the closest farm?"

Rifling through his pack, Grakt pulled out the primer in question and studied it intently, while they waited. After a time, he consulted his compasser and pointed one hand roughly north. "It is not far, north into the hills up there. We can be there in a couple days. Exactly 48.36 hours at our average rate of speed and accounting for 7.39 hours of sleep per night and—"

"That's great," interrupted Wren, both excited and apprehensive that they'd finally begun the quest in earnest to save their friend. She only hoped that they could survive the journey. Lost in their own private thoughts, they said little more.

The next two days passed slowly and quietly. They walked in relative silence, perhaps each concerned with what might greet them at the farm. On the second day, Wren and Mala rose to the wonderful aroma of Grakt's earthy tea, cactus sprouts and taters cooking on the fire. Wren stretched and realized that she was starting to adjust to the long hours of walking and sleeping on the cold ground. She felt stronger and wilder, as if the natural world was filling her with a power she didn't know she possessed. Mala, as ever, just went about her day as if nothing could rattle her. After several hours of walking, Grakt pulled them up and said, "It is just ahead. Let me reconnoiter the situation while you two wait here."

They both gawked up at his towering form.

Wren said, "I appreciate the thought, Grakt, but you seem to be the least natively endowed to reconnoiter in a subtle sort of fashion."

"Well, yes, perhaps you are right," he said, looking down as if noticing his bulk for the first time. "But I will not wait here while the two of you risk your lives."

"OK," said Wren, exasperated with his chivalry, "we'll go together, Grakt. Just try to make yourself seem...smaller."

Wren recognized the look of wry humor on Grakt's oversized features.

As they approached the farm, Wren began to think that it was abandoned. The pens were empty, the fields overgrown with tall grasses. The warm afternoon air sparkled with floating pollen and an overabundance of flying insects.

"Where are the animals?" she whispered. No one answered, so she crept closer to the nearest structure, a low barn that ran the length of a long empty paddock. A malignant effluence crept from the gutter into the farmyard, and Wren detected the odor of outhouse and something worse. This farm emitted the sickly-sweet stench of slaughter–of death. Was it an abattoir?

"Where are all the animals?" she asked again, her voice tense. "Where are the crops? What kind of farm is this?"

When no one else appeared willing to go forward, Grakt took the lead. He did his best to act small and Wren would have laughed had she not been filled with such overwhelming dread. He led them cautiously through the open barn doors of the nearest shed.

What Wren saw when she entered pushed the breath from her lungs, and she had trouble getting the air back into them, as if they were no longer willing to give a home to such contaminated malodors.

The gutter that spewed its putrid sludge into the barnyard led back up into the barn itself, and with great reluctance, they followed it in. A long line of stanchions lay before them, like those on a dairy farm, but no female herdbeasts were ensconced here. Cringing back as if the sights and smells that assailed her were too much to bear, Mala doubled over, retching into the nearest gutter. When she at last rose on trembling legs, Wren took her hand and pulled her forward.

"We've got to finish this," she said, but heard the quaver in her voice and wasn't at all sure if her own will to continue was any stronger than Mala's.

"Look at them," Mala cried. "How could they do this?"

Grakt said, his tone laced with cynicism, "The drakyn code has very little in the way of moral or ethical parameters. In fact, I'm not sure they have a moral code at all."

Wren just stood staring for a long time, her expression blank. Finally, she realized that the drakyn overseer could be near, in his own form or something seemingly benign. She didn't think for a minute that they would pretend to be one of the creatures in the stanchions. No proud drakyn would stoop so low or appear to be a victim, even for a moment. She searched the shadows but saw only the poor creatures hanging before them.

The rusting metal stanchions each held up the lolling head of a naked and unconscious human. Their skin was so pale that at first she thought they were dead, then she saw the slight rise and fall of thin chests as they took in shallow breaths. Their lower bodies were covered in ocherous and brown crusted stains. Apparently, the captives were not allowed to leave the stanchions to relieve themselves, hence the gutters that were filled with human excrement. Each had one arm attached to a slender bamboo tube that dripped a thick magenta liquid from their arms into buckets on the floor.

Blood farms, she thought. Not animal farms at all, but places where human beings were milked for their blood. The delicacies that Teeka had prepared, the blood that arrived daily from the farms, it wasn't animal blood at all, but the blood of human beings.

"Oh, no!" she gasped, then felt the dizziness and horror overtaking her. She swayed and Grakt was there to support her, helping her to sit down against a stone pillar.

"Are they killing them?" she asked

"I don't think so," replied Grakt. "At least not immediately. A living heart is required to pump blood, and the drakyn are nothing but efficient. I would bet they bleed their victims only so long, then let them recover, then start it all over again until eventually their victims lack the strength or will to go on."

Anger cauterized her fear until it was but a tiny ember at the back of her brain, while the rage that rampaged within her promised to leave desolation and destruction in its wake. Then it all collapsed into an unbearable sense of despair for what she saw before her.

"It's ghastly! We've got to stop this!"

"Yes!" said Grakt and Mala in unison.

"Let's get them out of here," said Wren through gritted teeth, as she reached toward the nearest stanchion.

"No!" cried Grakt, stopping her before she could pull the tube from the closest victim.

"You might kill them! What if removing the tubes precipitates their death? We do not know how this system functions yet. We need to find out more before we rush in with our tails swinging before us!"

Wren wasn't sure exactly what he meant about her nonexistent tail, but she calmed down enough to realize that he was right.

"OK," Wren admitted, a little ashamed by her rash reaction. "Let's hide outside and watch what happens next."

"Where are the drakyn who tend them?" Grakt inquired, but no one offered an answer.

He pulled Wren and Mala back out the door and they hid just outside, watching the barn's interior. After a few minutes, a tune began to play, eerie and dissonant. It was a disquietingly unnatural sound. Soon the back door opened and several bulky creatures shambled in, but they were not drakyn as they expected, but dageki, like Grakt. They stumbled in blindly, as if they were sleepwalking. In surprise, Wren turned to Grakt to ask, or accuse him, but of what she didn't quite know. But Grakt stared ahead unblinking, the look on his face as blank as the other dageki in the barn.

Without a word, Grakt stood up and stepped into the barn, taking his place among the other dageki. Wren grabbed at him, but he was too strong for her to stop him.

Mala pulled her back down and whispered, "No, wait. Let's see what happens. There are too many of them to fight."

One is too many of these creatures to fight, thought Wren, thinking of the incredible strength that Grakt had shown on the rare occasions when he'd seen fit to use it.

As they watched, the dageki stepped forward to the stanchions. They applied a sticky salve to the point where the bamboo tubes entered human veins. They quickly pulled the tubes out and gripped the arm of each unresponsive victim. After a few seconds, they tied each arm with a cloth bandage. Wren saw that they pulled a lever somewhere at the back of the stanchion and it opened with the creak, allowing the human to fall backward. She gasped aloud, sure that they would hit the floor, but each dageki caught his charge before they'd fallen. The entire operation was done in perfect synchrony, as if this was some grotesque ballet of the unimaginable. Half the dageki carried their charges back through the door, while the others gathered the buckets and dumped the viscous liquid into drums lined up along the wall.

Wren felt nausea and disgust rising in her. This had to be stopped, and now their strongest ally had just deserted them to join this abomination! How could Grakt have done this? She looked at Mala in disbelief, but Mala only shrugged and pulled her away from the door to a safe place in the high grass where they could hide and gather their wits.

"What's going on here?" whispered Wren, more to herself than Mala.

Mala looked thoughtful, then said, "Remember what Grakt told us about the dageki who are disappearing? How one told him of a disquieting sound that affected the dageki in his village?"

Wren said nothing, but it was starting to make sense to her. What if the drakyn had found a way to hypnotize the dageki with this uncanny music?

"I suppose it's possible," said Wren. "It's just like the drakyn to find a way to manipulate others to do the work for them."

"If so," Mala continued, "how do we free them, and why was Grakt caught in it? Why didn't that slaver use it on him when you two escaped?"

"I don't know. Maybe he didn't have time. I got the feeling his son wasn't really into the abuse of these creatures. I wouldn't doubt that Bryn hid the instrument from his father that night when we escaped."

"OK. But we're going to have to find this thing and disable it or steal it if we can. We haven't even seen the drakyn yet. We'll have to avoid them somehow. And I didn't see Poppet. Did you?"

"No, not yet, but there are more barns, so I assume there are more victims."

She was interrupted as the rear door opened and the group of dageki appeared, each carrying an unconscious human. They worked in a reverse dance of what they'd done earlier, attaching the unresisting humans to the stanchions.

"It appears you were correct that there are more victims," whispered Mala.

"Yes," said Wren, dejected. "How can we help them all?"

"Well," began Mala in a brisk voice, "first, we need to find out how many there are."

As if in a trance herself, Wren mumbled, "How many? How many are dying? How many farms are there? How many humans are suffering right now?"

"Don't think about that! It only leads to despair, and we don't have time for that! Let's deal with one problem at a time."

Pushing down her panic in the face of Mala's unrelenting logic, Wren retrieved an errant strand of silver hair and pushed it behind her ear with a shaking hand. She said, "OK, first we have to find out where that sound is coming from and somehow stop it. If we had Grakt and the rest of the dageki on our side, it would sure help."

"I say we split up," said Mala. "Let's check out the other buildings. That way, only one of us can be caught at a time."

"That makes sense," replied Wren. "Let's meet back here when the sun is at its zenith."

With that, they crept off, one heading to the southern buildings and the other around to the north and west. The first building Wren encountered was the one the dageki must have retreated to with their human captors. Through a small, greasy window, she could see orderly lines of pallets, and each held a drowsing human.

Dirty blankets had been thrown over them haphazardly. A lone dageki sat on guard against the far wall, slumped and clearly not much more aware than its charges. Not seeing anything that she thought might make the noise she'd heard, she moved on to the next building, another milking barn, much like the first. She saw no one she recognized among these captives. Wren began to despair of finding anything, when the sound began again, this time much closer to her. She ducked back under cover, as a stream of dageki exited the nearest barn with humans in their arms. Behind them, she saw the instrument that was controlling them. It was in the hands of a firstform drakyn, the first she'd seen since her escape from the palace. She cringed at the sight of it but saw no gold stripe that would indicate that it was Kodo, at least. What would he be doing here anyway? Surely the son of the queen would not be forced to perform such an ignoble task as herding dageki and milking humans of their blood.

She paid more attention to the instrument, for this was what they had to disable or steal, if they had any hope of freeing Grakt and the others. It looked like someone had thrown a dozen flutes into a bag and glued them in place where they'd fallen in a tangle. To play the notes it needed to, the drakyn was using both hands, clawed fingers stretched to their max to reach the correct holes, while it blew air into the bag. When the drakyn squeezed the bag, the sound it created was like nothing Wren had ever heard. Certainly not music, but beyond dissonance. The twisted notes grated at her ears and filled her thoughts with despair and exhaustion. All she wanted was to get as far away from this cacophony as she could. How could it put the dageki into such a trance, so receptive to suggestion that they would do anything the drakyn asked of them? Another thought occurred to Wren; even if they were able to destroy the instrument, did the drakyn have another one? If not, how quickly could another be brought in? She sighed in exasperation. First, she had to be sure that only one drakyn guarded this farm.

Wren had finished her reconnaissance of the barns and was sneaking through the tall grass at the back of the far building, when she saw the grass rustle ahead of her. She stopped abruptly, fearful of what unknown creature might be stalking her. She exhaled in relief when she saw that it was only Mala. They shared what they'd seen, and Wren described the drakyn and the bizarre instrument it wielded that appeared to control the dageki.

"I didn't see any other drakyn," Mala said. "There must be only the one. This drakyn must sleep sometimes. Maybe I can slip in and steal that thing while it sleeps. I don't think the drakyn have as acute a sense of smell and hearing as the dageki do."

"You? No," replied Wren. "I'll do it."

"No, I will," said Mala. "I'm smaller, less likely to be noticed."

"OK, we'll both do it. That way, if it wakes up, one of us can distract it while the other absconds with that flute thing."

"Then what?" asked Mala.

"Well, Grakt is stronger than any drakyn."

"Yes, but the drakyn are transmogrifers."

"Do you think they would send their most talented to perform this hapless job?"

"No, I suppose not," mused Mala. "OK, then tonight—"

"No!" interrupted Wren. "They sleep the deepest during the day, in the sun. I've seen it. You couldn't wake them with a farrier's hammer."

"So how do we know when?"

"Well, I suppose at the heat of the day. In a couple hours, I would guess."

"OK," said Mala. "Let's go out in the grass and rest until then."

When they woke, the sun was at three or four o'clock and its touch soaked the grass and soil around them, creating a rich, earthly perfume that rose, filling them with warmth and hope.

"I guess it's time to check on the frucking drakyn," said Wren, dispelling all the wellbeing the warmth had created. Mala said nothing but stretched her short limbs and rubbed her round face vigorously. "Let's do it," she replied.

The two of them crept up to the dusty window of the barn, where they'd seen the drakyn retreat to after the last milking. Wren spotted the creature sound asleep, it's ugly features awash in the sunlight that flowed in from the tiny window. She knew this was their best chance.

"OK, I'll go in and grab that flute thing. You wait here and guard the door." She slipped through and pulled the door shut behind her before Mala could follow.

Mala gave the door a look of chagrin but didn't follow. Perhaps Wren was right that they needed a lookout.

After closing the door quietly behind her, Wren crept forward, sure that with every step the creature would wake to tear her apart or deliver some worse fate that only a transmogrifer could imagine. She crept up to the sleeping form and extended her hand slowly, grasping the lumpy instrument in shaking hands. She moved back cautiously, congratulated herself on how easy this theft had been, when the instrument emitted a sound. Sure she hadn't pressed anything, she stood still, aghast that it had betrayed her. The drakyn stirred, grunted quietly and released gas with a loud *ploop* sound. Terrified that the creature would wake, Wren abandoned all caution and ran back out through the door in a rush. She ran past Mala, not resting until she was deep in the tall grass. When she at last turned around, Mala was behind her, giggling with relief.

"You did it!" Mala exclaimed

"Yep," she gulped, as her breathing returned to normal. "What do we do now, destroy it?"

"No," exclaimed Mala. "Grakt and his people may be able to figure it out. He would want us to keep it, I'm sure."

"OK, but now what? How long do we have to wait until the dageki are free of this compulsion?"

"I don't know, but I think we should get it away from here. Do you think the drakyn has the ability to track it?" When Wren didn't answer, Mala said, "I'll hide it in the woods. Then all we have to do is wait for the dageki to wake. If they ever do," she added lamely.

"I think they will. The ones that Dolman captured were alert, talking normally and not under any trance that I could tell. They were as communicative as a dageki ever gets, I guess. I don't know how long it took them to wake from its effects. I got there after they were all caged."

Mala took the instrument from Wren and headed toward the woods.

"Careful," warned Wren. "It sometimes plays itself."

As Mala disappeared, Wren turned back to the barns and gritted her teeth, prepared for the long wait and whatever mayhem would surely result when the drakyn and dageki awoke from their respective slumbers.

Drenka woke slowly, scratching her itchy hide with dry, splintered claws and once again railing at the totally unfair circumstances that had brought her to this miserable, stinking outpost on the edge of nowhere. If she hadn't made that comment about the queen's unfortunate choice of gowns for her figure to the acquaintance of a friend of an acquaintance of a friend of the queen, none of this would have happened. She could have assumed that she had only herself to blame, but she would never accept that possibility. She thought, quite rightly, that only morons and lowborns were capable of accepting blame.

Snorting in disgust, she reached down for the shambolika, but it must have slipped from her grasp during her nap. Her groping claws found nothing but air. Blinking her sleep-caked eyes and struggling to wake fully, she rummaged around on the dusty floor, but the instrument was nowhere to be found.

Drenka stood and took a deep breath, imagining what the queen would do to her if she lost something as precious as a shambolika. The instrument was complex and just one took their most talented transmogrifers weeks to duplicate. Then another fear gripped her. The dageki would eventually wake from the effects of the instrument. The trance had to be reinforced every few hours. Drenka was perhaps not the most talented of her kind. In fact, she worried that if she wasted her limited skills defending herself from a pack of angry dageki, she wouldn't have the energy to transform into the sturdy winged avatar she used for her trips to the palace. Then what would she tell the queen when she arrived? That she'd lost her most valuable charge, not even knowing who or what had stolen the device?

In sudden decision, or just sheer panic, she staggered out the door into the fading light of the farmyard, transforming as she went into a new winged shape, a sleek and efficient form, built not for short hops, but for long distances. She rose into the air quickly and was soon just a black speck dwindling on the horizon, heading not for the palace, but in the exact opposite direction.

From her place of concealment, Wren watched the drakyn transmoger and fly away, not really knowing the exact direction that the palace lay from where they were now but thinking it might be going the wrong way. She worried the drakyn would bring reinforcements. In a panic, she ran to the building where the dageki were housed, hoping she had time to wake them before the drakyn returned with others of its kind. When she opened the barn door, a double dozen sparkling eyes stared back at her from the gloom.

"Grakt?" she called tentatively.

Nothing.

"Are you in here?"

A grunt. Then she heard one of the dageki clearing its throat.

"Wren? What has transpired? Why are we here?"

"Grakt, is that you? What's the last thing you remember?"

"We were at the blood farm, in the barn," Grakt replied slowly. "We were about to reconnoiter when several of my people appeared. There was a sound...then...and the..."

"That's the last thing you remember?"

"Yes."

"You were taken in by the same kind of device that Dolman used. The instrument you theorized the drakyn use to control your race.

It's an intriguing device. It looks as if it would produce music, but the sound it makes is the farthest thing from music I've ever heard. Mala and I stole the one the drakyn used here, then the beast just transformed and flew away, I assume to bring more of its kind."

"Maybe," said Grakt, "though the drakyn are not known for their bravery when alone or under duress."

"We can hope, but I wouldn't count on it. I will never underestimate those creatures. We need to get out of here quickly, if your people are up to it."

Grakt disappeared and she could hear him talking to the other dageki. They seemed slow to respond.

"It appears that the device has a cumulative effect. I believe that I woke first because I was under its control for a shorter period. They are starting to wake, but it may take some time."

Impatiently, Wren said, "We need to get your people out of here before the drakyn returns."

Under Grakt's prodding, the others slowly stumbled forward. As they walked, Wren said, "Maybe with a sample of this instrument you can figure out how it works and how to stop it."

"Perhaps not me," said Grakt, "but Mageki Kyni Gouzuni may be able to find a way to counter its effects."

"Your scientist? She's here?"

At the sound of her name, one of the dageki turned to Grakt and spoke to him in their keening tongue. After a while, Grakt said to Wren, "Yes, she is here. When I didn't find her among the captives of the slaver Dolman, I despaired that she had been killed, but it turns out she was captured long before to serve the drakyn here. I don't know how you have achieved our release, but I am forever grateful."

At first, the dageki were confused, dizzy and slow moving, but as they walked, the creatures stood up straighter and began to talk among themselves. One dageki was intimidating enough, but with twelve of them shambling along behind her, Wren began to wonder what they were discussing. She pulled Grakt aside and asked, "What are they saying? Is everything OK?"

Grakt looked at her, his head tipping slightly, a movement that she'd come to understand meant he was trying to frame his response in a way that a skragling might understand.

"It is of no importance."

"Grakt, I really need you now. We risked our lives to save you. To save them."

"There is no question of my loyalty to you and Mala, but I am dageki, after all."

"What does that mean?"

"Well," he paused, looking back at the other dageki huddled to-gether en mass. "Humans have been poisonous to us, enslaving or killing our people. Now you ask us to be your partners in a war against the vilest creatures on the planet. It is difficult for my people to adjust to other cultures. Even in these extreme conditions, dageki are slow to change. There need to be discussions, committees formed. There are decisions to be made and stratagems to be agreed upon."

"What decisions?" asked Wren, exasperated.

"I am so sorry," said Grakt, wringing his small hands. "After we help the humans recover, most of them wish to proceed from here to our capital city of Dmisi."

"Now? Before we go to the next farm?"

Grakt looked uncomfortable. "We are not an especially brave race, I regret to admit."

"I understand completely. The drakyn scare me to death, too. But what about you? Will you continue with us or go with your people back to the city?"

He paused for a long while and Wren thought that he'd decided to leave them. His hands flailed about, as if following the tortured route of his thoughts. They flowed this way and that, until finally coming to rest at his sides.

"I am torn, my human friend. If Mageki Kyni Gouzuni has the weapon, she will most likely be able to find an antidote in her laboratory in Dmisi."

"Well. Tell her to be careful," Wren laughed nervously. "I don't want your entire tribe enslaved by the thing."

Grakt drew his head back sharply, anger writ plainly on his features. "You think of us as a primitive tribe?"

"Well, no. I mean..."

Grakt pulled away from her and rose to his full height. It was an intimidating sight.

"We are not primitives. We are the most technologically advanced race that this planet has ever—"

"No, no. I'm so sorry," cried Wren. "I don't think that at all. It was just an incredibly poor choice of words," she hurried to add. "You're the most amazing people I've ever met. I'm really sorry." Wren fell silent, sure she'd driven her new friend away for good and embarrassed by the evidence of her own bias. Was she a bigot? She hoped not. She vowed to be more sensitive toward Grakt and his people in the future.

Grakt said carefully, all emotion wrung from his voice, "You understand our predicament, I am sure. There is a very high probability that we would all fall under the thrall of this instrument at the next farm. If they are using it here, I am sure they are using it on all the farms. Efficiency. That is the drakyn way, as I have previously pointed out."

"Of course. I wouldn't ask your people to risk themselves again. If Mageki Kyni Gouzuni needs her laboratory, then you should make sure she gets back to your city. What did you call it? Demisen, Demissie. Dimu..."

"Dmisi."

"Yes," agreed Wren, still not quite sure how to pronounce it. "This is so important for your people. More important than any of us."

Grakt bent down toward her, touching his cheek with one delicate hand as he looked back at the group of dageki, then back at Wren and Mala. "The odds are excellent that Mageki Kyni Gouzuni and the group will make it back to Dmisi unharmed. The odds of you two..." Wren could see him assessing the two of them critically, "...being successful in finding your friend Poppet and rescuing him on your own, are—"

"Are what, Grakt?"

"The odds are 99.98 to..." Seeing their expressions, he amended, "They are close to nil."

Wren thought for a second. "But we don't always make our decisions based on the odds, do we? There are other factors. Mala and I are determined to go on, no matter what. You don't owe us anything. These are your people. You should go with them to ensure they arrive safely."

Grakt shook his head. "No, I owe you my life, but that is not why I should accompany you. There are enough capable dageki in the group, they will assure that Mageki Kyni Gouzuni arrives home safely. My designation is as a diplomat. How can I be a diplomat, hiding in the safety of Dmisi? How can I cower at home while this plague of drakyn advances on the world? I was given a mission: To find other races, to contact new civilizations, to go where no dageki has gone before. Except, I didn't expect it to be so trying," he added meekly, his chest visibly deflating.

"I agree, Grakt. This whole thing has become more than I can handle. At times, I just want to go back to my cabin and grow taters, but I can't. It's too late for that. I've seen too much to turn back now. The thought of Poppet suffering like those poor wretches in the barns..."

She continued in a stronger voice, "But if you think your people will be all right, why not accompany us a little longer, just to the next farm?"

Grakt said nothing, turning away to look at the huddled group of dageki. Wren was certain he would decide to stay with his people. She couldn't blame him. If she were in his situation, wouldn't she choose the easy way? Wouldn't she decide to stay with her own kind?

Wren turned to Mala to discuss what they were going to do without Grakt to guide them, when she was lifted off her feet, her face covered with something dark and slick. Without light or breath, she started to struggle. As suddenly, she was released and dropped to the ground unceremoniously. Grakt towered over her.

"Sorry," he said quickly. "That was a pathetically inadequate representation of a human gesture. I saw you engage in it with Mala when she returned. I had hoped it would express my desire to help you. I am so sorry if I frightened you."

Taking a deep breath, Wren laughed. "No, no, Grakt. That was the most perfectly executed hug I have ever experienced. It just caught me off guard, that's all. So, you're willing to help us find the next farm?"

"Assuredly. I will tell Mageki Kyni Gouzuni that I have made my decision. She will understand. Despite many of our kind, with their isolationist leanings, she agrees with my desire to seek out species with some potential for intelligence."

Abruptly, Grakt was gone again. Wren turned to Mala, who remarked dryly, "Thank the gods we're members of a species with some potential for intelligence. Our odds just improved by approximately 99.982 percent." They both laughed.

CHAPTER FIFTEEN

Escaping Notice

P oppet had, for once in his life, been lucky. Normally, the new stock were immediately placed into a milking cohort, but the drakyn who brought him here was less than attentive, too eager to escape the smelly barns and get home to the palace for the fitting of a new gown for her debutante ball that evening, so instead of being hooked up to the milkers, Poppet had been dumped unceremoniously into the recovery barn, where humans were fed and cared for, at least as much as was required to keep them alive until they were well enough to be milked again.

Poppet had seen the milking barn as he was brought in and knew what fate awaited him. He could have panicked then but told himself that if he were to have a chance of escape, he would need all his wits and luck to get out of this predicament. Poppet realized quickly that the humans around him were dazed and weak. Instinctively he mimicked their stricken faces, even holding his breath to make his skin look as pale as the others.

Lying still on his mat, he pretended to close his eyes, while watching everything through hooded lids. A drakyn and a group of their dageki servants entered the room. Though he'd never seen a dageki, he'd heard the drakyn speak of those gentle, malleable souls in denigrating terms. Poppet didn't have time to consider how or why they were working for the drakyn. All he knew was that as long as they did, he had to consider them his enemies too.

He watched as the impressively massive dageki made their rounds. With surprising delicacy, they fed each human a tin of soup followed by a paste that looked and smelled unappetizing to Poppet. The other humans were so docile and dazed that they made no effort to resist. Poppet reasoned that the paste must contain herbs to calm the humans, while the soup provided nourishment to keep them alive. He couldn't be sure, but he had to take the chance. As far as he knew it could be the other way around: the soup was the drug and the paste the actual food, but he didn't think so. When Poppet got his thin soup, he drank it down, but when they offered the paste, he made the motions of swallowing but stored the evil-tasting lump in his cheek. When they'd gone, he spit it out on the floor.

He survived this way for several days, checking out the camp as best he could without being seen. While the others slept, he planned his escape. He wanted to take some of them with him, but they were so weak and disoriented that he didn't think they would make it very far before the drakyn tracked them down. He knew that there were three drakyn guarding this farm, unlike the smaller farm that Wren had visited, though he couldn't know that.

Watching the rotations of the various barns, he reasoned that his group was about to be moved into the milking barn next, and he couldn't afford that. As soon as he went through the process, he would end up like the others, barely kept alive until the next blooding. When the body had given all it could give, he would end up like the rest, dumped into a pit downwind from the farm and covered with dirt by the sleepwalking dageki. Then more humans would be brought in to replace those lost, and the cycle would continue. Poppet was not willing to see his life end this way. He'd already survived so much for his young age; a seemingly never-ending war and the death of his family. His story had more chapters. He was sure of that.

When a loud altercation broke out in the milking barn, Poppet took it as a signal to make his escape. A distraction was the impetus he needed to act. Some of the bigger humans didn't always stay under the effects of the herbs. Sometimes, one of them would rise up and try to fight off the dageki, who were forcing him or her into the stanchion, perhaps for the last time. The will to live was strong, but none had succeeded in escape that he'd seen. How could they? The dageki were stronger than ten men. If they did manage to escape the barns, the drakyn could easily transform and take wing, tracking down the hapless escapee before they got even a short distance.

When Poppet heard the shouting, he immediately went into action. From under his pallet, he pulled out the bundle of food and the water skin he'd stolen. He crept silently from the barn. He'd seen how one of the humans had tried to escape, taking the easy route downhill into the open fields below the farm. Poppet went the opposite direction, uphill into the rocky scrublands. It would take him much longer this way, but there was more cover. He was almost sure that no one would notice he was gone. Most of the potential escapees tried to run from the milking barns. No one had the strength afterwards to run from the recovery beds. It made this line of escape less likely to be noticed.

Tamping down his terror, Poppet edged forward. He knew that this was the point of greatest danger. If anyone saw him running from the barn to the bushes, his escape attempt would end quickly. He could still hear the sharp sounds of the altercation emanating from the milking barn. He had no time to spare for the wretched soul who was grasping so desperately at life, only to be denied everything in the end. At least his unknowing sacrifice had given Poppet a chance. He intended not to waste it. With all the strength he could gather, he rushed into the bushes and began his arduous climb uphill. His only conscious thought was to escape this foul place, the source of the horrific nightmares he would surely suffer for the rest of his life.

Chapter Sixteen

An Unfortunate Rescue

As Poppet was escaping the blood farm through the back exit, Grakt, Wren and Mala approached it with trepidation from the front.

After giving what aid they could to the survivors of the first farm, Wren had been amazed at how quickly they'd recovered. No doubt urged on by the threat of more drakyn arriving soon, they'd gathered up food and water for the journey and carried those who couldn't walk. Sure that the drakyn would return soon, Wren pushed them to prepare quickly. When the drakyn didn't returned, Wren started to believe that, as Grakt had surmised, the lone drakyn had run, rather than face the wrath of her queen. Still, it would only be a matter of time before others arrived to carry the casks of blood back to the palace. They would soon discover that there was no new blood to collect and begin a search for their missing "livestock." The humans needed to be far away by that time.

The survivors left them to continue on to the nearest settlement. None of them, save Grakt, chose to follow Wren to the next farm, and she couldn't blame them. They'd just escaped from hell, and they had no desire to revisit it. As Wren watched them go, ambling into the trees, she could only hope that they would make it safely.

At first sight, the second farm was larger than the last one, and the terrain was much different. This farm, rather than being situated on a flat plane, was set up against a rugged hillside. Each barn lay in a separate tier of layered dirt with trails leading down between them. The largest building, Wren reasoned, must be the milking barn. Dageki were everywhere, moving humans to and from the barns. With so many dageki, she had to assume there were more drakyn to guard them as well. How were they going to figure out what schedule they were on? They couldn't hope that all the drakyn would sleep at once.

"We already have one of the instruments," she said. "Do we need another?"

"No, I do not believe so," replied Grakt. "I think the one will be enough. I want to save your people, and free mine, but now is not the time to act rashly. We need to look for your friend, and if he is not here, move on. I do not see how the three of us can have any chance of freeing all of these people."

Reluctantly, Wren agreed. "You're right, I guess. It's just so hard to walk away when this is going on."

"Once Mageki Kyni Gouzuni comes up with a way to counter the shambolika, we can release all my people. My hope is that, without the dageki, the drakyn will be unable or unwilling to sustain these farms."

"I hope you're right, Grakt. I suppose it's all we can do right now. But we need to check every barn for Poppet. And you need to stay here. We can't risk you getting sucked in by that instrument again."

Grakt lowered his head. "I understand. I do apologize for my weakness."

"It's not a weakness. It's no fault of yours, is it? You can't choose *not* to hear it."

Grakt looked at her intently, saying nothing.

Wren continued, "Mala and I will go around the barns and look for Poppet, just like we did at the first farm."

"Yes, of course," replied Grakt, seemingly distracted by his own thoughts. "It is just that I wonder, did centuries of complacency by dageki leadership bring us to the situation we now face?"

Unable to answer that question, Wren turned away to begin planning their foray into the farm.

Wren went left and Mala went right, leaving Grakt to hide in the brush while they searched the buildings. Looking back as she reached the first building safely, Wren could not see Grakt. She hoped he'd retreated into the scrub where he would be safe from the sound of the shambolika. Grakt had been able to name the device after talking to their scientist, Mageki Kyni Gouzuni. She'd surmised that it was actually an ancient tool, not for making music, but for torture and control. The dageki were exceptionally susceptible to its mind control. The construction of such instruments had long been banned in dageki territories. That it had been rediscovered and was now being used to enslave her people did not bode well for the likelihood they could avoid being drawn into this war. Mageki Kyni Gouzuni had also been worried that the isolation of her leadership might be leading them to disaster. Here was the evidence, she reasoned, for the dageki were now subjugated by two races, humans and drakyn.

Wren was almost finished with her search and had found no trace of Poppet. A shadow passed over her head, growing larger until it disappeared. Instinctively she stood totally still. When her heart rate returned to something closer to normal, she peeked around the corner of the building to see what was going on, just in time to see a winged drakyn drop a bundle at the door of the nearest milking barn. A dageki worker stumbled out to retrieve the limp form. Once the drakyn had flown away, Wren continued her search, now feeling sure that they wouldn't find Poppet here. As she came around the corner of the milking barn, a shattering scream pierced the quiet. Not even thinking, she ran at full tilt into the barn.

When she stepped inside, a scene of total mayhem met her eyes. Mala, still screaming, struggled ineffectually in the arms of a dageki, while another held the limp form of an oddly familiar woman.

Mala yelled, "Let her go! Let her go!" Her next words were muffled as the dageki held her closer, trying to quiet her struggles.

Wren could only imagine that Mala had lost her mind. Of any of them, Mala was always the calmest, the most practical. Why had she run into the barn, to be captured so easily? Wren then recognized the human the other dageki held and understood.

"Teeka!" she shouted, running forward. All the commotion had drawn another dageki over and this one intercepted Wren, grabbing her arm with so much force that she feared it would break. It was only a matter of time before the drakyn made his way in behind them. Teeka the cook hung in the arms of the first dageki, stunned. She made no effort to struggle, only staring at the stanchions in horror. Wren heard her whisper something that sounded like, "I thought eet was peeg's blood."

Wren screamed in desperation and fear. Had all their trials led them to this; slow death at the hands of the creatures they had already risked their lives to escape? Something huge rushed past Wren, but it moved so quickly that it was a blur. Before she could make sense of it, she'd been released and fell to the floor on her rump with a thud.

All she could do was stare as a giant form attacked the dageki holding Mala and Teeka. The other dageki gave little resistance, as the trance took away their initiative and judgment. They made no effort to fight against this unknown quantity who pushed them back and tore the two captives from their grasps.

The figure ran past Wren toward the open door, yelling, "Run!"

Wren realized that the creature was Grakt, but surely that wasn't possible. As soon as he got within hearing range of the shambolika, he would have become a zombie, like the others. With no time to figure out how he'd done it, Wren got to her feet and stumbled out of the barn. She looked downhill, but Grakt and the others had disappeared. In a panic, Wren searched the fields below them. Then she heard a distant voice call out and saw a tiny arm gesturing from the scrub to her right.

"This way."

Wren just caught sight of a dageki tail disappearing into the brush. In relief, she followed, looking back as she ran to see if they were being followed. She reasoned that it was only a matter of time before the drakyn figured out that they'd lost a captive and came searching for them, but in truth, the drakyn were disinclined to launch a full on search for one slave, who would likely last only a few weeks anyway.

When she caught up to the group, she whispered to Grakt, "How did you do that? That was amazing!"

He said nothing in reply. They continued, hurrying through the brush until Teeka stumbled and fell. Wren rushed up to help her, but Teeka pushed her away.

"What kind of hell ees these? I am rescued from the gardamn blood farm by two nincompoops and a giant slug with pretty scales."

"Well," replied Wren dryly, "I'm sure Grakt would be happy to take you back, wouldn't you, Grakt?"

Teeka fumed, and Grakt said nothing, looking away into the scrub.

Wren grabbed his arm, suddenly worried that the instrument had put him into a trance.

As if something had just occurred to him, he quickly raised his hands to his head. When he pulled his hands away, two tufts of tightly wrapped grass lay in his palms.

"Excuse me. In the excitement, I forgot."

"What? Grakt, that's brilliant! Why didn't we think of earplugs?"

"I believe that if the situation had affected you as it did me, you would have been more inclined toward a solution."

"That was a rhetorical question, Grakt."

"Sorry. I do apologize."

Teeka looked at them as if she were watching a puppet show that had gone horribly wrong.

"Eef you are feenished conversing at length with theese giant slug, do you theenk we could get thee fruck out of 'ere?"

Wren shot her a look of cool wrath.

"Communicating with Grakt requires a certain amount of patience. Since he just saved your life, I'm sure you're eager to show him the respect he deserves. And he's not a slug. He's a dageki, a member of an advanced race."

Teeka looked only slightly mollified.

"Let us keep moving," said Grakt. "We do not know how much effort they will expend to retrieve their lost livestock."

Wren grumbled, "If they knew Teeka better, they probably would have begged us to take her."

Mala, who had been unusually quiet so far, said, "No, I think they would have paid us in gold and jewels to take her. Next time I risk my life to save her, please hit me over the head with a log, would you?"

Teeka glared at no one in particular, saying nothing.

CHAPTER SEVENTEEN

The Worst of all Possible Worlds

K odo was growing tired of spending all his spare time with the queen, but he dared not leave her alone for too long. Jelebron had, unfortunately, been less than discreet with her plans for him to be announced emperor on her passing. He had enemies on the court, any one of whom might believe that by prematurely ending his mother's life, they could grab the throne for themselves. Unfortunately, the one he feared most was his own brother.

Semli would never challenge Kodo openly, it just wasn't his style. Besides, if he was perceived as plotting against his brother, it wouldn't gain him any cachet among the highest-ranking females. They would see it as just another tiff among two overly emotional males. Kodo was their obvious favorite, but that would mean nothing when it came down to choosing a new ruler. If they were forced to remove Kodo, Semli might be able to worm his way into their graces. At least that was what Semli probably reasoned. The truth was that the court would never accept Semli either. His firstform deformities would always relegate him to nothing more than an embarrassing lapdog to the court. Whoever challenged and fought off the others to claim the crown next, after Kodo's inevitable dethronement, would not have even the limited tolerance that his mother had shown to Semli, but Semli wouldn't figure that out until it was too late. Koto feared it was useless to try to reason with him. Semli resented his brother, not just because Koto was the favorite, but because Koto had saved his life when he was born ill and poorly formed. Semli simply couldn't face the fact that he owed Kodo a debt, if indeed he considered it a debt and not a punishment to have been saved, relegating him to a life that was far less than what Semli felt he deserved.

Kodo started, realizing with chagrin that Jelebron had been speaking and he hadn't heard a word.

"Are you listening to me, Kodo? I know what you're doing," croaked the ancient drakyn, wheezing out the words.

"You're spending this much time with me to protect me. You think I'm a target now that I've chosen you to be heir to the throne. You always were their favorite, you know. Perhaps they rush to celebrate your ascension. Or perhaps they're merely impatient for the crowning ceremony and the subsequent parties," she added with a chuckle.

"Mother," sighed Kodo, worn out by her delusions, "there's no way they will accept me as emperor. If you were thinking clearly, you'd realize that. I will be eliminated before your body grows cold."

Regretting his choice of words, Kodo added, "Not that you're due to leave us anytime soon." Knowing it was a lie, he added, "Mother, you look as young to me as the day I was hatched."

"Ah, yes," laughed the queen, preening her ragged and fading ear cartilage. "You were a part of that batch, weren't you? Perhaps the eggs have an advantage over the live born. Do you think? More time to mature. Semli was liveborn, you know."

"Yes, I remember, Mother. I've also been thinking of the others. It is so regrettable that Semli and I are the only two of your progeny to survive through this brutal war."

"Too bad, too bad, poor things." Kodo didn't think for a moment that she meant it. "But the war is necessary, child. You know that. We must rule with a strong hand. We must be given respect by the lesser races. It is the way. I only regret that I won't live to see the day we ultimately succeed in subjugating these upstart skraglings once and for all."

Kodo was starting to have doubts that an easy or painless end to the conflict was near, but he said, "I'm sure you will live to celebrate our success."

"Don't lie to me, son. I know my death is near. I can feel its breath on my neck in my chambers at night. I feel the chill of it deep in my bones. It doesn't matter how long I sit in the sun, this cold won't leave me until it's able to drag me down with it into the underworld. At least there it's supposed to be warm, if you don't mind the fires of Asmiroff burning your scales off over and over again through eternity." She cackled, the laughter turning into a hacking cough. "Now leave me for a while, little one. I've got plans to make."

"Yes, Mother. I'll be near if you need me."

With a perfunctory bow, Kodo left the chamber, his thoughts clouded by worry. So lost in reflection was he that he almost ran over Semli in the hall.

Semli, who today wore a form he favored, a handsomely dressed man of a skragling era called "Edwardian," dodged with grace and spoke lightly, "Whoa, brother, you're going to have to watch where you're going. You wouldn't want to step into an open well or something, especially before you're crowned 'emperor.'" Semli spit out the last word with total disdain. "After that, *lacta alea est.* Let the dice be cast, brother. It's been nice knowing ya."

Kodo thought it was so like Semli to find such an obscure quote; the words of an ancient emperor speaking in a dead skragling language, from a supposedly great civilization of their otherworld.

Ignoring the flippant words, Kodo said, "Your comprehension of skragling languages and culture is indeed impressive. You really should create a compendium of skragling knowledge. I hear the dageki are devising a way to manufacture several identical versions of a primer at once. It could change the world, this duplication of ideas that can be shared by many."

"Yes, or it could lead to our downfall. Let the rabble agree and we are doomed."

"Who said that?"

"I did, just now."

Kodo laughed. "You are so confusing, Semli. You follow skragling culture more closely than even I do, yet you pretend they mean nothing to you."

"As they do. None of it means a thing to me. Haven't you figured that out yet? I sleep with the slaves. I live recklessly, fighting without fear, as if life means nothing to me. Get it? Since I almost lost my life before it began, it's just silly to care. It's all a game."

"All your life, I've protected you, petitioned for you. In the beginning, I even breathed for you, and you—"

"I never asked you to do any of that. In your own best interests, you should've let me die. I owe you nothing."

"I didn't mean to infer that you did—"

"Yes, you did." Semli laughed, but there was no humor in it. "In your infinite do-gooder, holier than thou, everlasting gardcrap, you believed that you were helping me. Did I ask you to pull me from the teeth of my own mother? Did I ask you to hide me away until she'd forgotten that I still lived? It's all a ghastly joke. I'm now a cautionary tale told to quaking skragling brats, hiding beneath their beds in fear of the monster more monstrous than any who have come before."

"That's not true, you're making that up so you can feed your own self-pity. It could be different, you could value the life you almost lost, use what you've been through to live a full life. We could make Drakonia a better place, a world where study and enlightenment are the norm, not the exception."

"Do you even hear yourself? A better place? You must be jesting, surely. Drakonia will never be a 'better' place. Since the beginning of time, we've lived to kill, then survived the consequences. This world is made up of killers, survivors and victims. Have you lost the guts to kill? If so, will you be one of the survivors? I think not. I think you'll be a victim."

Kodo looked at him thoughtfully, seeing Semli for the first time as perhaps the quintessential representative of his own race. "I've been thinking about that lately. Can we afford to go on this way? This war is killing off our brightest thinkers, the strongest and most talented transmogrifers among us. Though no one has done an actual count, it's obvious that our numbers have been declining over the last few generations. Just look at all the empty palaces in the north. Though, when they first arrived, the skraglings had no transmogrifee talent, they have learned quickly, as if they were born to it. And these skraglings reproduce at a rate we can't match, despite the war and the farms. I fear they will just outlast us."

"Ask me if I care a gardamn about our survival as a race, brother. Besides, you've done your share of killing. Everything you touch comes to death, in the end. Just think about that pretty little drudge you brought in. She's gone, and it's your fault. I heard rumors that her and that little marm tossed themselves into the sewers to be drowned in shite, rather than spend another minute with you. Though I did get a taste before she offed herself. Not bad, not bad at all."

"What?" Kodo clenched his fists.

"Did you think you could keep her to yourself? Come on, Kodo. Brothers share, don't they?"

"What did you do to her?"

"For some reason, she was extremely susceptible to my charms. You know that humans lack the vomeronasal organ that we possess, right? But she seemed to be unusually sensitive to the pheromones I can produce. I took her, of course. They're just animals. Stop deluding yourself that they're anything more. Thinking like that will lead you to ruin. You can sleep in the sty with the pigs, but only a fool would fall in love with one."

At Semli's words, Kodo felt a seething anger rise in his gullet like volcanic magma, pushing upward past the point where any reason could contain it. No wonder Wren had been so distant toward the end. Did she throw herself into the sewers to die? No, she wouldn't do that. There was too much life in her to just give up, too much strength to stop trying. So he told himself. So he hoped. He approached Semli, with murder in his eyes, knowing that his brother was intentionally provoking him, but past caring. Then the bells started to ring.

When Kodo turned away, cocking his head to listen, Semli murmured, "Oh, oh, gotta go," quickly slipping away down the corridor before Kodo could react.

Counting the bells as he ran, Kodo opened the doors to his mother's chamber to find several of her servants leaning over her. As he entered, the twelfth bell pealed, and they turned away from the body of his dead mother. As if controlled by one mind, they bent low to bow before him, chanting over and over the words he most dreaded, "Hail, Emperor Kodo!"

CHAPTER EIGHTEEN

One Good Wing Deserves Another

The trail was becoming increasingly steep and treacherous. Wren knew from the maps Grakt had described that they must be well into the region called the Glyn. He'd translated it as "little hills."

Some little hills, she thought as she gasped for breath at the top of another steep incline. She looked back to see that the terrain was changing as they rose in elevation. The trees here were stunted and sparse, but the sky was an intense shade of sapphire blue and the air smelled crisp and pure.

She was pulled out of her reveries abruptly when Grakt stopped ahead of her. She stumbled, and he reached down with his short forearm to steady her.

He said, "We are now entering the territory of the leijong. They are basically friendly at this time of year, but they are easily riled. If we meet a flock, we must be on our best diplomatic behavior. I will do the speaking."

"A flock?" exclaimed Mala. "You said they were human!"

"More or less," replied the dageki enigmatically. "Legends say that they are descendants of a drakyn transmogrifee that did not have the desired effect. Instead of becoming a tool for the drakyn, the leijong became one of their greatest enemies. It seems that the qualities given to them also made them fiercely independent, as well as endowing them with great strength and endurance. No one has been able to undo what was done to them, and the leijong have no desire to go back to being totally human, or whatever their firstform might have been. Whoever did this had a great transmogrifee talent. It is highly unusual for changelings like these to breed true to form, generation after generation. The leijong have prospered and multiplied in this valley."

Wren was still pondering what "more or less human" might mean, when her attention was drawn away suddenly and completely by the scene before them. They'd reached the rim of a high mountain valley. The trail led down into the most bizarre village she'd ever seen. Frail-looking stick houses reached high into the sky, gently swaying and creaking in the breeze. They were propped up by sturdy living vines that twined through and around the buildings, and by a patchwork of guy ropes, made of the same vines. There appeared to be no logic or plan to the construction, one level precariously thrown together on top of another. In places, it appeared that they'd moved on to a new level before the lower level had been finished. Each level consisted of a single room, often with large open windows, and no doors. Through the windows Wren saw neither people nor furniture, nor were there any signs of life on the ground—no people, no livestock, not even cultivated fields.

Wren murmured, "But where are all the people?"

"The lupines are blooming in the mountains," said Grakt quietly, as if this explained it all.

"But—"

"We had better get going," continued Grakt. "I want to reach the flying river before half the daylight is gone. The winds will pick up toward evening. There," he said, pointing up and to their left. "Up there is the source."

Wren followed the line of his arm to a trickle flowing from the rocks high above. It flowed past the leijong city, into a shallow lake, and out the other side. She lost sight of it in a misty haze that covered the horizon.

"It looks harmless enough to me," she said uncertainly.

"It is just a stream when it enters the lake," said Grakt. "But by the time it reaches the boil, it is a raging torrent. You can't see the falls from here. It is all but suicidal to attempt the trip alone. Fortunately, I am acquainted with a leijong boatman who will guide us."

"Can't we go around the falls?" pleaded Wren.

Grakt glanced down at her with a long-suffering look. "There is no other logical route to Dmisi from here. To go through the mountains on foot could take months, and winter would catch us there. Many rivers there are to forge if we take the southern route. But we have argued over this twelve times, thirteen if you count this conversation. We all agreed on this route. Do you wish to change our plans now?"

"Of course not!" she said, exasperated. "I know it's the only sensible way. Still, I just have a bad feeling about this."

"There is nothing to worry about."

Wren obediently followed as Grakt led them down the steep path. As they descended, the leijong houses appeared even taller. When they reached the valley floor, the tops of the rickety structures were lost high in the sky. No one approached them. The village appeared deserted. She looked into the dark rooms of the bottom levels as they passed. Seeing what she thought was motion, she pulled away from the group without being noticed, and ducked into a wide opening.

She heard the structure creaking above her as she waited for her eyes to adjust to the dim interior. She stood for a moment on the simple mud floor, choking on the smell of rot. She looked down and found a tiny butterfly wing, once brightly colored, but now faded and ruined by water. It had a single yellow seed tied at its base, cracked and discolored. It smelled of death. She tossed it aside and wiped her hands. She was about to leave when a frail voice reached her from a dark corner.

"Have you come to wait with us?" it asked.

Wren jumped, unaware that the room was occupied. Then she saw them, cowering against the back wall, an elderly man and woman, gray-haired and thin, with sharp faces and oddly hunched backs. They wore no clothing and sat in the mud shivering, their arms around each other. Wren felt sudden pity and concern. What kind of people would leave these two like this?

"Are you leijong?" she asked gently, squatting before them.

To her surprise, the woman's clucking laugh resonated in the empty room.

"Once we were proud leijong. No more. Now we are food for the sucking mud. What did you think? This is the last level. Soon the autumn floods will come to take us to the mountain home. It is the way."

Wren could only stare at them. "But why doesn't your family care for you, help you up to a higher room above the rising water level?"

"Don't speak blasphemy!" snarled the woman. "It was our children who brought us here. It is the way, and all should know that, unless you are an enemy."

The emaciated form leaned forward, and Wren saw the gleam of yellow fangs and bulging, inhuman eyes. A sharp brown tongue darted toward her face, jutting from a mouth dripping with thick saliva. Terrified, Wren scrambled away and broke out into the sunlight. The others were far ahead, and she stumbled to catch up, not waiting for her eyes to fully adjust to the light. When she reached them, she caught Grakt by the arm and pulled him aside.

"Back there," she stammered, "I found–they need help!"

"I know. I should have warned you, but there is nothing we can do about it. It is their custom. The old and sick are sent to the lower levels where the water rises. It is their choice to end their lives this way. They are a very proud people. If we interfered, we would bring down the wrath of the entire leijong nation." He glanced at her. "It is hard the first time you see it."

"We can't just leave them like that—"

"We cannot interfere. To do so is a crime, and you do not want to see leijong justice in action. I know how difficult it is to accept, but you cannot feel responsible for every life. This valley only provides food for so many, and that is hard-won. If they expend energy on the old and dying, they might all starve."

Wren was silent as they walked through the empty village. Though she saw no more leijong in the lower rooms, she couldn't clear her mind of the vision of them sitting alone in the frigid mud, waiting to die. She knew she would see their faces in her dreams for a long time to come.

The group continued through the village and around the lake. They followed the stream into the mist they'd seen from the heights. Wren could hear the river beside them, a gentle, reassuring gurgle. From the distance ahead came an indefinable noise, a rumble and a rushing that never quite grew into the realm of hearing. She could feel something massive and powerful looming ahead of them.

They came to another haphazardly built structure, obviously of leijong stick construction, but this one, rather than being built into the sky, was built long and low, stretching out over the water. It was open on the end facing the water and the prow of a sleek craft poked out onto the river, where the current gently burbled around it. Unlike the building, the boat was well-crafted of a sturdy reddish wood. It sat high and proud in the water.

Wren turned her attention back to the building when she heard a whimpering sound. Against the shaded wall of the boathouse sat a crying man.

As they approached, the man made no attempt to rise, but only looked up into their faces with deep, liquid eyes. Tears rolled down his cheeks and his lower lip quivered. Wren couldn't help but stare, not because the man was crying, but because he was the most handsome man she'd ever seen.

It wasn't just the features of his face, or their shape that made him attractive to Wren. Perhaps it was the piercing look of freedom in his gray eyes, or the strength of his jaw. It wasn't entirely a human face, but it held a purity of nature that she'd never seen before, except perhaps in the eyes of the goshawk who hunted the high peaks above her home forest.

His clothing was plain and unadorned, of muted sepia and juniper green, except for a cape of some unknown iridescent fabric, covering a hump on his shoulder. He appeared to be in excellent condition. His skin was smooth and brown, and muscles bulged from his simple tunic. His hands were broad and capable. Wren believed he could have built this boat himself, or many others. She wondered what such a man could have to be so sad about.

Grakt stepped up to him, and a slow light grew in the eyes of the leijong.

"Kree," said Grakt, "you may remember me from the university diplomatic expedition last year. I am Grakt Si Tageki Ki Jorfa Kera Ri Jorfa. Please forgive my lack of formal speech, but we have no time for such niceties now. We need your services as boatman to navigate the falls. I have brought two bags of this year's poppy seed and the finest dageki damask for trade. Will you guide us?"

"Don't want the cloth," Kree replied gracelessly, as he stood. "But I'll take the seed."

When he stood, Wren noticed the cape he wore, how it moved with his body, conforming to the lump on his shoulder. She thought of the two old people she'd found in the village, realizing that this must be a traditional leijong garment.

He caught her stare and his deep eyes flared, then as quickly cooled.

"Of course, you're curious about my deformity," he said with a note of resignation. "I can't blame you, being a stranger. Everyone asks, and eventually, I must show them. Better now than later."

Wren stumbled backward as the air crackled and something brilliant unfolded above her. She raised her hands to shield her eyes from the light, but no shade could hide its brilliance. It was twice the height of a man and glowed in colors of transparent, glistening mother-of-pearl and quartz, deep magenta and sunturn yellow. It dazzled them in the sunlight. Wren was breathless at the sheer beauty of it. What she'd thought was a lump on Kree's shoulder had unfolded into a powerful wing that looked like a cross between a butterfly's and a hawk's, except that it had a powerful curve. She thought she'd never seen anything so beautiful.

"Wh–what deformity?" she stammered. "It's the most amazing thing I've ever seen!"

"Don't patronize me," he sneered. "Are you blind? I was born with only one. I should have been sent to the lower levels at that moment, but my parents were weak, and I have paid the price for their foolishness every day since. At least I've found a skill as a waterman that gives me some peace. I may kill myself yet; I think about it every day."

"But you're young and strong, with four limbs and a healthy body."

"Four limbs may be enough for you, a mere skragling, who has never joined the ritual flight to the alpine wildflower bloom, but for me, it's a disgrace and a loss beyond bearing."

Kree turned from them abruptly. Folded his wing with a snap, he entered the boathouse, slamming the rickety door behind him without a word.

Wren turned to Grakt. "I hope I haven't ruined our chances. Will he refuse to take us now?"

"I doubt that," replied Grakt. "He lives for his fares. Don't worry, his mood will improve."

Wren nodded, secretly thinking that it would take a miracle to improve this one's mood. She turned around to find Mala looking past her to the river with longing.

They settled down on the grass to wait. She was beginning to hope that they wouldn't have to go by boat after all, when the prow of the craft began to edge its way out of the boathouse and onto the water. Kree appeared, sitting in the rear of the boat, and steering with a long wooden oar. At the dock, he waited silently as his fares climbed into the boat gingerly. When they were all seated he said, "You'll want to tie yourselves in. There are tie lines on each bench. It's going to be a rough ride. The water demons have been active of late."

Wren thought she saw his upper lip curl as if he laughed at some secret joke, but she told herself it could only be her imagination. When she looked again his face was still, and, for the first time, almost serene.

They quickly followed his instructions, while Kree himself anchored his feet securely under the bench and maneuvered the craft out into the main channel.

As they slipped gently into the current, she looked down at her hands, white and gripped on the bench, and tried to force herself to relax. Looking around, she saw only calm faces, except perhaps for Mala, whose look verged on rapture.

After a while, she began to think that Grakt had been teasing her about the dangers of the river, if teasing were a thing Grakt might be capable of doing. The wide river slipped under them with a silken rustle, and Kree maneuvered the channel with practiced ease.

She turned her attention to the banks of the river as a stag raised his head from drinking at their approach, thundering off into the brush in alarm. Above and behind him the trees gave way to steep rocky cliffs that reminded Wren of the peaks beyond her home, which in turn brought her to thoughts of what her life had been and what it was now likely to become.

The world around her faded and she saw a meadow in a deep wood where tiny figures fought, striking and falling back, some not rising again. The metal rang out when the swords collided with a sound like the chiming of miniature bells. Then a strange blue lightning lit the meadow in stark contrasts. As soon as it had begun, the vision faded, leaving Wren with a deep and inexplicable sense of foreboding.

She'd been so involved in her thoughts that she hadn't noticed that the cliffs had fallen away beneath them. The river had risen from its bed and was flowing out over the open sky. Far below them the mountains descended toward the sea at a dizzying rate. She screamed.

"Beckle save us!" shouted Mala above the roaring water. "You scared me half to death! What's wrong?"

"Th–the river. What's holding it in the air?" she whimpered.

"I thought you understood," Grakt said in an exasperated tone. "Gonjigen means flying river in leijong."

"Yes, but I didn't think you meant that it really *flew*! I thought the rapids were fast...or something. And when you said falls, I didn't think it meant that the *land* would fall away!"

Teeka snorted. "You 'ave much to learn about zee wild world, girl. Zees was zee sight of a violent challenge between our kind and zee drakyn. Zee leijong are one result, and zees river another. Eet has not flowed naturally for many years."

"Are we safe?" Wren asked in a small voice.

"Perfectly," Grakt responded. "Just hold on. Look at Kree. Does he look worried?"

Wren glanced back at the boatman. His one wing was opened wide to catch the wind and steady him. He negotiated the rapids, guiding the boat with sure motions of the long oar. His glistening arm and leg muscles strained. Sweat covered his handsome face, a face transformed by wild joy. Wren realized that in his own way, Kree was flying.

When the river finally settled to earth and they pulled the boat into shore that evening, Wren felt rattled and ill-at-ease, as well as a little bit ashamed of herself. Who knew that she had a fear of heights?

Just add it to my 'fear of everything' list, she thought in disgust.

Trying to put the day behind her and steady her shaken nerves, she scoured the shore for wood to make a fire, while Mala had, amazingly, gone back to the river to swim.

"Haven't you had enough of the river?" Wren mumbled. When she looked again Mala had popped to the surface with a fat, wriggling trout in her hands.

"Ah," said Grakt, "drakynfruit and fish head stew for dinner tonight?" He looked at Teeka expectantly.

She beamed. "It just so 'appens to be one of my specialties."

Of course, Teeka was happy to share a new recipe and insisted that Wren record the particulars in her notebook. As Teeka read out the ingredients and instructions, Wren was amazed that the cook had a recipe for every microclimate they'd traveled through.

Wren wrote in her notebook:

Drakynfruit and Fish Head Stew
By Teeka Boideau

Ingredients:
5 cups of river water
3 dried or fresh (if available) drakynfruit flowers, containing the active drakynfruit pulp

1 fish head

5 or 6 river tongue bulbs

A dash of eel sauce

Sea salt

4 or 5 leaves of swamp cress

Instructions:

Bring the water to a boil. Add the fish head. Do not remove brains or eyes. Tear off the yellow-green leaves of the drakynfruit. Avoid cutting your hands on the razor barbs. Leave only the petals and the flower core. Scoop out the wriggling mass of the core and mash it in your hands. Add to stew. Add the swamp cress and tongue bulbs. Season with eel sauce and sea salt. Cook until the eyes of the fish grow cloudy and no longer appear to be watching you. Decorate with drakynfruit flowers just before serving.

After dinner, they sat around the fire listening to Grakt talk about his adventures since leaving the dageki capitol. He was almost giddy–at least for a dageki–now that he was on his way home. Kree sat apart, after he'd helped himself to a large bowl of stew and taken it to eat alone somewhere in the darkness. His dour mood had returned.

Wren saw figures materialize from the corner of her eye, and several of the tall leijong approached their campfire. Wren had not heard them walking up, but there was a swishing noise, like an owl's semi-silent wing strokes when bearing down on prey in the dark. As they drew near, Wren saw that they were similar in stature and bearing to Kree, but if it were possible, they were even more imperious and haughty in their bearing. There were four males and three females.

The females appeared to be slightly taller than the males, and their wings wrapped elegantly around their torsos, as if in modesty, but Wren wondered if it were not sheer vanity, to show off the stunning beauty of them. Beneath their wings she saw that the men each wore an azure blue sash and the women, a sash of the deepest cardinal red.

Grakt did a double-take as he observed their visitors, then rose and spoke solemnly. "Welcome, lords and ladies of the alpine fields. It is a consummate honor that you visit us here. But if I may be so rude as to ask without preamble, why have you come, the highest leaders of your people, to meet us, as we are the humblest of travelers and surely undeserving of such an audience?"

"Relax, Grakt," said one, "we're not here to raise the river fares." The apparent leader of the leijong spoke casually. The others made a lyric sound that Wren assumed was leijong laughter. He introduced himself as Aquilinus. "We're here to discuss something pressing for all our races. We are quite isolated in this valley, but we can't live with our heads in the sand like longneck pekkarinas any longer. The drakyn have gone too far, attacking our outposts, stealing our young, burning our wildflower fields. Now that the war with the skraglings is not going their way, they are at their most desperate and most volatile, and it's time that the other races made an alliance to do something about them, once and for all."

Grakt bowed. Looking behind him he realized that the others had stood and gathered more logs for the leijong to sit on. All but the leader ignored the proffered seating, and they squatted gracefully in the sand. They were as unmoving as stone. Wren thought they could probably hold this pose with ease long after she would have had to move her cramped limbs. In one way they appeared almost brittle, like glass sculptures but in another they had the strength of gale winds flowing in their veins. They took great pride in what they were. Wren thought that she wanted to be like that. Some day.

Grakt said, "We too have our problems with the drakyn. They have found a way to subjugate our people using a shambolika, an ancient weapon, capable of enslavement."

"I've heard of it," said Aquilinus. "An evil weapon from the early drakyn wars. They were all destroyed. I'm surprised that they found a way to recreate them. The drakyn are not prone to scientific endeavors."

Grakt looked at his feet, and Wren gazed up at him sharply, in sudden understanding. "You knew of this weapon, even before we discovered that the drakyn were using it, didn't you?"

"I do apologize, Wren. I could not bring myself to tell you. It is my fault that the dageki are enslaved."

"What? How? What did you have to do with it?"

"As you know, my fields of interest include historical research and engineering development. I found the plans for this device—"

"You recreated the deadliest threat that your people have ever faced?"

"It was not quite like that—"

Aquilinus interrupted. "We can discuss the culpability of the dageki in their own peril another time. Right now, it is imperative that your people and mine come to an agreement."

But Aquilinus wasn't looking at Grakt. He was staring at Wren.

"What? My people?" Wren pointed to her own chest.

"Yes, the skraglings," said Aquilinus slowly, as if he were speaking to a child.

"But I have no say in what they do. I have no power—"

As Wren spoke, another leijong came forward and handed Aquilinus some ragged pages that floated in the evening breeze like whisps of snakeskin.

"We have inherited–or should I say, been burdened with–an exceptional vision."

"You mean, like the eyesight of a hawk?"

Again, that melodic laughter from the leijong.

"No, something more. It's not always very accurate. Imagine grabbing pollen as it floats by, but this pollen consists of bits of time and pieces of the light with which we see the story of our future."

"Wow."

"You don't have to believe me. You're young. You have a lot to learn about who you are and who you can be, but we would like to be a part of that, perhaps only a single petal in the flower that you are becoming."

"How?"

Aquilinus pulled an amulet from his vest and offered it to Wren. "All I ask is that you wear this. It is an amethista, the lavender stone of our people."

"What does it do?"

"We believe that there will come a time when the war reaches a tipping point, when skragling, dageki and leijong destinies reside in flux together. When that time comes, call us with the stone and we will come to your aid. Not one of us, not a few, but the entire leijong nation. For now, we follow the wisdom of these visions, as written down in the leijong way."

What Wren could see on the pages looked like chicker's scratching to her. She stood in shock, feeling that something important was happening, but not having the slightest idea what it was.

"How? How will I call you? How will I know when the time is right? What if—"

"It's late. We don't happily fly at night. We'll go now to rest. At dawn, we'll be gone, helping Kree get his longboat back to the city. Good night."

After they'd melted into the darkness, Wren sat in silence, not wanting to talk to Grakt–not wanting to believe that the leijong had put her in such an untenable position. When would this happen? How would she know how and when to call them? What the fruck were they talking about?

Finally giving up in frustration, she crawled into her bed with her dubious gift feeling heavy around her neck. She pretended to sleep, only to spend the night tossing and turning in clouds of soft, drifting pollen that became a horde of screeching, biting insects, buzzing frantically as they erupted from behind her nightmare eyes.

CHAPTER NINETEEN

The Emperor Has no Hopes

K odo felt the fool; the clown and his crown; the throne soon to be overthrown. The whole gardamn thing was a joke that had no humor and meant nothing!

I'm starting to sound almost as cheery as Semli, he thought with self-disgust.

Akriast the senior had performed the ceremony, substituting "emperor" for "queen" with only the slightest sneer every time the alternate word was required. Of course, the court was nothing but enthusiastic...to his face. What was said behind his back was another matter.

Semli had been conspicuously absent, perhaps gloating from a distance over whatever hideous fate awaited Kodo, so that when it all fell apart, Semli would be clean of the whole uncomfortable affair.

"Oh, no! My dear brother has been deposed, you say. But of course, you know I had nothing to do with that. I was on the coast the whole time, training with my sailfish for the annual regatta. The poor boy! But I could have warned him. Our society will never accept a male leader at this level. I know my place and will of course serve the new queen with eternal loyalty and admiration."

Or something to that effect. Kodo shuddered. What should he do next? Where could he go? His whole life had revolved around the court, the war, the subjugation of a species that he now realized he'd come to admire, even above his own.

There, he'd admitted it. The skraglings had won him over. Perhaps he'd just spent too much time emulating them, learning from them and about them. Their ways and their spirit had infested him to the point that he couldn't remain as he was, living the life of a lazy, bloated drakyn lord, consuming the blood of the vanquished and the insincere admiration of his cronies. Did he possess no purpose greater than to wage war, to eat and shite and fornicate? If so, then he was only an animal, a beast better off deceased.

And what of Wren? What had become of her? Was she dead, or had she managed to escape? He chose to believe that she lived. There was something about her, not just the disturbing vibration he felt in her presence. He suspected an aberration in the balance that transmogrifers used when performing their art, or perhaps it was just her beauty that left him agog. He needed more time to figure that out–to figure her out. She had a strength of character that he wanted to emulate. Yes, he wanted to be more like a slave! How his mother would have laughed. Wren was extraordinary to him, a perfect form, like a butterfly, or a fox, but with the will of a badger. A smile creased his face at the thought.

With a sigh, Kodo straightened his uncomfortable robes and set about the task of formulating a plan of escape that would maintain his honor, if that were even possible. If he wanted to survive until he could find Wren, he'd better get his arse in gear and off this throne before it became the death of him.

An hour later, his thoughts were broken by the sounds of an argument outside the throne room.

He sat up straight. *Already?*

Loud, strident voices echoed in the hall outside, in tones that did not bode well for his long and uneventful reign. He realized that he'd waited too long. If he'd just left the palace as soon as the bells had rung announcing his mother's death, he wouldn't be in this situation now.

As if on cue, the double doors of the "queen's" throne room were thrown open and three furious drakyn females strode in. Kodo recognized them from the cult of Parthenos, those deluded creatures who practiced parthenogenesis, where females do not need males to reproduce. Kodo was sure it would be the death of all drakyn if they were allowed to continue, leading to more and more deformities and disease. When not enough material was available for the transmogrifee, errors in the twisted staircase–the pattern that was the basis of living matter–increased over time, like a juggler making small errors that grew and grew until the objects flew out of control.

Kodo said meekly, "Er, does this mean that I'm no longer emperor? It really does break my heart. I so wanted to be of service to the drakyn people, in some small way. I do have some skills, you know, and this room desperately needs redecorating, don't you think? Just dreary."

He laughed nervously, but there was no answering laughter. Drakyn females were not renowned for their sense of humor, especially not these cult members.

"You are an abomination that requires our immediate attention," spoke the largest of the three, in a strident tone. "The fate of our empire now lies in the hands of a male, who is also a buffoon. It is our duty to remove you before your delicate male sensibilities can negatively affect morale and discipline. Our most honored traditions, as well as the very structure of our society, have been put at risk by this farce. Males are not capable of rule. Therefore, you will be removed."

The drakyn warriors stepped forward.

Kodo raised his hands ineffectually to ward off the approach of the three massive forms. "This was not my idea, believe me," he croaked. "I'll be out of your way shortly; I just need to—"

The drakyn females reached the throne, but Kodo was no longer there. Before they could react, a sleek black-winged form passed over their heads and flew at great speed from the palace. The emperor was gone. The buffoon had left the room.

CHAPTER TWENTY

The Wastrel Gathers Moss

Poppet felt the muscles in his thighs cramp, wondering again how much longer he could hold this position. Wild grape thorns poked him in the back and his feet had gone numb fifteen minutes ago. The only sounds were the susurrations of leaves in the breeze, the chittering of birds, the occasional irate shout of a territorially aggrieved tree squirrel and the dedicated rhythmic ripping and munching of the grazing pony. Still, the man did not wake.

Who sleeps until high sun on the trail? Poppet wondered for the hundredth time. Surely this lone man snoring in his bedroll was no threat. But Poppet hadn't reached his advanced teenage years by being rash.

With a heavy sigh, Poppet rose from his place of concealment and crept down the hill, grimacing at the tingling pain in his feet and legs. As he reached the messy camp, the munching stopped and the pony raised his shaggy head, watching Poppet curiously with expressive brown eyes. From beneath the worn blanket, Poppet heard a muffled grunt.

"So, you finally decided to join us, eh?"

Poppet started and stepped back, prepared to run.

The man on the ground threw his blanket back to reveal that he was fully dressed in a rumpled shirt that might once have been white and stained wool trousers that had also seen better days. He pushed the wide-brimmed hat back where it had covered his face and revealed features that might have been handsome before the wrinkles and sun and general wear and tear had stolen its youth. Several days' worth of speckled gray beard decorated his chin and lazy blue eyes casually assessed his visitor.

Poppet stood motionless, not knowing what to do. He was hungry and thirsty and so tired of running, and that may have made the decision for him. The man looked like he'd been "sleeping one off," as Poppet's second dad had claimed, when he didn't get up in time to do the chores that Poppet had already completed for him. Poppet didn't see any weapons on or near the man. He looked harmless enough.

As if reading his mind, the man said, "Don't worry boy, I'm harmless. I can't say as much for Pollux though, he packs a wicked left rear kick if'n yur not careful."

"Pollux?" Poppet whimpered and was embarrassed by the timid sound of his own voice.

"Yeah, the donklet," explained the man, pointing at the animal that Poppet had assumed was a pony.

"A donklet? What's that, and what happened to his ear?"

"A donklet is a cross between a gardlandian donkey and a drakonian zoobilet."

"Ah," breathed Poppet, not really knowing whether to believe it or not.

"He was born without one ear, I'm afraid. Sports like 'im are often gifted with weird traits like that. An' who might you be?"

"P–Poppet."

"Well met, Sir P–Poppet."

"No, just Poppet," he laughed.

"My name is Duo Wastrellini. Just Duo is fine but call me 'the Wastrel' at your own peril. You look hungry–and thirsty. Let's sit by the fire that you're gonna light for us, and I'll see if there's any wine left from the party that Pollux and I had last night."

"You had a party with your donkey–donklet?"

"Well, pickin's 're a little slim out here, unless you brought a few lovely young ladies with you in yur back pockets."

"No, 'fraid not," laughed Poppet. "But I'll gather the wood to make up for it. Be right back."

When Poppet returned, the Wastrel–Poppet couldn't help but think of him by the epithet that he obviously disliked–had pulled out some jerky, dried fruit, a chunk of moldy cheese and a shabby-looking bottle of red wine. Poppet believed that he liked wine but had not as yet been able to test his theory by actually tasting it.

"Sorry," said the Wastrel, "this ain't the best vintage, I's afraid. Ran out o' the good stuff just past the leijong nation. We gotta make it to Maddog afore the rest o' this plonk evaporates too."

"Maddog? Is that a town?"

"Yeah, it's just down the river a ways. It's a bit of a dump. Depending on the wind direction, it either reeks of rottin' fish or herdbeast dung. There's a decent pub, the Silent Wife. And there's Miranda, the flower o' the western lands; eyes the color of the Westersea at highsun and breasts like..." The Wastrel's eyes took on a faraway glaze as he abstractedly chewed a piece of rock-hard jerky, lost in thoughts of some future pleasure.

After a tentative taste, Poppet changed his mind about liking wine. He found a dusty packet of aromatic tea in the bottom of the Wastrel's provisions and brewed himself a cup on the fire. Warming his fingers on the mug and stretching his toes out to the blaze, he felt halfway human for the first time in a long while.

"So, lad," began the man, "you look like you done had a rough slog o' it. Out here alone. No pack. No bedroll. Nothin in yur waterskin. In my extensive experience, that means leavin' in a hurry. A l'il farmer's daughter trouble, eh?"

"What? Farmer's daughter? Oh no, nothing like that," stammered Poppet. "I mean, I *did* escape, but—" Poppet stopped, unsure how much he should tell a man he barely knew.

"Hey, that's OK, friend. There's plenty o' time for swappin' stories. I get the feelin' you got a few t' tell, even for one as young as y'are."

Poppet nodded, thinking how right the man was.

"I'll make you a prop-o-sition." The Wastrel spread out the one word into three. He leaned back on his bedding with the bottle of wine in his hand. "Do some chores 'round camp, fetch wood an' water, pack the donklet—you can cook, can't ya? And Pollux and me will be y'ur guides to the skragling towns ahead. Some of 'em might be a bit rough, 'specially for an untried young farm boy such as y'urself. All kinds o' diseases, an' pitfalls for a young man to fall victim to, without the proper local knowledge—meanin' me an' Pollux, o' course. Deal?"

Poppet didn't even stop to think about it. His feet were warm. They said 'yes' before he could think it through. Though he wondered if he might later reconsider the wisdom of listening to your feet where the Wastrel was concerned.

CHAPTER TWENTY-ONE

Rats in the Stew

Wren had to admit that Teeka was an excellent cook. Maybe it was the spices, shrooms and tubers she gathered along the way, exotic tastes that turned even bland groundroot and fish into a culinary delight. Or maybe it was only the fact that Wren hadn't had much of an appetite after their encounter with the leijong, and her hunger had caught up with her.

Even Mala had seconds, though she was noticeably silent during the meal.

They'd followed the river southeast, crossing a shallow tributary that, Grakt explained, was their last water crossing until they reached Dmisi. He didn't seem as happy about their proximity to the city now, and Wren wondered what was on his mind.

Despite walking hours every day, Wren's body was in much better shape than she would have expected, but her emotions were another matter. She felt disjointed, abstracted from her fears, and her hopes. *What hopes exactly?* The leijong had placed a weight on her shoulders that she feared would prove too great for her.

Wren realized that dinner was over. Teeka went down to the creek to clean Grakt's precious pots, while the others sat with Wren by the fire. When Teeka returned, they sat silently, each lost in thought. Wren became aware that a waiting quiet had settled over their faces; all eyes were on her. Were they looking for her to tell them what they should do next?

For an instant, the panic of her dreams rose in her again, but she forced it down. Her decision was simple; she must continue with her attempt to free both the dageki and her people from the farms, even though the chances were very slim that she could succeed.

She said, with as much certainty as she could muster, "I've decided to continue my journey with Grakt to Dmisi, and eventually to find a counter to the weapon that binds them to the drakyn. It's going to be a possibly futile journey, and I don't expect any of you to go with me. Now that you're free of the dangers of the palace, there's no reason that you can't have a life of your own."

Mala said nothing but turned to stare intently at the fading horizon light, as if the sky would answer her questions for her, if only she looked hard enough. She said, "I'll continue with you and Grakt, if you think I will be of any use."

"Of course, silly girl," Wren said, realizing that she'd been holding her breath.

Teeka spoke. "Eventuallee, I would like to return to my home een New Marseille, but I cannot forget what I saw back there. Eet ees an abomination, and eet must be stopped. I don't know what help I may be. As you know, my talent at transmogrifee ees leettle more than useless, as eet ees for the rest of you." Teeka studied the ground, as if grappling with the confession she'd perhaps made for the first time.

Grakt spoke quietly to the fire. "All things will reveal themselves in time, of that I have no doubt. Now you must all sleep. I will guard the camp tonight. We should try to reach the River Cyn by tomorrow evening, and it will be a long day."

Wren wondered why he was staying up to guard them, since they hadn't set a guard so far. Wren was too tired to be frightened by his new level of caution.

The River Cyn wasn't much of a river, at least as Wren had expected. Although it lay in a wide bed, it was shallow, snaking its way through a flat, sandy plain at a lethargic pace. They splashed their faces and filled their water bags with the warm water, and though they were all exhausted, Grakt led them from the river's edge, making for a gentle rise just ahead. Wren hurried to catch up to the dageki.

"Why don't we camp close to the river? It would be nice not to have to trudge so far to get water and wash the dishes."

"Rain could make this a dangerous place to sleep."

Wren trusted Grakt. After all, this was his territory so he must know it, but she couldn't imagine rain as a possibility when the sky was so clear and blue, the ground chokingly devoid of moisture. And even if it did rain, what possible danger could there be from flooding here, with this gentle current?

Before she could ask, he continued, "There are dangers in the wild, even this close to the provinces. You must keep your eyes open and your tail ready. If you do not, you will not live long in the wastes, or anywhere else." Without another word he pulled ahead of the group, scouring the ground.

Grakt finally stopped at his chosen campsite, after carefully perusing several spots. When they caught up with him, Wren sat down in the dirt and stared at her hands, too exhausted to move. Grakt asked Mala and Teeka to gather firewood, but not to wander too far.

When they had trudged off, he said, "I didn't want to alarm the others, but we are being followed. That's one reason I set such a pace today, the other is that we are in grave danger as long as we stay out here in the open near the river. Storms are coming–my inner ear has registered the pressure drop."

"Why didn't you say something earlier? Who is following us?"

"I admit that I am befuddled. Sometimes when I look back, there is a wolf, then a man, or a grella. Once I looked and there was a tree where there had been no tree a second before."

"What? Who could be following us?" Wren stood up abruptly, her agitated steps creating clouds of dust in the slanting sunlight.

"You are probably more equipped to come up with that answer than am I."

Wren was about to protest, when she thought back to Mistra and their narrow escape. It was not impossible to think that one of the talented had followed them, to eliminate them for good. Or could it even be Jelebron? Despite the warm evening, she shuddered.

"It could be someone who trailed us from Mistra," she admitted.

At his blank look, she explained, "Mistra is where Benna and I are from. Before we left, there was a conflict. Someone could be following us."

"Thank you for informing me of this danger in a timely manner."

At first, Wren thought that Grakt was being sarcastic, but the dageki where such literal beings, she had to take his comment at face value.

"I'm sorry I didn't think of it earlier, but I have to say that we really appreciate having you with us, Grakt; you've been invaluable. There's something else I should say. I was angry at you at first, about recreating the shambolika, but I realized that you are a scientist. Without that scientific curiosity, where would we be now? Besides, it's not your fault that the drakyn are evil incarnate..." Wren trailed off.

"Your apology is acknowledged and accepted," said Grakt in a distracted tone, before turning to begin preparations for dinner.

Wren couldn't sleep. Grakt had been right about the weather. The stars were obliterated by dark clouds that had marched in from the east just after sunset. The air was still but filled with the portent of rain. Despite her fatigue, it made her restless. They'd done the best they could to protect themselves from the storm that was surely on its way, but Teeka said that when it rained in the plains, it was no gentle sprinkle. They were bound to get wet, but somehow, Wren didn't mind. She thought the rain would feel good, cleansing the air and her muddled thoughts at once. At least so she hoped.

She glanced over to find that Grakt had dozed off on his watch. It was just as well, the dageki needed sleep as much as anyone and she was awake now. The land was still, with a waiting air about it. Darkly silhouetted plants appeared to be reaching, their limbs outstretched, as if they too looked forward to the rain.

Wren got up and wandered a little way into the brush, wrapping her blanket around her shoulders. Something flashed on the distant horizon, below the clouds. Lightning, followed by the grumbling roar of thunder. She hoped the storm wasn't coming this way. If lightning started to hit the ground near them, they would have nowhere to hide in this flat land.

In the distance she thought she saw a house with no roof, just a square, and out of it stepped a human figure. Then all was dark again. When it flashed once more, the house and figure were gone.

Had she imagined them?

Before she had time to consider what she had seen, lightning flashed again, and this time she saw a loping, four-legged figure on a distant rise, loping toward her. She stood frozen in fear. Why did the wolf frighten her so? Was he a relative of the fox, the one who had been her friend? She thought not, feeling only menace from this creature. She tried to scream, but she was unable to move or speak. Another flash and he was right in front of her, looking across at her from a low hillock not twenty yards away. His eyes glowed, little fires in a matted mass of fur. His teeth gleamed yellow in the dark as he snarled at her. Then he spoke and his words hit her with searing pain. There was something familiar about his tone and syntax, but in her panic, she couldn't place it.

"Now you're mine, little one. There's no need to hurry now." He howled, the laughter of a jackal.

"It's a shame you have no power. It might have been fun to challenge you. You have the will if not the skill. I've got to be realistic. Afterward, I guess I'll have to kill you. It's too bad, you really are a pretty thing."

He started to advance, then everything happened at once. It began to rain, great droplets hitting the soil, slowly at first, then with an increasing rhythm that drowned out all other sound. The wind picked up, gusting through their camp with a wild fury, carrying with it something unnatural, a sucking force that pulled the color from life. Very close to her now, the wolf howled again, this time in raging agony, as his breath was ripped from him. He lifted his feet absurdly, as if they were on fire. Wren laughed, a wild guffaw at his misery, until she too was lost in the vortex of the storm.

As soon as the wind hit, it collapsed whatever held her companions in thrall. Mala leaped through the night in a blur of speed and fury. Teeka was instantly in action as well. The drawing of her large kitchen knife made a slick sound that cut through the darkness. They arrived almost together at the spot where the wolf had been, though the wolf was already far away, running for the distant hills in a desperate attempt to escape from his agony.

Mala started to follow the wolf, but Grakt called her back, screaming over the noise of the wind and driving rain. "Wait! He is gone. We must stay together!" Then to Wren and the others: "The storm will become more disorienting as it intensifies. This is no ordinary gale! Form a ring in the center of camp. Hold hands. Do not let go *for any reason!*"

The others did as he commanded, and none too soon, as the sky began to moan. Warped shapes flowing in great spirals, dipping and diving around them. Then they saw translucent faces and deformed bodies in agony. The screaming entered their minds and tore at their sanity. Wren lost all feeling in her hands. She couldn't see if the others were still beside her, or even if they still held her hands. Her body was lost, her mind on a tortuous journey that threatened to drag her down into insanity. She only wanted release. She found herself begging for death, to be let go and freed of the pain, but the sky answered with a grotesque mockery of laughter. The sound grated at her, denying order and life itself, ripping at her painfully exposed mind.

Wren became aware of sobbing, and then realized that it came from her own mouth. She sat alone in the mud; rain stung her face, and it was cold, so cold. She hugged her shoulders and rocked back and forth in misery.

After a time, the rain stopped, and the air cleared. Wren stood on unstable legs and looked around her. Their campfire had gone out in the rain and lay smoking. Pale starlight revealed Teeka and Mala, unconscious beside her.

She went first to Mala, rubbing her hands until the sensation brought the girl around. Mala sat up, holding her head, and moaned. Her face was covered with mud and tears.

"I hope I don't look half as bad as you do," said Wren.

"I hope you don't feel half as bad either," Mala replied.

Seeing that Mala would recover, she went to Teeka, who appeared to have suffered the most from the storm. She would not respond for some time, and then she was withdrawn. When Wren was finally able to get a word out of her, Teeka started to sob. Wren hugged her until the sobbing passed. Teeka finally pulled away from her with an embarrassed moan.

"You're alright now," Wren soothed.

Wren noticed that Grakt had been less affected than the others.

"Grakt, what *was* that?" she asked.

"It's called a psy storm. Our scientists believe that it is a buildup of errant transmogering matter from an intense battle. It reacts to electricity in the storm, creating a field of uncertainty that is very dangerous, especially if transmogrifee is attempted within the affected area. Those without transmogering talent fare better. No one has less of that than a dageki, so it had little effect on me."

"From what I've seen, transmogrifee isn't a talent you should covet. It brings out nothing but pure evil in the drakyn."

Wren turned back to Teeka. "If the talented are more affected by these remnant storms than others, perhaps you have hidden talents, after all."

"I doubt that," replied Teeka in a shaking voice. "But thanks."

Wren turned from her, scanning the glowing horizon with a worried expression. If only she had talent, she could protect them all. But what was she thinking? Did she really want a skill that only led to death and could warp its practitioners into monsters?

Grakt said, "I tracked the wolf as far as I could in the dark. Then the tracks became very confusing, as if I followed a creature that was half reptile, half wolf. Then the sign just disappeared. I only hope that it was disabled permanently by the storm. I fear that we are still in danger, but not from the wolf. We're going to have to break camp and leave this place, now."

"Now? Teeka is ill and—"

"No, I'm fine," interrupted Teeka, and then spoke quietly to Wren, "I think we should trust eem, after all ee's all we've got for a guide to theese lands, and ee's been right so far."

"All right," said Wren. "But there's something he's not telling us."

"If we are done wasting time, we should be going," said Grakt brusquely.

It was a long night. When the sun finally started to warm the sky, they were still walking. Repeated questions received increasingly short, enigmatic answers from the dageki. Wren gave up, trudging along in silence through the wet terrain in a waking bad dream. Often, they were forced to wade rushing streamlets, newly formed by the rains, and one was larger than the River Cyn that they had crossed earlier in the day. Wren could well imagine the raging torrent it must now be, and she was grateful at least for the presence of Grakt, for his knowledge of these lands.

After several more hours of walking, Grakt stopped abruptly, surveying the ground with a frown. "This will have to do. We can go no further without sleep. I only hope we have gone far enough. I may be worrying over nothing. They say they don't wake with every rain. Conditions must be precise."

"*What* doesn't wake with every rain?" asked Wren, but Grakt offered no reply and Wren was too tired to worry about one more thing. She threw herself down on her blanket and was deeply asleep in minutes. She didn't even have the energy for dreams, and she was grateful for their absence.

Wren woke with the sun on her face. It felt good to be warm after the misery of last night, although her clothes were still damp, clinging uncomfortably to her skin. She stretched and yawned, feeling rested, but stiff and sore. From the height of the sun, she guessed that it must be late morning. Beside her, Mala and Teeka started to stir from their sleep. Grakt stood silent guard at the edge of camp, his nose in the air and his eyes scanning the horizon. Wren couldn't help thinking that she should be there instead of him. She hadn't seen him sleep in some time.

Wren rose and looked around her. Their campsite was revealed by the sunlight as nothing more than a slight rise in the valley floor. Shale showed through the sand in places, forming the shallow ledge on which they were camped. Around her the sandy ground steamed away the remaining moisture from last night's rain. As she walked out to where Grakt stood, she wondered how far they were from Dmisi, but Grakt would surely have an idea. He seemed to know this country well.

Grakt turned to her as she approached, saying, "I hope you were able to get a little sleep."

"Yes, I feel much better, but I don't think I've yet seen you close your eyes, except for last night, and then only for a few minutes."

"There are ways of postponing the needs of the body when other demands are more pressing. It is a skill I learned in my training at university. At the time I thought it was the most useless class I had ever taken. Now I know that I was wrong. I will sleep soon, when we reach more friendly territory."

"I hope this sovereign of yours pays her diplomats–diplomat–well."

"My reward will be the rescue of my people, and my own survival, of course."

"Of course," laughed Wren, but then her expression turned serious.

"I don't know what I'm doing, pretending to be some savior of my race–and yours. I've been nothing but a kitchen drudge, and now I'm an outcast; powerless and with little hope of succeeding–in a quest that seems hopeless. I don't even know if I have the strength to continue this journey."

"You will find strength along the way. Of that, I am sure. Perhaps I am no great judge of human character, but I have been trained to assess others quickly and accurately. It is the most important part of diplomacy, and I would not choose to be at odds with you. You have hidden reserves. You are a survivor, and there is more..."

"What more?"

"Last night the storm arrived just when we needed it. The one thing that could have saved us from the transmogrifer's attack–if that is what it was–did not happen one second before or after the moment we needed it. We both know that life does not work that way."

"What are you suggesting?"

"I am not sure, but I believe that some greater force is at work in your life, perhaps more than one. It would almost seem that the gods are fighting for you, if I believed in such nonsense."

"It was only a coincidence; there is no omnipotent force in my life."

"Perhaps," mused the dageki. "Perhaps."

After a brief breakfast of dried fish and a handful of the pale green and bitter grossberries, Grakt insisted that they get moving again. Mala moaned, but Teeka was uncharacteristically quiet. She looked pale and drawn, her face pinched.

Wren asked, "Are you up to it, Teeka?"

"Of course. I'm just a leettle tired, that ees all. Last night took eet out of me."

"We can all rest tonight," said Grakt, and then almost to himself, "We are still in the range of the kygarid. It does not look like there will be an outbreak, even with last night's rain, but I do not want to take any chances."

"Kygarid? What are—" began Wren, but she stopped herself when she saw the expression on Teeka's face. It was a look of sheer terror. She couldn't imagine anything that would cause such a reaction in Teeka, who had been stalwart and imperturbable through experiences that might have brought another to her knees.

Grakt whispered to Wren, "I did not want to worry the group. I thought it better to tell you all less, especially if we are able to avoid them completely. Worry's only use is to sap the strength of the worrier."

Wren thought better of further questions. With any luck she would never have to learn more about the kygarid.

They started down the gentle slope of shale. When they reached the sandy valley floor, Wren found it softer than she'd expected. Perhaps the recent rains had caused the sponginess, but she wasn't encouraged by Grakt's expression.

He said, "We should traverse this depression quickly. There is firmer ground ahead."

Wren was more than willing to oblige. The sand here had an evil smell, something rotting and living both. It had a sickly-sweet and cloying odor that made her nauseous. Teeka had drawn her short knife. Her face was pale, but her mouth was set in a determined line. Mala just looked confused.

The sand began to emit popping sounds, as those of long confined gases escaping. This was followed by a sound like a hundred ripping gowns and the desert came hideously alive. In an instant, they were surrounded by writhing shapes, vaguely human, but mostly monstrous.

As the creatures slithered toward them from all sides, Wren's eyes were drawn to their faces. They all bore ghastly expressions of anguish, but warped and frozen in position inside a cocoon of gelatinous flesh. Human torsos were barely visible inside these semi-transparent, segmented masses. Arms were truncated versions of human arms, with

wriggling cilia where hands should have been. Hundreds of the creatures popped out of the sand at once, fully formed and hideous. Out of
twisted faces grew wailing mouths, and Wren shrank from the sound,
not language, not song, but some primitive and animal need. After a
second, she realized that they were pleading, begging for help. Wren
leaned forward to listen, to gaze into their faces.

"Don't look at thee faces! Don't leesten to them," yelled Teeka.

"But they want something, need something," Mala cried.

Wren was overwhelmed by a desire to help them, to give them
what they asked.

"Yes, they need food." yelled Teeka.

"What do they eat?" Mala asked innocently.

Teeka barked, "*Enfant*, were you born to ask stupeed questions,
or ees eet a recently developed talent?"

"Oh," Mala stammered. "You don't mean they eat—"

"Yes, they eat flesh," interjected Grakt, "and they will be dining
well tonight if we do not act quickly. We must reach that rock outcrop
ahead. If anyone falls, leave them. Do not let them touch you. Their
touch or contact with their blood will kill as surely as a sword, but with
more pain."

"Mala, no!" cried Wren, as she saw her friend leaning toward the
keening creatures. "If you touch them, you die." Mala got her message,
and retreated to Wren's side, but a low grunt indicated her displeasure
and confusion.

Teeka raised her kitchen knife uncertainly. Wren wondered if she
could kill a creature with a human face, no matter how ghastly, but the
monsters gave them no time to consider. One of them lunged at Teeka
and her long hours of cutting practice seemed to take over. She took
off the hideous head with one deft slice of her small but lethally sharp

weapon. With a high-pitched squeal of escaping gases, the kygarid curled in upon itself, disappearing into the sand from which it had been spawned. Then there were more, and their responses became automatic.

Teeka fought at their backs, her knife slicing easily through several of their attackers. She worked at a constant, unfaltering pace and they were slowly making their way toward the rocks, but it was too far. Wren's muscles were already burning with pain. Even if the brave cook could keep up the pace forever, Wren knew that the others could not. Knowing that she was as good as dead if she didn't keep moving gave her a burst of energy. She kept on, ignoring the pain in her legs and arms and somehow finding the reserves she needed.

Mala was also helping now, stabbing at the aberrations with a stick she'd picked up as they retreated. Wren took a step backward to escape one that leaned dangerously close to her. Her heel hit stone and she fell backwards.

Stone! Somehow, they had reached the shale outcrop. She scrambled up onto the ledge. Another creature lunged at her but was unable to scale the rock. Grakt and Mala leapt up beside her, followed by Teeka, who was the last to clamber up, as the creatures reached after her with their waving, tentacle-like arms. Unable to follow and realizing that their meal had escaped, they began a pitiful wailing at the edge of the stone.

The group scurried higher up to safety and collapsed in exhaustion.

"Can they reach us here?" asked a breathless Wren.

"No," replied Grakt. "They are bound to the sand. Like a fungus in the soil, all are netted together below the surface. One cannot separate itself from the others, any more than a limb can jump from a tree."

Teeka started to laugh, and they gaped at her in horror. She extended a shaking hand on which a drop of yellow fluid bubbled. From it ran spreading streaks of purple just below the surface of her skin. It laced up her arm like the gnarled branches of a corkscrew willow in winter.

"Eet seems that I 'ave taken a drop of their blood on my hand," said Teeka, with a vibrato in her usually strong voice.

Wren rushed to her, tearing a piece of her shirt to wipe away the drop. She tossed the fabric from her in disgust, but the purple streaks remained on Teeka's arm, visibly spreading.

"You must kill me now," said the cook in a tragic tone. "I weell die, being separated from them, but I weell develop their appetites before I do so. None weell be safe."

In a shaking voice, Teeka began what sounded like a tavern song, though not sung as it was meant, but soft and slow like a funeral dirge.

"The cook laid down her ladle
And gazed upon the table
This'll be my end, she cried
For the lord have I defied

'Cook with grace and panache'
The lord had so entreated
But Grace was off with a nasty cough
And panache was out of season

Oh, Gard, my end is nigh
These lords and ladies of ease
Are taters lacking eyes

And peapods short a few peas

So the cook she improvised
As on no recipe could she rely
A bit of cress and a couple rats
It all went splash into the vat

Until the lord was burping vermin
Now he's got a cook named Herman
So, let's lift a glass to n'er forget
That cook with a noose about her neck

Oh Gard, my end is...is..."

Teeka's voice faltered, then ran down the scale. The notes cascaded with her as she fell, ceasing with a jolt as her stiff body hit the ground. There she lay unconscious, and Wren imagined she could see Teeka's life escaping with every tortured breath.

Chapter Twenty-Two

I Regret to Inform You

A fter many hours of walking over open grassland, low rolling hills began to appear. Grakt carried Teeka in his arms, where she resembled a child, dwarfed by the great bulk of the dageki. Grakt had explained that the sovereign of the dageki was also a great healer and might be able to cure Teeka of the kygarid infection, if only they could reach her in time. So they hurried, Grakt setting a pace that had even resilient Mala showing signs of fatigue. Wren felt like she would collapse at any moment.

Pausing for breath at the top of an unusually long incline, a large valley opened up before them. It was patterned by the delineations of neatly marked fields, dotted by regular and symmetrical shapes that Wren assumed were the houses of the field workers. Below them they could make out the arrow-straight length of a broad road that disappeared into the distance.

"That is the Spoke," Grakt said, pointing. "Each province has its own such way. All six roads run into the capital city, like the spokes of a great wheel. They are as ancient as civilization itself."

When she could breathe normally again, Wren said, "Everything is so neat and organized."

"Many generations of cooperation led to this," said Grakt proudly. "All progress is based on balance, and the needs of individuals must come second to the requirements of the larger organism of society. Krasa Ktel has erupted thirty-two times in the last two-hundred years, while the rules of conduct for court acolytes have existed unchanged for over two-thousand years. Perhaps you can see why we honor conformity, and why individual action is so dangerous."

"But such a society might be ill-equipped to adapt, when change is inevitable."

"Up until now, there has been little need."

"It must have taken years just to make all the tiles in this road," observed Mala. She pointed to a sinuous shape formed of lustrous red tiles in many different shades. The effect caused the form to visually leap from the road. Wren looked at it in awe, appreciation, and fear.

"That image, it's a drakyn," she murmured. "Why would the ancient dageki honor them in this way? I thought the drakyn and dageki were enemies."

"I believe that our ancestors made a pact with the aggressors," explained Grakt, "to prevent further conflict. These patterns were made to honor the symbolic victors."

Mala asked in disgust, "You mean that the dageki leaders capitulated, without even putting up a fight?"

"Who can now judge the wisdom of our ancestors? However, the drakyn are now fewer and may eventually face extinction, while the dageki thrive."

"I see your point," said Mala. "But humans chose to fight, and they survived, with their pride intact."

Grakt tipped his head in a curious gesture. "If I understand human history correctly, much of their culture was destroyed by the drakyn wars, technology and social order lost, their numbers decimated as well. Where is the pride in this?"

Mala, red-faced, was about to reply. Wren thought it a good time to intercede. "There is little enough ground for understanding between us, *friends*," she stressed the last word. "Let's not dwell on the past, but on the hopes we have for our future as allies."

"Well said," muttered Mala. "You could run for magistrate with lines like that."

Wren jabbed her in the ribs, then whispered, "In case you haven't noticed, we have just entered an unknown country of very intelligent, excessively strong giants, among whom, Grakt is our only friend. We need to learn and adapt to their customs without offending them. And we need to get help for Teeka. Get it?"

"Got it," said Mala, but her expression remained defiant.

They continued in silence, and Wren noticed that, while they passed many dageki, none of them approached the group, or showed any interest in them. She had to believe that the humans must be an unusual sight in this provincial area. When she asked Grakt about it, his reply was enigmatic.

"Curiosity does not harvest the grain," he began. "These are farmers, with their own duties to perform. News of our presence has by now reached the social regulators in Dmisi. No doubt we will be met by someone as we get closer to the city."

The Spoke led them on, through increasingly compact farming communities and into more residential areas. The integration of farm and city was so complete that Wren could not see where one ended and the other began. Everyone, down to the poorest householder had a small garden to produce vegetables and grains, which were the staples of their vegetarian and pescatarian diets.

As they walked, the buildings became so packed that two and three-story houses began to appear, and even the small gardens disappeared. The slope of the land rose, and they followed the narrowing street into the center of the tightly packed city. A massive building was revealed before them. At its base were wooden gates as tall as a house themselves, ornately carved and enameled in bright reds and blues. Wren wondered where they'd gotten the wood. Was this area once forested? Before the gates stood several dageki wearing the first clothing that Wren had seen worn by these creatures, brightly woven brocade robes that must have some ceremonial function.

Grakt stopped, motioning for the humans to wait as he went forward to speak to the guards at the gate. After a time, Wren began to worry. What could be taking them so long?

When he returned to them, Wren thought that the color had drained from his body plates.

He turned to her apologetically. "I regret to inform you that you are under arrest."

"What!" she shouted. "What are we being held for?"

"I'm sorry, Wren. I'm not sure what the charge is. Perhaps it has to do with the fact that you are aliens and you traveled with the slavers."

"But we saved your lives!"

"I am very much aware of that, but appeal now can only go to the sovereign."

"Well, just go in and tell her. She is your grandmother, isn't she?"

"I'm afraid it's not as simple as that. I too have been ostracized for my actions."

"For doing what?"

"It is a very serious breach of etiquette. My crime was to speak to you without introduction."

"That's ridiculous—"

"Now, now," interrupted Mala. "Remember what you said about staying cool and trying to understand their customs?"

"This is no time to be cute!" Wren growled.

"Can we fight our way out of this?" asked Mala quietly.

"Maybe we could get out of here, but what about Teeka? We need the sovereign's willing help to save her life. We'll just have to go along with this, and hope that Grakt can get in to see his grandmother soon."

"There is another problem," began Grakt reluctantly. "In the struggle with the kygarid, I lost the tip of my tail–not a major portion–but enough to preclude me from court duties until it regenerates."

"Grakt, we must see your grandmother, it's the only hope that Teeka has to survive!"

"If I am acquitted, I will be allowed to work my way back through the levels, after my tail regenerates, of course."

"How long will all this take?"

"Perhaps a couple of seasons; it could be more. It depends on individual metabolism, and—"

"By the moons, Grakt, we can't wait that long!"

"I will do what I can, but it will help if you seem to be cooperating with me. Will you please follow me to your cell?"

Wren was amazed at the dageki idea of a cell; it was hardly an appropriate name for the large elaborate suite of rooms that Grakt had shown them into. Every effort had been made to make the room appear *not* to be a cell. There were elegant, silk covered couches, backless, and fitted with extended platforms for the dageki tail. High, ornate windows let in light and the patterns played across a long table covered with foods of every kind. Apparently, crime was rarely anything more than a social matter, and criminals were treated with exaggerated courtesy. "In the event that the accusations prove unfounded," Grakt had said.

The dageki had even brought Teeka in, laying her gently on one of the couches.

"More food will be brought to you," said Grakt, through the small decorative window of the door. "I will be back as soon as I can."

The dageki disappeared, leaving them with the stillness, the labored breathing of their ill friend, and their own worries. Wren sat alone, feeling responsible again for their predicament, wracking her thoughts for a solution to their dilemma.

As they waited, the silence was broken by a monotone dageki voice coming from outside the door. Wren went to the window, standing on her toes to see the visitor. A tall dageki stood in a floor-length robe with a long elaborate train, like a skragling wedding gown, facing away from her and reading from an obsidian dageki primer. He appeared unconcerned or unaware that what he said was unintelligible to them. He droned on for some time, then left abruptly.

Their next visitor was Grakt, and if Wren was really learning to read his expressions, then she was sure that he didn't bear good news.

"I have had no luck in getting you freed," he groaned. "Unfortunately, as extradrakonians, you rank lower than native groups and—"

"Wait, Grakt. What's an extradrakonian?"

"That should be obvious. Anyone not native to our world, newcomers–interlopers."

"And therefore, undeserving of civil treatment?"

"I am so sorry. I do not personally hold such prejudice. I fear that such attitudes are a universal malady here. And there is more bad news. My own petition has been stalled by an old adversary at the university.

It seems he covets my position. He must be unaware of what the work actually entails. There is nothing more I can do for now."

Wren thought for a moment. Before Grakt had arrived, she'd been on the verge of an idea. Something that might help them...*ah!*

"Grakt, I think I have an idea," Wren began excitedly. "There was an official here earlier, wearing a long robe with a train. He read from one of your primers, then disappeared."

"That was probably Ty Si Tageki Komaros Ni Hasa, instructing you on your duties and rights as visitors to the dageki empire. It is one of his functions in the Visitor Resources Department. Because we have few guests, he does not get to perform it very often; I am afraid he makes quite a show of it when he does."

"Yes, but that robe he was wearing, it covered his entire tail. Is it worn for any other official duties?"

Grakt gave her a blank stare.

She asked, "Could one be worn for a visit to the sovereign?"

"Well, there is an old clause. I do not think it has been used in centuries. It is an ambassadorial duty. If one is carrying official communications from the leader or representative of another realm in time of crisis, normal court procedures are waved. But what does that have to do with– "

"That's it, Grakt! I'm the queen of the northlands!"

"Well, yes, but to wear the ceremonial robes without proper clearance would be a crime punishable by banishment. What if one of her guards has learned of my tail debacle? I cannot risk it."

Grakt pulled away from the window. She could see his front limbs quivering with fear or indecision.

"Grakt, don't leave! You've already come so far! Just take the next step with me, make a decision for yourself and for your people. Once we can talk with your grandmother, I'm sure she'll understand!"

Grakt only looked at her with his head tilted in that vaguely bird-like manner that was characteristic of him when in deep thought. Then he began to back away.

"Grakt, wait! You promised us that you would help. Does a dageki promise mean so little? I risked my life to free you, and now, for my reward, you treat us little better than the slavers treated you! If you refuse, then you are no better than they are. Maybe the dageki are already enslaved—by their utter complacency!"

Wren turned away, before she could say more that she would regret. She stalked away from the window without looking back. She couldn't watch him walk away with all their hopes. He lacked the strength to defy his own rigid society. Because of her misplaced trust in him, Teeka would die, after killing her and Mala, of course. Hot tears stung her face.

Mala touched her arm gently, Wren thought to console her, but her eyes led back to the window. To her amazement, Grakt was still there.

"You were right," he began contritely, "I have been weak. Our society does need to change, and only I have seen the full extent of the dangers before us. It is up to me to start an avalanche of knowledge with the pebble that I am, one small dageki..."

Wren just couldn't think of Grakt as a small pebble, no matter how hard she tried.

He was still speaking. "But my chances of reaching the sovereign are very slim. I will try. I owe you that, and more, and I owe it to my own people as well."

After Grakt had gone, Mala let out a long sigh. "Whew, you took a calculated chance, Wren, trying to provoke him like that. How did you know it would work? He could have just gotten mad and walked away, leaving us here to rot."

Somehow Wren couldn't bring herself to tell Mala that she'd merely reacted in anger and frustration. Her only reply was an enigmatic, but worried smile.

Time passed and Grakt did not return. Their guards brought them more food, even though they'd hardly touched the table, but Wren had no appetite.

Teeka was getting worse, sometimes sitting up and speaking clearly, but when questioned she made no response, lost in the nightmare world of her own fever dreams. Wren kept her hand poised at the knife she'd taken from Teeka, remembering the last coherent words of the cook before the disease had overtaken her. The last thing Wren wanted was to kill the one who had sacrificed herself to save them from the kygarid, but if Teeka went berserk in these close quarters, she could kill them both.

The guards returned. When they opened the door, Wren thought that Grakt must have succeeded and they would be freed, but it wasn't to be. The guards had come for Teeka. One lifted her like a doll, cradling her in his arms, while the other watched the prisoners silently. They left without a word. Wren's spirits plummeted to a new low. She wondered if they would ever see Teeka again. She didn't think that the woman would survive another day without medical attention. Perhaps she wouldn't even make it that long.

After a couple hours, the guards returned for them. Opening the door wide, a squat dageki in ceremonial robes gestured for the humans to follow.

It was the longest walk Wren had ever taken, not knowing if it led to death or salvation. She blamed herself for getting them all into this position. Had Grakt reached his grandmother? Had he been arrested instead?

Following their captors, they left the guardhouse, crossed a wide tile courtyard, and entered another elaborate circular building. Wren was vaguely aware of the ornate architecture around them. She followed in a daze, telling herself she could see it all later, if they lived.

They followed a long straight corridor that led into the center of the building, following the same hub and spokes wheel pattern that pervaded this orderly and hierarchical society.

Entering a massive central chamber, they were led to a round platform at its middle, where curved steps led up from all directions. Wren could see nothing at the top. Was this a royal throne room, or a platform for ritual murder?

She heard a muffled voice, vaguely familiar, but she couldn't place where it was coming from. Her ears told her it was emanating from inside the platform, but logic wouldn't allow her to believe it possible.

Recognition of the voice began to sink through the fog of her thoughts as they were urged up the curving steps of the platform. For a second the steps took all her attention, as the rise and run had been spaced for dageki, not skragling anatomy.

As they reached the top, she realized that they were on the lip of a massive stone bowl, with steps leading back down to a pool at its bottom. There she recognized the voice she'd heard as that of Grakt, who stood in his ceremonial robe at the edge of the pool. He was now speaking to an immense dageki.

The creature was easily twice the size of Grakt, with a girth so great, that walking must be difficult, if not impossible. It floated in a fluid that, while resembling water, was thicker, clinging and gently rolling to the creature's tiniest movement in a spreading circle.

Cradled in its arms was a naked human woman. *Teeka!* thought Wren with relief, until it occurred to her that the woman looked dead. Then she saw the gentle rise and fall of Teeka's chest. She was alive, and the look of peace on her face, as well as the color in her cheeks, brought Wren new hope.

The giant dageki leaned its massive equine head over Teeka. It held a cup to her lips, speaking gently. From the water around them rose a scent that Wren could only describe as *healing*. It filled her with new energy. She remained silent, looking to Grakt, hoping he would lead them in the required protocol when speaking to this creature, who must be TyKoro, sovereign of the dageki.

Grakt began to speak in dageki, rattling on until Wren thought she would fall asleep standing up, then he turned to them.

"The sovereign now wishes to speak to Queen Wren Weatherspring DragonFlower Nightbird, ruler of the human race. The other is to remain silent. Because of the state of emergency that exists, the normal introductory period will be waved for her alone. It is necessary to remove all clothing and adornment when entering the speaking pool."

Wren hesitated, not so much because she was afraid to remove her clothing–this was no time to be shy–but the thought of being in such close quarters with this hulk of a dageki was daunting. She saw the twitch of Grakt's lip and realized that hesitation might be taken as insult. She quickly undid her clothes, dropping them behind her as she stepped into the pool. She'd expected the water to be cool, but it was neither cool nor warm. The sensation was like nothing she'd ever experienced. The fluid picked up her emotions, radiating them out across the water. To her consternation, she felt her own fear of the dageki flowing out toward the sovereign.

"Fear no," said TyKoro in a heavy accent.

"You also speak the common tongue!" exclaimed Wren.

"*I* speak the common tongue. *You* speak English." The sovereign gurgled out a laugh.

At least she has a sense of humor.

"Grakt teaches me some of your language as we wait."

In a matter of hours! thought Wren. What an intellect these creatures must possess. She could feel the sturdy presence of the sovereign's personality echoing in the water around her: highly intelligent, thoughtful, curious, maternal and incisive all at once. Here was a remarkable creature, for any race. She felt her own awe and appreciation emanating back toward the sovereign and realized that, more than anything she could have said, this convinced TyKoro of their good will.

The sovereign said a few words in dageki to Grakt, which he quickly translated.

"Unfortunately, my skills are not yet at the level of our young language expert. He will speak for me," said the sovereign through Grakt.

"Your companion is cured of the kygarid infection," she continued. "But she is very weak. She has an amazing constitution for so small a creature. It will be a few days until she is fully recovered. Until then, you are guests of the empire. I hope that you will accept our apologies for the less than civil treatment that you received upon your arrival. We have much to learn about the undeveloped world outside our territories. I suggest an exchange of knowledge. Grakt will be our liaison.

"Grakt has told me of some of your adventures together. I find it ironic that the same race who enslaves our people would include individuals who have done so much to help us. He has also delivered your message of concern over the numbers of dageki captives being taken and the necessity for urgent action against the threats presented by your own race, as well as the drakyn on these blood farms.

"I also appreciate your generous offer of help in ending the slavery of our people.

What the moons had Grakt told her?

The sovereign continued, misinterpreting Wren's concern. Wren made a concerted effort to control her emotions, and the pool's emanations stilled.

"Your concern is appreciated," continued the sovereign. "Unfortunately, support from the full council may be slow in coming. The irony is that being in a position of power can lessen one's own personal influence at times. It may take a while for me to convince the council of our dilemma. Unlike many of my compatriots, I do not believe that heavy dependence upon tradition and etiquette is necessarily good for our society in the long run. It would help if I had more information about the numbers and condition of our people in captivity. If Grakt is unsuccessful in his mission to free our people on his own—"

Grakt's voice faltered, then he regained control and continued his translation.

"He is to report to me on these things. Perhaps the urgency of our situation can be impressed upon the council with his report. If he is allowed, I would like him to accompany you to these farms, where he can help you deliver your own people from captivity. I am fully aware of his complicity in their fate. Recreating the shambolika was a grievous error, and it must be righted."

Grakt hung his head and his voice again faltered.

"Of course, Grakt is welcome to travel with us," said Wren in as positive a voice as she could muster.

The dageki sovereign spluttered. *Was that a sigh?* thought Wren.

"That is good," said TyKoro, through Grakt. "This has been an exhausting day for all of us. Grakt will show you to quarters more befitting one of your exalted position."

Wren climbed from the pool, understanding that they had been dismissed, and quickly dressed.

She had so many questions for Grakt that she could barely hold them back until they were out of the temple.

"Grakt, you did it, but how?" she asked when they were at last walking alone.

"Yes," he replied. "Your ruse worked, although it took me some time to convince her of the seriousness of our situation."

"But what did you tell her? Don't you think we should have gotten our stories straight first?"

"There was no such opportunity. However, I think you did quite well."

Mala interrupted, "But free all the dageki in captivity? Do you realize what a task that would be? It will probably take nothing less than the entire dageki race to end it. How can a few humans and one dageki be expected to accomplish it?"

"She puts great confidence in me," beamed Grakt.

"Or maybe she is ridding the empire of a bothersome troublemaker, plus some annoying extradrakonians," Mala murmured.

Grakt made no reply, but his body plates turned pale, and he said no more as he led them to their new quarters.

CHAPTER TWENTY-THREE

Wine Anyone?

D usty and tired, Poppet followed the Wastrel and a plodding Pollux down the hill into Maddog, his apprehension growing. The place did indeed smell, even from up here. On one side, the plains rolled themselves out into the distant east, dotted with clumps of herdbeasts and low scrub as far as Poppet could see. Nearer town, extensive corrals filled with the lowing beasts jostled each other for limited space. Below them, like a twisting snake, the River Dudge slithered its way south toward the Westersea, its shores pricked by hundreds of dingy, algae-covered fishing boats.

"What do they fish for hereabouts?" Poppet asked as they strode along.

"Oh, the usual," replied the Wastrel. "Mostly lumpstuckers, a few guttarfish and wobbledung, me personal favorite. Great fried with a little eel sauce an' topped with roadstools. A cul-in-iary delight I highly recommends."

"But how are we going to pay for food? I have nothing and—"

"Just leave it t' me. We'll get by. I got a few gravures to bankroll us in a game o' scridge, and you gots two strong young arms, ain't ya?"

Now Poppet was even more worried. Not that he minded manual labor, but the Wastrel had gotten only lazier–if that were possible–as the journey went on, giving Poppet more of the tasks required to get them through the day. Once, in exasperation, Poppet had asked, "So you have no talent at all? Is there nothing you can do to help?"

The Wastrel had looked thoughtful for a moment, then grunted, "Sure I got talent, but it's a shame to waste it out here, dontcha think? We're not in any danger. Transmogering is for the war, ain't it?"

Poppet's ears pricked up. "So, you been in the war? What was it like? What can you transmoger? Do you think—"

"Furgit it boy. Y'ur too young. Why'd you wanna waste your life to that miserable rabble, anyways? More fun gamblin' an drinkin' an whorin', in my humble oh–pinion."

As they made their way down to the valley floor, they came out on a wide, well-used road. As they approached the town, the Wastrel led them off onto a rough trail leading down to the river's edge. The man scoured the rocky ground as he walked. He bent to carefully choose small round river rocks that he put in his pockets, one at a time.

He handed one to Poppet, saying "Try to pick ones about this same size an' weight. Don't haves to be perfect, just close."

Poppet stared at the smooth round stone in his hand, wondering what his friend was up to, but following his instructions silently. If he'd learned anything being around the man, it was that he would tell you what you needed to know and no more, unless he was telling one of his fantastical stories. Then you couldn't shut him up.

He gave the handful he'd gathered to the Wastrel, and they made their way up the bank to the main road.

Though Maddog wasn't big enough to be called a city, it was much bigger than the villages that Poppet had known in the north. There, transmogrifee muat be a rarer talent, because they passed several businesses that were unfamiliar to Poppet. One sign read "Pigments 'n Grit .3 grav. per hect. each." Another said, "Staples Base, converted for 5 Gravure per Hecter." One building had a small notice in the window that read, "WANTED: Klean, Good Lookin' Bar Maide Desired. Must be Profitient in Convurting of River Waters to Palatiable Wine and Ales. Fish Duping not Required (We Gots Plenty of Those). Apply Inside."

They arrived at a large brick building with a decorative sign swinging from an iron bracket. It read "The Silent Wife Inn, Pub and Eatery" and in smaller letters at the bottom "Ale and Wine, Sweet Liquors. Vittles, Bath and Bed, 10 Gravure. Stables in back."

The wooden sign bore a faded painting of a large-bosomed woman in a plunging purple dress with white lace trim. She might have been quite attractive, were it not for the fact that she appeared to be holding her own severed head in her hands.

The Wastrel saw him gawking at the sign and said, laughing, "Now ya knows why they calls it the Silent Wife, eh?"

Poppet was aghast. "Does it represent something that actually happened?"

"The legend is that 'er husband cut it off when he got tired o' her naggin', but the lady was such a great transmoger, she picked 'er 'ead right up and stuck it back on 'er shoulders, none the worse fur wear. So, I assumes she weren't silent for that long."

"Oh," was all that Poppet could manage.

"Let's take Pollux out back so's he can get a comfy stall and a bale o' drygrass. He loves the stuff an I's thinkin' he deserves a break from 'is labours."

Pollux turned his sad eyes to the Wastrel as if he understood and let out a series of loud brays.

Poppet laughed. "He's more human than some folk I've known."

The Wastrel only smiled. The stable was large, but the stalls were mostly empty. Poppet assumed it must be the slow season. A scruffy attendant rose reluctantly from a straw bale to take the Wastrel's stable fee. Poppet was amazed when the Wastrel pulled a few glimmering gold coins from the pocket that he'd earlier filled with river stones. It looked like Poppet wasn't going to have to work for his dinner after all.

If the Wastrel truly had transmogered the coins from stones, he was a more powerful transmogrifer than even his boasting had indicated. Poppet knew that gravures and silvers were made of a metal that was practically impossible to transmoger. If everyone with talent could create their own currency, the system would fail.

"Take good care of 'im, boy, he be precious t' me," said the Wastrel.

"Aye, ee'l git the royal treatment 'ere, sir."

The Wastrel led them back around to the front of the inn and they entered the dim interior. A few mostly empty tables dotted the large space, and a long bar ran the length of the room. Behind the bar was the largest and most diverse collection of bottles that Poppet had ever seen. Row after row sparkled in every color and design imaginable. One was even shaped like a firstform drakyn, with the cork stuffed ingloriously in its upturned mouth. While Poppet stared, the Wastrel approached the barman, a squat greasy man, who wiped the grungy bar as if he believed it was doing some good.

The bartender looked up and said, "Well, if it ain't the Wastrel. Back to lose yur shirt agin inta back room? Or t'is it Miranda what draws yur dirty ass out o' the wilderness?"

The Wastrel frowned. "I hope yur referrin' to Pollux, an' I don't know how many times I told you Breck, me name's Wastrellini."

"Ah, and so glad I am to be havin' you correct me once agin'. And who might be this fine young gentleman ya brung wit' ya?"

"This here is Poppet. No last name. It's a long story I'm sure he'd be willin' to tell ya, after a few. Ain't that right, m'boy? Go ahead, pick yer poison. Drinks on me, fur all the help you gived us on the trail, and later, a bit a' supper wouldn't shrink me kippers, neither."

Poppet just stared at the many glittering bottles, seemingly the only clean things in the bar. *How could he choose?*

The Wastrel ran out of patience and said, "Give up a couple pints o' the Maiden's Kiss fur starters, and a shot o' Ol' Dead Man's Fingers fir both ta us too."

"Isn't it a little early to be drinking?" asked Poppet in an uncertain whisper.

"Naw," said the Wastrel in a voice as loud and garrulous as Poppet's had been meek and quiet. "You's gotta start early if'n you's gonna try em all, before you becomes unconscionable, eh?"

Poppet didn't know what to say to that, so he pulled up a worn stool and prepared to meet his maker.

Two hours later, after taking the Wastrel's bags to their rooms and enjoying a dinner that, Poppet had to admit, was delicious, the duo returned to the bar for a "Knee-capper" as the Wastrel called it.

"There's a wine yur gonna love, trust me. Breck, pour us a glass of the '96 Verminchelli, wun't ya?"

The barman gave him a quizzical look that Poppet incorrectly interpreted as an unwillingness to get them any more drunk—if that were possible.

After a few sips, Poppet slurred, "'Snot bad, not bad a t'all."

"Aye and yur getting yur protein at the same time from dem baby mice, ya know. A rodent in every glass, that's as I says."

"Excuse me...from the...what?"

"The mice. 'Ere, Breck, show 'im yonder bottle."

Poppet only got a glimpse of pale pinkish bodies with naked tails stuffed into the bottom of a wine bottle before he was running to the back alley to quickly relieve himself of the offending vintage.

Angry with the Wastrel for deceiving him so cruelly, he didn't go back into the inn, but staggered down the main street aimlessly for a while until he found himself at the door of another pub. *Oh, well*, he thought. *This night can't get any worse.*

Fortunately, the Wastrel had given him a few silvers for spending money. He opened the simple wooden door adorned with the crudely drawn words "Arse Whistle, Grog n' Gab."

At the bar he asked a pretty barmaid about the pub's name.

"It used to be called the Stagger Inn, but the new owners thought that wernt appropriate. What can I getcha?"

"Anything without mice in it," he replied emphatically.

The barmaid laughed. "You musta been drinkin' at the Silent Wife. That Breck, 'es such a joker."

"You mean the mice aren't real?"

"Oh, theys' real, all right."

"I'm sorry I asked."

After that, Poppet sat quietly, nursing his beer. This pub was busier than the Silent Wife, with a raucous group of young men drinking at a table behind him. They were discussing something about the transmogrifee wars. Poppet's large ears perked up and he listened intently.

One of them said, "Just got back from the eastern front. That Kemp, he's a genius at the challenge. I saw him transmoger a sword in an instant and took the drakyn's head right off with one clean swipe. Like nothing I've ever seen!"

Another said, "Yah, I'd give anything to be a part of his unit, but I hear it's only the best he takes on. You gotta pass his transmogering test to join, and even then, if you fail in battle you're out."

"If you fail in battle, you're dead, Grimes," said another of the men.

They all laughed at that.

Poppet couldn't stand it any longer and turned around to address the group.

"Excuse me," he said, "I apologize for listening in, but I couldn't help it. I've always wanted to join the resistance, you see and—"

One of the men, who appeared older than the others asked, "You look pretty young to me. You got any talent then? What can you do?"

"Nothing," admitted Poppet, "I've never been trained. I thought I could serve some other purpose, support the troops or somewhat..." His voice trailed off into uncertainty.

"Don't know 'bout that. Most in the service got some talent, if only for self-defense. No doubt they need any bodies they can get, but you'd be taking your chances. Even getting to the volcano lands is dangerous."

"The volcano lands?"

"Yah, it's to the east of here, a ways beyond the dageki lands. Once you get to Droop, someone can give you better directions, but I wouldn't make that journey alone, that's sure. It's perilous country beyond Droop. But that's where Kemp and his troops are based. There's quite a big contingent there. They've even built up a small community to support the troops, so you might have a chance to be of some use."

"OK, thanks," said Poppet and turned back to his drink. He pondered the possibility of making his way to the volcano lands alone, and he wondered if the Wastrel would agree to go with him.

It couldn't hurt to ask. If they've got a pub or a brothel there, I might have a chance of convincing him.

CHAPTER TWENTY-FOUR

We're Counting on You

While Teeka recovered in their new, even more opulent quarters, Grakt gave them a tour of some of the wonders of the dageki capital city. He was an excellent tour guide, showing them the marvels of technology and social organization that made the dageki society such an enduring one. Wren was amazed by the drakyn bowl, a device that could predict the smallest tremor long before it could be felt by dageki senses. When a tremor activated a balanced beam inside a large bowl, one of a series of carved flet drakyns on its rim would drop a small stone ball from his mouth into a tiny bell-shaped chamber of the bowl, with segments for every direction of the compasser. When the bell rang out, the dageki would know the direction of the tremor and have time to prepare for the inevitable quake or eruption.

Of all the wonders there, Wren was fascinated most by the university, where cutting-edge research was being conducted, according to Grakt, anyway.

Though the primers that Wren had studied since childhood described amazing devices and capabilities that the skragling world had long ago lost, in the dageki, science had found a new home. They had translated all the human primers they could acquire and built upon that knowledge to an amazing degree. The only problem was that, in their isolationist society, sharing with the other races just wasn't an option.

As they walked the tall halls of the science building, Grakt droned on about everything from the development of economical farming practices to micro research, whatever that was.

They passed a door with a sign in the regimental script of the dageki language.

"Grakt, what's in here?"

"Oh, that is the genetrical engineering department. You would not be interested. It is all rather dull and boring."

Anything that could seem dull and boring to Grakt must be beyond the pale.

He continued, "It is a complex study involving the formulae for counting and precise arrangement of elemental particles that form the patterns of living matter. It is the basis of transmogrifee in living things. Though, as dageki, we don't possess the skill ourselves, we can study how it works, as we do with many of the world's mysteries."

"I think I might like to see this, Grakt. I may not have any talent either, but transmogrifee rules us all, does it not?"

"Yes, your people more than mine, perhaps, but it is an arcane and esoteric area of research."

"Let's have a look anyway," she insisted, struggling to open the heavy door.

Mala reluctantly followed them in, looking as bored as she could manage.

A large, messy room met them. It was filled with equipment and the walls were lined with shelves housing crystal and obsidian primers of every shape and size, some of them half as tall as a man. Several dageki sat around desks, peering into contorted metal devices of unknown purpose. At the center of the room sat a large, intricate mechanism. She didn't know what function it might perform, but there was no doubt that it was a thing of sublime beauty. Hundreds of tiny colorful twisting staircases revolved on poles. Glinting beads of every imaginable color ran in rows, forming the steps. A delicate metal and glass cage was positioned at the base of each staircase, each containing a small plant or insect. Wren gasped in delight.

One of the researchers reluctantly left his station and approached Grakt. Their conversation carried on for so long that Mala was starting to edge toward the door.

Finally, Grakt turned to them. "Tinkoro Si Tageki Kys Se Gravis Tyo is a bit of a revolutionary," said Grakt apologetically. "It seems he does not hold with the tradition of the three-day ceremony of introduction. He says its only purpose is to hold us back from collaboration with other races."

"I like this guy already," said Wren, under her breath.

"He has agreed to discuss his research with us. I will translate."

"Great! First, what is that thing?"

"It takes some explanation. It is called the abacusian. It is a device for counting the number and making small changes to the elements in the base structure of a living being. The devices on the table allow us to see what transmogrifers use instinctively when they perform their art on living things, the most complex and demanding form of transmogrifee. We believe it can also be viewed as a science, and that one day, we, the dageki will be able to transmoger, using the data we are accumulating here."

"Wow, that's incredible, but how does it work?"

Again, Grakt translated for her as Tinkoro approached the abacusian, pointing first to the devices on the tables and then to the
abacusian itself.

"With my team, I have developed a spyglass that enlarges minute,
rather than distant objects. It is so powerful that it allows us to see the
tiny, twisted staircases in living matter. From here, all we need do is
apply the formula to the device. Each scientist is studying a different
form of life. This mageki here is looking at the pattern of a grub moth."
Wren saw a dull gray insect with plain whitish wings in the cage to
which Tinkoro pointed. The large moth fluttered against the glass of
the cage, then it changed, its wings turning for a second to the most
brilliant electric blue.

She asked in amazement, "They can transmoger?"

"Yes," replied Tinkoro. "It is a primitive form of the art, and their
skills are limited to only this one slight color change, but they do
indeed possess the talent. Now we will show what science can do."

Tinkoro motioned to the dageki he had pointed out, who rose
and, referring to scratched notes on a glassine sheet, started to move
some of the beads on that particular staircase, sliding them deftly and
quickly, as if she'd done this many times before. They watched in
amazement as the moth transformed. Its dull white wings grew, taking
on the delicate outline of a butterfly's wing. The wings sprouted bright
colors of blood-red, cerulean blue, and sunflower yellow. These tiny
lakes of color grew shorelines in rich, velvety black.

"It's beautiful!" cried Wren, moving forward to touch the glass of
the cage.

The instant the tip of her finger made contact with the glass, the
device ground to a halt, and an electric buzz filled her ears. As the
power built within her, Wren felt something break, as if her fear and

caution had been rent asunder with one flick of a mighty hand. She was no longer Wren. Perhaps, she was no longer human. The heat built up to an unbearable level. As quickly as she could, she pulled her hand away, but it was too late.

Their nostrils burned with an acrid sting, as the newly formed butterfly sizzled, then exploded in a plume of smoke. Only tiny remnants fizzled and popped where it had been. The others stood entrapped by their shock at what had happened. Then the lead researcher waved his diminutive arms, gesticulating wildly as he jabbered at Wren.

Grakt translated his words. "I don't know what it did, but your human transmogrifer just killed our specimen, and caused untold damage to the abacusian."

Wren stumbled away in shock. Whatever had consumed her was gone as quickly as it had overtaken her. She stood staring at her hands, shaking and afraid. At last, she said in a small voice, "I didn't do anything. It wasn't me."

Grakt said, "They insist it was you."

"But, Grakt, tell them I couldn't have done anything. I'm not a transmogrifer, I have no talent."

Grakt did so and Tinkoro was silent for a full minute, then he spoke again. "We must research this phenomenon. Nothing like this has ever happened before." He turned to consult his colleagues, and Grakt took the opportunity to urge his guests from the room, as he gibbered something that muat have been an effuse apology to the scientists.

Mala was the last to leave the room and she looked back to see that the abacusian had resumed its movement. "Now that was interesting," she muttered, suddenly not bored at all.

CHAPTER TWENTY-FIVE

Tandem Entanglement

Mala couldn't seem to let go of the disturbing events that had transpired in the hall of genetrical engineering. She'd always known that there was something different about Wren, but how strange that it took a dageki instrument to bring it to the surface, if that was what had happened. She'd tried to convince Wren to go back and try again, but Wren was uncharacteristically intractable when it came to the abacusian. So, Mala gave up on Wren and worked instead on convincing Grakt.

"You saw it, Grakt. The thing responded to her."

"Responded, yes. It exploded in front of us."

"But when she left the room, everything returned to normal."

"Not everything. The moth was gone, and now Tinkoro tells me that they can find no more of this particular species to replace the specimen lost."

"What? Surely you don't mean that she destroyed every grub moth in existence?"

"I fear so. This is an effect that Tinkoro calls tandem entanglement, where like organisms are affected in the same way, though they may be separated by great distances."

"That's almost unbelievable, but he is a dageki scientist, after all. You think that by killing the moth in the machine, Wren killed *them all?*"

"I do not know. Tinkoro says it is possible."

Wren paused, rubbing her forehead in thought. "So," she began slowly, "does the machine need the whole organism, or can it work from a part–say the wing of a moth, or the blood of a drakyn?"

"I see what you are thinking, Mala. You are a very bright sea-going mammal."

Ignoring the distraction, Mala continued her thought.

"But in theory, is it possible?"

"In theory yes. From what I have learned of the science involved, it could be possible."

"Then we've got to get Wren back in there and try again."

"She seems very reluctant to return to the genetrics lab, even though Tinkoro has asked me to bring her back. He has an experiment he wants to run."

"Then we've got to get through to her."

Grakt looked over at Wren, who sat at Teeka's bedside, conversing with the cook. Teeka did look better than she had the day before.

Grakt said, "Though I have not known her long, it appears to me that your friend the cook has changed since surviving the kygarid."

Mala considered this. "You're right, but not about her being our friend–not in the beginning at least, but she *has* changed, or at least mellowed some."

"Do you think she could talk Wren into returning to the lab?"

"I don't know anyone who feels stronger about ending the farms than Teeka does. Since she found out the truth, she's been as adamant as any of us to find a way to end them. I think she feels responsible for Poppet being sent to one. If anyone wants to stop the drakyn, it's Teeka."

"It is worth a try," said Grakt, but he didn't sound very hopeful.

Teeka was out of bed and taking cautious steps. She still looked frail. She'd lost weight and, on her stick-like frame it appeared even more extreme. Though her hands shook, the color had gradually returned to her face, and perhaps a little bit of her old attitude, as well.

"*Putain de merde!* What are you talking about? Are you a feinting limpet, or a woman?"

"Teeka, it's just too dangerous."

"Dangerous? Dangerous ees letting our people spend one more meenute een those gardamn farms!"

"I know, I know, but how can we be sure I can control this machine? What if I kill us all?"

"You won't."

"You don't know that."

"Yes, I do. You want to know how I know? Because you are the beeggest bleeding heart in zee history of humanity, that eez how. You would not hurt a fly." Teeka immediately regretted her choice of words.

"I killed off the grub moths," whispered Wren.

"I keelled a poor defenseless leettle moth," Teeka mocked. "So what? So what? If you can stop zee fruckin' drakyn weeth thees device, *you must try.*"

They were both silent for a long time. At last, Wren sighed.

Teeka said, "Yes! I knew you would see reason."

Wren laughed nervously, then turned serious. "I just hope I don't turn us all into the next species that I might accidentally wipe off the face of the planet."

Teeka only snorted.

The genetrics lab was almost identical to what it had been; the same dageki sitting at their same desks. The ladders of the abacusian twisted gently. The only thing missing was the specimens. All the cages were empty, and one cage had been replaced by a small, double plate of glass on a stand below the foremost staircase. Next to it was a human-hand sized handle of black metal.

As they entered, Wren was surprised when Tinkoro addressed her.

"Greetings. I will attempt to communicate in your language. It will save time. Grakt will translate when this new language fails me."

Grakt nodded.

Once again, Wren was amazed at the speed with which these creatures could learn. Nothing could stop the dageki from comprehending something when they turned their focus to it.

Wren leaned forward in what she hoped was the correct dageki bow to indicate honor and gratefulness. She'd learned that there were several hundred forms of address when bowing. She only hoped she hadn't performed one that meant, "Your mother is a sand grubber."

She said, "We are honored by your interest in our species, Tinkoro, and the effect I may or may not have had on your machine. But I must tell you that I doubt that what happened was anything more than an unfortunate coincidence. My granpapa was a teacher and primer-keeper. He tested me when I was young and found no aptitude for transmogrifee in me whatsoever. I simply have no talent. Also, I refuse to do anything that might endanger another creature. If I did cause the death of these grub moths—"

"You did. After extensive testing, I'm totally sure of that." Tinkoro quickly added, "But I believe we have found a way to experiment with your effect on the abacusian without harming a living thing."

"Really?" said Wren, looking hopefully at the device.

Tinkoro led her forward. "If you will bear with us, we will take some readings and do some calculations."

Wren was hesitant at first but relaxed when she realized that no specimens were in danger. Delicately, she touched the very tip of her index finger to the black handle. All motion in the staircases came to an abrupt halt.

"Fascinating!" said Tinkoro. "Take a firm grip, please. We need to get a temperature reading."

Wren did as she was told. Her head was immediately filled with a painful buzzing and the glass plate began to smoke.

"Please let go now," instructed Tinkoro, with perhaps more urgency than he'd meant to exhibit.

He glanced at one of the technicians, who shook his head slowly.

"Wren, we need to get this temperature down. There is a creature, called the Krasa piglet, that lives in lava-heated pools in the volcano lands. We believe it is the most heat-tolerant species on the planet. If you can get the temperature below 300 fergin, we can advance to testing on a living creature."

"But I can't," cried Wren, her frustration showing.

"There must be a way. If I understand the processes involved in transmogrifee correctly, you must first control the inner landscape before you can make changes to the outer world. In simple terms, you need to relax."

Relax? thought Wren. *How am I supposed to relax when so much depends on me?*

But she tried anyway, and after a time the buzzing in her head seemed to lessen, if only slightly.

"Good! That is it. Keep going."

Mala interrupted, "I don't think she should try to do so much at once, do you? We don't want her to burn out–er, grow too tired on her first try."

Tinkoro looked disappointed but agreed.

After that Wren spent time every day perfecting her interactions with the abacusian. She was learning that it responded to her mood and thoughts, and the most difficult thing was learning to control her own heart rate and emotions. Wren was surprised when Grakt offered to teach her a mind control method the dageki called "still thinking." At first, the idea of thinking about nothing only made her ruminate on everything, but with practice, she was able to enter a state where her deeper mind took over and time slowed. She got so into the practice, that once Mala had trouble rousing her for dinner. She found herself flying high above Drakonia, the round shape of the giant world turning beneath her. She looked across, and saw the double moons, Beckle and Meika, seemingly so close she reached out a hand to touch them. Then she heard Mala calling to her from a great distance. Coming back down to the planet's surface was a slow journey. As she descended, the frantic words grew louder. She opened her eyes and stared into Mala's round face. Mala pulled away from her with a sharp intake of breath.

"Your eyes!"

"What is it, Mala? I'm fine. I was just far away, and it took a minute to come down."

"Well, good, but your eyes looked like they were on fire, little specs of silver flames in them."

Wren closed her eyes and felt her metaphysical feet touching down.

"I'm back now. Just a little out-of-body trip."

"Huh. No shrooms for you with dinner then," said Mala. "I've heard some of them can take you on a mystery tour, and then you throw up."

Wren laughed. "We don't have any of that kind here, silly. I'm just practicing Grakt's 'still thinking.' I think I'm starting to get the hang of it."

The next day at the genetrics lab, Tinkoro was effusive with his praise.

"You've really come a long way. Look at these figures." He pointed at a scratchy glassine sheet that Wren couldn't read. "You've got the temperature under control. I think it's time to try it with the Krasa piglet."

"Oh no, I'm sure I'm not ready—"

"But you are, Wren. We need to take the next step. You can't put this off indefinitely."

Wren studied her hands. She said, "Alright, but I want you to monitor this very carefully. If you see the slightest—"

"Yes, yes. We are ready. We have been ready. We have just been waiting for you to realize that you are ready as well."

Wren went back to their quarters to gather her friends. Over time, they had stopped coming to her practice out of sheer boredom, she assumed.

When they got back to the lab, Wren thought she could read anticipation or excitement in the faces and movements of the dageki. She told herself to ignore her own fear, taking deep breaths until the "still thinking" state could take over.

She approached the device. The double glass plate was there, but only a greenish fluid could be seen smashed between the plates.

"Where is the piglet?" she asked.

"He is there," replied Tinkoro. "The Krasa piglet–I believe your people called it a tardigrade in your primers–is a micro being, too small to be seen with your eyes alone. Through our reverse spyglass, he appears as a tiny piglet with eight legs and claws for hands. His eyes are like nipples. We do not really think they are eyes, but perhaps gills. He has a little snout like a porker, thus the name."

"Sounds adorable," commented Mala dryly.

Tinkoro gave her a silencing motion with his little arm and turned back to Wren.

"These creatures can survive much hotter temperatures than you will be delivering. It is perfectly safe. Shall we continue?"

Wren nodded, glancing at her friends. Their faces showed nothing but confidence in her. *Misplaced?* she wondered.

Pulling a strand of silver hair from her eyes she nodded at Tinkoro, saying, "OK, let's do this. What do we have to lose?"

Tinkoro, taking her literally, began, "Well, among the many things that could go wr—"

"Whoa, Tinkoro," interrupted Mala. "We need to introduce you to the concept of a rhetorical question. I'm sure Grakt could explain it later."

"Yes, yes," said Tinkoro, excitement in his tone. "Stand over here, Wren."

Wren closed her eyes and reached for the black handle.

"Wait!" said Grakt. Stepping forward, he handed Wren a small, round stone.

"What's this?" she asked.

"It's called a worry stone."

"Do you really think I need anything more to worry about?"

"Oh no, it does not cause worry, it *absorbs* it. Not being a super-stitious being, I believe it works by distracting the conscious mind, so that deeper thoughts can surface."

"Alright, Grakt, I'll try it."

She took the stone and rubbed it in her fingers, while she concentrated on stilling her mind. The stone did seem to help. When she felt her thoughts wandering toward fear, she rubbed the stone and focused only on the sensation, the smooth warm surface, rolling through her fingers.

She reached forward to touch the black handle. She'd done it so many times that she didn't even need to open her eyes. As her fingers made contact, a whole new world was revealed to her. She saw the Krasa piglet—it really was an adorable little creature—swimming about in its little lake of algae water under the glass. Did it realize that its home had been relocated to a scientist's lab?

As she watched the piglet, she was vaguely aware of one of the technicians beside her, entering numbers into the abacusian. She waited for the piglet to respond, sprouting wings or another set of legs or whatever he was programming into it, but nothing happened. The piglet just swam on in total oblivion to the fact that its life lay in the balance.

Then her head started to buzz. She could feel the heat growing in her mind. The tiny elements of matter that every transmogrifer could see, she could now see too, but they were in frantic motion, bouncing off one another, gaining speed. The miniature lake began to steam. She almost pulled back, but she wasn't ready to give up so soon, when she'd worked so hard to find control. She concentrated on slowing the bits of matter, harnessing their frantic motion. With great effort, she thought cooling thoughts and gradually, almost imperceptibly, the water returned to a normal temperature. She heaved a great sigh of relief and opened her eyes.

"You did it!" exclaimed Mala. "I knew you could."

"Now let us try something else," said Tinkoro. "Take your hand from the abacusian, Wren."

She did so, and the technician returned to the station. He input the formula again. Wren couldn't see any change to the muddy turquoise liquid under the glass, but Tinkoro motioned her over to one of the inverse spyglasses. After she'd adjusted it for her eyes, she was able to focus on the Krasa piglet in his tiny lake. The poor creature looked confused, shaking his head and struggling wildly, as if he were trying to escape the effects of the abacusian. His tiny shoulders–all eight of them–had sprouted wings, the glorious, iridescent curving wings of the leijong, perfectly duplicated, but in microscopic detail.

The piglet floundered about the lake in what, Wren believed, was great distress.

She cried, "Make this stop. Change him back!"

Tinkoro's alien face took on what Wren interpreted as a devious look.

He said, "Go back to the machine. Return the piglet to his firstform yourself."

"But I can't do that...can I?"

Tinkoro said nothing but led her back to the abacusian. She touched the handle, and another level was revealed to her. She wasn't a mathematician like the dageki, or an artist like the transmogrifers, but through the abacusian she could understand what each of them did and how they achieved it. From the artist came the flow, the golden rectangle, perspective, and the sublime shapes, from the mathematician came the formulas that defined these things in a different, but similar language. They worked together to mold the malleable stuff of nature on Drakonia. It looked so simple, at least at that moment.

Eventually, her epiphany faded, and she realized, to her amazement, that she'd returned the piglet to his original form. He swam, oblivious to the grand joke that had been played on him, *sans* his leijong wings, with nothing but those things that made him happy and whole. A work of art, before he had been reworked into a disaster of neither art nor balance.

Wren pulled away from the device. She realized then that she'd been crying and tried to wipe the copious tears from her face.

Tinkoro said, "I believe I knew this about you, perhaps from the first time you stepped into this lab. Wren, you are a destroyer, yes, but you also have the potential to return our world to one of balance, to one where chaos is ameliorated by stability, where that stability is honed by careful adaptation. Where art and science are joined and stronger together."

"Oh my," commented Mala. "This is all way too meterphysical for me."

Teeka said, "Girl, you don't even know what meterphysical means, do you?"

Wren ran a nervous hand through her long silver hair. Pulling Tinkoro and Grakt aside she said, "Tinkoro, there's something I've been meaning to ask you about. When I use the abacusian, I feel something—it's hard to explain. It's as if the world sits at a tipping point, and what we're doing here could lead to total chaos, the destruction of everything, if we're not careful. Is that possible?"

Grakt helped Tinkoro with a few words he didn't know the meaning of and eventually, Tinkoro responded, with translating help from Grakt.

"Yes, what you sense, it is called entrofee; the second law of transmogering thermodynamism. In layman's terms, it states that all matter in the universe is inevitably headed toward a state of chaos. Whenever an act of transmogrifee is performed, a small amount of order is lost and can never be regained. It is possible that, if you were to overreach using the device, you could speed up the process of entrofee to the point of catastrophe. It could lead to what your people call Armageddon. Premature Armageddon, that is."

"But how do I know where the line is, if I want to avoid crossing it?"

Tinkoro looked thoughtful for a moment, his massive head tilted in consideration. "I would not be entrusting you with this power if I did not believe that you were the best individual to wield it. You showed us that in your concern over the grub moth. If you can be so concerned over the loss of one small insect, then I am sure that you will be circumspect in your use of this ability. I regret that I cannot tell you where this line is that you wish not to cross, but I have confidence that you will know, before stepping over it."

Wren didn't feel comforted at all by his words. She sighed, resigning herself to a task she wanted nothing to do with.

She asked, "But what does all this really mean? How can we use the abacusian against the drakyn, safely?"

"That is what we need to figure out, now that we know you can block transmogrifee, and return a being to its firstform. To see if this will work using drakyn blood or tissue, we will need to take the abacusion to a place where it can be gathered. I believe the front lines, where your people are fighting the drakyn right now, would be the best place to start. The sample needs to be fresh, so bringing the specimen back here to Dmisi is out of the question."

"But I can't take this device from you, Tinkoro. How will you continue your research?"

"The truth is that this is just a prototype. I have been working on a much larger version of the abacusian. I have no more need of this one."

Teeka asked, "But even eef Wren can stop zee drakyn from transmogering, how weell thees help us end zee farms?"

Grakt said, "If it were only the farms, I believe that being unable to transmoger would end them quickly. The drakyn would be in disarray and confusion. They have relied on their transmogering arts for millennia. Suddenly having to survive without it will throw their society into turmoil. For one thing, they would not be able to fly to the farms to collect the human blood.

"My problem is the dageki in slavery, not only on the farms but under human control as well. Mageki Kyni Gouzuni is still working on a way to cancel the effects of the shambolika. Until we have that, there is not much I can do here. If you decide to travel to the volcano lands, I would like to be allowed to travel with you. I believe I could be of some use."

"Of course," said Wren, "I'd love to have you with me."

She looked speculatively at the others. As one they said something like, "We're going too."

Wren smiled, then frowned, looking at the abacusian critically.

"How are we going to take this thing? It's too big, even for Grakt to carry all the way to the volcano lands."

Tinkoro was thoughtful. "I may have an idea about that."

Wren laughed. "The day you *don't* have an idea will be a very cold day in gardland."

CHAPTER TWENTY-SIX

Maddog Leads to Droop

Poppet eventually convinced the Wastrel to accompany him east, but only as far as Droop, which did have a pub. Along the way, they began to see more dageki settlements and farms. At the top of a particularly high vista, they were able to see the road below them. A few human travelers accompanied a lone dageki, and Poppet couldn't make out details, but he could see the considerable size difference between the dageki and his companions.

"Are they dangerous?" he asked the Wastrel.

"Dangerous? Dageki? 'Course not. They's the most gentlest creatures in the world."

"Oh, that's good, I guess."

"'Sept' they could rip yur head right off if they had a hankerin' to. Strongern a herdbeast–two herdbeasts–an' smell 'bout as bad as ten dead ones."

"And the drakyn?"

"What 'bouts 'em?"

"Where do they live? Besides in the far north, and the blood farms of course."

The Wastrel eyed him critically. "Knows 'bout the farms, does ya?"

"Intimately," replied Poppet in a sardonic tone.

"Ah, a resident, eh? Well, sorry 'bout that. I mean, not that I's the one sent ya there, or nothin'," added the Wastrel, "I's heard ain't many what escapes them places. Ya must'a been real brave or real lucky—"

"Or both? And the drakyn?" he prodded, not willing to let the Wastrel distract him from his original query.

"Well," continued the Wastrel, "they's spread out. More in the north, of course, 'cause that's where they comes from, 'parently. But they prefers flyin' forms, ya know, so they can be just 'bout anywhere. They's a bunch of 'em in the mountains north of the volcano lands, I recon. Prob'ly why yur famous Kemp is there."

"What about this 'challenge' thing? What's that all about?"

The Wastrel paused to scratch his scruffy beard, which he'd allowed to grow again after shaving it off in Maddog, before his evening with the lovely Miranda. "The drakyn's a queer lot, I recon. They pretend to be believin' in honor an' fair play and all that rubbish. They's only s'posed to use as much skill as their opponent, kinda like a handicappin' system or whatnot. Truth bein' they cheats like they's no tomorrow. It's one-on-one combat theys prefer and they's always a gallery of drakyn watchers, ta keep 'em honest, I 'spose. I recon they'd just kill us outright ifn they really got angry.

"They gots the challenge thing from ancient skragling–I means human–stories, I guess from the primers. Sometin' called a 'duel,' me thinks. Anyways, the idea stuck, and the drakyn 'ave paid the price. Over time, we's managed to beat 'em back. Fighters like this Kemp 'ave takin' out 'underds of 'em, Humans may not be old hands at this shite, but somehow, we's all got a talent fur it, or so it seems.

"Even me?"

"Prob'ly. Most ever human what came through the gardamn cubes 'ad some talent er other, even if 'twere just fur settin' a l'il fire."

"That's odd isn't it, everyone sent here having talent?"

"Yeah, no co-in-cer-dense, I's thinkin'."

"You mean whoever–or whatever–sent us here—"

"Maybe they was preparin' the way fur sometin' else."

"But what?"

"This conversion's gettin' too deep fur me, son. I's just a simple jester, travelin' the world with me loyal donklet."

A spluttering laugh burst from Poppet. He'd come to see that no matter what silly thing the Wastrel said or did, there was depth and wisdom beneath the surface. He hid behind his jokes, but there was more to learn about this man. He was sure of that.

They spent that night at a little roadside inn, coincidentally named the Plodding Donkey. When the pudgy, diminutive innkeeper came out to greet them, he saw Pollux and let out a gust of laughter, the sound too large for such a little man. "Oh, me stars! If it ain't me own beloved long-lost ass come to spend the night in me barn!"

"I hope yur referrin' to Pollux," joked the Wastrel, then corrected the man. "But 'es much more'n any ol' donkey sir, this ere's a *donklet*."

The wastrel was compelled to spend several minutes cataloguing the differences and similarities between a donkey and a zoobilet, while Poppet ruminated on his sore feet. At last, the situation was made clear, coins were proffered, and Poppet lead the donklet to a humble but neat stall in the tiny barn behind the porker sty, where the animal was given oats and a rubdown by the innkeeper's portly, enthusiastic daughter.

After a simple stew of taters and shrooms, with little bits of porker mixed in that the Wastrel called "bits o' bacon," the innkeeper offered them a glass of his own brew; a dark, frothy ale that proved exceedingly tasty to the exhausted Poppet. The innkeeper's daughter, fortunately too young to interest the Wastrel in after dinner activities, brought them a couple small cakes she called "afterteasers". Poppet was pretty sure she was using the words wrong, for, as far as he knew, afterteasers were eaten *before* dinner, which was odd, considering the name.

"Aperitifers, you say? What may these be?" asked the Wastrel in delight.

"I makes 'em meself, sir, from me own recipe." The red-cheeked girl made an elegant gesture and proudly placed a delicate yellow cakelet before each of her guests.

Poppet took a cautious sniff. His time with the Wastrel had instilled in him a healthy circumspection concerning anything offered them to eat or drink. It smelled fine, but that might mean nothing; the baby mice wine had tasted like honey, before he found out how it was vinted.

"What's in it?" Poppet asked cautiously.

"It's a secretive recipe, ya know," said the girl, wiping her hands on her apron. "But I can tell you a few o' the 'gredients, if you be curious."

"Yes, please," said Poppet, not touching his cake, while the Wastrel wolfed his down.

"Well...there's forest honey."

"Yes," snapped Poppet, his impatience showing. "What else?"

"An' rye flour. I's afraid that's alls I can tell ya without revealin' me recipe. There's inns in Droop that'd kill to know how to make these li'l gems." With that she skipped back to the kitchen, balancing her tray with grace and panache.

Poppet gave in and took a tiny taste of his cake. It was delicious, so he ate the whole thing.

The next day, as they set out to continue their journey to Droop, the innkeeper came out to see them off. Apparently, they had been the only guests that night.

"Purty quiet on the road right now, eh?" asked the Wastrel. "I 'spose we's the only group you seen in a bit."

"Funny you should mention it," replied the thick man, scratching his bald head. "Yesterday, jus' before yous arrived, the weirdest group was just leavin'; a pretty blonde woman 'an her servants, or I assume they were, accompanied by a dageki, of all things. I never see 'em with other races, normally. Very odd, i'twas."

"That is strange," mused the Wastrel. "Well, we best be off. Please give our regards to yur talented daughter, an' be thankin' her for the lovely cakes last night."

"Oh," preened the innkeeper, raising his chubby hands in a negating gesture. "It's nutin' I's sure. She loves to experiment on the guests wit' 'er recipes. She'll be so glad to hear yous liked 'em. They's not much call for her lard n' bore's snot cakes these days. Can't imagines why."

It was too late for Poppet to throw up, so he gagged his way down the road to Droop.

Droop didn't have everything that Maddog had offered. For one thing it lacked the stench of dung and fish guts. Instead, the neat high-plains town was redolent of desert flowers, planted in boxes along the streets, hanging from planters on almost every house, and peeking their round, bright faces out from among the vegetables and herbs growing in the omnipresent gardens.

"Wow," said Poppet in relief. "This is a change."

"Not the fragrant bovid town o' yur dreams, eh?" mocked the Wastrel.

"Nightmares, more like," said Poppet with a grin. "I can't say I'm not happy to put those endless dung fields behind us, with a herdbeast peeing on ever bush."

"Well, at least they's got a plant to piss in," quipped the Wastrel.

Poppet groaned.

"I knows, I knows! Even me jokes 'ave gone lame. Me thinks the road is startin' to wear on me, takin me sense o' humor, as well as the souls o' me shoes." He raised a foot to show Poppet the hole worn in the bottom of his boot.

"You could've ridden the donkey."

"Donklet, and no, one does not ride a donklet. Its indigner-fied, in'it? Especially fur the donklet. Sensitive creatures, they is. Got lots o' pride. Won't carry just any ol' thing, ya know."

"Well then," said Poppet in a sardonic tone, "I'm so glad they're willing to carry two cases of cheap wine."

"Yes, it's extremely most fortunate," the Wastrel agreed in all seriousness.

They spent the night at an inn Poppet was pleased to find was simply called, "The Inn." After breakfast, they went to check on Pollux, who was unusually restless in his stall, flipping his large head and kicking the stall door as if trying to tell them something.

"What is it, boy?" asked the Wastrel, ruffing the donklet's stiff mane. "Have the stable boys been mistreatin' ya?"

To Poppet's amazement, the ass was shaking his head side-to-side as if to say "no."

"What the fruck? Did he just—?" Poppet began, but the Wastrel interrupted impatiently.

"O' course not, 'e's just an ass, aint 'e? But I do be wonderin' what's wrong with 'im, poor sod. You might have to spend the night with 'im, just to be safe."

"What, me?"

"Well, the stable boys sleep out here, doesn't they? I'd think it'd be the least you could do fur our poor, hard workin' beast. Unless yous askin' to carry our provisions instead?"

Poppet mumbled his grudging agreement to spend the night in the barn but moped his way out of the stables and all the way down the street. He was paying so little attention that he literally bounced off the dageki when he walked into him, despite the Wastrel's shouted warning.

CHAPTER TWENTY-SEVEN

The Tortured Bagpipe

T he next day, Tinkoro took Wren to the stables, where he
introduced her to Kinzi Koro Ty Nee Hey. The name went
on but that was all that Wren could remember. The little bay pony
nuzzled them with his elegant muzzle from behind the gate of
his stall, his nose barely reaching the top. His long black mane
and forelock had a slight wave and shone with silver highlights.
Kinzi eyed her through his overhanging forelock with gentle but
wise brown eyes. Wren fell in love immediately, having dreamed of
equines since she was a child and her granpapa had taken her to a
neighbor's farm. The farmer had let her sit on the back of his giant
white work equine. She remembered the great strength and calm
that emanated from the equine's warm hide, and when he walked,
she felt like she was ensconced in a thousand-pound rocking chair.

"But how would he carry it," asked Wren, "and is there a
danger of damaging it? The abacusian seems fragile."

"It really is not," replied Tinkoro. "As in nature, there seems to
be a force that holds the parts together, beyond even our excellent
construction methods."

"Ah," was all Wren could say to that.

He continued, "But Kinzi Koro Ty Nee Hey has a little wagon that he has been trained to pull. We will pad it and hide the device under cover. It should serve you well."

"I don't know how to thank you for everything you've done, Tinkoro."

"It is I who should thank you. You have helped us advance our research tenfold, and with great alacrity. I wish you success on your journey."

Wren wanted to hug him, but couldn't figure out the logistics, so she bowed instead.

Tinkoro laughed.

"What?" she asked.

"You just told me that you celebrate my pregnancy."

"Oh, my," laughed Wren.

The next day, Wren and the group were packed up and heading off for the town of Droop by mid-morning. As Grakt explained, Droop was a gateway to the volcano lands. Beyond that, they would be in more dangerous territory. Grakt had also been able to scrounge up some coins, called gravures, that humans in this area used for transactions. It was a mostly uneventful journey, their only break when they stayed at a charming little inn called the Plodding Donkey.

When they arrived in Droop, they were pleasantly impressed with the general cleanliness and beauty of the town. When Wren commented on it, Grakt said, "Droop is more the exception than the rule, I fear. Many of these border towns are full of rabble-rousers, gamblers, and general malcontents. We may run into some in our travels. I would suggest you not talk to them and let them go on their way. We do not need that kind of trouble."

The first thing they did was to take Kinzi to the stables so he could have a rest and eat some grain. He deserved it, having pulled his little wagon with calm, capable surety and good humor the whole way. They paid the stable hand and started out the door, when Wren heard a strange, alarming noise. It sounded like a bagpipe being tortured.

"What's that?"

"Sounds like a donkey," said Teeka. "You don't know? I thought you were a farm girl."

"We never had a donkey. Let's go meet her."

As they approached the stall, Pollux excitedly raised his head, gazing at Wren with deep, intelligent eyes. She rubbed his neck and noticed that he was missing an ear, as if he'd been born without it.

"What's your name then, One Ear?" she joked. In response, the donklet hung his head.

"Oh, I'm sorry, I didn't mean to be cruel."

"I don't think he understands you," noted Mala, obviously anxious to be moving on.

Wren rubbed him on the neck a few more times, and she noticed that her hand came away with something dark and oily, like shoe polish.

"Well, your master needs to give you a nice bath, doesn't he?"

They left the barn and headed down the street to find an inn. *Hopefully with a bath and a good meal*, Wren mused. As they walked, Wren saw an oddly familiar figure just rounding the building in front of them, but she didn't have time to think about it when they noticed a couple men coming toward them. She saw a tall, scruffy looking man wearing dusty, travel-worn clothes and a wide-brimmed hat. Beside him strode a young man with red hair. The boy was not looking where he was going, his gaze glued to the dusty ground as he jabbered on to his companion. Before anyone could stop him, he ran right into Grakt, and Wren had to laugh when the boy literally bounced off the huge dageki. Then she realized that there was something familiar about his freckled face.

"Poppet?"

The boy picked himself up and formed clouds of dust as he slapped his clothes. He looked at them, and recognition slowly overtook him.

"Wren? Mala!"

Wren had never seen Mala cry, until now. They were all in tears, except stalwart Grakt and Poppet's companion, who just stood grinning in silence as he watched the curious reunion. They tried to catch up, right there in the street, but Poppet's companion said, "Wouldn't this whole conversation go down better over a nice ale?"

Poppet broke off from explaining his escape from the blood farm, realizing that he hadn't introduced them.

"Oh boy, sorry, this is the Wastr–I mean Duo Wastrellini. He saved my life, basically, and we've been traveling together ever since."

Mala snickered, "Bet you get called the Wastrel all the time, eh?"

The Wastrel gave her a look that could have turned fire to ice.

Ignoring the jibe, Wren said, "That's an excellent plan, though my tastes go more toward a dry chardonnay, or a Willamette Valley pinot noir."

"As do mine, actually," said the Wastrel as he led them toward the pub. Poppet noticed that the Wastrel was already acting oddly toward Wren. Normally, he should have been making lewd comments and falling all over her. The Wastrel let no beautiful woman go to waste. But not this time. He was oddly quiet and polite. Poppet briefly wondered why, but then he lost the thought in his joy at seeing his friends again.

CHAPTER TWENTY-EIGHT

All Spies, Please Step Forward

They agreed to spend the night in Droop, stock up on provisions for the road and leave first thing in the morning. The Wastrel insisted on packing twice as much water as Wren thought necessary but refused to remove any of his wine to make room for other provisions when she made the suggestion.

Wren could tell that the dageki wasn't happy to have the Wastrel accompanying them, but she just couldn't say no. Poppet had become attached to the rough-looking man, and Wren suspected he wasn't as bad as he looked. Despite his gruff, irreverent manner she sensed a kind heart in him.

They were only a couple hours out of Droop when the terrain began to change. Arid lands gave way to sand, scrub turned into cactus and other equally prickly, unfriendly denizens of a desert landscape. She started to see why the Wastrel had insisted on extra water, though she thought they could have eliminated his allotment, seeing the volume of wine he consumed. He appeared to take most of his liquid in the form of a '43 Happy Hor Merlot.

"Got it cheap," he'd explained, "when they got the label back from the transmoger artist, they found that he'd forgotten the "u" in 'Hour.'"

"That's not very funny," said Wren, but she turned away to hide her smile.

They camped for the night and Wren was glad they'd also brought grain for the animals. While Pollux tried to graze on the unpalatable grasses that looked more like rubber tubes swollen with water, the pony just ignored them, looking forlorn. Wren watched Pollux take a bite of the almost-grass and spit it out on the ground.

She laughed. "You're a tough one, Pollux, but I don't think even you can find anything to eat in this nasty place."

"Talking to me ass now, are ya?"

Wren started, realizing that the Wastrel had managed to sneak up on her.

"Oh, just commenting on his taste in succulents. Not much for them to graze on out here. I'm glad we had space for the grain."

"As I am ever so glad we had room fur a case o' '79 Pisse d'Ane chardonnay."

"You know I'm going to ask Teeka to translate that."

"Go fur it," he replied, laughing. "You'll find out it's an aromatic, golden varietal."

Not really listening, Wren's mind had traveled far out over the flat desert terrain. The Wastrel could see worry etched on her features.

"Somethin' botherin' you?"

Wren snorted. "What isn't bothering me? I'm carrying the weight of the world on my shoulders." She almost said more, then stopped herself.

The Wastrel opened his mouth as if to say something, then closed it abruptly.

"Well, come on back to camp. Yur gonna miss a real treat. Teeka's cookin' a big butt ant saute with maggot cheese."

"I think I'll just chew on some contail jerky, but thanks."

"OK, but it's yur loss. T'morrow, I'm guessin' we'll be injoyin' fried desert rat, so you better git some wholesome camp food wilst ya still can."

"Thanks, I'll take my chances."

As he left her alone, she mumbled, "Too bad there wasn't room for taters once we got all that wine loaded."

Wren ran her fingers through her long, tussled hair. *Better get Mala to braid it for me*, she thought. *These desert winds are brutal.* She realized that she'd almost told a stranger her deepest fears. What was she thinking? She didn't know the Wastrel, and even though Poppet had vouched for him, she still couldn't trust him completely, not yet anyway.

As the evening settled in, tiny desert birds flitted about the cactus singing, *whipper, whipper, whipper, whip*. In a heat mirage, Drakonia's golden sun sunk to the horizon, spreading itself into horizontal pats, like melting butter. This world was so solid, despite the malleable nature of its tiniest elements. It had always been able to rebound from the worst its little beings could do to it. But now she might have the power to change everything, and not necessarily for the better.

There was a game she'd played as a child, a simple one with painted chips of wood set on end in rows. If you toppled one, all the rest would fall. Every decision she made now was fraught with the possibility of spreading disaster. Very few roads showed her a route that did not affect everything and everyone. If she changed one little thing, everything else might be affected. Like the child's game of topple sticks, did she now hold in her fingertips the power to topple the world?

The next few days they trudged through the unblinking, unchanging desert. There were some changes, hollows where the cactus grew closer, as if there were more water beneath the surface to fight over. There were rocky ridges and outcrops sprouting out of the sand. There were fields of sage and airplant floating gently on the breeze. The only thing total absent was habitation of any kind.

Wren asked Grakt, "Where's the next city?"

"You never listen."

"And you sound like my papa."

"He must have been a very wise man."

"Grakt!"

"All right. There are no cities out here. The next thing we will reach is the outskirts of the resistance encampment, if it has not moved."

"Why would it move?"

"Would you want the drakyn to learn exactly where you were sleeping?"

"OK, I get the point."

"There is a river coming up. At least, it is a river in the winter. At this season, it may be flowing with only rocks and sand."

"We'll need more water soon."

"There are springs ahead of us. When we get to the volcano lands, this desert will turn to pine forest, and we'll have all the water we could desire. How are the animals doing?"

"Fine. I think Pollux is more suited to this climate than Kinzi. Pollux seems to need hardly any water, and the heat just loosens his muscles."

"And Kinzi?"

"He's struggling. Maybe he's just not made for this kind of environment, but you know him, he's a trooper. He's got more heart than his little chest can hold."

"He is indeed an admirable, if diminutive equine."

The dageki paused, then asked, "What do you think of Poppet's friend?"

"What do I think?" asked Wren, alarmed by the non sequitur and stalling for time to think.

"Well, I don't know him very well yet," she replied tentatively.

"Exactly!" said the dageki, perhaps with more vehemence than he'd intended.

"Grakt, let's give him a chance. He's been a great help to us so far, and I think Poppet almost idolizes him—"

"That might be the problem. Poppet met the man when he needed a way out of the wilderness. He didn't really have time to understand him. Many of these wanderers are thieves, con men, or worse."

"But the Wastrel saved Poppet from gard knows what, then took him along and showed him the ropes, when he could have just left him to fend for himself. Despite his rough exterior, I think there is a good man inside."

"Still, I do not trust him. There is something not quite right about him and that donkey. I will be watching him."

"That's fair, just try to have an open mind."

"My mind is open to the celestial song of the heavens, but my feet are rooted here in the world, a world where no one can be trusted."

"You trusted me, Grakt."

"Yes, and look where it has gotten me."

Was that a joke? She couldn't be sure what amounted to humor with the dageki.

"Let's just wait and see. Perhaps the Wastrel will prove a friend in need when–as my granpapa used to say–the dung hits the road."

"What an odd colloquialism," said Grakt, rubbing his hands on his sides as if to remove any metaphorical dung that might be clinging to them.

As they walked the next day, Wren noticed a gradual change. The moisture in the ground began to show its face, not in open water, but in the plants that were a little greener, a little more social. Then the cactuses gave way to sage and chokeberry. Stunted pines soon joined the bushes. Wren was starting to feel good about the day, when she heard and felt a rumble in the ground. It made her teeth chatter, and her limbs go weak. *Was it a volcanic eruption?*

"What is it?" she entreated the others.

The Wastrel was the first to answer. "Equines. Don't run, whatever ya do. They'll run you down an' stick you like wild porkers."

Wren didn't know what he was talking about, but obeyed, hearing an earnestness in his tone that she hadn't heard before. Everyone stood still but Teeka, who panicked and took off running. She hadn't gotten very far before a group of mounted men and women surrounded them, their swords and bows drawn.

"Please don't kill her!" Wren cried, as two of the soldiers deftly caught the cook and drew her up by her arms between them.

Teeka screamed, *"Laissez-moi passer!"*, but the men ignored her pleas, dumping her unceremoniously with the others.

Poppet helped her up and the cook pushed him away indignantly.

"I can stand for myself, *idiote*. Leave me be."

Wren stepped forward to speak, then realized that the Wastrel was already addressing them. "Duo Wastrellini and company, reporting for duty, *sir!*"

A stout, ruddy faced man rode forward. Perhaps he didn't look like a leader at first, with his bald head and short limbs, but there was an aura of strength and endurance about him that Wren had seen in few men of greater stature.

"Wastrellini?" he grunted. "Perchance I remember you. Weren't you a deserter?"

"Deserter? Me?" said the Wastrel indignantly. "I was Kemp's main lieutenant in me day. I may appear worse for wear these days, but it don't mean I ain't still loyal to the cause."

The man urged his roan forward, scrutinizing the group.

He said, "Can this be real? I can't imagine an odder lookin' group o' recruits than this; a retired, I mean *really* retired soldier, with a dageki, a blackie, a skag, and a whore."

Wren could feel Mala bristling at her side and reached for her hand, whispering, "He doesn't know your true value yet, so don't take his insults to heart." With a lifted eyebrow, Mala relaxed.

"Besides," Wren continued, "I'm more offended to be called a skag."

"I think you're the whore," Mala whispered. Turning to Teeka, whose turn it was to bristle, "Teeka, that makes you the skag."

Noticing all this unwarranted interaction among his captives, the leader shouted to regain control of his snickering men. "Get 'em back to camp for the testing, *now*."

Wren didn't know what testing entailed, but she was sure they wouldn't like it. Not. One. Bit.

The leader of the troupe yanked brutally on the bridle of his tall roan gelding, whose mouth was so scarred by this frequent abuse that he felt nothing. The equine obeyed out of habit and the others followed them with their captives into a copse of sparse pines, where resided the seventh camp of the advance guard for the resistance.

The camp was a disorganized mix of worn tents and haphazardly constructed lean-tos. A few more ragged-looking soldiers milled about, some wearing bandages, others limping from sprains or broken bones. Some were missing limbs.

Is this where the wounded come to recover? thought Wren.

"Why don't they just send them home?" Wren didn't realize she'd spoken aloud until the Wastrel answered, "'Cause they'll be sent back to the front soon as they's healed."

Wren didn't have time to consider this before the leader strode up with his arms swinging. He had the gait of a great bear advancing on its prey.

"My name is Aaron Windstrom. I'm in charge here. New conscripts must pass the test before proceeding on to the main encampment, if that is their desire."

"What test?" asked Wren.

"My gran's the truthsayer here. We've sent for her."

With no more words to share, he stood before them with his arms crossed over his broad chest. Wren could see muscles bulging from his forearms and shoulders. At his waist a short sword in a worn scabbard hung from a wide leather belt. His face was built like a jumble of boulders, his beard reddish-blond and his eyes a piercing hazel.

They waited. Their belongs had yet to be searched, and Wren was grateful. She didn't know how to explain the abacusian. *What if they confiscated it?*

The pony and his little wagon waited at the picket line, where Kinzi appeared to be flirting with a large bay mare. Pollux the donklet was nowhere to be seen. That was unusual. She hoped he hadn't wandered off, though she couldn't imagine him doing so. She'd never seen a line on the animal, yet he followed the Wastrel as if they were attached at the hip.

After a few minutes, a small, wizened creature approached them slowly, each step tentative, as if she were feeling her way. Wren thought "creature" because she couldn't determine its gender for sure with what she could see of it. *Female*, she decided eventually, *and very old*. The woman wore a long, black, mud-spattered cloak. Her leathery skin was almost as dark and speckled as the cloth.

This is Aaron's gran? He must be adopted, thought Wren.

A hood hid any features that might have told Wren more about her.

Aaron took her frail hand and helped the woman forward. She pulled back her hood and Wren couldn't help but gasp. The woman's large eyes were clouded and unfocused. She was blind.

Aaron said in a reverent tone, "This is Granny Anya Windstrom. She'll be doing your truthsaying."

"Truthsaying? What's that?" asked Poppet.

"She has a special talent, and one that's precious to us. It's not so much transmogering as such, but she can detect talent in another, and more importantly, she can detect what your firstform was–if you are attempting to infiltrate us as a drakyn spy."

"A spy?" gasped Teeka indignantly. "You think us *spies*?"

Aaron replied, "Everyone is suspect until Anya says otherwise."

"But that's just ridiculous," said Wren. "Why would the drakyn send spies into your camps?"

"It has been rumored," replied Aaron. "I'm not sure myself what's going on. Kemp can explain it to you, if you make it that far, of course."

The old woman reached toward them. Her arms looked like sticks covered in worn brown canvas. They shook slightly. When she spoke, the strength of her voice belied her frail appearance.

"You first," she said, reaching for Teeka.

The woman approached the cook and gently touched her fingers to Teeka's forehead. Anya breathed deeply.

Pulling her fingers away abruptly she declared, "Firstform. Very little talent, at least not any of use to us."

Teeka stood up straighter and said, "I'll have you know I'm the best cook in the northlands and—"

Aaron laughed. "Well, you're not in the northlands now, but the resistance can always use a good cook, if you're any good with fried contail, contail soup and contail everything else."

Wren only hoped she wouldn't spring her baby eel with bladder sauce on them right away.

Anya moved to her next victim, the dageki. She couldn't reach his forehead, so she touched one of his iridescent body plates instead.

"Just a dageki," she said in a bored tone. "Full of logic and tradition and not much else."

Wren could tell that Grakt was offended by her words, but he stayed silent. Not even a dageki could fight a camp full of soldiers with swords and bows, even if he'd been prone to violence, which Grakt definitely was not.

Poppet was next. He fidgeted his fingers while his arms stood rigid at his sides.

What could Poppet have to be afraid of? thought Wren.

She grew concerned when Anya took a long time with her analysis of the boy.

Pulling her long fingers slowly from his forehead, a look of puzzlement twisted her already wrinkled features.

Wren noticed that Aaron's hand had strayed to the sword at his belt.

Anya spoke, "You've got talent, boy, but totally untrained, I see. You're a seer. You can't transmoger but, like me, you'll be able to see those who do."

"Is that all?" asked a disappointed Poppet.

"Is that all?" mocked the seer. "Don't you get it, boy? You've got something more important than a legion of soldiers. You can rout out the enemy hiding in our midst. You'll need training, of course." She appeared to think before continuing, "I'm getting old." She said this as if it were news to anyone. "When you've sown these wild oats you so yearn to plant, come back to me and I'll teach you what you need to know. Someday, you could be my replacement."

Poppet stood in obvious shock and disappointment, as if unable to grasp what Anya was telling him. Before he could respond, the seer had moved on to Wren.

Wren felt cool fingers on her forehead, and the familiar buzz she'd experienced when first working on the abacusian came back to her. It happened so fast, she didn't have time to implement her thought-calming techniques. Anya's fingers began to smoke, then sprouted little flames.

Anya screeched and grabbed her arm tightly, as if to choke off the pain. Aaron ran forward and latched on to her damaged hand. Wren could see red blisters forming on the tip of each finger.

"I'm sorry!" Wren cried, "I mean, I didn't do that, did I?"

Aaron ignored her, his concentration completely on his gran. His eyes closed and the buzzing in Wren's head was replaced with a vision of a cool pond in the moonlight.

When Wren looked again, the blisters on Anya's fingers were gone.

Aaron is a healer.

"Is she a spy?" Aaron asked.

"No, she is firstform human, that's sure, and there's no talent that I can recognize. There's something amiss with this one, though. Dangerous perhaps, but not at transmogrifee. I would need more time to figure it out."

"That's fine, gran, let's save your fingers."

The old woman chuckled and moved on to the next in line. The Wastrel stood still and quiet, possessed of utter calm. In fact, if anything, he appeared to be far away, his eyes unfocused and his breathing slow and rhythmic.

As soon as Anya touched his skin, she exclaimed, "A great deal of talent in this one."

Wren noticed that several of the soldiers had joined Aaron, moving closer with their hands near their weapons.

"But there's nothing much else. A burn out from the wars, I figure. He's just hollow inside."

Next to them, Mala snickered, "That's our Wastrel, all right."

Now Anya turned to the last of the prospective conscripts, little Mala. As Anya reached for Mala's forehead, Wren saw the women's fingers tremble even more. She wondered if the woman was reaching the end of her endurance. She imagined that truth-saying might take a lot out of you.

After a moment's touch on Mala, the woman screeched in a strident tone, "This one is not wearing its firstform."

Before they could react, the soldiers had rushed forward, and various knives and swords were being pointed at the slight girl. Wren could only imagine what transmograffic attacks they were also preparing.

Wren jumped between them and Mala, shouting, "No, Mala isn't a spy! She's a marm."

Most everyone looked at her in confusion. Only Poppet said, "Of course! That explains a lot."

Anya held up an arm to stop the soldiers, then reached out to touch Mala again.

After a moment, Anya said, "She's right, this one has a great transmogering talent, but of her past life, I hear only waves crashing, see only the endless cerulean sea and taste these disgusting things called 'herrins.' Nasty life. No wonder she left it. This one also has the potential to be a great healer, with the right training."

"Gard knows we need more of those," said Aaron, glancing back at the injured men.

Aaron visibly relaxed, but said to Mala, "OK, then show us your talent. Change back to your firstform now."

Mala just stared, no words escaping her.

"She can't," explained Wren. "It's incredibly painful for her. I've seen it. To force her to transmoger again would be torture."

"I chose to be human, and never go back," said Mala in a small, embarrassed voice.

"Are you done with the interrogations for tonight?" asked Wren, her anger at their treatment of Mala and the others growing. "If so, our animals need food and water, and we are tired."

"That you express concern for your animals first speaks well for you, Wren Weatherspring."

Aaron motioned to his men with a flick of his hand, and they dissolved into the twilight. Aaron helped Anya back to her tent. When he returned his expression bore no mistrust, or less, anyway.

"Welcome to Windstrom camp number seven. After the marking, you're allowed to stay until you're ready to continue on to Kempstown, if that is your choice."

The Wastrel muttered, "Kempstown, is it now?" But Aaron appeared not to hear.

"Wait a second, what 'marking?'" asked Teeka warily.

"Oh, don't worry," said Aaron casually. "It hardly hurts a'tall."

To Teeka that wasn't reassuring. She jumped when Aaron let out a long, loud whistle.

A scraggly-looking young man trotted up from where he sat by the campfire.

Aaron said, "Gritt, here's a few new recruits for ya."

"Sure," agreed Gritt in a bored tone that said he'd done this many times before. He explained to the newcomers, "One of my talents is indelible ink, I mean *indelible*. Nothin' takes it off and another inker can tell a counterfeit from a mile off, so fakin' it jus' don't work. The thing is, we used to do the wrist or ankle. Soon enough we figured out both of d'em limbs is too easy to lose, so now we do it on the neck, like so." He turned his head to show a tiny tattoo on the back of his neck.

"If'n you lose it here, chanced are you won't be needin' no replacement mark." Gritt chuckled at his dark humor, but no one joined him.

"OK, jus' hold still," he said. With nothing in his hands, he simply touched their guests and they each bore a tiny mark on their necks when he was done.

When the Wastrel noticed that the symbol was a tiny, decorative 'K,' he mumbled,

"For Kemp, I suppose. How humble." But he accepted his mark like everyone else.

Aaron said, "We've got hay and grain for your ponies, and venison, taters and wild onions cooking for dinner. You can camp out there past the picket line after."

Aaron pointed to a stretch of dry grass just beyond the camp. It seemed that Aaron's trust only went so far, having them set up their tent outside the camp instead of in it. Wren didn't care. Trust went both ways, and after what they'd just been through, she wouldn't trust these men not to slit their throats in the middle of the night, just to be doubly sure that they weren't spies.

Chapter Twenty-Nine

The Wastrel Shows his True Colors

Wren was happy to leave Windstrom camp number seven the next morning. Though Aaron had shown nothing but the utmost hospitality toward them after the test, she couldn't throw off the oppressive sense of suffering and death just waiting in the wings, when these brave transmogrifers healed enough to return to the battle.

That afternoon they reached the Humptulips river. Even before they reached it, Wren could feel a looming presence ahead of them. A distant rustle reached them first, like a hundred mumbled conversationalists talking over each other. She felt moisture in the air and breathed deep as it refreshed her lungs. Swarms of tiny insects circled her head and she heard the cry of a fisherbird in the distance.

She glanced at Grakt. "You said it would most likely be filled with only stones at this time of year."

"It appears that there have been heavy rains up in the Hartbone Range to the north."

Mala nodded her head, smiling happily.

"What the fruck are you talking about?" asked Teeka, who was totally oblivious to the subject of this discussion.

Grakt explained, "The river is just ahead of us. It's called the Humptulips."

Poppet snorted, but there was little humor in the sound. "I've been to some odd places on this journey, but that takes the cake for the weirdest name I've heard so far. What does it mean? Impassable? Full of bloodsucking leeches with fangs? Or loaded with fish-gilled harpies whose preferred delicacy is redhead?" His eyes shone a little too brightly and his voice had a brittle tone. Wren wondered if the revelations of the truthsayer had been overwhelming for Poppet. He needed time to process his new talent and consider his role in the war. She doubted he would get that chance anytime soon.

"Nothing like that," replied Grakt, taking Poppet's words literally. "At least not in this river. Humptulips simply means 'hard to navigate,' but it should be tame now, despite the rains. It will not be nearly as treacherous as a winter crossing would be. Trust me."

Poppet grunted but remained silent.

At the water's edge, Wren was uncertain. It looked too deep for the little pony, especially towing his cart.

Grakt considered, "I could carry the cart across first, then the abacusi–"

He stopped suddenly as Wren waved him to silence, grasping quickly that she didn't want to share knowledge of the abacusian with the Wastrel.

"Our provisions," he amended. "Then the rest of you can lead the animals across."

"Pollux can swim quite well," offered the Wastrel.

"And of course, I swim fairly well, myself," piped Mala with a mischievous grin. "I'll lead the pony across. He won't be afraid beside me."

Grakt left them repacking their gear for the crossing, first going upstream and then downstream. When he returned, he said, "There is a spot downriver that should be ideal. The bottom is relatively flat, and it is somewhat shallower than it is here."

Following his lead, they went farther down the river. It didn't look any different to Wren than the first spot, but she trusted the dageki.

He had no trouble ferrying their gear and the abacusian, hidden in its canvas cover, across the current.

When it was time for the pony to cross, Wren realized that her hands were balled into fists, and she told herself to relax. Animals could read tension and fear, she knew. Kinzi didn't resist as Mala led him into the water, with Teeka on the other side, and Poppet in the back in case he needed help. Everything looked fine until Kinzi reached the point where his barrel-shaped torso started to float. He raised his head and Wren could see the effort in his shoulders and hips as his little legs pumped hard beneath the surface. She laughed. Kinzi was a born swimmer. He cruised across, even pulling away from Mala to beat her to shore.

"*Bravo, petit equus!*" shouted the Wastrel.

"Now wait," said Wren, "my granpapa was the language expert, but I think you just said, 'Well done, little equine' using three different human languages."

"I got excited, I guess," said the Wastrel sheepishly. But Wren had to wonder. There was more to the Wastrel than there appeared, and she was beginning to have suspicions that she knew him, somehow.

Mala was laughing as she jumped out of the water to pat the pony, who was shaking himself like a dog.

"Good boy! You were born for water, little one." In his ear she whispered, "Just like me."

Since the Wastrel had–reluctantly–left a case of wine with Aaron as a parting gift, and the first case had been decimated by the rigors of the trail, Pollux had little to carry. The few bottles left had been loaded into the back of Kinzi's cart. Pollux was ready to go. As usual, he exuded confidence and calm.

As they entered the river, Wren began to relax, realizing that Pollux was a good swimmer and perfectly at home. He almost pulled them across with his sure strokes, as if trotting in the water.

When they reached the far shore, Wren was amazed that the river crossing hadn't turned into a disaster, as she'd feared. She reasoned that not every bad feeling she got was an accurate premonition, though a good number did turn out to be true.

As she patted the donklet's dripping neck, her hand came away with a greasy feel, as it had at the stable in Droop. She looked more closely at the faint stripes on his coat. She'd assumed they were the result of his zoobilet parent, but now, one of the stripes was standing out in an odd color, a color that didn't occur naturally in either a zoobilet or a donkey. It was gold.

She turned to the Wastrel. Before he could react she pulled off his hat, the hat she now realized he *never* removed.

"What?"

There was no stripe in the Wastrel's hair, but she still knew now who he really was.

He looked sheepishly at Wren. "I can explain—"

She turned back to the donklet, fear and disbelief waging war for her sanity. She looked at the animal, pleading, "Are you Kodo?" as if the animal would talk to her, explain that she was just imagining this. She realized that expecting a donklet to talk was quite insane enough. She fell silent.

"No, he is not," said the Wastrel. "Well, not entirely. Pollux holds my mass, and occasionally my consciousness, in an emergency."

"Like at the truthsayer's test?"

"Yes."

"And this body you also wear, the Wastrel, did you create him too?"

"No, not entirely. I needed someone who could pass the truthsayer's test as a firstform. I knew there would be guards at the border."

"So, you took his life?"

"No, no, he was dead already, well, dying anyway. When I found him in his camp, he was minutes from death. Liver poisoning, I'm afraid. Unfortunately, I may have inherited a few of his vices, along with his good looks. Meeting up with Poppet was just a lucky coincidence."

"And the donkey? Why him?"

"Donklet," he corrected automatically. "I thought, since I had been an ass and a jester my whole life, why not take their form for a while? I believed it might teach me humility."

"And has it?"

"I'm a work in progress, but I'm doing my best, Wren. Please, just give me a chance."

"I hate you!" She knew she sounded childish, but she couldn't help it. She was starting to like the Wastrel, and she was afraid she'd *loved* the donklet. Now it was all a terrible joke that had been played on her, on Poppet, on all of them.

"Please, Wren, I've changed. All this time in human form, it's changed me. Like Mala, I don't want to go back."

"But you're still a killer on the inside, one of *them*. Like Semli."

Kodo–the Wastrel–examined his waterlogged boots. "I'm not like Semli. I never have been, really. You must understand. I'm so sorry for what he did to you. I want to make it up to you. If you'll tell me what you and the dageki are up to with that device, maybe I can help you—"

"Oh no, no way! Now who's the spy? How do I know you wouldn't take that knowledge right back to the palace? You're not going to like what we have in store for you and your kind, that's for sure."

Wren realized that the others had gotten far ahead of them as they argued, so she was surprised when she heard a new voice behind her.

"And what might that be, little bird?"

Not turning around, she saw the expression on Kodo's face and felt the color drain from her's as well.

She whispered, "Semli?"

"Yes," Kodo said through gritted teeth. "Follow my lead, I'll protect you."

Despite her fear, Wren bristled. "Protect *me*? I don't think so, but you can help. I need a drop of his blood, or a piece of skin."

"What?" He looked at her as if she had gone mad.

"Just do it. Hold him off until I can bring the abacusian."

"Aba–what?"

As Kodo dithered, Semli attacked, abruptly ending their conversation. He wore his samurai form and a curved sword glinted in his muscular hand. Wren fell back, pushed out of the way by Kodo. She tripped over a branch and fell hard. It was all a blur. She was amazed at the speed with which these two drakyn could transform. She'd never seen drakyn fight each other, but given their combative natures, she assumed it was inevitable.

The Wastrel, cum Kodo, had eased his way near Pollux. What happened next made Wren almost nauseous. It was as if the Wastrel was absorbed into Pollux, or vice versa. As his hand reached out to the donklet, the arm grew fur, while Pollux's head widened and flattened, merging into the Wastrel's side. Now, the Wastrel was gone, but so was Pollux. A few ounces of dust fell from the new creature as it spread broad wings. A giant eagle met Semli as he attacked, swinging his samurai sword with an inarticulate cry of rage. The sword merely bounced off the claws of the eagle, being forged of stone. As Semli realized that his chosen weapon was inadequate, he became something else. This time, he took a form even larger than that which Kodo had chosen, a steaming rock giant, spouting smoke and flames from its mouth. It lifted a hand like a small mountain to crush the eagle's feathered head, but the raptor was gone.

Below the giant's ample belly stood the human warrior that Wren had first met at her cabin, and the form that Kodo had taken at the palace. This visage was more frightening to Wren than any monstrous form could be, because it reminded her of her humiliation at the hands of the drakyn lord, and the mistreatment she'd endured while supposedly under his care.

The ploy proved a smart one for Kodo, since his opponent was momentarily blinded by his own girth. From the rock giant's perspective, his prey had simply disappeared, and Semli faced another problem; to create a creature as large as the giant from his available mass, he had to use some shortcuts. Some areas had to be stronger than others. Semli had placed the bulk of his strength in the head and arms of the creature, allowing other spaces to act as a shell, a stretching of what material was available. He'd left a gap where a sword might penetrate.

Kodo's weapon came around in a great arch, slashing through the giant's stomach as if it were room-temperature butter.

Where she lay, Wren felt liquid splatter her face but ignored it in her rush to get out from under the feet of these screaming monstrosities. All she could do was skitter backwards on her hands, unable to find the time or strength to stand.

With blood squirting from its rent abdomen, the rock giant showed amazing resiliency, swiping his massive fist toward the face of the warrior Kodo. The swing hit Kodo's jaw at a glancing blow, but that was enough to spray blood from the reeling warrior's mouth toward her.

Wren finally came to her senses. Now in a panic to escape before they turned to her, she rose on shaky legs and ran at top speed to catch up to the others.

"Drakyn!" was all she was able to get out before stumbling and falling into Teeka's arms.

Wren breathed hard and spluttered, "I need the abacusian. I've got to take it back to the battle and—"

Mala bent down to her, asking, "Are you hurt?" as she felt for wounds. She found none, despite the fact that Wren's face was decorated by a sprinkling of red droplets.

"How many?" asked Grakt calmly.

"Just one. Kodo, I mean the Wastrel, is holding him off. It's Semli. The drakyn has found us. Please hurry, I've got to get back."

"Why?" asked the dageki.

"Why? To save us all—"

"No, I mean why go back? You have the blood."

Wren lifted a hand to her face and stopped herself before she could smear it.

"Blood?" she asked, feeling foolish despite her panic.

"On your face. It is not yours, so it must belong to one or both of the combatants."

"Oh," said Wren, starting to think at last. "But I don't know which one," she said.

"Does it matter?" asked Mala, a chill in her voice. "You've got to try. If it's the drakyn's blood, you can kill them all."

"I can't do that, Mala, not yet. It's too much. It could upset the balance and kill everyone."

"OK, so kill only this one. Just do *something!*" exclaimed Mala.

The sounds of weapons clashing were growing closer.

Teeka yelled, "Just do it, girl! What does it matter? At least take the transmogrifee from him."

A look of decision crossed Wren's features and she turned to the cart, where Grakt had already uncovered the abacusian. He delicately wiped a drop of blood from her forehead.

She mumbled, "At least we have a fifty/fifty chance it will be Semli's blood."

"Then thank gard I'm not choosing," said Poppet. "I can turn a fifty/fifty chance into twenty/eighty at the drop of a hat. It's my one transmogering ability."

Ignoring Poppet's self-pity, Wren concentrated on slowing her breathing and lowering her heart rate. It was one thing to use her new skill in the controlled setting of the dageki university lab, but she wasn't sure she could do it out here, under incredible pressure and uncertainty. She thought of the worry stone and pulled it from her pocket. Touching it brought memories of the Krasa piglet and the joy she'd felt at bringing it back to balance, back to itself.

Her thoughts calmed. She closed her eyes and touched the black handle, knowing immediately which drakyn's blood Grakt had taken from her forehead and placed on the glass. In her shock, she almost pulled her hand from the abacusian.

"Oh, no," she whispered in horror.

Back at the river's edge, Kodo was reeling from the blows of the bleeding rock giant. Though his sword had caused mortal damage to Semli, his brother could heal himself faster than any fighter. He had to keep Semli distracted from healing his wounds.

Despite its copious blood loss, the rock giant still came at him, delivering blow after blow. Kodo had transmogered into several different forms, but he hadn't found one that gave him any advantage. Sure, he could transmoger into a will-o-the-wisper and sneak away on the breeze, but then what would happen to his friends–he really thought of them as his friends now. They would be left to die at Semli's hands.

He couldn't allow that. He couldn't understand Semli's hatred of Wren. He could see why Semli resented him. He was one of the only drakyn who had ever seen Semli's firstform, years ago. Come to think of it, all the others were dead.

Semli hit him again and Kodo felt a tooth fly from his mouth. Another hit like that and he might lose consciousness. He couldn't afford that.

Raising all the strength he had left, he charged toward the rock giant with a guttural cry, forming in his hands his fallen sword as he ran. He struck with all the force he could muster, but his sword hit nothing. The rock giant was gone.

Wren turned her full attention to the pathetic creature she saw in the abacusian. She let her pity fall away and focused on returning it to its firstform, but could she do it? What she saw was truly hideous. When she'd encountered Semli in the tunnels below the palace, she'd had only a glimpse of his firstform, and that in almost total darkness. What she saw now in the light of day and in minute detail made her feel ill.

How can he even stay alive with these deformities?

Restoring a Krasa piglet to his relative perfection had been a joy. She felt no joy in forcing Semli to return to a form that had, at least in part, made him the bitter, hateful killer that he was now. She had no choice. Maybe it would be better just to let him burn as she had the grub moth in Tinkoro's lab, but she just didn't have the heart for it and, above all, she feared the consequences of playing god, not just for herself, but for the balance the world needed to survive. She dampened her fear and concentrated on limiting the effects of the abacusian to this one individual. She wasn't ready to force an entire species to change, if she ever would be. Semli might die anyway, if forced to live for long in his firstform. Now, it was either him, or all of them. In the end she did what she had to do.

Semli screamed as sunlight burned his lidless eyes. This body wasn't made for sunlight. *It wasn't made for anything but misery*, he thought through the pain. He tried again to transmoger, but nothing happened. He was trapped in his worst nightmare, trapped in the grotesque body he loathed.

Forgetting the battle, he crawled away toward the trees where he could at least be unseen. He saw now how he'd failed. He'd underestimated the little silver-haired bitch. All along, she'd been the real threat. If he'd only cut her down, then dealt with Kodo. It was too late for that now. As he crawled, a few useless limbs trailed behind him, and he struggled to breathe.

Kodo stared, his mouth open in shock.

"Dear Semli," he whispered.

Semli only spat at him from his multiple throats, gurgling incoherently, like some undeveloped antediluvian beast.

"Get away! Leave me be! Go back to your perfect skragling."

Kodo stood, pity emanating from him, until he turned and ran, in the form of the Wastrel again, leaving Semli to his shame and misery.

Wren rubbed her eyes, trying to get rid of the images that Semli's firstform had burned into them. She heard footsteps in the gravel, moving toward them quickly.

Kodo stumbled forward, and Poppet helped him to sit.

"He's a mess!" cried Poppet, "Mala, can you help?" Mala brought out her first aid bag. As she worked on Kodo, she asked, "Where's Pollux?"

Kodo said through bloody lips, "He ran at the first sign of trouble. Smart one, is our Pollux, smartern' me anyways, tryin' to take on a drakyn as talented as that one."

"Are we safe?" asked Teeka. "Is eet over?"

"Yes," replied Wren. "Semli is--disabled. But—"

She'd been about to call out the Wastrel as Kodo, but then she saw how Poppet looked at him. How could she break the boy's heart, when it was already broken by the knowledge that he would never be a transmogrifer?

Let him have his friend for a little while longer, she reasoned, *I can deal with Kodo later.*

CHAPTER THIRTY

Double Trouble

P oppet didn't look any differently at the man he still assumed was the Wastrel, but the others probably sensed that something was wrong. They must have wondered why the Wastrel had returned without his donklet. They gave her odd looks, but said nothing, somehow sensing that she wasn't ready to discuss it. Eventually–no, sooner rather than later, Kodo would have to explain himself.

For now, her only concern was to get them as far from Semli as possible. She didn't know if Semli had other drakyn with him, but she thought it wasn't his style. He was a loner. Of greater concern was how long the abacusian effect would last. At first, she'd thought it permanent, but then she considered Semli's great talent. Would he find a way to overcome it? If that happened, he would come for her in his full wrath. Wren feared his fury. She'd seen it before. Though she was grudgingly grateful for Kodo defending them against Semli, she wasn't sure that Kodo had the talent that Semli possessed.

And now, Kodo posing as the Wastrel was a complication she didn't want to deal with. What would the dageki do when he found out? Or Teeka? She assumed that it had been Kodo who sent the cook to the farms after her and Mala escaped. And Mala must hate Kodo almost as much as she did. Not to mention that Kodo had seen the abacusian. He had admitted that he'd wondered about the devise from the beginning of their journey. Wren decided to explain the basics of how it functioned, saying only that with it she could return one drakyn to his firstform. She didn't yet trust him with the knowledge of its true power.

Wren was pulled rudely from her thoughts when she tripped over a fallen tree limb.

Looking around her, she realized that the terrain had turned bizarre. Branches lay everywhere, over the trail, over each other, or sticking straight up in the air as if they had been hurled like spears, to bury themselves deep in the ground.

The others had gotten ahead of them. Kodo walked beside her.

"What happened here?" she asked, not sure she wanted to hear the answer.

Wren suddenly realized that there was more wrong with the trees. She knew and loved the elegant branching pattern of oaks, but these trees no longer adhered to that pattern. Some gnarled branches twisted wildly, their ends tipped in bulbous appendages, which, to her horror, were moving.

"No wind right now," she observed nervously.

Kodo nodded, unconcerned. "Yeah, it's an ugly mess, eh? But you should see some of the battle sites closer to the front. Trees walk off by themselves sometimes, or they just screams and screams until—"

"What are you saying?" demanded Wren, frustrated by his hints.

"It can get messy, that's all I's sayin'."

"And quit with the country bumpkin accent, will you?" Wren loud-whispered at him, anger evident in her tone.

"Gotta keep up 'pearances don't we? Fur Poppet's sake?"

"Look," she began, "the others already suspect something isn't right, no matter what you say or how you say it."

CHRONICLES OF THE DRAKYN WAR   275

"They're all wondering what happened to Pollux."

"We'll say he ran off to safety. I'll find you a real donklet, if you miss him so badly."

"It's not about the donkey!" she cried.

"Donklet. Look, Wren, just give it time, please."

The last word had an odd wheedling sound to it, and she had to wonder about Kodo. What did he really want? Was he a spy for the drakyn? Was she leading the enemy right into the camp of humanity's greatest leader? Was he only being kind to her to elicit more information about the abacusian? If so, why hadn't he just killed her outright, or destroyed the machine? Maybe the drakyn didn't yet know that she was–so far–the only one who could wield it, or that this was the only working model. She prayed this was true.

She made the decision then and there to fabricate a lie, a lie that she hoped might become true when she got the abacusian to Kemp.

"Sorry," she began, "I guess I'm a little bit on edge. I think I'll feel more at ease when we get the abacusian to their leader, Kemp. He is renowned for his transmogering ability. I'm sure he'll be able to do much more with the machine than I have achieved with my feeble attempts."

"I don't know, I thought what you did to Semli was impressive. Plus, you saved my life. Thank you." He said these last words quietly, almost grudgingly.

"What?" she asked brusquely. "Never had your life saved before?"

"No. Well, maybe once, when I met someone who made me rethink who and what I was."

Wren was silent. She didn't want to know, didn't want to hear his lies.

They caught up to the others and traveled in relative silence for a few more miles, until a man stepped out from the trees to greet them. He was dressed neatly in khaki pants with red suspenders and a pale blue shirt. He had sandy brown hair and was clean shaven. When he turned his head, Wren noted the tattooed "K" on his neck.

"Welcome. Aaron Windstrom sent word by flet that you were on your way. My name's Cutter."

First or last name? Wren wondered.

The man exclaimed, "Is that the Wastrel? By the moons, if it ain't Duo Wastrellini, back from the dead to rejoin the fight. I'm surprised to see you, old friend. To be truthful, many of your age succumb to the transmogering disease, or take their own lives to be free of the memories."

"No, not me," said the Wastrel. "I mean, it *is* me, but I'm not here to fight. I's more of a guide for these fine folk."

Wren stepped forward.

"We're here to see Kemp. We've got a device that could turn the tide of the war in our favor."

"Win the war, eh? Only way to stop those fruckin' lizards is to kill every gardamn one of 'em, in my humble opinion."

Wren stared at him, then said softly, "Only as a last resort."

Kodo looked at her with wide eyes but said nothing.

Cutter said, "Well you might be in luck. Kemp's here to speak to the troops tonight." As he spoke, he checked the tattoos on each of them. "I'll see if he'll grant you an audience."

"Grant us an audience?" muttered Mala. "What is this guy, a fruckin' emperor?"

The Wastrel chuckled. "I think if'n you offered him the crown, he'd prob'ly take it."

"So you know him well?" asked Grakt.

"I did. It's been a while. Seems like he ain't changed much, though."

Cutter led them to a large tent set up in the clearing at the center of a large, well-organized camp. Grakt stayed outside with Kinzi and the wagon, to guard the abacusian. They had agreed to guard it day and night from now on. When they entered the tent, they were amazed by the opulent objects that had been hauled out here into the wilderness. The oversized rug they stood on was intricately woven with stylized images of all kinds. Equines leaped, birds soared, and lions roared, all bordered in ornate flowers and twining vines. The colors were a rich blend of cobalt, gold and black, with highlights of the deepest burgundy.

Above them, hanging from the tent supports, was an impossibly ornate gold candle chandelier, every candle lit and filling the space with the scent of gardenias. At the end of the rug sat a massive carved wooden chair on a slightly raised platform. A handsome, dark-haired man of middle years was sitting on it, wearing a black, double-breasted coat over tan britches. Every polished gold button on his jacket glittered in the light of the chandelier.

As they approached, the man's features became clear, features that were all too familiar to most of them.

As one, Wren, Mala, Teeka and Poppet cried out, "Kodo!"

After a moment of confusion on the face of their host, Wren exclaimed, "No, wait! He doesn't have a gold stripe in his hair. Kodo always had that, no matter what body he wears–I mean, wore."

The handsome man on the dais nodded his head. "I think I remember that one. Fought it a couple years ago. I thought I killed it. It was mortally wounded, for sure, but the thing managed to escape and fly west to die, or so I assumed. They can be hard to kill. Probably not the first or last drakyn that will mimic my form. Should be flattered, I guess."

Wren stepped toward him. "The four of us were held captive by him. He called himself Kodo, and he often wore your shape and manner. It is quite uncanny how much like you he looked and acted. Anyway, we all managed to escape, in different ways. We had the help of a dageki called Grakt, and I spent time in their capital city, Dmisi. He's outside, guarding the device."

"Yes, Cutter tells me you have some kind of weapon to show me."

Kemp's attention was drawn to a figure who hung back at the rear of the group.

"Wastrellini, is that you?"

The Wastrel stepped forward reluctantly, saying, "It's me. Kemp, how ya' been?"

"Glad to have you back. We'll catch up later."

The Wastrel said nothing, and Kemp turned his attention back to Wren.

"So, as you can imagine, I've seen my share of new ideas for weapons. Last week it was a crossbow that shot spinning saw blades and darts with tips that exploded into flowers, 'sposed to distract them, I guess. Truth is, there's no substitute for talent and fast thinking. No weapon can replace that."

"This one can," Wren said, with no doubt in her voice.

Kemp frowned. "Well, it's almost dinner time. Please join me at table and we can discuss this more."

Wren got the feeling he wasn't inviting the whole group, just her. Her suspicions were confirmed when he added, "Your companions width:967px; height:1585px;

will be shown to your quarters. Cutter will get them settled and feed them and your animals."

Kemp stepped down and taking her hand, led her from the tent, not giving the others another glance.

"Seems more interested in Wren than the device," Poppet observed.

The Wastrel frowned. "Kemp's never met a lovely lady he couldn't bedazzle, me thinks."

"Well, he better take her seriously," replied Poppet, thoughtfully. "Wren has changed since our days at the palace; she's stronger, more serious, and maybe harder somehow."

"Yes, she is," agreed the Wastrel, then realizing his mistake said, "I mean from what you've told me about your time there."

Poppet frowned. The Wastrel had changed too, since he'd met Wren. His accent was different, and he didn't joke as much. The Wastrel had taken a serious turn himself.

CHAPTER THIRTY-ONE

A Limited Skill Set

Kemp proved to be a charming, intelligent dinner companion. Wren felt herself relaxing for the first time in weeks. It was so good to talk to someone who had read the classics, the primers her granpapa had read to her each night as a child. They discussed *The Art of War*, *The Brothers Karamazov* and the *1962 Rambler Technical Service Manual*, the latter she assumed was some kind of literary travel guide. She hadn't read it, but it was obviously a great work. She pretended she'd read and enjoyed it along with other works they had in common.

"So, your granpapa was a teacher and primer-keeper," said Kemp. "What a coincidence! Mine was too. I inherited his books, but I couldn't be a teacher, not when I discovered I had this talent. Transmogrifee is a great joy, the culmination of everything you are and everything you can create out of your life. From the first time I changed a stone into a butterfly, I was hooked, and I never looked back."

"How old were you?"

"Five, I think."

"That's amazing. I've never been able to do anything like that."

Kemp looked at her with pity on his face. "It's possible you just have a block. I've heard of it before. Sometimes it happens in those who have a trauma in their childhood. They appear talentless, then one day, the dam breaks and all that pent-up creativity comes gushing out."

"I don't think I have a dam to break. If I have any talent at all, it's for destruction, not creation. Instead of encouraging change, I inhibit it, and I can only do that with the abacusian."

"Hmm," he said, taking another sip of the excellent merlot he'd poured for them after a delightful dinner that had consisted of pheasant with goldenbell shrooms and goosefoot salad.

"We will look at this device tomorrow. I'm sure we can figure it out."

Wren was encouraged by his confidence. Maybe he really could get more out of the thing than she had. The thought of giving up the responsibility for it was more than a little bit tempting. She felt the weight of it on her shoulders. How good would it feel to cast if off, to be free of this overwhelming burden? But could she trust someone else to make those decisions? Mala and Teeka wanted her to obliterate the drakyn, every last one of them. What would that do to the balance? She sensed a grave danger there. Even if she couldn't yet define it, she felt it looming, as if something much worse than the drakyn was just waiting, ready to rush in to fill the void. What if the next person to use the abacusian wanted to eliminate a rival, or a lover who'd rejected them? What if Poppet, in his despair over not having talent, decided to take the talent away from everyone else?

The possibilities for disaster were endless. Perhaps the device was better off with her, someone with no talent and no one to hate, really. She couldn't even hate Semli, though she wanted to. All she could feel for him was pity. And then there was Kodo. She didn't know how to feel about him. She should have betrayed him to her friends, and then to Kemp, but hadn't. She was horribly confused. The good she'd felt in the Wastrel had been real, she knew that. Maybe Kodo *had* changed. Or maybe he would betray them all and it would be her fault.

"Lost in thought?" asked Kemp.

"Sorry. I'm afraid I'm a little tired. It's been a long slog getting here."

"Oh, of course! Where are my manners? I asked Seleen to prepare you a warm bath before bed. She's excellent at heating water, but I'm afraid not good at much else, poor woman."

"Oh, thank you!" gushed Wren sincerely. "A bath would be so wonderful. I feel like the road dust has replaced my skin."

"Well, it still looks quite lovely to me. Your skin, that is."

Wren wondered if Kemp was flirting with her. Surely a man like this would have a lover–or two–or maybe one in every camp. Surely, he would pick someone with talent, someone who could bring her unique abilities to their bed. She decided he was being polite and ignored his compliment.

Kemp showed her to a large tent where, to her amazement, she would be the only occupant.

Seleen proved to be both burly and maternal. Her biceps bulged as she poured cold water into the metal tub. As she closed her eyes, the water began to steam before it even touched the surface. Her stout body and deep brown eyes exuded a sense of warmth and safety.

Swishing her hand in the water, she said, "Come in, child, the temperature's just about perfect. But look at you, he let you dine without first washing off the grime of the road?"

"Well, I did wash up first—"

"And look at these clothes! Why are you dressed like a boy? No, I take that back, like a lost boy who's been to gardamn hell and back."

"Actually, that's a fairly accurate description of the last couple weeks," said Wren dryly.

"We'll do something about that. When I was a girl, there was this..."

Wren stopped listening as she stripped off her filthy clothes and sank into the delicious, silken joy that was hot water. It was perhaps her favorite thing in the whole world. She guessed that you couldn't really appreciate it unless you'd grown up with it being a rare event, a treat better than the finest dessert.

"Ahhh..."

"It's good to find someone who appreciates my talents, m'lady."

"Appreciate it? Are you kidding? If I leaned that way, I'd ask you to marry me!"

Seleen turned away, and Wren could tell by the bunching of her shoulders that something was wrong.

"Oh, Seleen, I didn't mean to offend you—"

"You didn't," said the large woman in a small voice. "You just reminded me of my partner, Geery."

"I'm so sorry. Was he killed in the challenges?"

Seleen gave her a suffering look, and Wren immediately regretted her curiosity.

"No, she was a victim of what Kemp calls 'collateral damage.'"

"So, she was caught in the crossfire of one of Kemp's challenges? That's sad. I'm so sorry."

Seleen said no more on the subject, but Wren vowed to find out more about what had happened to Geery.

The next day, she found clothes befitting a princess on a chair beside her bed. Her old clothes were gone, and Seleen was nowhere to be found, so she had to wear the new ones. She didn't like how the gray dress impeded her movements, and she wondered how the long white duster that went with it would stay white with her wearing it.

Her grungy boots had been replaced with slippers that would be worthless if she had to flee or fight.

With a heavy sigh, she pulled back the flap on her tent and met her first day in the camp of the resistance.

The first thing she heard was the distressed sounds of Grakt as he spoke to several soldiers who had surrounded the abacusian.

Hurrying to his side, she found that Kemp was already there. Kodo and the others either hadn't risen yet or had found something more interesting than her and her "act" to follow.

Grakt was saying, "No, this is not a weapon, at least not as you think of them."

"What's the handle for then?" asked one of them.

A slight, compact woman asked, "How does it fire?"

"It does not–Ah, Wren, I am so glad you are here to demonstrate."

"OK," said Kemp, raising his arms to shoo his people away. "Clear out and give us some room to work. It isn't a circus."

Not yet, anyway, thought Wren.

To Grakt, he said, "I've seen some of the inventions you people have developed; pretty impressive for a species without any talent at all."

Grakt bristled. "I assure you that we have many talents—"

"Grakt," said Wren, "he doesn't mean anything by it. Shall we show him how it works?"

Grakt just nodded. In his best professorial voice, he began, "I have placed a princeling salamander in the cage here. As you know the princeling salamander can change colors using a primitive form of transmogrifee. Wren will demonstrate her ability to block the act of transmogrifee. To demonstrate her power even over our science, I will now input the formula to change this creature to another. I am going to use the code for a hairy desert frog. It is a simple formula." Grakt referred to one of his primers that, as Wren had learned, contained the genetrical formulas for many different species.

Wren's head buzzed and she felt the heat starting in her forehead. Calming her mind, she reached for the black handle. She was a little late grabbing it and the poor salamander struggled, half of him frog and half salamander. Wren quickly returned him to his firstform and stepped away from the abacusian.

"That doesn't prove anything," said Kemp in a chiding tone. "How do we know the machine did anything–that you did anything but a little simple transmogering?"

Grakt nodded. "Of course, you need to see it for yourself. Wren will now prevent you from transmogering the salamander." He nodded toward her, but she had a bad feeling about using the abacusian against Kemp. He was so proud. Realizing that they had to show him how it worked, one way or another, she grabbed the black handle again, concentrating hard.

Kemp waved his arms with a flourish, an actor on his favorite stage. He turned back to the machine and the watchers were surprised when nothing happened.

He tried again, more urgency in his movements now. Sweat broke out on his brow.

"What the—"

"As you can see," said Grakt, "she is able to completely mute the effects of your transmogrifee. As far as we know, she can do it with anyone. She is also able to return a creature to its firstform. She can control an individual, as in this case, or the entire species. All she needs is a specimen, blood, or tissue, from a drakyn and she should be able to control them all, prevent them from transmogering. We're not yet sure how long the effects will last, but if she has access to the machine, she will be in control. I guess, in her way, she is a transmogrifer, at least with the abacusian to aid her, but with a level of power that no transmogrifer has ever displayed."

Wren noticed that Grakt didn't mention her destruction of an entire species when she'd killed off all the grub moths. She was infinitely grateful for this. Grakt knew that she didn't want to use that option on the drakyn, if there was any way to avoid it.

Kemp looked stunned. "Are you trying to tell me—"

"Sir," said Grakt, "I have been trying to explain this to you all morning."

Kemp turned to Wren. "And you can return any transmogrifer to their firstform?"

"Yes," she replied. "Even you, were you to take another shape. I could show you—"

"No!" he cried, then said more softly, "No, no, that won't be necessary. I see the power in this thing. Let me try it."

"OK," she began, "I'll show you—"

"I think I can figure it out," he said curtly as he shouldered her out of the way to stand before the machine. He took the black handle.

After a few minutes, he stepped back, asking in a deadly voice, "What kind of game are you two playing?"

"What game?" asked Wren, truly confused by his reaction.

"There is nothing. There is no power in this thing, yet you, *you* can do something that no one should be able to do. The power must be in you, not in the abacusian. Why are you deceiving us?"

"No, Kemp, it's not like that. It was a miracle that we even discovered this. I had hoped that you would be able to take over for me. With your great skill. Now I see that won't be possible. If I am the only one who can wield this thing, then so be it. Don't you see what this will mean for the resistance? The war will be over!"

Kemp looked at her, his eyes revealing the battle going on behind them. Finally, he took a deep breath and said, "Of course, yes, that is our goal, isn't it, to stop the drakyn in their tracks. If you're successful, there will be no more need for the resistance. We will be free to...live ordinary lives."

Kemp continued after a minute of thinking, "You and this device must be hidden. No one else is to know about this. I have feared spies in our camp for some time now. We are all in mortal danger. This one who attacked you at the river, what if he lives? He and others will be coming for you. If the drakyn realize the power of this weapon, they will do everything they can to stop you. They will send spies to infiltrate the camps, to find you and assassinate you, and if that fails, they will abandon the challenges and come at us in their full force and fury. They have been playing at war so far. If they find out about you, they will attack with deadly intent to destroy us all. Will one of us be able to get the specimen you need before that? And if we fail, will you defend us against the entire drakyn nation, if they come for us *en masse*?"

She didn't know the answer to that, but the hairs standing on end on her arms spoke to the terror she was feeling.

CHAPTER THIRTY-TWO

Hubris, Thy Name is Drakyn

To his infinite frustration, Semli was unable to get an audience with the new queen, Akriast. He'd even told her attendants that the very existence of the drakyn race hung in the balance, but they had only sniggered at him in derision. Even the end of life as they knew it was not enough to pull the stupid female away from her endless courtly duties, cotillions, and tea parties.

In the end, he went with the only option left to him, deception. Though the frilly regency-era dress itched, and the corset had obviously been designed by that skragling genius whom he idolized, the Marquis de Sade.

"Frella, you look exquisite this evening," said Akriast, "such detail. I haven't seen this level of artistry since Semli left for the front."

"Forget him," said Frella quickly, "there's something we need to discuss. The skraglings have invented a weapon that—"

"The skraglings are always inventing *a weapon*," interrupted the queen in disgust. "Remember when Goslin was in such an uproar over this new thing which turned out to be nothing but a sword with feet. It was supposed to sneak into our camps in the middle of the night and what? Trim our toes?"

"This is different."

Akriast stopped on the path, eyeing her companion critically.

"All right, Semli, you can drop the disguise. I'd know you any-where."

"Yes, Your Majesty. This dress is a little tight."

The queen sighed and said, "Just tell me what this weapon is and what you want from the crown."

"This time, it's the real thing. The dageki have developed a device that can transmoger for them. They are collaborating with a skragling who possesses unusual powers. She can block the act of transmogrifee and even return her opponents to their firstform. Were it not for my immense talent, I might have been permanently locked in mine. I only managed to escape because of Kodo's weakness. He hesitated to kill me, and for that I will destroy him. Right now, this skragling is the only one who can wield the device. She is small and weak and untrained in its use. We need to eliminate her and the machine now, before she gains more abilities or they find others who can use this machine against us, or, in the worst case, the dageki have time to create more of these things they call abacusians."

"Semli, if any of this is true—"

"Unfortunately, it is all true, Your Majesty."

"Then why didn't you kill her yourself?"

"Kodo prevented me."

"Kodo, Kodo, always a thorn in your side is this brother of yours, eh? Our former emperor? What was Jelebron thinking? I wonder if your familial ties do not stay your hand when it comes to him."

"Not at all," growled Semli from between gritted teeth. "The next time I see him, he will die."

Akriast was silent for a while as they walked the palace garden, its bright spring blooms at odds with Semli's dark thoughts. His gaze flitted around the idyllic scene, not really seeing any of it.

"This seems a trifling matter to me," she said. "Not even the dageki aligned with skraglings could hope to threaten our mastery of the transmogering arts and our iron control of this world. I will assign three of our best warriors to assist you. Your mission is to eliminate this skragling and her toy, and Kodo if he stands in your way."

"Th–three?" stuttered Semli.

"What, too many?"

"Your Highness, you are underestimating the threat this thing poses to drakynkind."

"Remember your place, male. It is not your purview to judge what the crown estimates to be a threat. If anything, I have overestimated the danger here. With these three warriors, you will galvanize the fighters we have in the mountains into an overwhelming force to use against these upstarts. Now leave me, before I grow impatient with your whining."

Semli slunk away, the long white train of his dress gathering mud, while his spirits sunk even lower.

CHAPTER THIRTY-THREE

Humanity Becomes You

"I wish to change my firstform to human–permanently."

"Is that even possible?" asked Wren. Kodo had led them to the edge of camp to discuss something important, or so he'd said. Was this one of the Wastrel's jokes?

"I believe that with your help, and the power of the abacusian, we could do it."

"So, you know all about the device, huh?"

"News travels fast in camp, plus, I eavesdropped on your little conversation with Kemp."

Wren relaxed, just a bit. "Well, I guess that proves your loyalty. If you wanted to destroy it, or me, you would have done so already."

Kodo looked hurt. "You don't really believe I would cause you harm, do you?"

Wren had to consider that. "When we first met, yes, but I must admit that you've changed. I didn't believe that people could change their basic nature, at least after the age of about four, but maybe drakyn are different."

"Not much, I'm afraid, but I have had a unique set of experiences, even for a drakyn, and my time as the Wastrel changed me even more."

"So, you're serious about this firstform change?"

"Yes, completely."

Wren thought about making a decision like that. Could she choose not to be human?

"How can you make that decision?"

"It's time. The truth is that I've been human for a long time, in here." He pointed to his own chest.

"And how will you accomplish this? Steal another body, like you did this one?"

"No, and I told you, the Wastrel was dying. There is a man here, just a boy really. He too is dying, this time of the transmogrifer's disease. He doesn't have long. The errant growth within him is taking his young life, a bit at a time. I'd like you to meet him."

"No, there's no way—"

"Please, Wren. We could save him. He would become a part of me, and me him, and the Wastrel would survive too. If we act soon, much more of him will remain than what I was able to salvage from the Wastrel. Please, just talk to him. His name is Trey. He's in the med tent."

"Does he know what you plan for him?"

"Yes, at least what he believes the Wastrel has planned for him. They knew each other. I guess the Wastrel was a bit of a mentor to him. They were friends."

"And the Wastrel, what becomes of his consciousness—and his body?"

"The Wastrel's consciousness will become a part of the new human we create. His body will have to disappear. He's a bit of a wanderer, you know, so he will decide to leave and continue his adventures alone. Poppet will understand that."

"Eventually, yes," said Wren, her thoughts in turmoil.

She told Kodo she would have to think about it, and indeed that was all she thought about for several days. When she couldn't resist any longer, she went to see the ailing soldier for herself.

The field hospital was an unmarked tent, that nonetheless announced its presence by its unique odor, a combination of disinfectant and death. Most of the injured she passed as she entered bore superficial wounds from accidents or injuries and deformities inflicted in the challenges.

At the back of the tent were a few beds reserved for the long-term sufferers of the transmogrifee disease, the name given a group of afflictions that took different forms, some highly visible, like the man with four arms, two of which were so resistant to removal that they grew back within seconds of being transmogered away.

In Trey's case, the disease had taken a more deadly form, an invisible disorder that affected his lungs, and that would inevitably lead to a miserable, protracted death, or so she'd been informed by the medic who pointed him out to her.

Wren was surprised to find Trey sitting up in bed, juggling three apples simultaneously. She wasn't so much surprised that he could juggle; Wren had tried it a few times and found it challenging but doable, with practice. But she knew that juggling while sitting was much more difficult, as you didn't have your whole body to adjust for the small errors you inevitably made. Trey wasn't making any errors. He must have exceptional coordination and focus.

He had a farm boy's fresh face, with a slightly bulbous nose and full lips. His eyebrows and hair were curly masses of gold.

Golden, of course. That's probably why Kodo chose you, to hide his stripe.

He saw her and looked up, his already bright features taking on a joyful radiance at seeing her.

"Hello, you must be Wren." His voice was mellow and had just a hint of amusement in every word, as if life were a subtle joke to him. "I'm Trey. Duo said you might be stopping by to see me."

"Yes, but we call him the Wastrel."

"Ha! Yes, I've heard him called that. He doesn't like it, though."

"I guess that's why we do it."

Laughing, Trey deftly gathered the balls in one hand and set them beside him on the bed.

Only then did Wren notice the bloody handkerchief crumpled on the blanket beside him. He saw her expression turn sad.

"Yah, 'fraid my days are numbered, and it's not a large number. I'm good right now. Clemper just administered my daily medicinal transmogering. Ironic, isn't it? That the only thing keeping me alive is what's given me the sickness in the first place. The more I take the 'cure,' the deader I get."

"I'm sorry."

"Don't be. I did what I loved. A lot of us don't live past thirty, you know. Some of the best of us."

"I've heard that." How could she deny this man the chance at life? His open, accepting expression was enough for her to decide right then, as Kodo had probably known she would, *the bastart!*

"But Duo, he has an idea," he continued, "I'm not sure I can believe it, or maybe I don't want to risk believing it."

She said slowly, "It may be possible. I don't want to get your hopes up, but he has more transmogering ability than anyone I've ever seen"–now was not the time to mention the even more talented Semli–"and I have a device that we may be able to use to—"

"To give me a new life, of sorts."

"Yes, but right now, it's a long shot. We've just begun to experiment with the possibility. I've never tried to create something with the abacusian, I've only used it to block transmogering. With that power I could probably pause your illness—"

"No!" said Trey with bitter certainty in his voice, "I've always been a doer. I can't spend my life in a state of suspended death. I want to live, whatever form that may take."

Wren was silent, staring at her new friend. He knew what he wanted.

"You would be sharing your consciousness with—no, that's not quite right—you would become a new personality, a combination of three, though Duo assures me that yours would be the dominant one. Are you up for that?"

"For a chance to live? To run again? To practice the bo staff and feel the sun on my face? Yes, of course I'm up for it!"

"OK," she said, rising to leave. "We've got a lot of work to do yet to make it happen, and not much time. I can't promise you anything, but we'll do our best."

"It doesn't matter. Don't worry about me. Whatever happens, I'll be free of this bed. That's all I desire."

Wren left the medics tent, her thoughts in turmoil. She wished she'd never gone in there. Now she'd met Trey and, as Kodo had foreseen, she couldn't let him down. She had to try.

CHAPTER THIRTY-FOUR

Change is in the Wind

K odo described it as tacking.

"Have you ever sailed without a sailfish?"

"Not something a farmgirl usually gets the opportunity to do–with or without a sailfish."

"I'll explain the concept to you, if I can. Tacking into the wind is the act of going forward, using the power of the wind that blows against you along with the angle of your keel to propel you forward."

"Sounds impossible."

"It would be, if the sailor didn't go at it obliquely. You can't face the wind head on, you can only approach at thirty-five or forty-five degrees at most. Then you tack as far in one direction as you can, then switch directions and go at it again from the new angle. The zig-zag pattern is called 'beating.' It works, trust me. I've been sailing since I was little. We compete every year in the annual drakyn regatta. At least we did."

"So, how does that apply to the abacusian? Do we sail it out to sea?"

"No, silly. I plan to tack against your ability to halt an act of transmogrifee. To lock Trey and me together permanently. Timing is the important thing. Too soon and we'll both be torn apart, too late and the Wastrel and I will die, and Trey too, from his disease."

"You don't ever make anything easy, do you?"

"I know we can do it. You've met Trey, you know he's all in, no matter what happens."

"I can understand Trey. He has nothing to lose, but you could lose everything, your very consciousness, your firstform–everything. I just don't understand why you'd take this risk."

Kodo looked as if he was about to say one thing, then changed his mind and said instead, "Eventually, perhaps you will understand what motivates me, but maybe you never will, because unlike me, you haven't squandered your time on this planet. You've spent your life so far caring for others. You think things through, consider how your actions will affect everyone and the balance that we must maintain if any of us wish to survive in the long-term. Always selfless. For me, this will be my last chance to be selfless too, to step out of the façade that I have fabricated and called a life. To step into my true self, whatever that may be. It's my chance to truly live, and I will do anything to make it happen. If I don't succeed at this, it's just better that Kodo fades from memory."

"And the Wastrel?"

"He wasted his life, as surely as I did, at first in the wars and then in his slow alcohol-soaked decline into forgetfulness. I merely interrupted his tedious and painful suicide by drink to give him a few more years. Now there's a chance for him to try again, to spend more time laughing and loving. This time around, I think his humanity will truly shine."

Wren thought she was beginning to understand. She sensed that Kodo was holding something back, but she could leave him his little secrets. Didn't she have her own?

"All right," she said firmly. "Let's do this, but we must prepare. We'll practice on an inanimate object until the timing is perfect. I don't want to fail because we didn't practice enough. I don't want to take unnecessary chances. Four lives hang in the balance."

Kodo's face erupted in a wide grin of relief, then he realized that she'd said "four lives."

"Four?"

"Yes," she said quietly. "I couldn't live with myself if I fail the three of you."

Their practice was delayed one morning, when Grakt came to her at dawn with news. She was just about to sneak out to meet Kodo before breakfast, when a shadow grew outside her tent.

"Ah–hem."

"What is it, Grakt?" She would recognize that massive form and distinctive voice anywhere.

"I need to speak with you."

Wren stepped outside. If Grakt was surprised that she was fully dressed so early, he didn't show it. The sun was peeking through the trees on the horizon and a chill stilled the camp. Sparkling jewels of dew dotted the tents.

Grakt began hesitantly, "I received a flet last night."

"A flet?"

"A messenger flet. We don't instill the message transmographically in the mind of the flet, as do the drakyn, of course. We simply wrap a flexible glass note around one of their tiny legs."

"How do they find you?"

"Several were imprinted with the sound of my voice and scent before I left Dmisi. Flets have amazing long-range sensory abilities, even superior to dageki."

When Grakt hesitated, Wren asked, "What did it say, Grakt? Out with it."

Grakt spluttered, the dageki equivalent of a sigh. "Mageki Kyni Gouzuni has developed a countering agent to the shambolika. I have been recalled to the capitol to head the expedition to free our people from the farms, but I do not want to go right now, with so much hanging in the balance here."

Wren didn't want him to go either, but she said, "Grakt, you must go, you know that. As much as I want you here, we need to save everyone from the farms, as soon as possible, before more die."

"Yes, that has weighed on me too. Will you be alright on your own? I will leave the abacusian with you, of course."

"It's no problem. I have the others to help me. When will you leave?"

"I will pack now and be ready to begin my journey tomorrow morning."

"Then we will have a going-away dinner for you tonight."

"That is not necessary. The complete ritual is thirteen days and there is no time for that."

"Grakt, it's only an evening. We don't know when we'll be together again. It's just human to want to say goodbye."

"All right," said Grakt, "we will do it the human way."

"This is perfect," said Kodo later, when they met in the woods for practice with the abacusian. "The Wastrel will leave with Grakt tomorrow. It'll be the perfect time for him to disappear."

"But we're not ready."

"Yes, we are. We've practiced this until we could do it in our sleep."

"That doesn't make it any easier."

"Wren, stop putting this off. We're ready. Let's meet back here before Grakt leaves in the morning. I'll sneak Trey out of the medical tent."

Reluctantly, Wren agreed. She couldn't admit that she was terrified.

When they met in the pre-dawn, Trey looked exhausted and excited at the same time. Kodo showed no emotion, except casual indifference.

"What did Grakt say when you told him it was just a ruse, the Wastrel leaving with him?"

Kodo snorted. "That dageki is smarter than he looks."

"What do you mean?" asked Wren, suddenly worried.

"He figured out who I was and even what we were up to. He wished me luck."

"That's amazing. I wonder how he figured it out."

"He said he'd known I was Kodo as soon as I returned from the battle with Semli, and apparently we haven't been secretive enough about our practices out here."

"I hope no one else has Grakt's reasoning abilities."

"I think we're safe. This will soon be over, and no one will be the wiser."

To Trey he asked, "Are you ready, son?"

Trey gave a mock salute and said, "Ready and willing, sir. Let's get this over with."

Wren only hoped it would be as quick and easy as the other two thought. They had practiced it to death with inanimate objects, but a living, breathing subject was another matter.

Marshalling her courage, she stepped up to the machine. It stood at eye level on the ingenious wheeled wooden stand that Poppet and the camp carpenter had fashioned for her. Kodo and Trey both placed a hand on the metal cage.

"Remember," she said, "don't begin the transmogrifee until I give the signal. First, I'll return Trey to his firstform, removing the disease from his body at the same instant that—"

"Yes, I know," said Kodo, sounding bored. "We've been over this a hundred times."

Frustrated with his ability to take everything so casually, Wren fumed, then realized that it was the last thing she needed to do right now.

Just relax.

She pulled the worry stone from her pocket and concentrated on the two images in her mind, separating Trey's energy from the others. She found the errors in the visual formula before her and corrected them as easily as erasing unwanted lines from a pencil drawing.

She heard a sharp intake of breath as Trey realized that his illness was gone. She knew it wouldn't last. After Semli, their experiments had shown that the effects of the abacusian had a time limit. If she wanted to keep his illness at bay, she would need to keep repeating this procedure, over and over, until it too eventually failed. He would succumb to his disease in the end anyway. If Kodo could transmoger at just the right time and in just the right way, he could turn her ability to destroy into an ability to create. Tacking against the wind. Then if she could bind them together at just the right instant. If, if, if. She had to stop thinking and just let it happen.

Kodo began his transmogery. The two men began to stretch and deform as two became one. Everything was going as planned until Trey began to scream. One thing they hadn't counted on was the self, and its overwhelming desire to continue being. Despite his conscious desire to do this, Trey's animal self fought it tooth and claw. None of the inanimate objects they had practiced on could have taught them this lesson. Her head began to burn with throbbing pain, and she could feel the effort that Kodo exerted to hold it all together. He couldn't continue like this for much longer, she saw.

In her desperation, an idea came to her. Unsure if it would work, she sent an image to the struggling soldier. Suddenly, juggling balls appeared in her mind, revolving in her invisible hands. Quickly, she tossed them to Trey, and out of habit, he grabbed for them, balancing them in a perfect arch in his mind as he'd done in his bed. It gave Kodo the instant he needed to complete the transformation. As he did, she used all her skill and energy to force the new being into its firstform—its newly minted firstform. After that, her memories were a blur. She felt herself releasing her hold on the abacusian, but then the ground came up at her at a dizzying rate and it hit her hard, knocking the consciousness from her.

She woke staring up into the pines. Birds flitted about in the branches and sunlight trickled through. A gently breeze had the trees talking softly, but all else was silence. Her head hurt.

"Are you rejoining us, then?"

Wren turned her head quickly at the sound and regretted it. "Ouch. Yes, I'm fine."

Kodo as the Wastrel was gone. She looked at Trey and was almost afraid to ask. "Are–are Kodo and Duo and—?"

"We're all here, but it doesn't really feel like that. It's more like being reborn with more knowledge and memories than I should have. It's a little confusing, but I think it will be become easier over time."

"Then you think we achieved it, a permanent firstform?"

"Yes, I believe so. Thank you, Wren. You saved my life–our lives."

"Oh, it was nothing," she answered dryly.

Chapter Thirty-Five

The Battle Within

Wren was beginning to wonder if the drakyn really were planning an attack, as Kemp had said. His advance camps and scouts had so far seen nothing unusual. Knowing that Semli would eventually recover from the effects of the abacusian left her certain that he would come for her again. The bastart just didn't give up.

She'd been kept busy helping the injured soldiers, who had heard about Trey's miraculous recovery. She tried to explain that what the abacusian did was only temporary, but she'd found herself unable to extinguish the hope in their eyes, so she did what she could for them.

Mala too had volunteered her healing services and had met a medic who was willing to teach her what he knew. Despite the dire nature of some of the injuries, she applied herself with her usual positivity and warmth, and Wren could see the soldiers' eyes light up whenever she entered the medic's tent.

Teeka had joined the group of cooks and was soon running the entire staff with her no-nonsense, dictatorial style.

Poppet had been aimless at first, unsure of what he would do in the camp, but eventually his industrious nature had won him a home with the men who maintained the day-to-day functions of the camp and had met a man who volunteered to teach him carpentry. Oswald was a squat, powerful man with black hair and calm brown eyes. Having no transmogering ability had been a handicap for Poppet at first, but the carpenter had found it useful to delegate the easier jobs to Poppet, thus saving himself the strain of using his talent on simple tasks. Poppet was losing some of his teenage clumsiness and was taking to his new craft with diligence and energy.

Trey's exuberance knew no bounds. Today he was teaching a group of would-be transmogrifers his bo staff technique, demonstrating basic moves and stances and what he called the bo staff kata. Each of his students had a make-shift bo staff, some of which were nothing more than a trimmed alder branch. Wren watched from a distance so as not to distract him.

"What's a kata?" asked a stout woman with an intent gaze who might have been in her early twenties.

"Kata means form," explained Trey patiently. "The kata is used to memorize and perfect the moves you will use in battle."

"But surely you won't use these exact moves in this order in the heat of battle," she commented, her tone skeptical.

"Of course not," replied Trey, "but the moves will become a part of your body, so that it will remember them quickly when they're needed. Plus, the practice will teach you focus and concentration, something every transmogrifer must possess in spades when entering a challenge."

Then he went step-by-step through the set up and moves.

"First, grip the staff in thirds. Be sure the weight is evenly distributed. Feel the balance This hand palm up and this one palm down, like so."

Then he demonstrated the most common stances, long front stance, equine stance, and cat stance. Wren really liked the last one. The cat stance was very light. About eighty percent of your weight was on the back leg, with your front foot lightly touching the ground. When she tried it herself, it felt like she was poised to pounce, like a cat. She also liked the equine stance. The fighter stood with knees bent and legs apart, as if riding an equine. It felt silly at first, but she could see how much power and stability it created.

Trey then demonstrated some common strikes.

"Here is the overhead front strike: Bring up your front knee, rest the bo on the right shoulder. The bo should be parallel to the ground. Step into a long front stance, rotate your forward hand, twisting the wrist, and sliding the left hand down to the 'pocket,' like so. The bo staff will come forward with incredible force, if executed correctly." As he demonstrated, the students gasped as one and stepped back.

"Now let's do the four-point strike. It consists of an up-down, side-to-side motion, like this. Make sure all strikes hit the same spot, and keep your elbows parallel to the ground, stay in a strong, long front stance." He demonstrated once more.

"Here is the overhead rib strike," he continued. "Start in an equine stance, bring your arms up over your head, and finish by swinging the front tip of the bo across, slamming the opposite end of the bo into your own rib. Be careful at first, I've seen someone break their own rib with a little too much enthusiasm." A few students laughed at this.

"Now, let's do the front thrust: Bring up your front knee, draw back the bo all the way in a straight line behind you, then step out into a deep long front stance and thrust the tip of the bo into your enemy."

"Lastly, here is the uppercut. It's much like the boxing move but draw the bo under. This will create a curving motion. Finish in the cat stance."

Trey then showed them a kata based on the stances and moves he'd just taught them. Each move flowed into the other, creating an intricate dance. It really was a joy to watch.

Wren was amazed by the power Trey generated with these moves. She heard his clothing snap and felt the bo smashing with great force on contact with his invisible foe. What looked like a simple exercise was obviously a deadly maneuver in the right hands.

One of the students asked, "But how do we use this in a challenge? I have yet to see any transmogrifee."

"Ah," said Trey, "I was just getting to that. This is where we add the next level. The actual transmogrifees are obviously up to your individual talent and preferences, but here are just a few. You might want to stand back."

Trey closed his eyes and his body stilled completely, making him a statue for a few seconds, then he began to move.

He thrust forward, using the overhead front strike, but as the bo was about to hit his imaginary opponent, the bo grew in length with incredible speed and force. It struck the air a good twenty feet above him with a resounding crack.

The students emitted a low "oohh" sound.

Then he demonstrated the overhead rib strike, but this time, when the staff came around, the tip formed a giant hammer that came down with incredible force. This would have knocked his opponent into the ground with the power it released. Indeed, the tip of the hammer buried itself deep in the ground.

When Trey signaled that he was done, Wren could tell that the students were impressed, as they surrounded him eagerly, drilling him with questions.

She knew that with the transmogering genius of Kodo, Trey could do much more than these relatively simple feats, but she was grateful that he was wise enough not to show the full gamut of his new abilities too soon.

That evening at dinner, Kemp was quiet and withdrawn.

"Is something bothering you tonight? You've been very quiet," she said as he poured her another glass of chardonnay. This time, Trey and several of his lieutenants shared the table.

He said nothing for a moment. "I'm not sure. Something feels off. It may be as I feared, we have not had a challenge from the drakyn since your group arrived."

"Is that unusual?"

"We should have heard from them by now. Something is going on. I believe they're marshalling their forces for a different kind of attack, a mass attack."

"Then we need to develop a battle plan to address that possibility," said Trey. "Wren, how are we going to incorporate your abacusian in the heat of such a battle? My guess is that it will be mayhem."

Kemp said, "I have already assigned a group of four to go to Wren's side and guard her when the battle begins. They will protect her in her tent until one of the fighters can deliver a sample of drakyn blood or tissue."

"Will four be enough to keep her safe?"

"I can't spare more. Even a few drakyn will be an overwhelming force. If we all fail, it won't do her any good."

"Unless we can get a specimen to her quickly, then she'll be able to hold them all in their firstform until we can dispatch them."

"That is the plan."

Wren looked at them in growing concern. She knew what happened to the best-laid plans of mice and men. Right then she wished she could be a mouse and hide under the bed until it was all over.

Their fears were realized the next day, when Semli and his forces attacked. It was total confusion. Wren was in her tent, getting ready to face the day, when she heard shouts and the sounds of frantic movement and running feet. She stepped out of her tent to a bizarre scene. The sky was filled with writhing shapes. Screeching cries echoed through the trees. The soldiers who had been assigned to her appeared at a run, forcing her back into the tent before she could take in much more of the wild scene.

"But I need to see!" she screamed at them.

"No," said one of her burly, six-foot enforcers, who happened to be a woman. "You must stay safe. You're the key to this battle, in case you've forgotten."

"No, of course not. It's just—I can't wait in here, not knowing what's going on out there."

"Believe me," said another, "you're better off not seeing what goes on out there."

A few miserably minutes passed, and the screams grew louder and more frantic, truncated by grunts and thuds. No warrior came to her tent with the drakyn blood she needed. She was about to make a break for the tent door, when Trey appeared there, covered in blood. She couldn't tell whose blood, but by the state he was in, she reasoned that most of it was his. She cried out, "Are you OK?"

"I'm fine," said Trey, his voice thin but determined. Then his eyes rolled back in his head. As he fell, he reached a hand toward her, but his downward motion pulled the object he proffered from her grasp. The object took to the air, floating gently as he went down hard. She knelt over Trey to try to help him, but the others pulled her away, pointing.

On the floor of her tent lay a feather.

One said, "He wouldn't have brought this in if it were not of the enemy." Another said, "Please, Wren, you must concentrate! The battle rests on you now. Forget Trey."

Easier said than done.

"The medics will care for him, if any medics survive," he added quietly.

Pulling herself away from Trey was the hardest thing Wren had ever done. If he died, she would not only lose Trey, but the Wastrel and Kodo, too. It was almost impossible to concentrate with her fear for him and the others yammering at her, but she pulled the worry stone from her pocket and forced herself into the right frame of mind. Nothing happened. She cried out in panic. The sounds of the battle filled her already suffering ears. The thought of Trey dying, the thought of Poppet or Mala or Teeka, suffering and dying. It was more than she could handle.

Then Trey was beside her, his bloody hand on hers. "Forget us," he croaked. "Forget us so you can do what you need to do."

His look broke her heart. How could he be so strong when she was so weak?

Pulling up her last reserves of strength, she managed a modicum of calm. The sounds of the battle demanded less of her consciousness.

When she at last felt ready, she touched the black handle of the abacusian.

What she saw brought her to the point of unseeing rage. This was not Semli's blood, but it didn't matter. It belonged to a female drakyn warrior, one of their strongest. She'd already killed five humans, had almost killed Trey. Her transmogering talent was immense. The second the human transmogrifers thought they had her cornered, she would rise up in a new, more deadly form, a sphynx, a giant bear, an eagle with the claws of a lion. She was unbeatable. Or she was until she met her match in Wren.

This time, she knew she couldn't limit her power to just one of the drakyn, as she'd done with Semli. If she was going to end this fight, then all the drakyn would need to be returned to their firstform. She didn't have the time or ability to pick out just the ones who battled here. All drakyn everywhere would need to be changed. She felt the immense power that would be required to do this, and her head buzzed and burned from the strain. As when she'd killed off the grub moths, something broke inside her. She screamed as the power entered her and seared away her fear, tearing through it as easily as a paper lantern adrift in a hurricane.

The new Wren tossed the creature back into her firstform as easily as tossing off an errant whisp of hair. What she saw confounded her ideas of what a drakyn should look like in its firstform. She wondered why so many drakyn were being born deformed. This creature reminded her of Semli. It choked and stumbled, trapped within itself, in a cage of misery and deformity. Around this drakyn, the others also returned to their firstforms, and the tone of the battle changed. The drakyn in these fragile, clumsy forms were no match for the human warriors who remained.

Kemp cried out, a primitive but effective rallying cry. The humans surged forward following his lead with renewed vigor. They delivered quick deaths to the drakyn who remained. Soon all the drakyn were dead and the camp folded itself into the cries of the injured and the weeping of survivors.

Wren stepped from her tent and called frantically for a medic to help Trey. Mala ran forward with her supplies and Wren helplessly watched her minister to the fallen warrior. After a minute, Mala said, "He's going to be OK. Not all this blood is his, and he's a tough one."

Wren went out to survey the chaos and destruction. The dead lay among remnants of their camp, the injured and dying everywhere. She felt warm tears on her cheeks.

As she approached him, Kemp was stuffing something into the pocket of his coat, but in the stress of the moment, it didn't occur to her to wonder what it was.

"Are the enemy all dead?" she asked through her tears.

"All but for a couple who were able to escape before you returned them to their firstform. Drakyn are not known for their bravery."

Wren surveyed the camp again. The dead drakyn lay in heaps where they had fallen. She counted ten at most. Survivors were busy removing their heads and tossing them on a raging fire.

"Why are they doing that?" she asked, aghast at the grotesque sight.

"It is rumored that in the past, very talented drakyn could reanimate their fellows, unless the head or heart were removed and destroyed. Even then, they say that some of the great ones could bring them back to life with just a drop of blood."

Wren was thoughtful at learning this. "So, perhaps the power I am able to access with the abacusian also resided in some drakyn, or at least it did at one time."

Kemp gave her an odd look but said nothing.

"Is something else still bothering you?" she asked.

"It just seems like there were too few of them. This was by no means the full force of the drakyn nation come to bear on us."

"Yes," she mused, "it does seem like too few, but look what damage these few were able to inflict on us."

As they surveyed the remnants of the drakyn, Kemp pointed to one grotesque heap of flesh. "I think this was Semli," he said. "He was badly deformed in his firstform, as you described him, but what a talent! It was all I could do to best him."

Wren didn't know what to feel about her arch enemy finally having been killed. Right now, she felt nothing but relief for the human fighters who had lived, and sorrow for those who had not.

Kemp asked, "Was your abacusian attack limited to just this group of drakyn?"

"I don't think so," she said. "I didn't have time for that. I believe that I sent all drakyn back to their firstforms."

"All drakyn," he said in awe. "No doubt, when they recover, they will now be motivated to move against us in larger numbers. Many will have died, especially those caught high in the air in their winged forms. Not even their queen will have been spared. They will be coming for you. This time, it'll be a much larger force, I have no doubt. What appears to be a victory may prove to be our undoing. I rue the day you brought that device into my camp."

Kemp stomped away, leaving Wren alone with her guilt and worry.

As she watched, the remaining injured human fighters were being carried to the medic's tent. The camp was in a shambles. After they had assessed the damage and the loss, Kemp brought her a list of the dead and missing. Two of her friends were unaccounted for. Both Poppet and Teeka.

Wren didn't believe this was a coincidence. Semli had known their value to her. Perhaps he had directed they be taken before his death. Were they hostages? She had to hope this was the case, and that her friends still lived, that they had not been killed out of revenge, or spite, or whatever vile tempers fueled the drakyn. Worried that they could have died when the drakyn who carried them had fallen, Kemp sent out scouts to search for them, but not a trace was found.

Chapter Thirty-Six

The Gypsy Jesters

Wren didn't have much time to worry about her lost friends in the next few days, as she was kept busy helping the wounded, burying the dead and restoring the camp. With Mala's help, Trey had recovered at a miraculous rate, no doubt helped along by the transmogering skills he'd inherited from Kodo and the Wastrel.

Not knowing how long it would take the drakyn to recover and launch another attack left everyone on edge. Wren knew she had to leave the camp, to take the danger away from the survivors, but Kemp disagreed.

"You're the most important weapon we have!" he yelled at her. "Do you think I'm gonna just let you wander off into the volcano lands alone? Are you crazy?"

"I won't be alone. Trey has agreed to go with me."

"Oh, great. Look, I agree that we need to move," he said a little more coolly. "They know our location now. But we'll move together. All of us."

"That won't work. We're too large a group. The drakyn will find us easily. Trey and I on our own can move quickly and quietly."

Kemp sat down gracelessly on a log by the fire and put his head in his hands.

"This weapon," he mumbled through his hands, "I wish you'd never brought it. We were winning this war."

"Were you really? It's gone on too long. You've lost too many of your best and most talented. They were just playing with us. You said so yourself."

"Yeah, well they're not gonna be playing anymore."

Wren said, "Before he left, Grakt and I were working on a way to make the abacusian effect last longer. I think that eventually, I may be able to sustain it."

"Sure. You've just got to survive until then, with the entire drakyn nation out to wipe you—and us—off the face of the planet! And when you're gone, do you think they'll go back to the gentleman's rules, as they call it? That the challenges will be enough for them after this?" He added quietly, as if talking to himself, "To spend my life perfecting this talent, only to have it end this way."

Wren was livid. "You're thinking about *yourself*, now? How you'll use your talent if not for war?"

"What do you know about talent? You. Have. None. In fact, if it weren't for that fruckin' machine, you'd be nothing."

"OK, Kemp, I think you need some rest."

Wren turned away, her face red, and ran into Trey, who pulled her after him, away from Kemp.

"Kemp is losing it," he said calmly.

"You heard that?"

"Yah, I've seen it before. They spend so much time on their craft, they start to lose contact with reality, whatever that is."

She gave him a quick sidelong glance.

"That was a joke," he said with a smirk that reminded her of the Wastrel. "You don't have to worry about me—us. I—we're just fine."

Wren started to laugh, despite her concerns. Then she frowned.

"What do you think? Is he right?"

"You're both right. We need to leave the camp, but we need to keep you and the abacusian safe at the same time."

"So, how?"

"Ah, the age-old ploy of multiple decoys."

Wren was intrigued. "How?"

"We split the camp personnel up into halves or thirds. Every group takes a pony or equine and a wagon with a canvas-covered object. Meanwhile, the abacusian takes another route."

"You're a genius!"

"Yes, I am."

"And humble too."

"Yes, that too." He smiled broadly.

She could see that he'd changed. He still had the fresh, farm boy face, but there were lines of care at the corners of his eyes and a wisdom in them that should have taken more than Trey's scant years of life to develop. He was at once an exciting new friend that she was just getting to know, and an old friend who filled her with the comfort of knowing what he was going to say next. Every day, his personalities melded more, and he grew in confidence and sangfroid. If she weren't so worried about her lost friends and the inevitable showdown with the drakyn, she would have taken great joy in getting to know her new–old–friend.

She thought again about his plan. "It still puts our soldiers in danger."

Trey sighed. "Wren, these soldiers have volunteered to be put in danger. Perhaps the most we can do is try to limit the casualties. It's what happens in war, I'm afraid."

"Yes, I see that. Let's discuss it tonight at dinner with Kemp, if he's still talking to me."

That evening, Kemp's mood had improved, and they said nothing about the earlier argument. With just her, Trey and Kemp at the table, they felt comfortable bringing up Trey's idea for the decoys. Kemp appeared to be excited by the concept. For the first time in a while, the light came back to his dark eyes.

"Yes!" he said, "I think it could work. But no one outside of this tent can know where the abacusian is cached. I still don't trust that there are no spies among us. They found us too easily last time, and they had the element of surprise, despite my numerous scouts."

They spent that evening planning, and the next few days preparing the decoys. Wren's constant fear was that they would be too late, but the day came for their four groups to leave the camp, and the drakyn still hadn't attacked.

Wren even used a henna and mashed blackberry rinse to darken her hair, just in case drakyn spies should sight her from above. The four groups took off in opposite directions, with plans to meet up near Krasa Ktel, after the conflict was over. Their agreed rendezvous spot was deep within the volcano lands, in the shadow of the mighty volcano.

Wren had never been so close to the mountain, and she worried about an eruption.

"Don't worry," Trey said. "It's been in a phase of small eruptions and mini quakes for the last few years. At worst, we'll have to put up with some ash fall, and a few temblors. It's nothing."

"It may be nothing to you, but I have no desire to be deep fried in molten lava."

Trey just laughed. "With all the threats we face right now, ol' Krasa Ktel is the least of our worries."

Wren only hoped he was right.

Wren, Trey and Kemp were the last to leave camp. Mala had elected to stay with the wagon that carried the wounded. Wren looked back in amazement at what they'd created in such a short time. Two equines, Aploosa and Crowbait, were hooked to the wagon, a gothic, overly decorative affair of elaborate wood carvings, inlaid false gold, beaded fringe and paintings of jugglers, mimes and musicians in a panel on each side.

Trey saw her inspecting his art. "Perhaps instead, we should have illustrated peddlers, beggars and thieves."

Wren laughed. "Haven't you heard of marketing? You never tell the buyer exactly what you're selling. Where would the fun be in that?"

"Nice. I'll make a traveler of you yet. Let's hope we don't run into that many we need to fool along the way. I know my juggling will pass muster, but I'm a little worried about you on the organetto."

"I can pass," she replied indignantly. "The soldiers and farmers out here are probably tone deaf anyway."

They packed the last of their things into the wagon and Kemp jumped agilely into the back. He had been quiet and reserved, but Wren assumed it was caused by his worry for his men.

Wren and Trey hauled themselves up unto the bench and Trey took the reins. He'd offered to let Wren try her hand at running the

team, but she'd never run a wagon before, so she was content
to learn from his solid hands and strong voice as he worked the
equines.

Wren asked, "Tell me again why you picked these particular two
equines?"

"Well, Aploosa is dependable and good natured…"

"And Crowbait?" she prodded.

After a moment in thought, he said, "Well, he adds visual interest. He has a unique personality… and he was the last equine left."

She chuckled at that. Despite many transmogering efforts to
heal him, Crowbait was still a swayback, roman-nosed, ill-tempered
gelding, *way* beyond his prime. He would try to bite your knee
when you mounted him. But if Aploosa walked beside him, he was
happy enough to do his job towing the wagon.

The first few days of travel were uneventful, and Wren began to
relax, at least a little. She worried most about Kemp. After dinner,
he usually disappeared for a few hours, scouting, he said. When he
returned, he plopped down without comment into his bed, to fall
almost immediately into exhausted sleep. When she asked him how
he was doing, he just mumbled and walked away.

Though they had tried to avoid populated areas, the wagon
limited them to navigable roads, and these eventually led them to
small settlements, mostly human, but there were a few small dageki
villages and farms. The dageki had little interest in them, and left
them to their own devices, which was fine with Wren. The less
questions she had to answer, the better.

One evening, they reached the end of the day and were forced to set up camp outside a little village called Upperton. What it was upper to, Wren couldn't fathom, as the area around them was devoid of any hints of civilization. She wondered how they survived out here on their own, but Trey told her that the population consisted of some highly talented transmogrifers who had objected to the war and refused to fight. For obvious reasons, they weren't very popular with the soldiers. Kemp refused to go into town with them.

As they walked the streets of the village, Wren was amazed at how clean and neat everything was. The wooden boardwalks were swept and the rough glass windows clear and sparkling, as if they had just been washed. The town smelled of lilacs and clean washing hanging on lines.

"Wow, this is quite the town. It's so well-kept," she mentioned to Trey as he pasted a notice to the window of a tailor and haberdashery.

She looked at the placard. "Are you sure we need to do this? I thought we were undercover."

"It's important we keep up appearances," Trey replied. "A traveling troupe of peddlers and performers which fails to peddle or perform will be more suspect than if we announced ourselves as fakes to all in the village square."

She wondered if he wasn't just enjoying himself.

"Yes, but you do like to juggle, don't you?"

"Just as you love to play the organetto, my dear."

"Yah, there's that," she said dryly.

"Don't worry, we're not far from the rendezvous point, just another day or two. Maybe the drakyn won't attack after all."

"I hope so. I just wonder what's going on. Why *haven't* they attacked? Kemp says he hasn't received any flet messages from the others yet, so where are the drakyn?"

"I don't know. They may be gathering their forces. After their last disaster, perhaps they're finally thinking in terms of strategy instead of reacting in rage. But let's not discuss it out here in public, all right?"

"Sure."

Wren was encouraged when, later that evening, only a few curious villagers showed up to watch them perform. Wren got out her organetto and put the leather strap over her shoulder. She'd polished the ornate pipes to a brilliant luster, and the bellows were soft and supple. She began to play a sprightly tune on the small keyboard to accompany Trey, who juggled three clubs and an apple. When he was done, they were rewarded with scattered applause. She began to play the folk song she'd been working on.

Wren played and sang along in a soft, melodic voice:

"A Gypsy Rover came over the hill
Down through the valley so shady.
He whistled and he sang 'til the green woods rang
And he won the heart of a Lady.

"She left her home her castle great
She left her fair young lover
She left her servants and her estate
To follow the Gypsy Rover

She left behind her velvet gown

And shoes of finest leather
They whistled and they sang 'till the green woods rang
As they rode off together

Last night, she slept on a goose feather bed
With silken sheets for cover
Tonight she'll sleep on the cold, cold ground
Beside her Gypsy Lover

Her father saddled up his fastest steed
And roamed the valleys all over.
Sought his daughter at great speed
And the whistlin' Gypsy Rover

"He came at last to a mansion fine
Down by the river Kyndry
And there was music and there was wine
For the Gypsy and his Lady

"Have you forsaken your house and home?
Have you forsaken your baby?
Have you forsaken your husband dear
For a gardamn Gypsy Rover?

He is no gypsy, Father dear, she sang
But Lorde of these lands all over.
And I shall stay 'til my dying day
With my whistlin' Gypsy Rover."

This time, the applause was more enthusiastic, and a few more coins were tossed into their collection hat.

Later, when they'd all gone, Trey said, "I think they have no idea how hard it is to juggle differently shaped items."

"You're just jealous because I earned more coins than you did."

He laughed. "Yes, you're right, I am. You were fantastic. You really missed your calling. Should've been a bard."

"I wish I could be just that, or anything else than what I am now," she said wistfully. "I don't relish this job, not at all. Last time I used the abacusian…"

"Last time, what?" he prodded.

"It was like the first time I touched it." She hated even talking about that. "Something happened to me, like a burst of light or an explosion in my mind. But I don't like what it revealed, what I might be capable of."

She was silent until he finally asked, "So what do you think is happening?"

"I don't know. It's like a demon within me, an anger that I can't control. It scares me."

He was quiet for a bit. "The power you have is indeed frightening, but you've done an admirable job of controlling and channeling it so far."

"Yeah, so far," she replied grimly. "Trey, you must promise me. If I get out of control, you must stop me, whatever it takes."

She could tell he was about to make light of it, but he saw her serious expression and said, "Yes, I will do what you ask, if I can, but I will never desert you or harm you ever again. I will sacrifice my own life before doing that."

"Trey—"

"Wren, there's something I need to tell you, about Kodo, and I guess about me and the Wastrel too. All of us, we—"

Trey was interrupted by a frightful scream coming from the woods behind them. Both realized at once that Kemp hadn't returned from his scouting. As one they yelled "Kemp!" and took off toward the sound.

They found him in a small clearing in the woods beyond their camp. In an instant it was obvious that Kemp hadn't been scouting. Trey lifted a fallen branch, transmogering heat at its tip until he had a makeshift torch. What it revealed set Wren's hair on end.

Kemp lay on the ground with a small glass beaker in his hand. A trickle of blood ran from it onto the ground. Then they saw the thing that lay beside him, a grotesque, gray, writhing figure, ill-formed and keening loudly in its misery.

Trey realized what was happening before Wren and ran forward, but he was too late. Before he could transmoger himself, the figure had transformed and stood before them, looking down at Kemp in disgust. The figure lifted a glittering samurai sword and swung at the prone man, eviscerating him with one deft swipe of the blade.

Kemp cried out, but the words melted into a gurgled gasp as he attempted to replace his own spilled intestines. His pain was ended abruptly as the sword half-severed his head from his body. His head lolled to the side and blood spurted from the wound. Not even a sword this sharp could slice through vertebrae in one attempt.

The figure grunted and said, "Gotta work on that. Just not pretty when I can't remove the head in one swipe, like in your ancient otherworld battle stories, but those tales aren't real, are they?"

He turned toward them, and Wren finally realized who he was.

DAP DAHLSTROM

"Semli!" she cried in horror.

"Yes, dear one, thanks to the hubris of your friend, Kemp, I am back among the living."

Semli turned to Trey. "You seem familiar to me, skragling. Have we fought before?"

"In a way," said Trey through gritted teeth. As he spoke, he pushed Wren behind him.

"Ah, you see you have a choice here, don't you?" snarled Semli. "Before you so rudely interrupted us, the skragling told me where this abacusian device is hidden. How ingenious to conceal it in the shape of an organetto. But back to your choices. As I see it, you can save the woman, or the weapon. Which will it be?"

"Both."

"I think not." As Semli spoke he launched himself forward at Trey with incredible speed.

Trey transformed with equal alacrity, forming a wall to prevent Semli from reaching Wren, but when he reached up to engage with the drakyn, Semli was gone.

"The abacusian!" screamed Wren.

They hurried back to their camp, leaving Kemp where he lay. As far as Wren was concerned, the traitor deserved to have his body eaten by scavengers.

Semli was not in the camp when they ran up and little had changed. For a second, Wren hoped that he hadn't found it, then she saw the shattered pieces on the ground, twisted pipes and shredded keyboard mixed with the remnants of the colorful beaded staircases of the abacusian.

She knelt to gather the pieces, but Trey pulled her away.

"There's nothing we can do now. It's gone."

"Can't you repair it?"

"I can try, but I fear that the science is beyond my skill. For this, we need a dageki."

"Grakt is off on a mission. Gard knows where he is now, and Tinkoro is in Dmisi working on his experiments. There's no way we can get the pieces back to him in time."

Wren surveyed the sky, worried that Semli would soon be returning. Trey followed her gaze, but the sky was empty.

"Do you think he'll be back?" Wren asked. "And why didn't he stay to fight you?"

"Who knows," mused Trey. "Who knows what Semli is scheming. Perhaps he needs to gather his strength. He was just brought back from the dead. I think we'd better travel through the night and get to the meeting spot as soon as we can. I'll send a flet to both Grakt and Tinkoro, but I don't know what good it will do. It looks like we're on our own now."

Wren helped Trey gather up the broken pieces of the abacusian, all the while wondering if she'd just precipitated the end of humanity on Drakonia.

CHAPTER THIRTY-SEVEN

Back on the Farm

G rakt was exhausted, not so much by the physical demands of traveling between farms, or the inevitable conflicts at each, but the emotional toll of explaining over and over to the dazed dageki captives that they were free to walk away, to go home.

To his great relief, the last farm lay just ahead. When they were done here, then he too could go home. From here it was only a couple days to Dmisi. After reaching home, he was anxious to go on to the skragling soldiers camp, to rejoin Wren and the others. He feared they would need him soon, if they did not already.

After leaving the camp and arriving in Dmisi, he'd gone immediately to Mageki Kyni Gouzuni, the scientist working on the countering agent to the shambolika that enthralled his people on the farms, and elsewhere. He was grateful at least that others had been assigned to freeing further dageki being held by humans.

When he got to the lab and was shown her invention, he almost lost hope. There must have been a terrible mistake. The device she showed him was another shambolika that, as far as he could ascertain, was identical to all the others.

"Forgive my questioning of your immense abilities," he began, "but is this not a shambolika?"

"Yes, it is," replied the scientist.

Grakt waited for her to explain. When she did not, he launched into another detailed analysis of her skills and knowledge. After which, he asked, "Mageki Kyni Gouzuni, can you please explain to me how this will help us free our people from the shambolika?"

If Grakt hadn't known better, he would have thought that Mageki Kyni Gouzuni wore a smug expression on her broad features, but since dageki were incapable of such base emotions, he knew he must be mistaken.

Mageki Kyni Gouzuni motioned to a couple of her lab assistants, one carrying another identical shambolika.

"Now," she began in a commanding tone, "we will demonstrate the oppositional sound wave shambolika."

As Grakt gazed in confusion, she picked up one of the shambolikas, and her assistant the other. They began to play at almost the same time.

Grakt stepped back in fear of the effect it would have on them. He heard one discordant note from the assistant's shambolika, then silence. Even though their fingers moved, no sound was emitted by either instrument, and no one appeared to be under the trance inducing control the shambolika normally produced. To his amazement, Grakt felt nothing.

He blurted, "But this is magic!"

"No, not at all," countered Mageki Kyni Gouzuni. "This is science."

The bulky dageki went to a clear glass board and began to draw using a wax pencil. First, she drew a multiple curved line consisting of several peaks and valleys. Then she drew another on top of the first, identical except that it mirrored the other horizontally and intersected at the same point on every curve.

She explained, "Destructive interference is when similar sound waves line up, peak to trough, as in this diagram. The result is a cancellation of the waves. The noise-cancelling shambolika works on this principle. It detects the sounds coming into the ear and produces sounds with equal volume but with the peaks and troughs reversed, resulting in near silence. Our device emits sound waves of the same frequency but with an opposing pressure pattern to essentially cancel out the invading noise of the shambolika."

Grakt exhaled in relief. "That is truly amazing."

"Yes, it is," agreed Mageki Kyni Gouzuni with another smug smile. Grakt was sure of it this time, but he didn't mind, not at all.

Brought back to the present, Grakt surveyed the farm below them. It looked abandoned, but there was no way to be sure until they made their incursion. His people knew what to do without being told. By now, it was second nature. Everyone knew their jobs and what they might face when they entered the farm.

But this rescue mission had not been without casualties. At first, the drakyn minders fought back when they found their shambolikas inoperable. Though Grakt had brought a number of dageki with him to deal with such contingencies, the military dageki were hesitant to engage in violence, even to save the lives of others of their own kind. Grakt had learned this the hard way. Once a few of the dageki soldiers had been killed, they changed their minds and, to Grakt's amazement, fought fiercely and effectively. Usually, the drakyn minders saw they were outnumbered and chose to escape rather than fight, preferring to save their own tails rather than fight off thirty angry dageki.

As Grakt and his people progressed through the farms, he noticed a change. The last few farms had been empty of drakyn, as if they had all recently abandoned their posts and flown away.

Grakt couldn't figure out why this was happening, until he received a flet message from Dmisi, informing him that large numbers of drakyn had been flying east over the capital and amassing in the mountains above the skragling lands.

East, he thought in alarm, *where Wren and the skragling soldiers were camped!*

In a panic at this news, he pushed his forces hard to reach the final farm, and at last they were here. Like the previous ones, it was in disarray and chaos, with no drakyn minders present.

He led his group through, helping the dageki to recover from their trance and releasing the human victims who still lived.

In the last barn, he and his men came upon two humans who were familiar to him, and his heart sank.

Both Poppet and Teeka lay still and pale in their beds.

In growing trepidation, Grakt leaned forward to touch Poppet's arm. To his alarm, the boy opened his eyes wide in terror, not realizing that the dageki before him was a friend.

"No!" screamed Poppet. "I'm not going back in there. Just kill me now, I can't take it again."

"Please calm yourself, young man. It is I, Grakt, here to rescue you."

For a long moment, Poppet just stared at him with frantic eyes, then he began to cry. Through his tears, he said, "Oh, Grakt, I've never been so happy to gaze on your ugly dageki face, but please check on Teeka, she hasn't fared so well. I think her leg is broken, and she may have other injuries."

Grakt ignored Poppet's illogical comment about his face being ugly, since the boy was obviously delirious, and motioned his medical team forward. They set to work on the frail-looking cook.

After a while, he returned to Poppet, who was sitting up and looking around him, still a little dazed, as he watched them minister to Teeka.

Grakt said, "They say she was close to death, but our medical professionals have developed a tincture that is quite effective in countering the effects of blood loss. They've set her leg and there appear to be no more significant injuries, internal or otherwise. With some rest, you should both recover completely."

"Thank the gardlanders," said Poppet with a sigh.

"How did you end up here? Are you alone? We couldn't find Wren or Mala. Are they safe?"

Poppet had never heard the dageki ask so many questions at once.

"I can't tell you that for sure, but I think Teeka and I were the only ones taken. There was an attack on the camp. It looked like ten or so drakyn. I think Kemp was expecting more. Anyway, Teeka and I were outside, and we barely had a chance to run before one of the drakyn came for us, almost as if it had been assigned to take us alive. I'm not sure why. It grabbed us both in its front claws and carried us away from the battle.

"Then, the weirdest thing happened. The drakyn who was carrying us changed, in midair with no warning whatsoever. It reverted to its firstform. I'm sure it didn't choose to do that. It fell like a stone with us in its claws. I thought we would be crushed, but because it carried us in its front claws, I think that saved us. We were on top when it fell and fortunately, not that far from the ground. Still, it wasn't fun. Teeka was worse off than I was. We were both unconscious for some time, I think, because the drakyn must have recovered and brought us here. I woke up on a gardamn drakyn farm again. I felt like I was in my worst nightmare."

"You're safe now, but I am wondering what they had planned for you and why they let you live."

"I'm not sure," said Poppet, scratching his mop of red hair. "But Semli was always scheming, I learned that at the palace. Maybe we were to be hostages to stop Wren from using the abacusian. I heard the English-speaking drakyn say that the one who brought us asked them to try to keep us alive as long as possible. That gave us some hope, anyway, but no one ever came back for us, and they put us into one of the milking cohorts. I must assume that Wren was able to use the abacusian against them. More than that, I don't know."

"That explains much," said Grakt. "The drakyn have been abandoning the farms. Many have been seen flying east, toward your camps."

After a moment in thought, Grakt continued, "I am afraid you will not be allowed your time of rest just yet. I believe that the drakyn are gathering in the mountains for a massive offensive against your kind. Your people are in grave danger, even with the abacusian. I imagine they will send in their best operatives to find Wren and eliminate her before she can do more damage to them. We must return to Dmisi, and from there, to your camp to assist Wren and the others."

Poppet, his features grim but determined, agreed.

Fortunately, the dageki had wagons to carry the injured. Later that day, they were on their way back to Dmisi, and toward the war that no one wanted.

CHAPTER THIRTY-EIGHT

I'm Asleep, Aren't I?

W ren was in despair. So was Trey, she thought, but he just tried harder not to show it. Without the abacusian, their soldiers faced a terrible battle, especially if the drakyn attacked with all their fighters at once, which now seemed most likely.

She blamed herself completely for the state they found themselves in now. If she'd never used the abacusian in the first place, none of this would be happening. Everyone would be safe, or at least safer.

They rode the ornate wagon toward the meeting place, its gaudy raiment now at odds with her mood. The one thing she couldn't understand was why Kemp had betrayed them.

"I just don't understand it. Why did Kemp restore Semli?"

Trey replied, "I think he just couldn't resist the urge to recall a being from their blood alone, to do what no human transmogrifer had ever accomplished. Plus, I think he was jealous of you and what you could do with the abacusian. He'd been a transmogrifer his whole life, and one of the best. Then you came along and changed it all. In the end, his hubris proved greater than his common sense. He bested Semli once and assumed he could do it again. A critical error."

"Yes, and now the human race may well pay the price."

"We'll come up with a plan. We've fought the drakyn before without the abacusian. We can do it again."

Wren asked, "Do you think Kemp was collaborating with the drakyn? That he was the spy in our midst?"

"It's possible. Kemp lived for his craft. I think he wanted the war to continue because it was the best way for him to showcase his talent."

"That's ghastly! How could he betray his own people?"

"Pride is the most fearsome monster of all."

They rode on in silence, each trying to find a path that might lead to victory, or at least survival.

At the rendezvous point they found that the other groups were already there, setting up camp. If Wren hadn't been lost in her own concerns, she would have appreciated the beauty of the place more. The spot they had chosen for a campsite lay near a gentle stream in a lush forest. With more available water here than in the arid pine forests, giant firs were the grand masters of this land. They towered over all, except for the tip of Krasa Ktel, just peeking above the trees in the distance. Wren was amazed to see that the mountain was covered in snow.

"Snow?" she exclaimed looking up at the peak. "I would have thought it would be spitting hot lava and ash from its tip instead."

Trey said with a laugh, "Not even mighty Krasa can defeat the cold at three miles up."

"The mountain's that tall?"

"Yes, for now."

"What does that mean?"

"Let's just say that the volcanoes in this range are known for blowing their tops–but don't worry, we'll have plenty of warning if that happens, and we're far from the danger area anyway."

"That's good to know," she replied uncertainly.

The next few days were taken up with setting up fortifications and the planning of many diversely opposing strategies. To say that Kemp's lieutenants were unhappy to hear about the loss of their two greatest weapons, both the abacusian and their most talented transmogrifer, was a gross understatement. Many wept openly upon hearing that Kemp had fallen. Wren and Trey had agreed that it would be better to leave his legacy intact. As far as anyone knew, Kemp had died defending the abacusian. They didn't need to know the details. Morale was low enough already without adding the fact that Kemp had betrayed them all.

Trey had lobbied for a measured response; however many drakyn attacked their camp here would be met by an equal force of human transmogrifers. The rest would be immediately sent to the farms and settlements, where less skilled fighters might not be able to withstand the drakyn attack. Some others of Kemp's command argued that they had to make a stand here, with all their skilled transmogrifers in one place, if anyone were to survive the onslaught. Wren agreed with Trey. She felt that the fighters were just worried about making sure that *they* survived, and gardamn the settlements.

A few days later, scouts returned bearing bad news; a great number of drakyn were gathering in the mountains to the north. If there was any good news at all, it was that they were only risking short scouting flights, Wren assumed, in fear of her using the device again. That meant that Semli hadn't yet informed them of its destruction. When that happened, she was sure they would not hesitate to attack with everything they could muster. It was only a matter of time.

One day, Wren woke to shouting and stepped from her tent, groggy and sleepy-eyed. In the meadow, a fight had broken out between the "all in here" and "support the settlements" factions. Wren watched the confrontation, trying to fathom the unbelievable stupidity of mankind. How could they argue now, when everything hung in the balance? Were they or were they not on the same side?

Before she could intercede, other noises intruded; a whooshing of giant wings and the screeching of beasts in feral rage.

She looked up to see the sky black with winged shapes. Drakyn, and a lot of them, more than she'd ever seen in one place before, converged on the camp. Some wore only wings on their original bodies, but others had taken on their battleshapes; giant eagles, pterodactyls and flying vipers, plus worse things she couldn't name.

Instantly Trey was at her side. "You must hide!" he said, pushing her back toward her tent. "They must know the abacusian has been destroyed. They'll target you first, to eliminate the threat you pose."

Wren's first urge was to object, but then she realized that if she stayed, Trey could die trying to protect her. She turned to run but couldn't resist looking back.

The drakyn were everywhere. The human warriors fought valiantly, but the drakyn were in such a rage and they far outnumbered the humans.

So, the idea of sending transmogrifers to the settlements has been settled.

She looked for Trey in the melee and she eventually found him, having taken the shape of a lion-headed, clawed griffin with four wings. Even in her fear, she noticed the gold stripe that ran from his head to the tip of one wing.

Ah, Kodo, so you're still with us. You may yet regret changing sides.

Several of the drakyn must have recognized her because they broke from the battle and headed her way. Trey intercepted them just as she reached the tent.

What good is a tent going to do me?

Wren turned to face her fate. At least once she was gone, Trey could stop risking himself to defend her. She just didn't want to go this way, with no weapon to fight back. She saw the claws coming at her and heard a trumpet sound.

Then, only silence.

Wren woke on the floor of her tent. A creature was leaning over her, its giant head filling her vision. For a second, she saw drakyn. She sat up and scooted away in fear, only to realize that the massive head belonged to Grakt, not a blood-thirsty drakyn come to finish her off.

"Forgive me for frightening you, but you are urgently needed!" he began.

"What? Grakt? What are you doing here?"

"I was attempting to explain. As your people say, I have brought the cavalry. I believe the phrase means procuring the aid of skraglings riding equines, but in this case, they are dagcki on pachyd–but I can explain that later. How are you feeling? I'm afraid you took a nasty fall when Tinkoro removed the drakyn who were—"

"Tinkoro's here too?" Wren rubbed the back of her head and winced when she found the lump there.

"Yes, and he brought—"

Wren didn't hear the rest of his explanation as she rushed from the tent and straight into a giant, imposing face with gentle brown eyes and a massive tube attached where a nose should have been.

"What the—?"

"Yoo-hoo, Wren!" said a voice from somewhere above her. She looked around but saw no one. Finally, she caught a glimpse of a figure atop the creature she was hallucinating. For hallucination this must be, or the oddest transmogery she'd ever witnessed. For one thing, animals weren't usually gray. Brown, tan, even greenish gray, but rarely the gray of dried mud. When you added a tracing of wrinkles like a dry stream bed in a ten-year drought, you got...

The hallucination or dream or whatever it was got even weirder when Teeka and Poppet ran up to hug her.

"I'm asleep, aren't I?" she asked of no one in particular.

"I know, right?" said Poppet, excitement illuminating his voice. "This one is Bubba. He carried the abacusian, and that one over there, her name is Princess. Aren't they wonderful? They're called pachyderms."

"Princess," echoed Wren in a fog. "Yeah, sure."

She turned to go back to her bed so she could wake up, but Tinkoro had managed to make his way down a rope ladder on the side of the patient animal and had grabbed her arm. "Wren, I have urgent need of your attention, as I'm sure Grakt has explained."

She noticed that one of his diminutive hands was covered in bandages. Suddenly dizzy, she said, "I think I need to sit down. No wait, first I need to find Trey."

Grakt came up beside her to grab her other arm solicitously. "Trey is here. He's fine."

Wren looked around her, but the enemy was gone. "Where are the drakyn?"

"They have retreated, at least for now. Tinkoro does not have your skill with the device, but he was able to cause them enough distress with the new abacusian that they were unable or unwilling to fight any longer. They will be back soon, I fear."

"New abacusian?"

"Oh, yes. When we got back to Dmisi, we found that Tinkoro had been working on a larger, more powerful version. But enough, you must come."

Grakt and Tinkoro led her to a large angular object partially hidden under a canvas cover. Tinkoro pulled the cover away with a dramatic flourish.

Wren gasped. The object before her bore little resemblance to the abacusian that Kemp had destroyed. It was several times larger for one, and for another, the entire glowing, vibrating, kaleidoscopic mechanism was encased in glass.

"But how do you reach it?"

"You do not," explained Tinkoro proudly. "You no longer need to touch the mechanism, nor is there any need for a blood or tissue sample to activate it. The glass enclosure is unbreakable and should protect the device from most forms of physical damage."

"Then how?"

"You wear this." Tinkoro pointed to what appeared to be a red leather uniform or outfit, made of a patchwork of scale-like overlays. It was too small to fit a dageki. With it was a cape of the deepest aubergine. A wide belt of flexible silver chain mail cinched the waist. The oversized belt buckle was made of intricately filigreed gold and was adorned with a large chartreuse stone at its center. The round stone had a vertical black slit, reminding her of a drakyn's eye. Wren shivered.

"It's called a drakyn's eye, but it's actually a stone of unknown material and origin. They are very rare, and supposedly found only on an island in the Thousand Isles, far north. This one was in our museum of antiquities and dates back to the first dageki empire."

He handed her the outfit and belt.

Tinkoro continued, "We guessed your size, but we can make adjustments once you try it on."

Wren scoffed, "What's this? I don't need a new outfit."

Teeka mumbled under her breath, "A wardrobe intervention. Eet's about time."

Wren gave her a sour look.

"It is not clothing," explained the ever-patient Tinkoro. "The drakyn's eye stone in the belt amplifies power. It will allow you to activate the abacusian remotely. Guard the belt with your life. Though the abacusian is impervious to harm, the stone is not. I must caution you, do not lose the remote.

"The suit is made from the cast-off scales of the firegullet lizard, who have adapted their fire-resistant hides using the slow transmogrifee that your gardlandian ancestors called evolution. The suit will protect you from the considerable heat that is generated. There isn't time to explain the intricate scientific formulas that allowed us to create it. Just understand that it should allow you to connect with thousands, perhaps an infinite number of organisms at once, but control each of them separately. It is an immense step forward technologically from the first abacusian. Though it was regrettable that the first one was destroyed, this is not your father's abacusian."

Tinkoro paused and turned his head to the side as if considering the importance of what he was about to say. "Wren, you now have the power to control every creature on this planet."

Wren's mouth fell open and she said nothing.

Trey, who had just joined them, asked "But how can she keep all that straight? No one can visualize thousands of individuals at once, much less control them. I can transmoger only one thing at a time. I don't think what you're suggesting is possible for a human being."

Tinkoro looked hesitant for the first time. He said slowly, "In order for this to work as it was designed, the device will need to make some changes to the brain of the practitioner. At least that is the working theory. When I used the machine, even for the short time I was able to touch it, I felt the changes beginning to affect me, so I am reasonable sure that our hypothesis is correct."

"What?" shouted Trey, stepping forward to glare up at Tinkoro. "You don't know exactly what will happen to her, do you?"

"Oh, yes," began Tinkoro, "I mean no, not completely, no. Obviously, without a skragling subject to experiment on, we were not able to—"

Trey exploded. "She isn't a 'subject,' a 'user' or a 'skragling' to be experimented on! She is a living human being who deserves some say in this. What happens if it kills her or damages her beyond healing or tips the balance of some unseen scales in nature that we can't even imagine yet? If it has the power you say it does, we could all be in danger from this thing, everyone on the whole frucking planet. Am I right?"

Tinkoro's eyes flitted about nervously, finally coming to rest on Wren.

"Obviously, it is her decision, but the drakyn will be returning when they have recovered from the pain I was able to inflict on them in my feeble and fumbling attempt. I can do no more. Only Wren seems to have the unique aptitude to control the device. Yes, it is dangerous, but I fear the danger will be far greater if she does not try."

Wren, who had been silently observing the abacusian as they discussed her fate, said without turning, "Tinkoro, is there any way you can prepare me for what I will experience? Does this thing come with some kind of user's manual?"

"Not as such," he replied. "But we will do our best to prepare you and help you through the adjustment period."

Wren sighed. "Then I have to try." She looked at Trey. "There's no alternative. I don't want anyone else to die because of me. We must end this war, somehow."

Mala, who had hung back throughout the conversation, stepped forward to touch Wren's arm. "Wren, you didn't start this war; the drakyn did. No one could blame you if you backed out now. This looks very dangerous."

Teeka said, "There is another alternative we are forgetting. If this device has the same capabilities as the last one—"

Wren knew what she was referring to. "No, Teeka, I haven't forgotten what happened the first time I touched the abacusian, but we won't discuss that, not yet. That will be our very last resort. We're not murderers. I won't commit speciocide in the name of peace."

Trey looked at her oddly but said nothing. She'd not yet told him about killing off an entire species of grub moth by accident. What would he think of her when he found out? That the world wouldn't miss one specific type of dull gray insect? That she was playing with powers she couldn't hope to control? She decided then that she would have to tell him about it soon. He deserved to know.

Trey himself was another reason that she was hesitant to invoke this deadliest of solutions. Wasn't part of Trey's genetrical and psychological makeup still drakyn? What would happen to Trey if she killed all Kodo's kind? Would part of him die too? Or all of him? She couldn't live with that. There had to be a better way, a way for her to create instead of destroy. She looked again at the lovely spinning mechanism that she'd first viewed with awe and delight, but now she saw in it only darkness.

CHAPTER THIRTY-NINE

The Naming Ceremony

That night, after practicing all day with the abacusian, she was exhausted and slept better than she had in a long time, except for the dreams.

Trey had asked her to eat dinner with him, but she'd feigned fatigue. The truth was that she just couldn't bear the questions he would ask about her progress on the abacusian, *or lack thereof.*

She had to admit that she was terrified of the power she could feel within the object. Even the little that she'd ventured into its nature told her that it would be an infinitely powerful weapon, and she still wasn't sure that she was the one to wield it.

She knew she had to let go, to allow the machine into her mind, yet despite the urgency of their need, she hesitated. She was hiding like a frightened child at the periphery of the abyss she saw looming before her whenever she touched the stone.

Though Tinkoro showed nothing but patience and understanding when she faltered, she could nonetheless sense his worry. The drakyn would be returning, and she needed to be ready.

Tomorrow, she told herself. *Tomorrow I'll take the plunge.*

After that she remembered nothing but disturbing dreams. One of them, perhaps because it was the last one before she woke, was exceptionally vivid.

The sky was dark with wings and struggle, the air electric with cries of fear, rage and pain. She touched the amulet she'd worn every day since the leijong leader Aquilinus had given it to her. Then more wings joined the darkness, the shimmering arcs of jewel-toned pinions that could only belong to one kind of being.

The leijong had arrived.

The next day her worst fears were realized when she woke to the same sounds of panic that she'd heard in her dream, only now, they were infinitely real. The drakyn were here and she wasn't ready.

Then the leijong were there, just as in her dream. Their fierce fighting presence might give her the time she needed. If only she'd practiced more seriously, taken more chances with the abacusian. It was too late now. Whatever was meant to happen would happen.

Then the ground shuddered. She felt a series of explosions, like the sound the ice made on the river back home when it broke apart in spring, or the rumble of thunder, but deeper and stronger than any she'd ever heard. Soon the sky darkened, and great billowing clouds rose, moving at unbelievable speed toward them, thicker and darker than they should be. It started snowing hot ash. Long fingers of lightning lit the clouds in shades of dirty yellow.

Krasa Ktel had woken.

What great timing.

With fumbling fingers, she rushed to put on the lizard-scale garment that was supposed to protect her from the heat of the abacusian. Seeing the damage caused to Tinkoro's hand when he tried to use it unprotected, she knew she couldn't attempt it without shielding. Now she also hoped it might protect her from burning ash.

Urgency left her no choice but to jump headfirst into the uncertain future and immense power the abacusian offered.

Instead of the tentative steps she'd so far taken, this time she let go. Her mind took hold of the abacusian as if she were picking up a great flaming sword that was far too heavy for her to lift.

Her body vibrated with an overwhelming sense of power. She watched as a detached observer as her mind grew to fit the knowledge the machine offered. The buzzing that she felt every time she used the abacusian before had been but a foreshadowing of the true power she could wield with this device.

New compartments formed in her mind like buds opening on a tree. At the tips of each branch formed an infinite number of branch-lets and on each an infinite number of new buds. Each bud was a part of her spreading consciousness, all equal, none forgotten or unseen, none lesser and none greater.

Wren realized how small and blind to the wider reality she'd been. Before her, a new world opened up. She saw the drakyn in their entirety, the deformed, the stillborn, the mentally unbalanced, Semli being a prime example. The drakyn were transmogering their way into extinction. The more they used their talent, the sooner they brought the end upon themselves. The more fighters they lost to the challenges, the smaller their already anemic genetic pool became.

She knew what she had to do. Her hesitancy was gone. Kodo had chosen to become human, and it had changed him for the better. Instead of binding the drakyn into their firstforms to be slaughtered, she would give them the gift of humanity.

The grand experiment.

With the power she now held, it would be a relatively quick work to change all the drakyn into human beings. The challenge would be holding them in their new firstforms. Kodo, Trey and the Wastrel had been willing participants and had helped her to make the change permanent. She couldn't do that to the drakyn unless they were willing as well. She doubted that any of them would wish to transmoger permanently into what they viewed as inferior beings–the skraglings.

She didn't tell anyone what she was about to do. She didn't ask anyone's permission. It was too late for all that. It was time she grew out of her insecurities and fear of taking action, of making a mistake. It was time for her to grow into the destiny she now knew had awaited her all along.

Wren began creating personalities for each new human, not one at time, but all at once. Each new person was different, each one with a distinct persona and physicality. The buds of the tree she envisioned in her mind expanded and flowered. A new race of man was born, male, female and everything in between, young and old, creators and builders, shopkeepers and mothers, thieves and saints. All of them now human, except for one.

Semli had been attacked by the abacusian twice now, and with his genius at transmogrifee, he'd found a way to counter even her new, greater power.

Now he faced her on the empty battlefield, the lone drakyn left untethered to a new human life. He towered over her, his winged shape like nothing she'd ever seen before. It wasn't exactly an eagle or a griffin or any animal she recognized, but purely a new creation of his imagination. All she saw in the seconds she had were claws rotating like augers, limbs as wide as tree trunks and eyes spewing crimson flames.

Wren rose from the ground, floating in the current that now surged through her. Her silver-blonde hair had grown long, and it now stood out around her head like a dandelion gone to seed. Her scarlet suit glowed and smoked around the edges of each individual lizard scale. She touched the fingers of one hand to the stone, now glowing like a mini beacon in her belt. The long gloves Tinkoro had given her deflecting the heat as spears of white-hot fire spouted from the fingertips of her outstretched hand. Sweat broke out on her brow, dripping into her eyes–eyes that swirled like molten mercurum.

"You won't use your fledgling power to kill me," spit Semli. "I know you, poor little Wren, always the frucking bleeding heart. 'Oh please, no more deaths on my head.'" He imitated her voice poorly.

It didn't anger Wren as it might once have. She was beyond that. He expected her to engage with him, hesitate for the second it would take him to attack her. Saying nothing, she gathered all her strength for the last act she'd known in her heart would be asked of her. Semli would never give up. The venom of his hatred ate at him, yet somehow fueled him, giving him a strength and resilience no other drakyn could claim. The fire grew from her fingertips as Semli beat his wings ferociously. In a lightning-fast forward thrust, he charged her.

Wren let out a scream of animal rage and Semli cried out in pain as the heat hit him. His feathers burned to smoking stubs. His rotating claws melted. The inferno she sent at him grew and condensed into a cone of deadly white heat that scorched even the air between them. Semli ignited, burning to charcoal and carbon dust before their eyes. The ebony powder floated away on the breeze.

Gone for good? Let's hope so this time.

She felt suddenly exhausted and deflated. As she settled back down to the ground, she looked around her. The camp was a shambles, everything covered in ash. The meadow was filled with new humans who looked about in confusion and fear. It would take time to help them adjust. The job was done, but in truth it had also just begun. She would need a great part of her concentration to maintain the drakyn in their new forms, at least at first. There would also be the new casualties and wounded to deal with. As she reached the ground, she found that her legs were unwilling to support her. Trey was there to catch her when she keeled over.

Wren woke gratefully to a quiet camp. She could hear some distant conversation and the snap and hiss of a campfire, but no cries of pain, no battle noises and Krasa Ktel had gotten over its temper tantrum, at least for now. From the light glowing outside her tent, it must be early evening. They had let her sleep most of the day away. Oh well, she'd probably needed it. With a sigh, she rose and reluctantly slipped back into the red uniform. She wanted to check on the progress of her recently coined human beings, and there was one other set of tasks she wanted to complete.

Connecting to the abacusian was easier now, though she thought she would never get used to the surge of power and widened awareness it gave her. She found that the drakyn were adjusting to their new lives with more adaptability than she would have given them credit for. She'd begun the creation of villages for most of them, and they appeared content to go about their new lives as if they had always been this way. There were a few problems, of course. Some of the drakyn were more resistant to her influence than others, and some still clung to their violent natures, causing upset in their communities and trouble for themselves. Not that humans were a nonviolent species either, but the drakyn were capable of even more ruthless and wanton behavior. She adjusted where she needed, then turned from the drakyn to a few gifts she wished to bestow.

To Kree, the one-winged boatman of the leijong, she granted the wing he so desired. To the fox who had brought her a contail, saving her from starvation early in her journey, she gave a long life, a healthy mate and rich hunting grounds. For Poppet, she changed his transmogering gift to include the carpentry he so loved. For Mala, she removed the block that made transmogering so painful for her, allowing her to return to her family in the sea whenever the urge for water overcame her. For Grakt, she removed the burden of guilt he felt for recreating the shambolika, then freed any remaining dageki slaves from its power. For Tinkoro, she gifted the one thing he most wanted, a long life to pursue his precious science. For Teeka...Teeka was a tough one. For Teeka she removed the overwhelming guilt she felt for what she'd done to get Poppet sent to the farms and increased her cook-specific transmogering skills so she could commit even more egregious culinary crimes.

She realized that while she couldn't return Seleen's lost mate, Geery, she might be able to bring her new happiness. In a few days she would meet a new friend, who would eventually become much more than that.

At last, she thought about Trey. What could she possibly do for him? He was so happy in his skin. Unable to think of anything to give him, she set the thought aside to complete his gift another time. She just hoped he wouldn't be jealous when he saw what the others had received. She felt that the two of them were growing closer all the time, and it was something they could discuss openly. She wanted to give him something truly special for all he'd done for her.

A little later, she left her tent to find a somber group mourning the lost and adjusting to their new reality—a future without war and suffering. The ash had been cleared away, by transmogrifee she assumed. Several fires had been lit, and the leijong had set up camp away from the humans. Despite their commitment to helping her defeat the drakyn, the leijong were still a race who valued their privacy and didn't interact well with other species. When Aquilinus, the leijong leader saw her he came over to speak to her.

"Aquilinus, how did your people fare?" she asked.

"We lost two of our strongest, and there were some injured, but your healers have helped them recover with amazing speed. That small one, Mala, seems to have a great talent for healing."

"Yes, she's special. I'm so sorry to hear about your losses. You may have saved us all by showing up when you did, and I didn't even have time to call you—"

"But you did call us, last night."

The dream.

"I had a dream that you would arrive, almost exactly as you did today. I don't believe in magic, but—"

"Ah, perhaps the leijong also have a different way of perceiving reality. We believe that magic is just the craft that is yet to be discovered."

"I hope that's true. Otherwise, I might be losing my mind."

Aquilinus laughed in his musical way, then his expression turned serious. "The drakyn were a danger to us all. We are honored to have played even a minor role in eliminating the threat they posed. Our fighters who died, they dedicated their lives to protecting our people. They did so willingly and bravely and will be honored in our memories. Their battlenames will be engraved on the walls of our mountain temples and spoken with reverence until time itself ceases its flight."

"That's beautiful. Obviously, the leijong have rich and wise traditions."

"That brings me to the reason I wished to speak with you. I believe it is time to break with tradition, just a bit. We wish to celebrate you and your warriors tonight with a traditional leijong victory feast. Also, if you will allow it, we would like to present you and Trey with your own leijong battlenames. To other than leijong, it may seem frivolous or unnecessary, but trust me, it is a great honor among our kind."

"It would be an honor to receive such recognition from your people. We will gladly accept."

The leijong feast did not disappoint. Long tables had been laid out with venison, fish and clams, fresh vegetable and baked tubers for the humans, and more exotic fare for the leijong. Wren was amazed to find a bizarre selection of honey and nectar cakes, edible flowers, fertilized eggs, pickled rodents and tiny purple mountain shrooms. Wren tried a delicate cake that she was so impressed with that she asked for the recipe from Bridda the leijong cook, a tall, aquiline-faced woman. It was written in delicate English on the filmy parchment that she'd first seen covered with prophecy when they met the leijong on the banks of the flying river.

Bridda's War Cake Recipe

Ingredients:

1 lb. salt porker (all fat)

2 live duck eggs, incubated for 18 days

4 cups milkweed nectar water

½ cup aspen tree sap

½ cup poppy pollen

1 tsp. sinnerman spice

6 cups prairie bugwheat flour, sifted

1 lb. raisins (may be substituted with toasted grub moths or wooly aphids, if available)

Directions:

Boil duck eggs until dead. Remove beak and bones.

Chew porker fat until smooth.

Spit with tree sap into warmed milkweed water

Mix flour, poppy pollen and sinnerman spice

Add dry ingredients to wet, mix well and let stand to attract wild yeast

Cook in hot ashes until risen and fragrant

Note: Can be eaten immediately but will keep for years if stored in a musty place, such as the lower levels of a leijong stick house.

After reading the recipe, Wren decided against having seconds.

With the tasty and generous food, pared with the firebush nectar wine and traveler's ale that the leijong kept flowing, the mood in the group started to ease. Wren even heard some laughter. Realizing that Trey stood beside her, she smiled at his easy expression. "You're looking well pleased with yourself this evening," she said to him.

"Well, I guess we should all be relieved. It's just hard, taking in the ones we lost, both human and leijong, while at the same time I want to jump for joy that this frucking war is finally over. It hasn't sunk in yet, I guess."

"I know what you mean. It's been a long road, but I'm not sure it's entirely over yet."

"What do you mean by—"

Trey was interrupted as Aquilinus stood up to address the group.

"I don't make long speeches—" he began, but was interrupted by a sniggering from his fighters. "OK, so sometimes, I've been known to lean toward the long-winded address, but not tonight. We're all tired and weary of this conflict, and we need to withdraw tomorrow to our aeries to recover and care for our wounded. But now that it's over, it's important that we remember the fallen, and honor the bravest who made this victory possible. I know it has never been done before, but I believe it is time for the leijong to break with tradition and enter two non-leijong into the battlename registry."

A muttering began among the leijong.

"I know, I know, it goes against our traditions, but were it not for these two, all might have been lost—probably would have been. Join me in welcoming two new members to our ranks." At his nod, another leijong soldier handed him a medallion on a sparkling golden chain. The medal showed a golden eagle about to pounce on its prey. It was beautifully shaped, intricate, even delicate, yet solidly made.

Just like the leijong, she thought.

Trey bowed his head as Aquilinus placed the token around his neck.

"You, Trey Terraborne, have this day earned your battlename. From this time forward, you are Goldwing."

Wren thought that a perfect name for him, and it honored Kodo, as well.

Aquilinus turned to Wren and repeated the same words, then as he placed an exquisitely crafted silver medallion around her neck, added, "You, Wren Weatherspring, have earned the highest honor of the leijong. Your battlename is Silverfire."

Trey beamed at her. "Silverfire. It fits you perfectly. Now we are Goldwing and Silverfire."

The troops took up the cry, repeating "Goldwing and Silverfire" over and over. Wren was embarrassed, but at the same time thankful that they had something to celebrate. She only hoped that would continue to be true.

Over the next weeks, Wren noticed that Trey and Poppet were often away from the camp and had been less than transparent about what they were doing. Because Wren spent many of her days directing and controlling the new human drakyn, she was left with little time to worry about whatever project the two were involved with.

Her newly minted humans needed guidance and help when they strayed, and training in their new vocations. She'd not allowed them to use transmogrifee. It had already almost destroyed their race. Let them learn it all over, and perhaps future generations would find a way to limit the genetrical effects which would have eventually extinguished their kind completely. She had to believe that one day they could be drakyn again, when they learned compassion, constraint and humility. If that were even possible with this arrogant species.

She'd used Kodo as a model, and he'd turned out well, she reasoned. The drakyn possessed great talent and drive. If they could only direct it in positive ways. She hoped that in time, they could develop new habits that benefited not just themselves, but Drakonia as a whole. Perhaps she was being overly optimistic, but she had to believe it was possible, or else everything she'd done would eventually lead them back to disaster.

Wren was sad to see both the leijong and the dageki leave them, but they had their own lives to return to, and besides, every distraction made it harder for her to concentrate on the drakyn. Just this morning, she'd been interrupted several times by someone wanting something, a something she could not now recall. Even though, within the influence of the abacusian, she could observe almost infinite possibilities at once, she was still only human. When she went back, she noticed that small errors had intruded on the delicate balance of her network.

One morning, Trey bounced into her tent with an almost unbearable level of belligerent exuberance. He glanced at her sour expression.

"Too much leijong wine last night?" he asked too brightly.

It wasn't the wine, but she replied, "Yes, and could you please keep your voice down? The ridiculous gleefulness in your tone hurts my head."

"You're so lovely when you're hung-over–I mean, strung over my shoulder."

"What have *you* been drinking?"

"Nothing, my dear. It's just that Poppet and I are done with our project, and we'd be honored if you would accompany us to see it."

Wren couldn't help but catch his contagious glee. "Of course, I'll go with you."

"OK, good," he continued. "I'll just go hitch Crowbait and Aploosa to the wagon and we'll be off."

One thing that Trey hadn't kept from her was the redesign of the traveler's wagon. They had turned it into an open cart to accommodate the glass-encased abacusian, since Bubba and Princess had returned to Dmisi with the dageki.

"Are you sure the equines can handle it?" she asked. "It's really heavy."

"They're equines, m'dear. Each of 'em is stronger than an ox—well, just as strong anyway. And you know how Crowbait loves to work."

She snickered at that, but Crowbait did seem to be in a better mood when he was hitched to the wagon, and Aploosa was happy to entertain any enterprise that ended up at a barn with a bucket of grain.

They took the trail south from the volcano lands. As they traveled, Wren began to enjoy the scenery of this land even more than she had the forest to the north. There were deciduous trees interspersed with the firs and soon lush meadows appeared. Ash, poplars and alders lined the sparkling creek they followed. A doe and her two yearling fawns watched them pass without fear. A badger berated them loudly for intruding on his territory before disappearing into his burrow to sleep the rest of the day.

They continued on until they reached a broad, open meadow with a quiet stream meandering through it. A small farm lay before them. The evening sun lit the fields and the trees at its edges. The alpenglow was in full effect, turning the tall grasses to spears of gold. Fences demarked certain sections of the fields that would hold equines or porkers or goats, but were now empty. Apples adorned the orchard like fat rubies, gleaning in the evening light. A vegetable garden sported late-season crops in neat rows, and she could see equine stalls and a drygrass barn peeking out through the trees. From one of the pens, the pony Kinzi whinnied at them. From another a donkey saw them and brayed loudly.

"Pollux!" Wren exclaimed.

"No, not Pollux, I'm afraid, but his cousin. We haven't named him yet. We thought we'd leave that for you."

In awe, Wren thought they had come upon the gardlander's concept of heaven. Her eyes filled with tears.

"You don't like it?" asked Trey nervously.

"Like it! It's just so beautiful! But who lives here?"

"You do," sighed Trey in relief. "I'm so glad you like it. When I came upon this plot of land, I thought of you."

She gazed at him, her eyes bright. "Are you saying this is all for me?"

"Wait, there's more. Come around these trees. Poppet and I built you something."

He led her forward until she could see the cabin.

"You two built all this? So quickly?"

"Well, Poppet wanted to practice his new trade of transmograffic carpentry, and Oswald was happy to act as teacher and consultant. Together we cut the trees, dried and planed the wood. Poppet did that with his new talent alone, I'm really impressed with his progress."

At this, Poppet's face turned red.

"We built the cabin from the ground up. It's not huge, but it will be easier to heat in winter and—"

He stopped speaking when he realized that Wren was gone. He found her on the porch of the cabin with an odd look on her face.

She spoke slowly, looking around, "But this looks just like..."

Trey had an apologetic look on his face. "Yes, Kodo had something to do with this. He's still a part of me, you know. He wanted to somewhat recreate the home he took from you, as a way of saying he's sorry, to say that—"

"He–you didn't have to do that. It's been a long time and I wouldn't go back there now if I could. The truth is I couldn't have stayed there much longer anyway."

"Well, you're here now and we hope you like it," added Poppet. "We're just a few miles from a human settlement to the south, if you need supplies or anything. It's a little village called Skragsville—"

"Well, we're going to have to change that."

"Ha! Anyway, the point is that we wanted to give you something for everything you've done, and we've seen how much concentration it takes to control and direct the drakyn as you do. We thought you needed a place for peace and quiet." He looked embarrassed again, but forced himself to continue. "I personally owe you so much, Wren—"

"You owe me nothing!" Wren exclaimed. "I simply gave you a little boost along the way. It's entirely likely you would have developed a talent for transmograffic carpentry all on your own. You had the desire, the drive and the patience, and that's all it takes to succeed at anything."

"I don't know about that," he demurred, "but we hope you'll accept this gift from all of us. Mala and Teeka helped with the design. Hopefully, it's the cabin, the farm and the animals you've always wanted to be surrounded by."

"Oh, Poppet, it's so lovely, and just what I need. It's perfect!"

Both Trey and Poppet beamed.

Poppet said, "Come inside and see the kitches. We built some cabinets that—"

Trey interrupted, "Let's just show her, shall we?"

When she stepped into the kitchen and living area, Wren was overwhelmed. Comfy-looking chairs surrounded the glowing fireplace. A combined oven and woodstove took up the bulk of the open kitchen, with a large woodblock counter for preparing food, metal pans hanging on racks and actual cabinets on the walls. Her old cabin had only rough open shelves. These cabinets went to the ceiling, and Wren thought that she would need a ladder to get to the top ones.

Poppet followed her gaze and explained, "See this lever on the side? Just pull that and see what happens."

Wren did as she was told and was amazed when the topmost cabinet moved down to switch positions with the lowest one.

"Neat, huh?" asked Poppet. "That was Teeka's idea."

"That was so thoughtful, especially for her."

They all laughed.

Wren frowned. "But what about the abacusian? I can't just leave it in the wagon."

"We have a plan for that too," said Trey.

They led her to the back of the cabin, which to her surprise, opened up into a large light-filled space.

"Oswald calls it a sunroom," Poppet explained excitedly.

The length of the back of the cabin was taken up by a long open room, with glass panels on all sides, letting in light even as dusk fell upon the cabin. She could only imagine how much brightness and warmth the morning sun would bring.

"The glass is a design that Tinkoro came up with," said Trey. "The panes draw in heat when it's cold outside and expel heat in the summer. It's almost like magic, but he assured us that there is science behind it, of course."

"Of course," laughed Wren. "It's all so amazing, and a perfect place for me to work. Thank you."

They were all silent for a moment, then Trey said, "We wanted you to have a place to work without distractions, but even a country girl needs company once in a while, so we included a few extra beds in the loft, opposite your upstairs bedroom, for when you want to entertain guests."

He looked at her hopefully, but she didn't seem to notice his expression.

She laughed. "You are all welcome whenever and for as long as you wish to stay."

"Good." Trey gave her an enigmatic smile. "There is one caveat, I'm afraid."

Wren's thoughts immediately ran to the worst possible destinations.

"What's that?"

"I'm afraid you'll have to take in Crowbait, too. Nobody else wants him."

"Oh," she exclaimed in relief, "is that all?" She forced herself to frown. "I'm sure it will be an incredible burden for him. To be pampered, allowed to run free and eat grain every night, but I have faith that he'll forgive me eventually."

They laughed together and Wren felt a wave of peace and happiness wash over her. She just wondered how long it would last.

CHAPTER FORTY

Kree

K ree woke up to his miserable life as the one-winged boatman of the leijong, but something was wrong. More wrong than usual, that is. He thought at first that he'd come down with some illness. He felt dizzy and unbalanced. His lungs had to work harder than they had the day before. Sweat broke out on his pallid face.

He stumbled out of his rough bed in the boathouse and squinted into the glaring morning light. Leaning heavily on the coarse boards of the boathouse wall, he turned awkwardly to study the new lump on his wingless shoulder.

Great. Now he had some malignant growth to add to his litany of woes. He'd be forced to quit his job as boatman, to be left to die in the lower levels when they flooded, or worse, be exiled from his homeland, to wander the world until he died a painful death as a filthy, worthless, no-battlename vagrant. Life could only get worse, it seemed.

He leaned over and covered his face with his hands, weeping in despair. His one wing started to open reflexively and the lump on his right side expanded simultaneously. Kree fell forward and cried out in pain and disorientation. The new lump on his right shoulder was not a malignant growth after all, but a perfectly matched, arching and curling, beauteous leijong wing.

Kree was in shock. It appeared that the one thing he'd always wanted had, by some unimaginable means, been granted to him.

A wing.

But Kree had never flown before, had no idea how it was done. His natural balance was gone. Would he even be able to ferry the longboat now? Was his life as a boatman over?

Kree began to cry again, awash in this new, deeper, all-consuming mutation of his eternal sorrow.

CHAPTER FORTY-ONE

Crowbait and the Cube

Wren had killed a deer with her new bow, a gift from Trey, and the nice four-point buck was hanging out back by the chickers coup, skinned and gutted, but covered with cheesecloth to keep flies away. A few days passed before they deemed it ready to eat. Wren knew that you never ate meat before it had been "seasoned" by hanging, at least if you didn't want it to taste tough and gamy. Trey cut a few pieces of the meat that ran along the spine, what Teeka called "flaming minion," and Wren seared them on the stovetop.

Poppet picked spareguts from the garden and Wren steamed them in a pot on her new woodstove. Spareguts were, fortunately, much more appetizing than their name implied, having no guts and nothing spared at the end of the meal, because the spear-shaped vegetables were so delicious.

Wren felt sad, but only for a moment, that Teeka wasn't here to add her unique ingredients to the dinner.

After they'd eaten, Wren asked Poppet, "What will you do now? You seem to be really enjoying your new craft, and the apprenticeship with Oswald has given you some amazing new skills."

Poppet's eyes lit up. "It's so rewarding to actually 'make' something and to know that it's going to be around for decades, maybe generations."

"I'm sure your pieces will be loved and used for a long time to come. They're beautiful, and useful, too."

Poppet looked thoughtful. "When my apprenticeship with Oswald is over, I think I'd like to help build the drakyn–I mean the new humans'–houses and farms. It's a big project, but it's worth doing, don't you think?"

"Yes, it's worthwhile and a great gesture on your part, considering how the drakyn treated you."

"That's in the past. If our experiences taught me anything, it's that we need to move on from what we were to make room for what we can become."

Wren smiled. "I couldn't agree with you more. Thank you again, Poppet. Please come back and join us whenever you can."

"Us?" asked Poppet with a smirk.

"Well, yes. Trey has agreed to stay and help me with the farm. Do you object to that?"

"No, no, not at all. I mean, that's great. So, Trey must have told you tha—"

Trey interrupted them, balancing a basket of fresh brown eggs under her nose.

"Look," he said, "the hens are laying."

The next day, after Poppet had left to return to the camp, the fall weather was warm, and a gentle breeze had the grasses talking quietly among themselves.

Wren and Trey decided to go on a picnic. Finding a flat spot in the grass by the creek, they laid down a blanket and enjoyed a simple meal of cheese and fruit. Wren had included a few smoked herrins in honor of Mala, who had stayed at the camp to tend to the new ranks of the wounded. After some thought, she had decided not to honor Teeka by bringing any of her favorite treats. She didn't want to risk the indigestion.

After a glass of pinot noir–Trey and Poppet had brought a case with them from Kemp's hidden stores–they lay back on the grass to talk and laze in the filtered fall sun.

Trey sat up, suddenly looking nervous. The piece of straw he was chewing on started gyrating rapidly in his teeth.

"There's something I've been meaning to talk to you about," he began slowly. "I've been wanting to tell you that—"

"No, no, don't even try it," laughed Wren. "Every time you start to tell me something important, all gardlander's hell breaks loose and some disaster befalls us."

"Not this time. Not here. Look around. Isn't this the perfect spot?"

"For what?"

Trey took a deep, shaky breath. "To tell you that I love you, that me and the Wastrel and Kodo, we all love you."

Wren laughed and Trey turned red. Grabbing his arm, she said, "I've known that forever. What's the big secret?"

Trey looked down, embarrassed, and Wren leaned over and kissed him tenderly.

He smiled at her and said, "I'd like to do that again, and again and—"

She kissed him again, this time with more passion. Soon their bodies were naked and entwined, enjoying all the new terrain they had to explore. They made love under the warm sun, on a soft blanket in the lush, fragrant grass and it was the most luxurious feeling Wren had ever had. Joy filled her for the sake of joy and all her fears melted away. At least for a moment, the world was perfect.

After a while, Trey asked groggily, "Want another glass of wine?"

"Maybe later. Right now, I just want to—"

"Make love again?"

"I was going to say, 'enjoy the moment.'"

"That's what I just said."

They laughed together and did as he suggested.

Later, when they got back to the barn to feed the animals, they found that Crowbait was missing.

Wren looked worried but Trey reassured her, "He used to do this occasionally at camp. He'd chew through his tether and wander off. He'd show up again in a couple days for his evening grain as if nothing had happened."

"But there are wolf packs out there and he's not a colt anymore. What if he falls and breaks a leg, or—"

"OK, we'll find him. I'm a fair tracker."

"That's good, because I'm an excellent one."

"Point taken. Let's go."

They picked up Crowbait's trail at the back of the farm, near the creek where his hoofprints were clear in the mud.

"He doesn't seem to be in much of a hurry, just kind of meandering about."

"Yes, but he seems to be heading in a generally southern direction. What's that way?"

"Nothing special, that I know of."

They walked for a while through the woods, when Wren saw a large gray slab of what looked like stone ahead of them. "What's that?"

Trey didn't answer. As they drew closer, Wren said, "It's a cube, a gardlander cube!"

"I had no idea there was one out here," said Trey.

"I've never seen one. Can we look at it?"

"I don't see why not. From all I've heard, they're totally inert. Whatever power they used to bring humans here seems to be gone."

As they approached, they heard a ripping and munching sound. Crowbait peeked his head out from behind the cube.

"There you are, you naughty equine," chided Wren.

Trey approached the animal slowly, attaching the lead line to the equine's halter when Crowbait was munching away on the tender grass. Tying the line to a tree, Trey looked back at Wren, who was circling the cube.

"Look how smooth it is. What's it made of?"

"No one knows. The dageki hate to admit it, but it's probably technology beyond even their capabilities."

"Amazing!"

Wren came around to the open side. There was no door, or even a frame for a door. The entire side was just open to the air. Looking in, Wren noticed that the floor of the cube was devoid of leaves or dirt.

Wrinkling her brow, she asked, "Does someone clean them?"

"No, of course not. Who would have the time for that? They're always like this. They seem to repel dirt and leaves."

"Is it safe to go in?"

"Maybe. As far as we know, the cubes stopped transferring humans to Drakonia generations ago. I'm just not sure if you should."

"Why not?"

"It's just that you seem different from most people. You have powers that no human has ever possessed. It might be dangerous. Perhaps we shouldn't risk it."

"I think you're just being paranoid."

Knowing that she would do what she wanted, no matter what he said, he compromised. "At least let me go in first and check it out."

Trey stepped into the cube and turned to face her.

"Can you hear me?" he asked.

"Yes, no change, nothing. I'm coming in, too."

Before he could stop her, Wren stepped into the cube. She faced him, watching the expression on his face.

"See," she said, "Nothing happened." Then her head started to buzz, like it had at first when the abacusian was out of control.

She watched as Trey's face showed awe, and then increasing distress.

"You had better turn around," he said, his eyes wide.

Wren turned and her world literally changed forever.

The blur of images outside the cube was flipping so quickly that at first, she couldn't decipher what she was seeing. Then she started to see a pattern. The entire scene before them was at once white with stripes of gray, then vibrant greens, then bright yellows and greens, then muted oranges and browns and then back to the white with gray stripes, repeated over and over again. She concentrated on slowing the frantic pace of the images, not knowing if just her wanting it could make it so. To her amazement the scenes did slow, until she realized what it was they were seeing.

White with gray stripes were the deciduous trees in the coming winter, green the buds and young leaves of spring, bright yellow and green were the meadow flowers and grasses of summer, the oranges and browns, the leaves of fall.

"Seasons," she said in awe. "They're seasons passing."

"Can you stop it?" asked Trey. She could hear the concern in his voice.

"I'll try."

She concentrated until her head was throbbing, and the pictures slowed even more, until finally, they stopped completely.

She tried to turn to Trey, but her head wouldn't move. Wren started to panic, her fear rising with each moment she stood paralyzed. Then she realized that she'd stopped time, and a human body was subject to time. Wondering what Trey might be thinking, she thought at him, *It's OK. Don't be frightened. I think that time needs to be moving very slowly for us to move too.* To her infinite surprise he thought back to her, *Thank the gardlanders! I thought we were stuck. Please get us out of here!*

Wren very gently pushed the timeline forward, a second equaling a second, until she was able to move her body. She looked out at the scene before them, but very little had changed.

"This looks like fall, when we stepped into the cube," she said with relief. "Let's get out of here."

"OK, just let me go first," he said, "Let's do this in the order we went in, just in case that matters."

Trey stepped out of the cube and disappeared around the corner.

"Whew," she began, "at least we survived th—"

"Wren, you'd better see this." Trey's voice was tight.

She stepped over beside him to see him pointing at the trees.

The rope that had secured Crowbait to the tree was still there, but it looked more frayed and weather-worn than she remembered. Then she saw what was connected to it.

Crowbait was gone, replaced by the pale, moss encrusted skeleton of a long-dead equine.

"Where's Crowbait?"

"He's here. I think that's him." He pointed to the remains.

"But how?"

"Let's calm down and think about this. The cubes were placed here to transport humans from some other place..."

Trey's face was blank for a moment.

"Or place and *time*," he added. "Perhaps, if it were a long journey, they would need to be able to suspend time for the people within the cube, or change the *when* they got here for some reason. You seem to have power over the cube, like you do the abacusian, but here, it's time, not matter that you're able to control."

He was quiet again for long while and Wren was just about to speak when he said, "How far do you think we are from the abacusian?"

"Oh, I don't know, maybe half a mile, but what does that have to do with anything? I'm not even wearing the protective suit and the control belt." She didn't tell him that she'd started to feel the device even when she wasn't wearing it.

"I'm just wondering if the presence of the abacusian near the cube is causing this effect or increasing your powers somehow. You shouldn't be able to think at me as you did when time stopped, even with your powers. I just hope you can get us out of this predicament too. Do you think you could do that again, slow the seasons, and then send them back the other way? In reverse? You need to take us back to the autumn when Crowbait was–is–still alive."

Wren rubbed her eyes, then looked back at the cube. With a straightening of her shoulders, she said, "I really don't want to go back in there, but let's give it a try. We have all the time in the world to figure it out, right?"

"That's my Wren!"

Trey took her hand and they stepped into the cube, together this time. It wasn't quite as disorienting for Wren now, perhaps because she knew what to expect.

She was able to decrease the speed of the seasons flashing by and, with great effort, she slowly reversed the motion.

"How will I recognize the time we need to find?" she asked, more to herself than Trey.

He looked at her thoughtfully. "Remember how you told me you use landmarks to find your way home from hunting or shrooming? Isn't that instinctual for you now, to notice little details?"

"What landmarks? It's just trees and grass."

"Maybe there's something, even if you don't consciously remember it. Maybe your mind took a picture of the exact moment we stepped into the cube, what late-season wildflowers were blooming, a branch that had fallen, something like that."

"But how?"

"Just let your memories flow, until you find the scene that seems right. Give it a try, please?"

"OK, I'll try," she said uncertainly.

Wren started the timeline running backwards, cautiously at first, and then she remembered how long and how fast the scenes had advanced the first time and sped them up. When she felt she was getting close, she slowed and started watching for details that might trigger a forgotten detail from the day they sought.

Suddenly, she stopped the seasons rolling back and went forward a little. Was there something she recognized? Yes! Now she remembered the fading trillium flower that, with its three-leaf shape, had made her think of Trey. Three elegant white petals perfectly balanced on green leaves of almost the same shape. It had been twisted and spotted with brown by the heat of summer, but was amazingly, still blooming. Trilliums didn't bloom in the fall. That might never have happened before and might never happen again. Had it bloomed for her benefit alone? She found the bloom and then watched it fade until it was just as she remembered seeing it.

Tentatively, she said, "I think this is it."

"OK, let's check it out."

Trey led them out of the cube and hurried around the corner to look for Crowbait.

"He's here!" he shouted to her. "Alive," he added quietly.

"Trey, I'm not sure this is the exact day or time. It's close, I know that, but what if we're an hour–or even a day later? Could that change our reality in ways we don't yet understand?" Fear brought a chill to her tone.

"Let's not think about it. My brain's not big enough."

With a hesitant laugh, Wren said, "Yeah, but I know someone's brain that is."

"Tinkoro? Yes, he may be able to help us make sense of this," Trey said, perhaps planning a trip to Dmisi to consult the dageki scientist. Wren thought it might be a good idea.

When they returned to the farm, they were relieved to find that all was as they left it–and *when* they left it, except for a few little things that Wren noticed in the following days: a bridle on a different nail from where she had put it, the turnips ready to harvest when they hadn't been before their picnic. She vowed to ask Tinkoro what might be happening when she saw him next, then forgot all about it. She had indeed chosen the right day and even the correct time of day. The animals still needed feeding and told them so vociferously. The sun was setting gracefully, lighting up her little farm with an evening glow that brought contentment down on them like a gentle cloud.

"I hope I never have to leave here," she told Trey later. "It's the most perfect place, *and time* on the planet."

"I wish that as well, for both of us."

They fell asleep in her bedroom loft, warm in each other's arms. Wren tossed and turned, dreaming of an equine skeleton with hundreds of faded trillium blossoms poking up through the decaying ribs. As she watched, the blooms transmogered into a tiny flock of winged drakyn that flew up, buzzing like flies, and scattered on the breeze.

Chapter Forty-Two

Now I Lay Me Down

Trey had gone to Dmisi to talk to Tinkoro about their experiences in the cube and what use they might make of it. Wren returned to the cube to find out what she could do with it and the abacusian. She found that, with intense concentration, she could move the cube in both time *and space*. She used her new ability to make some small changes to the past, changes she hoped wouldn't topple the house of cards she believed that time was built upon. Only she knew that the first time, Teeka had died, not of the kygarid infection, but earlier in the psy storm that brought Semli in wolf's form, or that they hadn't met the Wastrel and Poppet in Droop, but that she had arranged that meeting.

For the most part, she was happy to tend to her animals and crops. With winter approaching, her spare time was spent putting up stores of jerky, smoked trout, taters, maize, onions, garlic and dried herbs. In the evenings she worked on her notebook, adding what she could remember about their journey and filling in the events that had been too hectic for her to make notes on at the time. Stretched out on her kitchen table, she organized the recipes and drawings she had made along the way. On a separate sheet of paper, she worked on a title for the notebook. Several had been scratched out, leaving only one remaining at the bottom:

Too Many Cooks: How the Complacency of Drakyn Leadership Lead to the Downfall of a Once-Great Nation

A Recipe for Disaster: How one War was Precipitated by a Humble Cook

Wren Weatherspring's Recountal of Events Leading to the Drakyn War

Bad Blood: A Compendium of Errors Leading to the Drakyn War

The Dageki Device That Changed the Fate of Three Races

Transmogrifee for Beginners, A Primer on Change

A Brief History of the Drakyn War

Goldwing & Silverfire

Chronicles of the Drakyn War

The rest of her time she struggled to keep the drakyn in line. She saw now that they fought her, not like they had as drakyn, but in more insidious ways, as their inherently scheming and duplicitous personalities fought for ascendancy. She supposed it was inevitable that the true natures of these creatures would not change overnight, but still she was frustrated that little advances were met with major setbacks. Every day, it was that much harder to concentrate on what she was doing with them, and sometimes in the morning, when she returned to the abacusian, some of what she'd done the day before had to be redone. She thought she was getting enough sleep yet felt tired all the time.

Trey returned, but he seemed oddly reticent to share with her what Tinkoro had said about the cube. What he did say was vague and incomplete to Wren.

"The nearest cube to Dmisi is far into the northern mountains, in what was drakyn territory. As a result, Tinkoro and his people haven't been able to do much research on them yet, but he said he would send a team to gather information from it soon. The stories of humans arriving in the cubes is nothing but hearsay to the dageki, since they never witnessed it happening. They are quite empirical in their gathering of knowledge, you know. Since the cubes have been inert for so long, the dageki haven't spent much energy studying them."

"But surely now he has a reason to study this one, after what happened with us?"

"Yes, he said he would come discuss it with you."

"When?"

"He has some urgent research he must complete first. He wouldn't go into it with me."

"It doesn't sound like you found out much of anything."

"No, I guess not. He did tell me one thing that I found a bit disturbing, though."

"What's that?"

Trey looked grim, and that worried Wren. "He told me about the grub moths. He was surprised that you hadn't told me about it. It's more than a bit embarrassing that I'm just about the only one who *didn't* know."

Wren immediately regretted not telling him the whole story sooner. "I've been meaning to tell you about that. It just wasn't an option I wanted to discuss with you."

"Why not?" Trey's tone was sharp. "Wouldn't it have been easier to eliminate the threat the drakyn posed early on? We could have saved many lives."

"Trey, you don't understand. There's more to it than that. When I use the abacusian, I feel the balance in the world–in all matter. Eliminating an entire species as integrated as the drakyn should not be done lightly. I've felt for a long time that Drakonia exists on a knife's edge.

Too much use of transmogrifee has brought us to the point where all matter–and maybe even time–could be disrupted beyond repair."

"So, what you're saying is that you just know better than us lower beings about what is best for us?"

"Trey—"

But she spoke to an empty room. Trey had left her.

Winter on the farm passed uneventfully. Trey took some time to get over being angry with her, but only after she'd spent hours explaining the balance of nature the abacusian demanded of her, and that she'd feared for his own life–or at least the drakyn part of him–if she'd invoked the ultimate solution. After that, he accepted, if only grudgingly, her reasons for not using it.

The first sprinkling of snow in early winter brought a quiet that Wren had never felt before. The flames burned bright in the fireplace, and she sat down to read in her favorite Poppet-constructed chair with a blanket on her knees and a hot cup of aromatic mint and dandelion tea steaming at her side.

She'd gathered some of the primers that Kemp had collected and spent her spare time studying them. New primers were great treasures to a primer-keeper like Wren. Her family had been gifted with only three small volumes, but Kemp had six, each one a treasure of knowledge from the past. Wren knew that occasionally, a work of fiction had been smuggled through from the gardlands, and Kemp had managed to find a couple of these impressive works. She turned each page as if it were made of gossamer glass as she read *David Copperfield* and *1984*, deciding that Charles Dickens was her new favorite gardland author, and George Orwell her second. The last primer she read was a torn and moldy thing that, she had to admit, was beyond her skill to comprehend. When she finally had time to peruse the *1969 Rambler Technical Service Manual,* she found that it was too profound and erudite for her to fathom, containing all sorts of esoteric terms that she just couldn't translate. Perhaps the dageki could make sense of that one, but Wren feared it was just beyond her limited intelligence to figure out.

At last, spring poked her head from the snow, and the short but burly crocuses popped up in her yard, bright harbingers of the summer warmth to come.

With spring, another group of visitors arrived at the farm. Wren was inside the cabin peeling taters but knew who it was as soon as a trumpet sounded outside. As she ran to the porch, she was greeted by Bubba and Princess, who took up most of her yard with their bulk. On top of them sat Tinkoro and Grakt.

"Welcome!" she called up to them.

Tinkoro came down his rope ladder and addressed Wren in his formal tone. "It is indeed an honor to see you again, abacusianist Wren Weatherspring. If you would accept our humble request to speak with you without the formal reintroduction ceremony, we wou—"

"Enough of that, Tinkoro. I'm so glad to see you both! Trey is out in the barn, but he'll have heard Princess announcing your arrival, that's for sure. Come in and have a cup of tea with us."

Wren was amazed by how much space the dageki took up in her cabin, making it seem more like a dollhouse than the spacious home she knew it to be. She started to worry if her human-sized chairs would support the dageki, when Trey showed up, rolling in a couple barrels for the dageki to sit on.

390 DAP DAHLSTROM

When they were all seated and enjoying her honey-blossom sweet tea, Grakt said, "I'm afraid this is not entirely a social call, dear friend. I'm sure that Trey has told you what Tinkoro has been working on—"

"No, wait," said Trey quickly. "Wren, I just didn't want you to worry, at least not until Tinkoro had finished his research. I hoped that his findings would be better than what he indicated to me whe—"

"Trey," began Tinkoro, his large eyes dark. "I'm afraid the news now is not any better than when you visited us last fall. In fact, the situation is now even more dire."

"What situation?" asked Wren in rising frustration.

Grakt stood and leaned down to take Wren's hands in his own. His deep eyes delved into hers. "Wren, the news we have is not good. I know how you like to be direct, so I will accommodate you now. The abacusian is killing you."

The room was silent for a good minute, before Trey said, "But you don't know for sure—"

"Yes, we do," said Tinkoro. "The abacusian was not designed for humans to control. The stress it is putting on Wren's system has resulted in certain aberrations within her genetrical makeup. We have not been able to find a way to slow or change this progression."

"I have felt tired," said Wren hesitantly.

"That is only part of it," explained Tinkoro. "The abacusian is drawing energy from you that you do not have. Eventually, it will begin to draw from your lifeforce."

Trey scoffed, "That's ridiculous! I thought dageki didn't believe in magic. Lifeforce is just a fantasy, an imaginary force that fairies and widgins are supposed to steal from babies, when they die unexpectedly in their cribs."

"It is real," said Tinkoro. "It is a force that is quantifiable. Each of us has only so much of it to spend, and when it is gone, life is gone."

"Wait!" said Trey suddenly. "What about the cube? Wren was able to control time within it. Isn't it possible that, in the cube, she could control or stop the progression of this disease?"

"Yes," agreed Grakt, his eyes sad. "But only while she stays within the cube, suspending time. The second she exits the cube and returns to the world's present, the progress of the disease will resume, leading to her premature death and the end of her control over the drakyn. Also, I would warn against using the cube again to reverse time. It goes against everything we know about the nature of time. It should only go in one direction, forward."

"But Wren managed to make it reverse, and nothing changed when we got back."

"That's not exactly true," interrupted Wren. "There were small changes." For some reason, she held back the fact that she had been to the cube again, to make even more changes to the past. Perhaps it was better that only one person knew what had changed.

Tinkoro nodded sagely. "Think of time as stirring honey in a cup of pudding. You can stir it in one direction, but when you stir it the opposite way it does not end up in the exact pattern that you started with. So it is with time."

"Just another way that I could bring about the end of life as we know it," said Wren in a defeated tone.

"Yes, I am afraid so."

Trey was silent, his expression grave.

Wren asked, "How long do I have?"

Tinkoro shook his head. "If you keep using the abacusian, maybe six months to a year, at the most."

Wren stood up, her features still. "Well, it's decided then. I'll go into the cube tomorrow. From there, in suspended time, I can control the drakyn until–if and when–Tinkoro or his ancestors can devise a less deadly form of the abacusian, or when a stronger abacusianist is born."

"And if none of those things happen?" asked Trey, watching her closely.

"Then I will have the choice to return and use the ultimate solution, destroying all the drakyn. But I won't take that course until all other options are exhausted."

"I am so sorry, Wren," said Tinkoro, lowering his head.

"No, don't be sad for me. It seems almost inevitable. After everything I've survived, it is the abacusian itself that is finally going to take me down." Wren laughed, but it had a hollow sound.

Trey stood alone, looking out the dark windows of the cabin, and Wren wondered what he was thinking. How could she say goodbye to him? In a short time he had become her whole world. Now they might be separated for eternity.

CHAPTER FORTY-THREE

Going it Alone, Almost

The next day, Wren prepared to enter the cube. She didn't want to put it off any longer, for fear she might lose her nerve.

She sent flet messages to Mala, Poppet, and Teeka, giving them and Trey joint rights to the farm, but only on the condition that they and their ancestors agreed to protect the abacusian at all costs.

She petted Pollux II, Kinzi, Aploosa and even Crowbait, who, surprisingly, didn't try to nip at her as she turned away.

At last, she sat on the porch of her cabin and gazed out at her farm, the happiest place she'd ever known. The tears rolled down her cheeks. Wasn't that the way life worked? The more you loved something, the more likely you were to lose it.

Trey was nowhere to be found. She couldn't really blame him. She didn't want to face him either.

She sat in silence until her tears and self-pity had run their course, then sat up with new determination. What did it matter to the cosmos if she lived or died? It was one small cook against the universe. She would do what she needed to do.

Wren approached the cube at dusk. It was an unusually silent night. No wind, no birds singing. Nothing. She turned back to gaze in the direction of her farm. She would miss it, but she knew she would miss Trey even more. But Wren was done crying about it.

She'd taken only a step toward the opening, when she heard a voice from behind the cube.

"You didn't think you could leave without me, did you?"

Trey poked his head out from behind the cube.

"Trey! You came to see me off after all."

"No, I didn't."

Trey came up to her and took her in his arms. Pulling back a little, he looked her in the eyes and said, "Wren Weatherspring, will you consent to be my princess and spend eternity with me?"

"What are you talking about? You want to get married? Now?"

"Well, no–I mean, yes, I think we should get married someday, but there isn't enough time right now, ironically. Wren, I'm going with you into the cube."

Wren pushed him away. "No, I can't let you do that. You can't give up your life for my sake. It's not right."

"It is right–for me. It's the only thing I want to do, and didn't I do it once already? What would the rest of my time be without you? If–when you come back, I could be long dead, or old enough to be your grandfather. I don't want to live this life alone."

"You'll meet someone else."

"I don't think so. Where am I going to find someone even remotely like you?"

"You have a point there."

"Wren, I love you, and I think you love me. If you do, then you can't leave me behind."

Wren sighed and said, "OK, we'll go together, but we should tell the others, so they don't wonder where you've gone."

"I sent a flet to everyone this afternoon."

"Pretty confident I'd say yes, eh?"

"I knew you wouldn't be able to resist my considerable charms," said Trey, visibly relaxing his shoulders. "There's just one thing we need to do before we can leave."

"What's that?" Wren asked curiously.

"Well, come back here, and I'll show you." Trey led her behind the cube, where he'd laid out a blanket, glasses, grapes and cheese, and a bottle of wine.

"It's not a very old vintage, but I was thinking you could take it into the cube and—"

"No way!" Wren cried, laughing as he pulled her down beside him.

They made love under the stars, and it was bittersweet and intense for both of them, knowing that it might very well be the last time.

As they lay together, Wren mumbled sleepily, "One more night won't matter, will it?"

"No, I don't think so. Plus, it gives me one more opportunity to enjoy your snoring."

"I don't snore; princesses never do."

"Ah," he said, kissing her gently on the forehead. Before he even pulled away, she was asleep. Trey lay watching her for a while, until sleep came for him as well.

Wren dreamed that the leijong leader Aquilinus was standing before her and Trey. He said, "This is not a dream."

"All right," said Wren. She stared, realizing that if this was a dream, it was a very detailed one. She could see the flying river behind him, and a fire burning a short distance away, where some of his warriors sat around laughing and talking. She could smell the smoke from the fire and feel the dampness in the riparian air.

"We've been given some new prophecies, and they concern you," he began. "What you're doing is the right thing, going into the cube, but the timing is not." Wren paused to wonder how he knew about the cube, but this was a dream, after all, where anything was possible. When she pulled her attention back to him, she realized he'd said something amazing.

"Sorry, what did you just say?"

"I was saying that the child you bear—"

"Child?"

"Are you unaware of your pregnancy?"

"Well, my schedule was off, but I thought it was just from stress."

"As I was saying, your progeny will have an ability far beyond anything we have seen before. When she—"

"It's a girl?" asked Trey, with awe in his voice. She turned to find Trey standing next to her.

"Please stop interrupting or I will never get through this dream," admonished the leijong.

"But you said it wasn't a dream!"

"Just. Be. Quiet."

Wren was silent, pouting. Trey grinned.

"The point is that you can't take the child into the cube with you. She must be allowed to mature, while you two remain in the cube to control the drakyn until the time comes that you can be replaced by another."

Trey said, "Are you saying, don't go into the cube until the baby is born, then just give her up? How can we do that?"

"I'm afraid that you must. There is no other way."

Epilogue

Mel and Toby had married young, younger than their parents wanted, but even Mel's anxious mother had finally agreed that they were meant for each other. There was true love here, a comfortable home, and a life to be envied, but in their secret dreams, they had always wanted more. Mel wanted a baby. Toby wanted a baby. It just wasn't to be. They had accepted that cruel fact and moved on, or so they thought.

Sometimes they fought for no reason. Sometimes Mel cried without knowing why, like tonight. Toby was out back, feeding the porkers. She was washing the dinner dishes, when the tears started to fall, all of their own accord. Without her permission, a tiny sob erupted from her lungs, then another. Then her cries were joined by other, smaller cries, like the whimpering of a child, or maybe the distant cry of a vixen in the woods behind their cabin. That's what it was, just a fox crying for her mate to come home and help her make adorable little cubs who would frolic about their den in the joy of discovering new life. Mel cried even more, then she abruptly stopped.

The cries outside had grown louder and more insistent. The sounds weren't coming from the back woods, but from their front porch.

Hesitantly, not knowing what she would find, she opened the front door. Below her lay a baby in a woven basket, bawling its little head off.

"Oh, my," she exclaimed, immediately thinking of the welfare of the baby. "You must be freezing out here!"

She picked up the basket, and the baby stopped crying immediately, eyeing her curiously with wide, wet gray eyes. Mel brought the basket in and set it on the kitchen table, just as her husband came in from the back.

"What's this?" he asked gruffly, then tempered his tone with a gentle hand on his wife's shoulder.

"I don't know. The poor thing was out in the cold, so I brought it in."

"What do you mean? Who gave it to you?"

"No one; it was just there, on the porch."

Toby looked uncertain, then said, "Well, I'm sorry, my dear, but you know we'll have to give it back. It's someone's baby. Not ours, that's for sure. Whomever it belongs to will want it. If it's an unwed mother, they change their minds, you know. We'll need to take it to the magistrate in town."

"Not tonight, surely."

"No, in the morning, I reckon."

Mel leaned down to adjust the blankets on the baby, which had fallen away to reveal tiny, perfect fingers and toes, and hair as silver as moonlight, with an odd streak of gold over one ear. As her fingers adjusted the blanket, she felt stiff resistance and heard a rustling, not the sound that fabric should make.

Her hand came out, and she held a too-heavy piece of parchment. When she unfolded it, she found a brilliant emerald stone inside. They both gasped in awe.

"It's so beautiful," murmured Mel.

"Yeah, and worth a pretty drakma, I'll wager."

Mel turned to him, frowning. "Don't even think about it, Toby Joseph Newman! This here stone is her legacy, a gift from her mother. You'll not be selling it to buy ale."

"All right, all right. I guess so, but what does the letter say?"

Being both primer-keepers, Toby and Mel could read. Their heads came together as they stared at the note.

It read:

I don't have a name yet. I'll leave that up to you.

Just know that I am the daughter of a transmogrifer and an abacusianist. Don't worry if you don't understand that last word. So far, there has been only one of these, my mother.

My parents regret, more than you will ever know, the necessity of leaving me behind, but where they go, I cannot follow.

My hope is that someday, if I grow up to be healthy and teachable, that I can develop certain abilities, abilities that have the potential to save the world from a dark future.

All I ask is that you allow me to be your daughter for as long as you choose to be my parents, and that you never let me take anything I'm given for granted or see anything I reach for as out of reach.

Please teach me that whatever is meant to be, will be, but only if I work hard every day to make it so, and that the rest is just icing on the war cake.

THE END

is just the beginning...

Keep Reading!

About the Author

Dap Dahlstrom is an American author and artist. Growing up in poverty on an isolated farm, she read her first book at a young age, a Little Golden Book titled *The Three Little Pigs*. Thus began a life-long love of books, writing and art.

Before starting her writing career, Dap was a successful copywriter and graphic designer, earning numerous national and international awards. Her passions include big game hunting, ocean fishing, martial arts, German shepherds, and reading, reading, reading!

Intricate world building, logical magic systems, and relatable characters who shine with humor and wit combine to make her books the complete package for fantasy fans everywhere.

Please leave a review on Amazon. Available in paperback and ebook formats. For bonus material, visit my website at

dapdahlstrom.com

If you'd like to be put on the mailing list to receive an alert for the publication date of the next book in the Drakonia series, contact me at **dapdahlstrom.com/contact**

www.ingramcontent.com/pod-product-compliance
Lightning Source LLC
Chambersburg PA
CBHW060142260626
47160CB00001B/80